THE DEBUTANTES

OLIVIA WORLEY

WEDNESDAY BOOKS
NEW YORK

This is a work of fiction. All of the characters, organizations, and events portrayed in this novel are either products of the author's imagination or are used fictitiously.

First published in the United States by Wednesday Books, an imprint of St. Martin's Publishing Group

 For information, address St. Martin's Publishing Group, 120 Broadway, New York, NY 10271.

www.wednesdaybooks.com

Designed by Devan Norman
Lace title page image © Sveta Aho/Shutterstock

Library of Congress Cataloging-in-Publication Data

Names: Worley, Olivia, author.
Title: The debutantes / Olivia Worley.
Description: First edition. | New York : Wednesday Books, 2024. | Audience: Ages 13–18.
Identifiers: LCCN 2024018643 | ISBN 9781250881465 (trade paperback) | ISBN 9781250881441 (hardcover) | ISBN 9781250881458 (ebook)
Subjects: CYAC: Mystery and detective stories. | Balls (Parties)—Fiction. Murder—Fiction. | Missing persons—Fiction. | New Orleans (La.)—Fiction. | LCGFT: Detective and mystery fiction. | Novels.
Classification: LCC PZ7.1.W676 De 2024 | DDC [Fic]—dc23
LC record available at https://lccn.loc.gov/2024018643

First Edition: 2024

10 9 8 7 6 5 4 3 2 1

For New Orleans—I love you. (I promise.)

THE DEBUTANTES

LILY

DECEMBER 30, 12:00 A.M.

Growing up in New Orleans, the first thing you have to learn is that we're all going to be underwater one day. Not just flooded, like we've been plenty of times before. I'm talking *underwater,* gone, like the map of America from one of those dystopian books I used to devour before I realized it was embarrassing. And people choose to live here anyway. Which shouldn't surprise me, because the second thing you have to learn is that if the hurricanes don't get to us first, there's plenty of other things that will.

I clutch my keys tightly, the sharp ends poking out from between my knuckles like claws. It's one of the things Mom taught me to do to protect myself, like never walking with my AirPods in at night, never making eye contact with men on the street. This is what we have to do to stay safe, she says, because this city isn't safe, not even our wealthy street in its tunnel of oak trees. Life isn't safe, so it's on us. We have to protect ourselves.

I know that now. More than ever.

The wind picks up, cutting through my hoodie. It's cold.

Colder than it should be in Louisiana in December, made worse by the humidity. That's what happens, I guess, when you build a city on the edge of a river that wants to swallow it up. I bury my hands in my sleeves, pressing them to my face for warmth. Even though I changed out of the ball gown a few hours ago, I can still feel the ghost of it on my skin, a red rash already formed from the tight corset.

My phone lights up with a message.

Where are you?

I let my fingers hover over the keyboard before changing my mind.

The Den rises in front of me behind its tall iron gate. It's just off the highway, in one of those run-down neighborhoods that makes my parents double-check the car locks when we drive through. Which is funny, considering what's inside: the Krewe of Deus home base, where the parade floats are built, gilded, and stored until they make their magnificent ride on Mardi Gras Day. Nothing inside is all that valuable—plastic beads and doubloons, wooden floats with papier-mâché decorations—but it's not about the things. It's what they represent. New Orleans royalty, locked behind a four-digit passcode.

I check over my shoulder out of habit, like Dad always does when he brings me here to visit. The coast is clear, nothing but the dark road disappearing into the night. I punch in the code and step through the gate, quickly walking up to the warehouse door.

Cracked open. Someone else already inside.

My heart starts to pound now, even though I'm technically supposed to be safe here, protected from the dangers outside.

But that's the thing I've learned about iron gates: they lock the danger in just as often as they keep it out.

The warehouse is cold and dark, casting the floats and their creatures in shadow. Jesters and kings, monsters, a whole kingdom made of paper and gold leaf. It isn't real, any of it—and still, in this light, it's terrifying.

It hits me how alone I am, how bad an idea this is. I squeeze my keys tighter. Suddenly, they seem like a ridiculous way to protect myself, no better than one of the wooden feathered spears they throw in the parades. What damage can I really do here, all by myself?

Enough, I think. And that has to be worth something.

I breathe out and send one last text.

Here

LES MASQUES CELEBRATES 60TH ANNUAL BALL

Society & Culture | Published Friday, December 29

Time to dust off your white gloves, ladies—the Les Masques Ball will proceed most merrily this evening at the Uptown Country Club. In grand Carnival tradition, the 60th Annual Ball will honor ten Maids and this year's Queen, Lily LeBlanc, daughter of Mr. and Mrs. George LeBlanc II.

A senior at Edward T. Beaumont School, Ms. LeBlanc is no stranger to the Les Masques tradition: her mother, Alice, reigned as Queen at the 30th Annual Ball, and her paternal grandfather, George LeBlanc Sr., is approaching the 10th anniversary of his rule as King of Deus in the annual parade.

For those fortunate enough to secure an invitation, the royal presentation will begin promptly at 8:00 P.M., followed by dancing and merriment.

A longstanding tribute to the elegance, gaiety, and culture of New Orleans, this year's Ball is particularly meaningful: tonight's festivities are dedicated to the memory of last year's Queen, Margot Landry.

Though some wondered whether the Ball would proceed in light of this tragic loss, Les Masques has decided to forge ahead. In the words of Ladies' Krewe Liaison Genevieve Johnson (Maid, 30th Annual Ball): "Like the city we call home, the Krewe of Les Masques will always persevere in the face of tragedy." And thankfully so—this year's Ball boasts a crop of young women worth celebrating.

1

APRIL

DECEMBER 29, 8:15 P.M.

I'm one breath away from losing a zipper. It wouldn't even have to be a deep one—just a normal-sized breath, which I can barely manage in this glorified torture device of a ball gown. With every inhale, the boning cuts into my skin like teeth, reminding me of two universal truths. One: debutantes aren't supposed to indulge, including in oxygen. And two: I'm pretty sure these dresses are designed to keep us from running away.

"Uh." Milford, my appointed escort, looks up from the phone he snuck into his suit pocket. "Are you gonna be sick or something?"

Heat rushes to my face as I realize I'm death-gripping my magnolia bouquet. Milford doesn't look especially worried, only disturbed, but my face gets hotter as I start to worry that he thinks I'm blushing because I have a crush on him. I don't—but does worrying about this anyway make me a narcissist or just socially anxious? Or both? Suddenly I'm layers deep in a nesting doll of anxiety, worrying about my worrying, and all I can do is force out "I'm fine."

I am decidedly not fine, but Milford goes back to his phone, thank god. I go back to breathing: in for four, hold for seven, out for eight. It's not easy, since my lungs are, you know, being squeezed to death by a custom-made prison.

I wince, thinking again of how much this dress must have cost Dad: a clean thousand that could have gone toward my college fund or literally anything else. If Dad just wanted to burn dollars, I would have happily used them for photo paper or film, since I've been blowing through Beaumont's darkroom supply. But according to Dad, it's "expected"—his favorite word when it comes to all of this debutante stuff. Every Maid here has a custom dress. I just so happen to be the only one with the figure of a wooden plank, hence the extreme measures taken to keep my strapless dress from becoming a belt. Like an unfriendly reminder, my skin starts to itch under the beaded top.

"I think we're next," I mumble. *I think,* as if we're not the only couple left in the hallway. The qualifiers always slip out before I can stop them, a knee-jerk apology for speaking.

Milford looks at the door to the ballroom, then sighs, slipping his phone back into his pocket and holding his gloved arm out for me. I take it, cringing at the forced formality. Apparently, we debutantes are also incapable of walking without a strong teenage boy to support us. Sorry, a strong teenage *Duke,* because that's their official title. One way New Orleans debutante nonsense is different from regular debutante nonsense is that celebrating how rich and important we are isn't enough. We have to literally be *royalty.* Maids, Dukes, Queens. It's a Mardi Gras thing.

Also, one could say, an asshole thing.

My own personal Duke, Milford Wilcox III, was assigned to me by either the debutante gods or the alphabetical order of our last names, whichever came first. He's also a senior at

Beaumont, but all I really know about him is that 1) he lives in a multimillion-dollar mansion, 2) his dad is running for mayor, and 3) he's probably not psyched to be escorting the most socially awkward Maid to ever disgrace this country club.

From the other side of the door, the jazz band's muted rendition of "Someone to Watch Over Me" beats like a death march. I picture Dad's beaming face in the audience and think of the mantra I've been repeating all night: *This means a lot to my dad. My dad means a lot to me.* Sure, debutante balls are historically racist, sexist, classist, and basically everything wrong with New Orleans and this country, but I can set aside my morals for one night. Right?

Wrong, says a louder voice in my head. Because now, in my too-tight dress and my too-big gloves, all I can think is that last year, Margot stood in this very ballroom less than a day before they found her body.

It rushes up in my throat: a plea, a panic, anything that will get me out of this. But it's too late. Inside the ballroom, the applause for the last Maid fades, and Mrs. Johnson's voice comes over the microphone like God, if He were an aging Southern belle.

"Presenting Maid April Whitman!"

I know I'm the one who was worried about missing our entrance, but now my shoes feel glued to the floor. But it's officially too late to run. Milford has to tug me out of the hallway and under the hot lights of the stage.

The country-club ballroom yawns in front of us, high ceilings dripping with chandeliers that look suddenly precarious, like they could come crashing down at any moment. There's a pitiful smattering of applause as we step onto the old wooden floor, white gloves against champagne flutes. I don't blame them for feeling lackluster. I'm the last Maid, and it's pretty hard to stay enthusiastic after watching nine other girls get paraded around like Wagyu cattle.

We round the stage, and the lights are blinding, turning the audience into shadowy shapes in folding chairs. I can still spot Dad, though. He gives an actual standing ovation as we pass, clapping with his hands up high, like this is one of his favorite operas and I'm the prima donna who just gave a career-defining performance. Next to him, Mom gives her best *I know you hate this and I'm sorry* smile, and I feel a bubble of warmth. We're doing this for Dad. I can do this for Dad.

As we near the center of the ballroom floor, my shoulders itch for the familiar weight of my Nikon strap. Instead, I catch a glimpse of another camera: the official event photographer, setting his aim. Sweat prickles in my armpits, heat rushing to my face. It's a special kind of panic, being the one on the other side of the lens. Being seen.

Milford clears his throat next to me, and I remember that I'm supposed to curtsy. Mrs. Johnson's words from this morning's rehearsal echo in my head: *Brighter smile, April. It's a ball, sweet pea, not a funeral.*

Sure, I wanted to tell her. *Until I die of oxygen deprivation.*

Now I dip down just like I did this morning, doing my best approximation of happiness while my pulse beats in my ears.

Flash.

And then it's over. Milford drops me off with the rest of the Maids, who ring the empty throne in the middle of the floor, before lumbering over to the makeshift backstage area. I breathe out shakily.

"Don't lock your knees," a voice next to me whispers, causing the tension to immediately reflood my body.

Vivian Atkins, one of the other two Maids in my class at Beaumont. At school, Vivian's usually in jeans and a T-shirt or her soccer uniform, but somehow, she's just as intimidating in a ball gown, her strawberry-blond hair cascading in a classy ponytail that she could probably use to strangle me. Maybe I'm projecting. While I disagree with popularity as a concept, Vivian is part of that crowd, and I don't trust any of them. She's also never spoken to me before.

I try to form a response, but my voice feels locked inside my throat, so all I manage is a barely audible "Thanks."

Vivian shrugs, eyeing Mrs. Johnson. "She'll go feral if a Maid passes out before Lily comes in."

As if to confirm, Mrs. Johnson shoots us both a smile that says *I will quite literally explode if y'all don't stop whispering during my debutante ball.* I guess I don't blame Mrs. Johnson for being so intense: this whole thing is like her Super Bowl, especially this year. Across the row of debutantes, Piper Johnson—the other Beaumont Maid—is an echo of her mother, looking like the child bride at a Kennedy wedding in her modest cap-sleeve gown, brown hair pinned up in a stuffy sixties updo.

To be fair, we all look like child brides in our white dresses. Which is sort of on purpose, I think. Historically, debutante balls were a way for the elites to announce to society that their daughters were ready to be married off before they hit the ripe old age of twenty-two. Here in New Orleans, this particular brand of hell goes all the way back to the 1850s, when a bunch of rich white supremacists got together to form one of the first Mardi Gras social clubs, the Krewe of Deus—pronounced "crew," and yes, all of the clubs spell it that way, because of course they do. As a secret society, Deus organized an extravagant, rowdy parade on Mardi Gras Day, followed by a superexclusive debutante ball at night—a lavish masquerade for only the richest and whitest in town.

Somewhere along the way, Deus spawned Les Masques, a debutante ball specifically for high-school girls, which is how I came to be standing here, craving the sweet release of the apocalypse.

Now, even though Mardi Gras clubs like Deus are technically open to anyone—as long as you've got money to pay the dues and another member to vouch for your worthiness—I still can't get past the rotten, gnarled roots of it. And looking around at the other Maids onstage, this ball doesn't look any less rich or white than they all did a century ago.

My chest tightens again, but I force myself to stay calm. It's too late now to panic, anyway, because it's almost the grand finale. The band's song ends, leaving a hush of anticipation before they start up a drumroll.

"Presenting Her Royal Highness . . ." Mrs. Johnson pauses, relishing in the ceremony of it. "Queen Lily LeBlanc!"

A trumpet plays royal fanfare as the spotlight swings to the ballroom entrance—the main one, the *grand* one. The Maids came out of the side door, but this is an entry fit for royalty. Two "pages"—the lucky ten-year-old boys whose parents forced them into page-boy costumes, complete with blond bowl-cut wigs and feathered hats—pull open the heavy wooden doors. The band starts up a dreamy instrumental cover of "La Vie en Rose," and every head in the room turns to see her.

Lily LeBlanc glides forward in her white ball gown, and somehow, despite all this, the pageantry, the absurdity, the room holds a collective breath. She's the picture of everything a Queen should be. Regal spine, sparkling crown balanced perfectly on her white-blond updo, two careful coils falling out to frame her heart-shaped face. Wyatt Johnson, Lily's boyfriend and Piper's twin brother, is escorting her, but he might as well be invisible, a golden shadow serving only to complement her glow. Everything about Lily sparkles, from her blue eyes and bright smile to her ridiculous scepter and heavy beaded cape.

But I know what the rest of them don't: it's a rhinestone glow, so convincing that you almost think it's real. Real enough that you don't know you've been fooled until it's too late.

The trumpet croons, punctuated by jazzy drum hits, as Lily and Wyatt parade to the throne at the center of the stage. He holds her gloved hand in his as she ascends the dais, watching her like he can't believe he gets the honor of helping her up three whole steps. When she makes it to the top, Lily gives Wyatt an adoring smile, and it's like a premonition of the wedding they'll no doubt have before Lily turns twenty-five—old-maid status, by Southern standards—only the weird funhouse version where she towers above him on her throne.

With a bow, Wyatt turns and goes offstage with the other guys, and Lily is alone to rule her kingdom. Just before she sits, she steps forward, eyes up, unafraid of tripping over her cape. Her focus seems soft, but then I realize she's looking at her parents, sitting front and center. Lily's mom smiles perfectly, looking every bit the mother of a Queen in purple satin. Her dad is proud, eyes glinting the same steel color as the Krewe of Deus medallion around his neck.

I wonder if they're thinking what I'm thinking, the terrible thought that just drifted into my head like one of the piano's glissandos: "La Vie en rose" is the song Margot entered to last year. They've used it for every Queen's entrance since god knows when, but some part of me thought maybe they'd change it. Now it feels cursed.

But if it's crossed Lily's mind, she doesn't show it. She lifts her scepter, and slowly, just like she rehearsed, she moves it over the crowd, one side to the other, like she's casting a spell. One that seems to be working. Time stops, the room enraptured. Then, in the last few measures of the song, she takes her seat, and the spell breaks. The applause is deafening.

I can't believe these assholes fell for it.

The clapping fades, and so does the music, as we all wait for the next part of the program. I try to hide my cringe at what I know is coming.

"And now," Mrs. Johnson announces, "presenting the Les Masques Jesters!"

If this whole thing wasn't already weird enough, *this* is the cherry on top of the Southern-bullshit sundae. The Dukes stumble onstage like a nightmare, now disguised as "Jesters" in the literal horror show we've normalized as Mardi Gras costumes: sparkly medieval-style outfits, jingly hats, and worst of all, peach-colored masks with painted red lips, obscuring everything but their eyes, which peek through two holes in the plastic.

The band starts up a circus-style number, and the boys launch into their unchoreographed dance—bouncing, thrusting, TikTok dances of varying skill level—while Lily looks on, laughing with a glove over her mouth. It's a tradition, the guys dancing around for the Queen, and everyone seems to think it's cute. *I,* however, would rather eat my own bouquet than watch two more minutes of this.

The band rolls into their big finish, and the boys hit their final pose, a bow to their Queen. I let out a breath. Finally, it's done. Only a few more minutes and I can leave this stage for good.

And then the lights go out.

There's a breath of shocked silence before the murmuring starts. I strain through the darkness to look at the Maids next to me, but they're all confused, too. We didn't rehearse this. My heart pounds against my dress.

"Everyone, stay calm." Mrs. Johnson's voice, swallowed now by the din of the crowd. Her microphone must not be working. Wait, why isn't it working?

And suddenly, light. *Click.* A projector shines from somewhere in the back of the darkened ballroom, its glow aimed right at Lily, making her shield her eyes. At first, I can't tell what it is. Moving images of some kind.

When I realize, my stomach plunges.

Margot. Photos, videos dancing across the throne. Margot at school, smiling, laughing, giving the camera the finger. Margot as Queen, her crown crooked on her dark-blond curls like a messier, realer version of Lily. Her ghost. The videos are all silent, but I can still hear her laugh echoing in my memory. I feel around for something to grab onto, but there's nothing but the limp flowers in my hands.

Through the panic, I try to be logical. Maybe this is some kind of tribute. They said tonight's ball was dedicated to Margot, didn't they? But then I see Lily's face, the strange look in her eyes. Something like confusion.

Something like fear.

The projection cuts off, shrouding the ballroom and Lily in darkness. For a second, there's nothing.

And then the room lights up. Bright red glows everywhere—on Lily's pale face and the deep velvet curtains behind us, aimed from somewhere up high, at me and all the Maids. I back away from the light, nearly tripping over my dress, and then I see it: movement near the throne. An arc of red, splashing against Lily's dress, her face.

Blood.

For a moment, there's stillness. Lily brings a gloved hand to her face, too stunned to scream, frozen like a photograph with crimson dripping down her gown.

And then, chaos.

2

VIVIAN

DECEMBER 29, 8:25 P.M.

I don't think. I move.

Balling my giant skirt in my fists, I run to the middle of the stage, only one thought in my head: my best friend is covered in blood.

But I've barely made it a few strides before the lights turn back on and I realize I was wrong. It isn't blood. Lily's dress is ruined, but the stain is too bright to be real. Paint, maybe. And suddenly, I feel a little stupid.

But also, what the hell just happened?

I look out at the crowd. Some people are still sitting and whispering into their gloves, but most are up and elbowing their way to the exits. Mrs. Johnson is trying to corral them with her still-dead mic, but it's a losing game. This is as much of a free-for-all as the canned-goods and bottled-water aisles when the city issues a hurricane warning. And maybe we *should* be running. Because even though everything seems fine, I can't shake the creeped-out feeling: someone just threw fake blood at Lily in a ballroom haunted by a dead girl. One who, just last year, was sitting on the same throne.

Someone waving pulls my attention. Mom, standing out from the crowd with the height and strawberry-blond hair her strong genes passed on to me. I wave back, and she grabs Dad's arm. They both look relieved. I'm far enough away that for a second, I could believe they aren't in the middle of an epic divorce, the kind the other debutante parents are probably gossiping about over wine and oysters at country-club brunch, even though it's not a huge shock. Mom and Dad stuck it out as long as they could, but now that my older brother, Spencer, is in his second year at LSU, and I'm a senior at Beaumont, I'm pretty sure they figured, *close enough*.

Just before I go to meet them, something flashes to my left. A jester hat. I stop in my tracks as one of the Dukes, a tall boy, slips out the ballroom door with what looks like a bucket tucked into his side. A bucket that, if I had to guess, just played a starring role in the newest sequel to *Carrie*.

Nice try, asshole. I pick up my speed to follow him. If only I could actually move in this dress. But just as I open the door, a hand grips my arm.

"Viv!" It's Savannah, worry all over her face. "Are you okay?"

"Yeah," I breathe, glancing into the hallway. *Shit*. The Jester's gone. And the door's blocked anyway, too many people spilling out. "I think so."

Sav sighs, folding her arms over her long emerald dress. "I knew I was in for some horror-movie crap when y'all made me come to this, but I didn't think it would be so . . ."

"*Carrie*?" I joke weakly.

"Oh my god." Her mouth hangs open. "They *Carrie*'d the debutante ball."

Normally, I would laugh, but I'm still coming down from

the panic. Looking back at the throne, I realize Lily and Wyatt are gone.

"We should find Lil," I say.

Sav nods. "But if she starts doing telekinetic murder, we're seriously going to have to revisit this friendship."

I know Sav's trying to break the tension like she always does, but I can still feel how freaked out we both were a few seconds ago. Reaching into the pocket of my dress, which is the only part I could really get behind, I grab my phone and shoot my parents a text to say I'm fine and going to check on Lily. Just as I hit SEND, mic feedback screeches.

"Everyone, may I have your attention, please." A familiar soft Southern accent: Mr. Pierce, standing at the announcer podium.

Besides being the Head of School at Beaumont, Mr. Pierce is also one of the leaders in the Krewe of Deus, the organization that runs Les Masques. Basically, if Les Masques is the debutante JV league, Deus is varsity, the real deal. If we're lucky, us Maids will all be invited to the Deus Ball when we're in college, but I'm not holding my breath. At that ball, the Queen is always a twenty-one-year-old debutante, and the King is a respected old dude from the Krewe, usually wearing tights. Which, you know . . . gross. For lots of reasons.

Mr. Pierce clears his throat. "On behalf of the Krewe of Deus, I want to sincerely apologize for the disturbance of tonight's presentation. Rest assured, whoever is behind this cruel and disrespectful joke will be punished. Country-club security is already taking measures to track these pranksters down."

Security? Looking around the room, all I see is one barely adult dude in a green country-club uniform mumbling into a walkie-talkie. Figures. If I had to bet, the biggest crime this guy's ever solved here was probably a drunk grandma misplacing her shawl.

"We hope this little blip won't derail such a fine evening. Genevieve and the Ladies' Krewe have worked so hard to make this a fantastic night." Mr. Pierce nods at Mrs. Johnson, who gives a smile that barely hides the rage in her eyes. "And we all know how much the young ladies of the court and their families have been looking forward to this honor."

Right, *this honor.* It's what everyone says about scoring a Les Masques invite, Dad included, but I'm pretty sure every senior girl with a dad in Deus is asked to be a Maid. Being a debutante is probably the closest I'll ever get to nepo-baby status.

Anyway, if this is such an *honor,* every Maid still onstage probably shouldn't look so close to bolting. Half the crowd, too. I spot Coach Davis sitting a couple rows behind my parents. He's here with his girlfriend, Ella or Emma or something, who was apparently a Deus Maid a few years ago. I'm a little embarrassed that he's here, honestly. Coach moved from Texas last year, when he got the job teaching PE and coaching soccer at Beaumont, so I can only imagine what this all looks like to him. There's deb stuff all over the South, but this is about as over-the-top as it gets.

Seeing me, Coach shoots a thumbs-up with a questioning look, like, *You good?* I shrug, and he gives a somber nod. At least someone gets it. I turn back to the stage.

"Please, continue enjoying your drinks and the music," Mr. Pierce says. "Let's give these young women the night they deserve."

He claps his gloved hands, sparking some weak applause from the half of the audience who hasn't escaped, and Mrs. Johnson snatches the mic.

"Laissez les bons temps rouler!"

She waves at the band, and they reach for their instruments, swinging into another jazz song. Everyone seems to relax a little, and I feel it, too, like I'm cooling down from a long run. Because this is a debutante ball. Sure, it's creepy as hell, but it's not like anything can go *that* wrong.

"Do you see her?" Sav asks, straining to see over the crowd.

One of the few nice things about being five foot nine and wearing heels is that I don't have the same problem. I spot them by the side door of the ballroom. Lily's ditched her crown, scepter, and cape, and her parents are shuffling her out, Wyatt trailing behind them like a golden retriever.

It takes a minute to push through the crowd, so when we finally catch up with them in the hallway, Wyatt is gone, and Lily's talking to her parents, their voices hushed. Right away, I get the sense we've walked in on something we shouldn't be seeing.

"I told you," Lily is saying. "He had the jester mask on. I couldn't see."

"Don't play dumb." Lily's dad, so harsh it makes me tense up.

"George." Lily's mom. "Can you lower your—"

"You saw his face, Lily."

But Lily isn't looking at her dad anymore. She sees us and folds her arms over the bright-red splatter on her dress. It's almost funny now, how fake it is, but something about the warning look in her eyes digs a pit in my stomach. Her parents clock us, too, and the pit gets even deeper.

"Girls." Mrs. LeBlanc's gloved hand brushes her pearls. "So good to see you."

"So sorry to interrupt, Mrs. LeBlanc," Sav says. "We just wanted to make sure Lily was okay."

"I'm fine." Lily closes her hand around her necklace, the

single diamond teardrop she's worn since her thirteenth birthday. The one she always touches when she's lying.

I've been Lily LeBlanc's best friend since kindergarten, and she hasn't gotten any better at hiding her tell.

Before I can say anything, the hallway door swings open and Mrs. Johnson runs out, kitten heels clacking.

"Lily! Goodness, I am *so* sorry, sweet pea. Are you okay? Are you hurt?"

In a flash, Lily's whole face changes with a bright smile that deepens her dimples. "I'm okay. I mean, that's what I get for wearing white, right?"

Mrs. Johnson laughs like she's Lily's number-one fan. I swear, the second Lily and Wyatt started dating sophomore year, his mom probably popped the champagne and fired up the future wedding Pinterest board. But Lily always knows how to get people in her pocket. It's one of my favorite things about her: one second, she's a debutante princess, and the next, she's a monster on the field, stealing the ball out from under the other player before they even know what hit them.

"So gracious. I swear, this girl was just *born* to be Queen," Mrs. Johnson gushes, hand on her heart. Then, noticing Sav and me, she gets a look on her face like she just smelled something bad.

Checks out. We've spent half of high school hanging around the Johnsons' house with Lily, Wyatt, and our other friends, but Mrs. Johnson has never liked us much. Me because my family isn't old-money enough, and Sav because her family is actively antidebutante. Which I don't blame them for: Sav's mom is Black, her dad white, and even though all this stuff apparently "isn't racist" anymore, I wouldn't touch it with a ten-foot pole if I were them. I didn't really want to touch it at all, but my parents insisted, and with the way things have been at home lately, I wasn't about to rock the boat. Sav's only here because Lily and I promised her a full year of aux privileges in exchange for coming, even if it means she'll blast *Six* the musical at all of our pregames.

"Speaking of our Queen," says Mrs. Johnson, bringing her attention back to Lily, "where's your consort gotten off to? Because if he up and left you here to deal with all this alone, he'll be getting a *stern* talking-to at home, believe me."

"He's getting the car," Lily says with a laugh. "Don't worry. He's learned from the best."

"Oh, hush," Mrs. Johnson teases, clearly thrilled to be buttered up. "Now I know it's such a chore, but you wouldn't mind coming with me for a few minutes, would you? Security has just a few questions."

"I'd love to help, but I really don't know if I can," Lily says, using the same tone that always gets her extensions on homework. "I barely saw anything. It was so quick, and then he was gone."

She touches her necklace again. Another lie. I watch Lily's face for some sign of what she's hiding, but she doesn't look my way.

"Of course," Mrs. Johnson says. "But anything you remember might help to—"

"We appreciate your diligence, Gen, but I think Lily would like to get home and rest." Mr. LeBlanc lays a broad hand on his daughter's shoulder. He's changed just as quickly as she did: the sharp tone and angry stare are gone. Now there's only a sympathetic smile. "I'm sure you can imagine that tonight hasn't quite been the royal treatment she was hoping for."

He says it like a joke, but there's a warning flare in his eyes. Mrs. Johnson picks up on it, her neck blotching.

"Of course. And again, I'm *so* sorry. If I'd had any idea that someone here was planning this sort of—"

"Thank you, Genevieve. You've been more than helpful." Lily's mom gives an icy smile, not even trying to hide it with charm like Mr. LeBlanc did.

"Well." Mrs. Johnson sniffs. "I'll let y'all get home, then."

"I'll let you know if I remember anything that might help," Lily says.

"Thanks, sweet pea." Mrs. Johnson turns to me and Sav again, like an afterthought. "And girls, if y'all saw anything, don't hesitate to let me know."

With another robotic smile, Mrs. Johnson clicks back down the hall and into the ballroom. As soon as she's gone, Lily drops the sweet look.

"I'll go see if Wyatt got the car," she mumbles to her parents. Then she heads for the exit, pushing her way through the double doors like a warrior princess leaving a bloody battle.

Lily's parents look at each other, like there's something they want to say but can't when me and Sav are still standing here.

"Well," Lily's mom starts. "Maybe we should—"

"Oh!" I blurt. "Um, I just remembered I have Lily's keys. I'll go catch up with her."

It's a lie, but I don't wait for anyone to stop me. From the look on her face, Sav knows what I'm really doing. As close as the three of us are now, Sav didn't start at Beaumont until middle school. I'm the one who's known Lily since we were in kindergarten, dreaming of the day we'd be tall enough to use the monkey bars on the playground. And whenever Lily has a secret, I'm the one who can pull it out of her.

Outside, it's colder than it was when the ball started. At

least, what passes for cold in New Orleans at the tail end of December, which is maybe fifty degrees.

Lily's about halfway down the path that leads to the front entrance of the country club, under a bending oak tree. Her phone lights up her face, and her gloves are off and balled up in the crook of her elbow.

"Lily."

Her head snaps up, scared, but then her shoulders loosen. "What's up, Viv?"

At the sound of my nickname, I relax, too. I walk toward her, my ugly white heels pinching at my blistered feet.

"Ugh." I stop, wincing. "Please tell me why I thought it was a good idea to run four miles this morning and then wear heels?"

Lily smirks. "Because you're in love with Coach and you want to be his favorite player of all time."

I laugh, even though the joke felt more like a dig. Too accurate. Not that I'm in love with Coach. He's not *un*attractive, I guess, but also, ew? He's, like, twenty-five. Still, I'd be lying if I said it wasn't his voice in my head when I went on my run earlier, that I wasn't thinking he'd be proud. I want to be pissed, but then Lily grins, and I can't do anything but let it go.

"Okay, first of all, his favorite player would be *you,*" I tell her. "And you're totally changing the subject."

"Which is?"

I sweep an arm at the building behind us. "What the hell?"

She's silent. I cross my arms and stare her down. Literally. I have about eight inches on her, so it's not hard.

"Who threw the fake blood at you?"

Her hand reaches up to her collarbone. "I don't know."

"You're touching your necklace."

She drops her hand. "So?"

"I've played, like, a hundred games of BS with you. I know when you're lying."

Her mouth opens, about to argue, but then her phone lights up. A text from an unsaved number. Before I can read it, I feel Lily staring. Her face is cool, almost unreadable, but it's obvious she caught me looking at her screen. I look away, guilty.

"Wyatt just texted," Lily says. "He got the car. I should go meet him."

"Okay."

We're quiet for a second, ignoring the truth, which is that we both know the text Lily just got wasn't from Wyatt. I'm supposed to be the person Lily tells everything to, and for some reason, we're both going along with this obvious lie.

Lily gathers up her skirt.

"I saw the guy leaving the room after everything happened," I tell her. "One of the Jesters. He had a bucket."

Lily sighs, and I can see the exhaustion on her face. I couldn't tell on the stage, but up close, dark circles shine through her under-eye concealer. It makes me uneasy all over again. Lily never looks anything but put together. It's her weird superpower, even in 8 A.M. physics.

"It was probably one of the Dukes being dumb." She shrugs. "Jason or someone. He seemed kind of wasted when y'all were up there."

"Oh, believe me, I know. He went way too hard at the pregame." I roll my eyes at the memory of him stumbling as we looped around the stage. "But I don't think he did this."

I can't explain how, but I know, and I can't deny the panic spilling through my veins like a tequila shot: Lily knows who did this to her, or has a guess, and for some reason, she's lying about it.

Before I can find it in me to call her out, Wyatt appears at the end of the path, walking toward us like Lily manifested him, TikTok–tarot girl style.

"You sure you're okay?" I ask Lily, lowering my voice so he can't hear. "Just, with all the Margot stuff, I would be a little freaked if I were you, so it's okay if you're not—"

"I'm fine, Viv." She reaches for the diamond again, then catches herself. "I promise. Go have fun, okay? I'll text when I get home."

Okay, now I'm a little annoyed. Does Lily seriously think I'll just go have *fun* when she's being this cagey? She's the one who actually cares about this deb stuff, not me. Sav and I would both rather be home in sweats, but here we are. Because even though I'm a Maid, everyone knows it's all about the Queen. This is Lily's night, not mine.

Wyatt catches up to us, sliding an arm around her tiny waist. A stray lock of golden hair falls onto his forehead, and I feel the stupid urge to brush it away, but I'm not supposed to be having thoughts like that about my best friend's boyfriend of almost two years. Anyway, Lily beats me to it. She tucks the hair behind his ear, and he kisses her wrist, blue eyes locked on her.

"Car's parked out front." He glances between us, like he's noticing me for the first time. "Everything okay?"

Lily smiles. "Yeah. Perfect."

But as he pulls her closer to his side, I catch it: a little twitch of her face, her muscles tensing.

I wish I didn't see it. I wish it didn't give me a little rush of hope.

"I'm going back in," I say. Too loud, like I need to announce it to all the ancient oak trees, too. "Text when you get home?"

"Of course," she says.

I turn and walk back inside in my uncomfortable shoes, everything I could have said going sour in my mouth like bad champagne.

3

PIPER

DECEMBER 29, 8:40 P.M.

When I envisioned my first-ever debutante ball, I had a very clear picture in mind.

Beautiful dress, check.

Mom and Dad beaming as I rounded the stage, check.

One night when everything was so perfect that for once, just once, I could let go and have fun? I should have known that was too much to hope for. Because even if tonight hadn't turned into such a disaster, relaxing has never been in my DNA.

Exhibit A: standing here in this ballroom, I feel closer than I've ever been to shoving a walkie-talkie down a grown man's throat.

"A Jester," I repeat, laser-focused on the security guard. "He was dressed as a Jester, and he had a bucket. I saw him slip out that door, but I lost him."

"Can you give a bit more of a description, Miss . . . ?"

"Johnson. Piper." One of the pins holding my hair in its Audrey Hepburn–inspired bun is stabbing my scalp, and I reach up to adjust it before stopping myself. I'd only mess it up. Not that it matters now. I was going for *Breakfast at Tiffany's,* but looking at all the other Maids with their half-up, half-down looks and fashion ponies or Lily's effortlessly stylish updo, I feel more stuffy than classic. "He was tall. But he had a mask on, so that's the best I can do."

"Thank you," the security guard says. "We'll be sure to keep that in mind."

Seriously? I want to yell, but I can't. I'm a Johnson, and Johnsons are calm and collected. Johnsons fix things. And it's time for me to step it up.

I give him my best blistering look, the one I've mastered from years of watching Mom. "Listen, if I were you, I would be a little more concerned about this entire situation, especially considering that it was Lily LeBlanc up there. Because if this isn't sorted out soon, it's on you, and her family will make sure you know it."

At that, his eyes bug out, his back straightening to attention. Finally. I don't know how to feel about the fact that I just sounded exactly like Mom, but I've got to admit that she always gets the job done. Hell hath no fury like a Johnson woman pissed. But I'll psychoanalyze that in my therapy session on Thursday.

"Of course, Miss Johnson," he says. "We'll be on the lookout."

They won't, but I've done my best to fix this mess. Now I just have to hope they figure out who pulled this stunt before Mom has an actual conniption.

Speaking of which, it's time to move on to phase two of my damage-control plan.

I do a quick loop of the ballroom, but I can't find her. Instead, I spot Dad at one of the tables bordering the dance floor, looking every one of his fifty-two years as he nurses a glass of his usual whiskey neat.

"Hi, peanut," he says wearily as I approach, kissing me on the forehead.

"Hey, Dad." I pull him in for a small hug. "Have you seen Mom?"

He squeezes me back for a moment before letting go. "I think she's engaged in damage control."

Like mother, like daughter.

"You didn't go with her?" I ask.

"You think she asked?"

"Touché."

"Gesundheit."

I roll my eyes at the classic Dad joke. I'm glad he doesn't seem angry right now, but also, I'm surprised he isn't. He's in Deus, so this disaster of a night reflects badly on him, too.

But Dad just sighs. "You look beautiful, peanut. I'm sorry this all went to hell in a handbasket."

His eyes are glossy, almost like he's on the verge of tears, and I realize what must be going through his head. Margot Landry. Of course. I kick myself for not seeing it before, how he might react to all those videos of her. In all his years as a psychiatrist, I'm pretty sure Margot's the only client he's ever lost.

"It's okay," I tell him, putting on a smile. "I'm having fun."

It's always my first instinct when his mood turns cloudy, like if I perform the role of perfect daughter more convincingly, it'll make everything better.

"I'll go make sure Mom's okay," I add.

Dad gives me another side-hug. "I'd bring reinforcements, if I were you."

"Already on it."

We both mean alcohol, of course. And I know how that sounds, but my parents are hardly alcoholics. They drink in the way every adult in New Orleans does: socially, which, in a city that's all about socializing, means pretty much always. Personally, I'm not a fan of alcohol, but I can't blame them. We have drive-through daiquiri stores, for god's sake. We're practically raised to be debaucherous.

Smoothing my gown, I march up to the bar and ask for a vodka tonic.

"That bad, huh?"

I turn to find Aiden Ortiz leaning against the bar, looking annoyingly tall in his suit.

"It's for my mom," I say snippily, both to him and the bartender, who's giving me a wary look. The bartender relents, making the drink, and I have to wonder if it's because he's met my mom already. Like I said, hell hath no fury like a Johnson woman pissed.

I turn back to Aiden, nodding at his own glass. "You're one to talk. Was being my Duke *that* difficult?"

"Shirley Temple," he says, swishing the drink. "But also, would you blame me? Escorting your royal highness around a ballroom was pretty taxing."

Aiden's eyes flash the exact color and stickiness of honey. They're another one of his irritatingly perfect qualities, along with his 4.7 weighted GPA and the Google internship he's got lined up for the summer before he starts at Stanford. He got in early action, because of course he did. I'm in early at Vanderbilt, which is just as good a school, but try telling that to everyone at Beaumont. They're all obsessed with the idea of their best and brightest leaving the South for four years at a flashy school, so long as they bring their diplomas back home to settle down, pop out some kids, send them to Beaumont, and start the cycle all over again.

I frown at his Shirley Temple. "Girly drink."

"Archaic gendering of beverages," he fires back.

My frown intensifies as I take Mom's drink from the bartender. For once, sneaking a sip doesn't sound like such a bad idea. But then I get a better one.

"You were up there with the Jesters. Did you see who did this?"

Aiden looks away. He knows something. Doesn't he?

But what he says is "I don't know. I was mostly trying not to die of embarrassment, and then everything happened so fast. All that Margot stuff . . ."

Aiden's stare flicks to the throne. He doesn't finish the thought.

I cross my arms, which are suddenly prickling with goose bumps. "You seriously didn't see anything?"

His eyes meet mine, and he shakes his head. "Seriously, Piper. I wish I had."

I chew the inside of my cheek. I don't know if I believe him, but I know the look on his face. It feels like a more sincere version of the look he gets in AP Gov just after making an annoyingly smart comment to shoot down an uninformed opinion. It's a look that means *end of discussion*.

"Fine," I say, walking away. "Bye."

"Always a pleasure, Piper Johnson," he calls after me, and I hear his annoying smirk without seeing it. I make a show of ignoring it, scanning the ballroom instead.

I spot Mom just in time. She's coming in through one of the side doors, looking very much like she needs this vodka tonic.

"Have they caught the guy yet?" I ask by way of greeting, handing her the glass.

"I knew you were my favorite daughter."

She takes a long sip, and I smile. I am her *only* daughter, so the competition is hardly fierce, but still, I feel a bubble of pride. I anticipated a need and filled it. That's what Johnsons do.

"And no," Mom sighs. "This entire thing is a disaster."

"Yeah, I know. I talked to security. They were zero help."

I catch a twitch above Mom's eyebrow—a telltale sign she's stressed.

"But the people who stayed seem to be having fun," I add quickly. I don't want to make her feel like this is her fault, even if it happened on her watch. "It looks like they got it all cleaned, too." I gesture at the throne area, which, aside from a conspicuous WET FLOOR sign, looks perfectly blood-free. "It's like it never even happened."

"Well, it did," Mom snaps. "And people aren't going to just forget that the presentation was vandalized with *blood* and"—she lowers her voice to a hiss—"and images of a *dead girl*."

I shrink slightly. "I know."

Mom softens, pressing a manicured hand to her temple. "I'm sorry, Pipes. It's just unbelievable. After what happened at the Den last year . . ."

I lower my voice. "You think this has something to do with the vandalism?"

Mom nearly gave herself an ulcer trying to deal with it last year. On the night of the ball, someone vandalized the Krewe of Deus Den, the warehouse where they store all of the parade floats in the months leading up to Mardi Gras. So many floats were ruined that they would have had to cancel the parade, if not for the battalion of volunteers Mom assembled to fix them with barely a month to spare. They never caught the vandal, but soon, no one really cared anymore—because the day after the ball, they found Margot's body, and a dead Queen tends to trump petty vandalism.

They found her in her car, parked near the levee. An overdose—which, though tragic, wasn't entirely surprising. Margot was a party girl, infamous for all the old clichés: cutting school, crashing Tulane frat parties, hiding a flask in her locker. There was even a rumor that she almost got arrested once for drunkenly cursing out a cop at Mardi Gras, before they realized who her family was and let her off with a warning. Her death was awful, obviously, but not unthinkable.

Mom sighs.

"Maybe," she says, but I can tell she's not too invested in my vandal theory. Her sharp green eyes scan the ballroom, distracted. "Have you seen your brother?"

"Not since the presentation. Why?"

She looks around as if to make sure no one's listening, then leads me by the elbow a few feet away from the crowd. When she speaks, her mouth barely opens, and she keeps a placid look on her face, like we could be talking about our dresses or the hors d'oeuvres.

"Lily's lying about what she saw."

"What?" I follow her lead, hiding my surprise. "Like, you think she knows who did this?"

Mom nods, adjusting her faultless low bun. "I can smell a lie from a mile away. I'm hoping your brother can pull it out of her, if he decides to reappear. Lily said he was getting the car, but who knows where he got off to. He won't answer my texts." She sips her drink, catching the eye of one of the other Les Masques moms from across the ballroom, who waves. Mom waves back. She whispers to me, "Shelby Fontaine. Her daughter, Eugenie, is one of the Maids from St. Anthony's. The husband is an insufferable ass, but I made Eugenie's dress, and she *does* look lovely in it. I should go play nice."

"I can find Wyatt," I tell her. "See if I can get him to ask Lily what's up."

She gives my cheek a light touch with her gloved hand. "Thank you, Pipes."

Watching Mom float over to Mrs. Fontaine and her *insufferable ass* of a husband, I smooth out the satin of my dress. It's also one of Mom's designs, and probably my favorite thing I've ever worn: cap sleeves, white-lace detailing spilling from the bodice to the hem of the floor-length skirt. Even though I'm doubting my hair choice now, this dress makes me feel exactly how I was hoping to: classic and beautiful, like a princess at a royal wedding.

Mom runs a full-time business designing dresses, and the debutante market is her biggest. Every Maid or Queen worth her salt wears a Genevieve Johnson original, Lily included—and sure, I'm a little jealous sometimes that I have to share Mom's designs, but I'm so proud of her. Because I know how my mom comes off to people. I've heard the other Maids giggle about her at rehearsals. They think she's some ridiculous, sycophantic Southern belle who'd do anything to please the powers that be. But what they don't see, what I wish they could respect, is that even though Mom can be a lot, she's not the butt of a joke. She's a shark with a goal, and she knows exactly what role she has to play to get there.

And so do I.

Straightening my spine, I focus on my mission: find Wyatt, figure out what Lily saw, and fix the catastrophe that this ball has become. Mom said Wyatt was getting the car, so I make my way outside.

I find them faster than I expected. They're standing on the path that leads to the main country-club entrance, but something seems wrong. Lily's glaring at Wyatt, her arms folded, and his hands are shoved deep in his pockets.

"I told you I'm fine." Lily's tone is so uncharacteristically cold that it makes me hesitate. I stop behind an oak tree, just out of their sight.

"Obviously you're not," Wyatt grumbles. "You won't even look at me, just your stupid phone."

"Do you need, like, a full log of who I'm texting now?"

I grit my teeth. Something's definitely off here, because Wyatt and Lily don't fight. As much as they get on my nerves, they're pretty much the perfect couple. It's *why* they get on my nerves. At home, Wyatt can be moody and hotheaded, but I've never heard him talk to Lily with anything but cartoon hearts in his eyes.

"You don't need to act like I'm some possessive creep!" he snaps. "All I'm saying is it would be nice if my *girlfriend* wouldn't act so—" He stops, pointing at Lily's phone. "There! See? You can't even go two seconds without looking." He steps closer, reaching out. "Who the fuck is—"

"Stop."

"I just want to—"

"Don't touch me."

And now I'm overcome with the protective instinct that's been ingrained in me since the day we were born, when I emerged fourteen minutes earlier and a whole lot wiser than my asshole brother. I march out from behind the tree.

"Hey," I call, laser-focused on Wyatt. "Mom's looking for you."

He and Lily jolt apart like magnets with the same charge. Wyatt stares at me, and I wonder if he can tell from my expression just how much I've overheard. But we've never had that twin-telepathy crap you see in movies. Besides the blue eyes, we barely even look related: he got Mom's golden coloring, and I got Dad's harsh combination of pale skin and brown hair.

"Are you Mom's bounty hunter now?" Wyatt asks bitingly. Now that he's recovered from the jump scare, he's pissed.

"If the price is right." I turn to Lily. "Hey."

"Hi." She doesn't look happy to see me, and I can't fight the little pulse of hurt. In the past, Lily's tolerated me—little more than a polite wave or small talk as she and Wyatt head up to his room—but ever since I started helping her with her college application essays a few months ago, I've felt like maybe, *maybe* we were becoming real friends.

Not that it matters anymore. I got into Vanderbilt, Lily didn't, and now it's obvious that all she ever wanted me for was the favor.

Fat lot of good that did her.

With a quick glance at Lily, Wyatt stomps over to me and pulls me out of her earshot.

"What are you doing?" he demands, voice low.

"What are *you* doing? I heard y'all fighting. What's going on?"

His jaw twitches. "We weren't fighting."

"Does she know something?" I press, even quieter. "Mom thinks she was lying about what she saw. Did she see who—"

"I know you're jealous that you're not Queen, or whatever, but can you stop trying to shove yourself in other people's business?"

My face heats. *That* he said loud enough for Lily to hear. And it's not even true. Sure, being Queen is an honor, but I never had the illusion that it would be me. Lily's had this in the bag from the day she was born a LeBlanc.

I cross my arms, trying not to let the hurt show. "You're in a mood."

"Yeah, wonder why."

"Fuck you."

"Fuck *you*."

Normally, those two words are a term of endearment, our best expression of sibling love, but now they feel charged. Real.

Wyatt sighs, running a hand through his hair. A truce. "Do you want a ride home? I'm driving Lily."

It's as close as he'll get to an apology, but it does nothing to soften the hurt still burning in my stomach.

"No," I tell him sharply. "I'll go with Mom and Dad." I start to leave, but something stops me. I spin around to face him again. "You may think all this is lame, but I don't. It's a family tradition, it's *important* to me, and someone tried to ruin it tonight. So even if you don't care, I'm going to deal with it. Like I always do."

I'm almost halfway back to the building before Wyatt calls after me.

"Right. Because who wouldn't want your help?"

It's like a current down my spine, making me stand up straighter. *Does he know?* When I turn back around, Wyatt's looking at me with that smug expression of his, the one that says he's won every battle before it even starts, because that's just how life works for him.

But he can't know. There's no way. Because if he did, we'd both have a shit ton more problems than we do right now.

I put on my best *bless your heart* smile, like the little Mom clone he thinks I am.

"Get home safe," I tell him, and then, murmuring to myself as I turn away, "Hope your relationship makes it past the first traffic light."

4

APRIL

DECEMBER 29, 9:30 P.M.

I press my forehead against the cool glass of the car window, watching the streets of Uptown pass in a green-and-golden blur. There's a dull throbbing behind my skull, but I try to ignore it, focusing on the fact that we'll be home in ten minutes. Then I'll get to peel this dress off and try to wipe the past two hours from my memory.

"How's the air?" Dad asks from the passenger seat. "Too hot? Too cold?"

"I think we're just right, Goldilocks." Mom reaches across the driver's side to squeeze his shoulder with a warm smile.

They're annoyingly cute for a couple who've been married almost twenty-five years. Sometimes, it feels like a slight from the universe that I, April Whitman, cynic extraordinaire, somehow ended up with two college-sweetheart parents who manage to run a real-estate business without becoming any less in love with each other. It defies the logic of both physics and America's divorce statistics.

I'm mostly kidding. I'm glad my parents have such a good

relationship. Really, it's just that the least-perfect thing about them seems to be me.

"How ya doing back there?" Dad asks me. "You've been awfully quiet."

"Just practicing my wistful gaze out the window," I say. "You know, for when I'm a debutante child bride and my husband goes off to war."

Dad laughs. "Well, you look beautiful."

"Good. They'll never know I'm hoping he dies in battle so I can inherit our massive country estate."

"There's the feminist, mildly sociopathic debutante I raised," Mom teases, but she glances at Dad in that way of hers, a telepathic temperature check. Instantly, I feel guilty, remembering Dad's beaming face as Milford dragged me around the ballroom. Dark humor has been my number-one defense mechanism through all this, but I'm worried it might actually be hurting Dad's feelings.

"I'm glad I did it, though," I say as convincingly as possible. Which is to say, not at all. I edit the statement, making it true. "I mean, before everything happened at the presentation, I'm glad we all got to hang out as a family, and stuff."

"Me, too." Dad smiles, but there's a twinge of sadness in it. "Look, April, I know you only did this for your old man, and I'm so sorry it turned out to be such a mess." He pauses, and I know he's doing his own temperature check on me, wondering if he should change the subject. "Did you have some fun before, at least? I saw you chatting with Vivian Atkins up there. Are y'all getting to be friends?"

"Chatting" is a generous description, considering I could barely produce a single syllable. I feel a twinge deep in my gut, the same mix of guilt, shame, and frustration I get whenever my parents try to save me from my own hermitlike behavior. It's no secret that I have no friends, which is due to a combination of social anxiety and, as I've told my parents hundreds of times, personal choice. The people at school aren't exactly my type, with their rich-kid conformism and total lack of interest in anything outside of the Beaumont bubble. And sure, maybe Vivian seems a little more down-to-earth than some of the other popular kids, but she's still one of Lily's minions. To them, I'm just the weird, quiet girl with the camera, if I'm anything at all—and that's the way I like it.

Because I've tried the alternative, and it was infinitely worse.

Still, I can't handle the barely disguised hope in Dad's voice.

"Yeah," I lie. "A little."

"That's great!" He grins at me in the mirror, but it's too put-on, fading as quickly as a camera flash. Already, I know what's coming next. "I just can't believe someone would pull a stunt like that. Those videos, like some kind of joke . . ."

The silence stretches, pressing against the windows like a palm print in the condensation.

Dad sighs. "I'm just really sorry it happened."

"Yeah," I say through a tightening throat. "Me, too."

I close my eyes again, but this time, I can't block out the images. The blood on Lily's dress. The red light. *Margot*. It's like my corset is getting tighter and tighter, so fast that I want to scream just to remind myself I still can.

Like she can sense it, Mom straightens. "Y'all want to take one last spin down St. Charles before they take all the lights down?"

I may be a cynic who wants nothing more than to get home right now, but I *am* a sucker for some good ol' capitalistic holiday cheer. Plus, I could really use the distraction.

"Hell yeah," I say. "Aux me?"

Dad hands me the cord, and I hit SHUFFLE on a playlist of Whitman Family Favorites—all the big holiday hits except for "The Christmas Shoes," because Dad can't listen to it without openly weeping—and shift around in my giant skirt until I have a good view.

I drive down this street every day on the way to school, but I'd be lying if I said it didn't still take my breath away. St. Charles Avenue is like something out of another world, old sepia-toned photographs come to life in full color. The long two-way street is split by the neutral ground—or the median, for the uninitiated—and the streetcar track, all of it shaded by a parade of gnarled old oaks, bending to each other as if in mutual adoration. Both sides of the street are lined with some of the grandest houses I've ever seen: old Victorians and colonials with wraparound porches, dangling lanterns, and big yards behind tiny iron fences that are hardly more than decorative, like the mansions themselves are imposing enough to ward off intruders.

Most are still decked out for the holidays, white lights wrapped around tree branches, ornaments dripping like red and gold dew drops. The St. Charles families always go all out, spending tens of thousands to hire decorators, like it's some kind of competition. Which I guess it is. Tourists flock to this street, snapping pictures from the sidewalk and the streetcars, dreaming about which fairy-tale home they'd choose.

And shining above them all is Lily LeBlanc's mansion.

I can't help looking as we pass it, some compulsion to capture it all. The house is a bright, flawless white, three stories trimmed with columns and cornices that make it look more like a wedding cake than a home, too perfect to cut into.

On instinct, my eyes track up to the window I know is Lily's bedroom. I haven't been there since last year, but it still lives in my head like an old photo, the contours clear if I focus hard enough. Her queen bed with its gauzy canopy, the covers and pillows as white as her ball gown. Bare, tidy walls, except for a single picture hanging there: Margot and Lily sitting in profile, the levee stretching behind them. Margot has her signature claw-clipped bun and smudge of black eyeliner, playfully giving the camera the finger. And Lily looks over her bony shoulder, head tilted like she's forgotten that I'm behind the lens. Like she's forgotten that I was Margot's friend first.

I can remember that night so clearly. Or maybe it's just that I remember the photo, which, sometimes, I think is the same thing. It was a few weeks before the start of our junior year, mine and Lily's—Margot was about to be a senior—and for the past month, we'd been something like a trio. Against my will, obviously, but I had no choice.

Margot and I had been friends since that January, even though hardly anyone knew about it, not even my parents. We never really hung out at school. She had her crowd, and I had my camera. But it wasn't that she wanted to keep me a secret. At least, I didn't think so. Because I felt that way, too—like she was this special hidden place I'd found, or a new favorite song by an underground band, something that would be ruined once everyone knew about it.

But then, that summer, Margot spent a few weeks at her family's beach house in Mississippi, which just so happened to be right next to the LeBlancs' new vacation home. When they got back, Margot and Lily were attached at the hip, and suddenly, whenever we hung out, she was there, too, whether I liked it or not.

I didn't, for the record. And neither did Lily. To her, I was just an unfortunate consequence of befriending Margot, the crawfish shell and spindly legs you have to deal with before sucking the good stuff straight from its head.

The night I took that photo, we were sitting in Margot's favorite spot on the levee, right along where St. Charles turns into River Road. We'd go all the time that summer, walking about ten minutes from Margot's house, crossing the train tracks, and then climbing up the grassy hill to the bike path on top of the levee, where we'd sit facing the other side: a concrete slope down to a tangle of grass, trees, and beyond that, the Mississippi River and a skyline marred by bridges, barges, and industrial plants. It wasn't much to look at. If St. Charles Avenue was a kingdom full of castles, then this was the drawbridge and moat, the last thing standing between us and destruction.

Maybe that's what Margot liked about it: it felt like the edge of the world.

"Y'all ever think about how the river could just kill you?" she'd asked that night, absent-mindedly rolling the spark wheel of her lighter, the fancy silver one engraved with a sad clown face. I never knew where she'd found it, but she always carried it around, more for the aesthetic than any actual smoking habit.

Lily laughed, genuine and bubbling.

"Thank you, Morbid Landry," she teased, taking a sip of her hard seltzer. "Please elaborate?"

"Like, the current is so strong it'd pull you under in seconds. It's filled with toxic sludge and definitely alligators and it could also flood us at any time, but we still built a city around it. That's pretty badass."

"Or a death wish," I added.

Margot's face lit up as she turned to me. "*Exactly.*"

I couldn't help smiling back.

"We're literally sinking into the ocean," I added. "It's kind of ridiculous that people still buy property here."

Lily glanced at me. "Well, you'll be out of here soon enough, right?"

Her tone was casual, but the question sent uneasy pinpricks down my spine.

"I mean, like, with college," she added, off my silence. "Didn't you say you're not applying anywhere in the South?"

I shrugged, deflecting. "It's still a whole year away."

But Lily was right. Seventeen years in the South felt like plenty, and I was already itching to get somewhere with seasons and a general public who wouldn't balk when I held a girl's hand, if I could ever get over my crippling anxiety enough to start dating one.

"Well, sinking or not, I'm sure as hell staying," Margot said. "Like, there has to be something spiritually wrong with you if you have the chance to go to a school with Mardi Gras break and don't take it." She looked at me again. "I love you, April, but you are disturbed."

She smiled, but there was something sad simmering beneath it—something I felt a sudden urge to capture, if only so I could examine it later.

"I never said I wasn't." I lifted my camera. "Smile."

Now I turn away from Lily's house, focusing intently on the trees bending above us until we get home. Before the engine's even off, I'm pulling off my clunky heels and climbing out of the car, desperate to unhook this dress and take my first gulp of unrestricted air in hours.

"Careful with your skirt!" Dad calls behind me. "The ground is dirty."

Shooting him a thumbs-up, I bundle the giant puff of fabric as I walk up our front steps, the brick chilly on my bare feet. As much as I can't wait to move out, our house *is* pretty cool. Like a lot of the homes in our neighborhood, it's at least a century old. It's a renovated double shotgun—a New Orleans classic, named because of their long, straight design, where you could stand in the entrance and, theoretically, shoot a bullet clean through the back door. It's got that famously colorful Uptown style: canary-yellow clapboard with a porch framed by bright white columns, an iron gas lantern hanging above the front door, which is painted the same robin's-egg blue as the window shutters. The colors don't match, but no one in New Orleans gives a shit. They match because we say they do.

I glance through the front window to see Mouse curled up on the piano bench, licking her mittened paws. I bend down and tap on the glass.

"Hey, gremlin. How about you, me, and a *Doctor Who* binge?"

Her tail flicks—as close as this cat will ever get to showing approval—and I smile. Just as I'm about to get back up, my phone buzzes. When I see the name on the screen, my dress feels even tighter.

Lily.

Meet me at the Deus Den tomorrow at noon, it says. We need to talk about Margot.

5

PIPER

DECEMBER 30, 11:55 A.M.

In the long list of things that piss me off, being left on read has got to crack the top ten, especially when it's about something this cryptic.

> Meet me at the Deus Den tomorrow at noon. We need to talk about Margot.

When Lily sent the message last night, I responded immediately to ask for more details, but she still hasn't gotten back to me, despite the very clear READ AT 9:50 P.M. banner beneath my text—which, as far as I'm concerned, could be classified as an act of psychological warfare.

I send her another text:

> I'm here

Five minutes early, I mentally add. *Not that anyone's counting.*

Shielding my eyes from the sun, I look up at the Den. From the outside, it's nothing special, just a long warehouse building with a high arched ceiling. But inside, the place is magical. Or it used to be. I haven't been here since I was little enough that Dad still held our hands as he walked me and Wyatt down the long aisles of floats, pointing out the one he'd be riding on in the parade: the Fool's Float, one of the first and most historic in the lineup, with the big laughing jester at the helm.

The floats used to scare Wyatt so much that he'd cry at the giant papier-mâché creatures staring down at him, but I loved them. I always ran ahead, eager to touch the gold-leaf flames and see if they'd really burn me, half-afraid they would.

I still love when Dad tells that story. Maybe because, for once, the roles are reversed: I'm the fun one, the carefree one, while Wyatt hangs back, overthinking.

I check my phone again, but Lily still hasn't read the message. I sigh. She's never been punctual, which she usually gets away with on account of being, well, Lily—pretty and popular and charming, all qualities that don't come naturally to me. Tardiness is also high on the list of things that piss me off, but I try to tamp down the frustration.

I'm not sure why Lily has summoned me to the Den, of all places, but if she knows something about who projected Margot Landry all over the ballroom last night, then this is an opportunity I can't pass up—even if it means waiting alone on a sketchy-looking street just off the highway.

"Piper?"

I spin around at the unexpected voice, instinctively grabbing for the pepper spray in my purse.

"Oh my god, it's me!" Vivian Atkins holds her hands up, blocking her eyes.

I lower the spray, suspicious. For all the times Vivian has

been at our house with my brother and their friends, I don't think we've ever really exchanged more than a casual hello.

"In my defense, you snuck up on me."

"Wait." She squints at my hand. "Is that *bedazzled*?"

I glance at my pepper spray, which is pink and—yes, okay, *fine*—sparkly, but I won't give her the satisfaction of embarrassment. "It was the cheapest one."

"Frugal of you." With a look of what can only be described as sociological fascination on her face, Vivian crosses her arms over her Beaumont soccer hoodie. "What are you doing here?"

I debate coming up with a lie, but then I notice the time—noon on the dot—and I wonder if this is purely coincidental.

"Did Lily text you, too?" I ask.

Vivian frowns. "Yeah. Wait, did she also text—"

Before she can finish, shoes shuffle on the sidewalk behind us, and we both turn to find April Whitman approaching the Den gate. She blinks at us, looking like a meerkat with her wide brown eyes and dangling arms, that ever-present camera slung over her shoulder.

"Um," she says. "Sorry, I . . ."

"Got a text from Lily? Welcome to the club," I finish, because it looks like the sheer act of talking is making April so nervous, she might explode. Which maybe it is. Already, this might be more words than I've heard her say in nearly thirteen years of going to school together.

I check the time on my Apple Watch.

"It's 12:02," I say. "She's late."

As I look up again, I catch Vivian making an expression I'm used to—one transmitting a very clear *Chill out, Piper.* All of Wyatt's little posse look at me like that, like it's some sort of crime to actually *care* about anything besides sports or hooking up or whoever scored the booze for this weekend.

I straighten my spine. "Should we go in?"

"Wait. Just—what did Lily say in her text to y'all?"

Vivian still looks skeptical, like she can't believe her best friend would deign to text the rest of us. Although to be fair, she might have a point. It's not like Lily has been seeking out my company lately, and I've never seen her even speak to April. There's nothing tying us together, besides school and Les Masques.

So this must be about the latter.

"She said we needed to talk about Margot, didn't she? This is probably about last night." I pause, watching Vivian's confused expression. "Did she tell y'all something different?"

April shakes her head.

"No," Vivian says.

"Well, then." I gesture at the gate. "Shall we? She could already be inside."

Doubtful, I think, but still, I'm not exactly dying to wait here in this awkward trio. I pull the gate handle. It doesn't budge.

"It's locked," Vivian says, oh so helpfully. "There's a code or something."

April fidgets with a piece of mousy-brown hair, cut bluntly just above her shoulders with choppy bangs she no doubt sheared herself. She looks even more eager to escape than usual—I'm sure because she can't bear to spend another second with anything or anyone debutante-related. Then, to my surprise, she steps up to the keypad and starts punching in numbers.

"Wait," I start. "You shouldn't—"

The keypad flashes green, and when April pushes, the gate swings open.

Vivian and I stare, open-mouthed.

"How did you know the code?" I ask.

"My dad." She hikes up her camera strap and steps inside. "He let me come shoot the floats for a project last year."

"And you just . . . remembered the code a year later?" I ask, still slightly in disbelief. I'm one of the best math students at Beaumont, but even *I* have trouble memorizing phone numbers, let alone a code I've only used once in my life.

April shrugs, red-faced. "I remember stuff."

I want to ask why she's not higher up in the class rank, but that would probably be considered rude, and anyway, she's already walking up to the warehouse door. It opens, unlocked, and we follow her inside, our footsteps echoing on the concrete floor of the big yawning space.

During Mardi Gras season, artists and Deus members are here most days, putting the finishing touches on the floats and making sure their parade throws are in order. Now, though, we're still about a week away from the official beginning of Carnival—the weeks-long period leading up to Mardi Gras Day—so the building is eerily quiet, empty except for the huge floats and their half-finished creatures staring down at us. I'm a little surprised, really, that they'd leave it all unattended after the vandalism last year.

"Hello?" Vivian calls out.

Silence.

My Apple Watch dings, and I look down at the screen. An email notification from Lily. Weird. She's never emailed me except to send drafts of her college essays.

And then I clock the subject line: *Delete After Reading.*

I click to open it and see the other recipients. "Y'all?"

They both turn to look at me.

"Check your email."

Vivian frowns. "Why?"

I thrust my phone in her direction. She gets closer to see it, April leaning in beside her.

> If you're getting this, something went wrong.
>
> Check the darkroom. April knows where.
>
> I'm sorry.
>
> Xx L

Before I can even say anything, Vivian has her phone out and pressed to her ear.

"Are you calling her?" I ask.

She doesn't have to answer. I hear it cut straight to Lily's voicemail greeting, tinny through Vivian's speaker.

"Hi, this is Lily, leave a message."

Vivian hangs up and dials again.

"Hi, this is—"

She jabs the END CALL button and types out a text instead.

"It won't send," Vivian says. "Like her phone is off, or something."

I turn to April. "What does that mean, 'check the darkroom'?"

"I—" Her voice cuts out sharply, like someone shut off the volume. April's eyes are trained on a spot of concrete floor a few feet away, the space cluttered with cardboard boxes, paint cans, and papier-mâché flowers still waiting to be attached to their floats.

And then I see what she's really looking at. A glimmer of something, catching the sun as it streams through the high warehouse windows. April bends down to pick it up, lifting it high enough for us to see the teardrop diamond on the gold chain.

I've seen that necklace before. I don't need April's weird

mathematical memory to remember where, either. Lily wears it every day, absent-mindedly fidgeting with the diamond, like she can't help showing it off.

"Is that . . ."

"Lily's." Vivian finishes my thought. She turns around, taking in the space around us. "Lily!"

But there's no answer.

A creeping dread starts up beneath my skin, like whenever I know I'm forgetting something on a test, only this is much worse—because right now, I'm not drawing a blank. It's the opposite. I have a feeling I know exactly what's about to happen.

"I'm calling her mom," Vivian announces, already holding the phone back to her ear.

Her foot taps frantically as it rings, the tone droning on until it's broken by a muffled "Hello?"

"Mrs. LeBlanc? It's Vivian. I'm here at the Den with Piper and April, and we're—" She pauses, listening as Lily's mom says something I can't make out. "The Deus Den, yeah. I'll put them on speaker, hold on." She does. "So Lily asked us to meet her here, but—"

"Wait, you heard from Lily?" Mrs. LeBlanc's voice is panicked, and the dread sinks its claws deeper. "When?"

"Last night," Vivian says. "And just now. She sent us this weird email, but she's not here, and we found her necklace. Has she—have you heard from her today?"

Lily's mom is quiet for what must only be a second or two, but already, I know. I can feel her answer in the weight of her silence, the crackle of her voice as it comes through the speaker again.

“I need y’all to stay right there. Don’t move, okay? George and I are on the way.”

“But have you seen—”

“No. We . . .” Lily’s mom takes a breath. “We haven’t seen her since the ball.”

6

VIVIAN

DECEMBER 30, 12:30 P.M.

When we were little, Lily used to have this weird obsession with fairy tales. But not the G-rated Disney stuff. The dark versions. The *real* versions. She'd hold court in the playhouse on the Beaumont playground and tell the other kindergarten girls the stories like a secret. Stuff like *Did you know that Ariel actually dies at the end of "The Little Mermaid"? Did you know that Cinderella's stepmother cut off the stepsisters' toes so they'd fit in the shoe, but they bled all over and that's how the Prince knew they lied?*

That's how it feels, searching the Den with Lily's parents. Like one of those screwed-up stories, some version of "Hansel and Gretel" where instead of breadcrumbs, all we have to go on are Lily's email, her necklace, and a warehouse full of monsters.

We look through everything. The floats, the costume racks and closets, even behind the boxes of old Deus memorabilia. Mr. LeBlanc unlocks the storage room at the back of the warehouse and calls inside, but there's no answer.

Lily isn't here.

Her parents make some calls. They ask us if we can meet back at their house to talk to a detective. A detective, like something out of Sav's guilty-pleasure *SVU* episodes. And then I'm driving, thinking the whole time that this can't be real, because Lily wouldn't go *missing.* That's not what this is. She's just . . . not here. She's somewhere else.

But that email.

If you're getting this, something went wrong.

I'm sorry.

I park in the LeBlancs' driveway, closing my eyes for a second to pull myself together. *Easy, Atkins,* I hear Coach's voice in my head. *Keep your head up.* This is just a misunderstanding. Maybe Lily will even be inside, lounging on the sofa and wondering why we're all so freaked out.

But she isn't.

The empty house is freezing. It always is. I clench my teeth as I settle into my usual spot on the living-room sofa, where I wait, watching my phone like a lifeline for a text, another email, anything, but it never comes.

And then the detective is here.

Detective Rutherford looks more like a Hollywood exec than a cop, with his bright white teeth, salt-and-pepper hair, and perfectly pressed button-down. He's probably the same age as Lily's dad, early fifties, or maybe a few years younger, but it's hard to tell. He's aging well in a way that only rich guys can pull off, and I pick up a definite old-money vibe as he smiles and says, "Please. Call me Marty."

He also has an accent. Most of the people I know in New Orleans don't have more than a hint of one, but Call-Me-Marty has that specific Louisiana twang, Southern mixed with something almost like New York. He goes down the line, shaking each of our hands and asking our names before settling down in the chair across from us.

"Thank you so much for coming," Lily's mom tells him.

"Of course. Anything for my oldest pals."

"Marty's a friend of the family," Lily's mom explains. "Lily's godfather."

"Her daddy and I go all the way back to Vanderbilt," Marty adds. "To you girls, though, I'm probably another one of those old Deus dinosaurs." He gives a small chuckle. "Y'all looked lovely last night, by the way."

"Thank you." Piper adjusts her Vanderbilt quarter-zip, obviously eager for Marty to know she'll be at the alma mater, too. She's been wearing it nonstop since early decisions came out a few weeks ago, and I know it pisses Lily off, even though she'd never say it. Vanderbilt had been Lily's plan for ages, so we were all kind of shocked when she got rejected, especially since she's a legacy.

April and I don't say anything, but judging from the look on her face, I feel like we're thinking the same thing. This Marty guy seems way too chill about all this, like he's sure it'll be sorted out before the Johnsons' big New Year's Eve party tomorrow. And maybe it will. Or maybe this is just some sort of detective strategy to keep everyone calm.

If you're getting this . . .

"Marty's with the NOPD, but he's helping us out informally today," Lily's dad explains. He's standing behind us, anxious in a way that makes me even *more* anxious, because I've never seen him be anything but confident. "It's still a little early to, well . . ." He clears his throat. "We're just hoping to get this sorted as quickly as possible."

Like this is just an inconvenience, and Lily will be back any minute now. And maybe she will. She has to be.

Lily's mom nods, gripping her cardigan so tightly that her

knuckles go white. Normally, Mrs. LeBlanc has this badass rich-lady elegance that Sav once described as *almond mom, but make it fashion*. Now, though, she just looks breakable, like she hasn't slept all night. Which, I realize, she probably hasn't.

"Please, girls, tell Marty anything you can," she says. "What you saw at the Den, and anything you might have heard from Lily since last night."

Marty gives us another Southern-charm smile. "That sound okay?"

We all nod silently, except for Piper, who gives a weirdly formal "Yes, sir."

Classic.

"Good," Marty says, shifting forward in his seat. "Now I understand y'all were at the Deus Den this morning. You were supposed to meet Lily there?"

"Right. She said—" Piper hesitates. "She said she wanted to talk about Margot."

April visibly tenses at the mention of her name. Marty, on the other hand, doesn't react, except for a small concerned frown.

"Margot Landry?"

We nod.

"Why would she want to talk to y'all about Margot Landry?" Marty asks.

I've been asking myself the same thing. All I know about Margot is what everyone knows: her family owned half the city, she was kind of a mess, and she was Queen of Les Masques last year. Then, the day after the ball, she died. An overdose, apparently.

She and Lily were friends, though, at least for a few months. They got close over the summer before our junior year, when both of their families were at their Mississippi houses. Usually, Lily's parents would let Sav and me tag along, but we'd both been busy that summer, Sav at a theater intensive, and me coaching kids' soccer at Beaumont's day camp, since I desperately needed the money and the résumé padding.

Pretty soon, though, I wished I had gone. Because when Lily got back, she and Margot were suddenly besties, making all these weekend plans that Lily never invited us to or even told us about. Sav and I had been kind of worried she'd ditch us completely.

But then, after junior year started, things were back to normal. Lily and Margot stopped hanging out. I don't really know what happened. Maybe Lily just lost interest, or she realized Margot was too intense. Sometimes, I think that whole thing was just Lily rebelling a little, being friends with someone older and cooler and more dangerous than me and Sav. Either way, it didn't last long. That December, Margot was Queen of Les Masques. And then she was gone.

After, Lily didn't talk about her much. No one did. It was like Margot became another ghost haunting Beaumont's old halls.

"We thought it might have had something to do with whoever sabotaged the ball last night," Piper finally answers for all of us. "Maybe Lily knew who did it."

Marty's smile flickers in a way that tells me Piper's baby-narc energy isn't working on him like it does on all the teachers at Beaumont. Which, in a way, I've got to respect.

"I appreciate that, of course," he says, "but you girls really shouldn't worry yourselves over a prank."

"You think it was a prank?"

Every stare in the room turns to April, who hasn't said a

word since the Den. Even Marty looks like he'd almost forgotten she's sitting here. But he recovers quickly, giving April a kind look.

"A prank may not be the right word, no. What happened last night was certainly in poor taste. Cruel, even." He pauses, glancing at Lily's mom and then back at us. "Alice says y'all got an email from Lily. Is that right?"

Piper nods, getting out her phone. "Here, I can show you."

She hands it over, and Marty reads the email, making a small humming noise before handing it back.

"'Check the darkroom,'" he repeats, a line creasing his eyebrows. "Any idea what Lily meant by that?"

April swallows. "I'm . . . not sure. I figure she means at Beaumont. Um. In the photo lab."

Marty softens, giving her a small smile. "You don't have to be shy, now. Y'all aren't in trouble." When April doesn't say anything else, he sighs. "I know this has been a stressful morning for y'all, but trust me, we're doing everything we can to bring her home safe. Cases like these, we usually have 'em back where they belong by nightfall."

"What do you mean, 'cases like these'?" It comes out more sharply than I meant it to, but I can't stop myself. Already, I can hear what he's implying, the story he's about to spin: pretty rich white girl runs away for attention, realizes she can't hack it away from Mommy and Daddy, and makes it home in time for dinner. And maybe that's better than the alternative, but something deep in my bones knows that isn't what this is. Because if there's one thing Lily has never been, it's reckless.

"Well," Marty starts carefully. "If Lily's sending an email, it's a good sign she's not in danger. Her car is missing, too, right?"

"Yes," Mrs. LeBlanc says. "It wasn't here this morning."

Her car? That's new. If Lily took her car, then maybe she really did just run away. But that doesn't explain the email, her necklace on the ground.

"Another good sign," Marty continues. "If Lily took her phone and her car with her, then it's likely she just ran off. Maybe it was stress from the ball or her boyfriend. He drove her home, didn't he?" He looks to Lily's parents, who nod. "Maybe they got into a tiff on the way home. Trust me, girls, we see this stuff all the time."

Piper stiffens slightly, and I wonder if she knows something I don't. Were Lily and Wyatt fighting? The way Lily tensed up when Wyatt touched her last night, that weird anonymous text . . . God, it seems so obvious now. Something was going on, and Lily didn't tell me.

"But what if she didn't send that email?" Piper asks. "Someone could have easily gotten into her account. Or the email could have been prescheduled. She could still be in danger." She hesitates. "I respect your professional expertise, Detective Rutherford, but I *do* think we should consider the alternative."

Despite the light undertone of kiss-assery, Piper has a point. And I'm glad someone else is backing me up here.

Marty, on the other hand, is obviously trying to hide how quickly he's running out of patience.

"Of course," he says, "we'll be considering all possibilities. And I know, given the mention of Margot Landry and last year's tragedy, that this is all a little . . . worrisome." For a second, he looks uncertain, but then he's back to detective mode. "But like I said, I'm confident that we'll bring Lily home in no time. She's a good girl, and we're going to find her."

A good girl. Meaning, Lily isn't Margot. And he's got a point: Lily follows her parents' rules, even when they're overly strict. She's polite and nice, at least when she's supposed to be, and she'd never do anything as dangerous as what Margot used to do. She's the perfect debutante. She doesn't go *missing.*

And somehow, it doesn't help at all.

It comes out of nowhere: my head swimming, like I'm running too hard on an empty stomach.

The blood on Lily's dress. Margot's face floating over it like a ghost. Last night starts to warp into last year, those same pictures of Margot on the news, people whispering about her all over town. Lily isn't Margot, I know, but a new fear digs its claws in so tight that I know it won't let me go: Lily could be in danger, and the last thing we ever did was lie to each other.

I stand up, little starbursts in my vision.

"I'm sorry, I just—I think I need some air."

I rush out of the cold room and out of their cold house, stopping on the front porch. It's cool out here, too, but somehow not as bad. I sit on the marble porch steps, listening to the gurgle of the fountain on the patio, the rumble of the streetcar out on St. Charles. I try to breathe the way I do after a game, shedding the adrenaline, grounding myself.

Marty's probably right. Lily isn't *missing.* But even as I try to convince myself, it feels less like the truth and more like a fairy tale. One of the cheap ones, the kind Lily used to roll her eyes at.

I slide my hands into my hoodie pocket, pulling out my phone to reread the text Lily sent me last night.

Meet me at the Krewe of Deus Den tomorrow at noon. We need to talk about what you did.

Piper and April both said that Lily wanted to talk about Margot, so I went along with it. I didn't tell them my text was different for the same reason I didn't tell Marty.

Because he was right. It doesn't make sense that Lily would want to talk about Margot Landry, a girl I barely even knew. There's another reason Lily texted me, why she's been pulling away from me, maybe even why she disappeared, and I'm afraid I know exactly what it is.

7

APRIL

DECEMBER 30, 1:30 P.M.

After the LeBlancs', all I want to do is go home, curl up with Mouse, and try to dissociate until Presidents' Day. In fact, that's exactly what I'm planning to do as I walk down the marble porch steps, aiming straight for my car, when I hear Piper behind me.

"Where are you going?"

I stop, turning to look at her there on the porch. Vivian's behind her, still as pale as she's been since she came back inside to finish answering Marty's questions.

"We have to go to the darkroom," Piper says, like it's the most obvious thing in the world. "We have to at least try to figure out what Lily meant."

I hike my camera strap up my shoulder. I don't like the thought of it, bringing Piper and Vivian to the darkroom. It's my own little cave, and like most trolls, I prefer to inhabit it in peace.

"I don't know what she was talking about," I say.

That's not true. I have an idea, but I don't like it. I don't like *anything* about this—how even now, from wherever the hell she is, Lily LeBlanc has managed to take control of my day and make it all about her.

Another memory from that summer burns through me: Margot bent over her phone, fist pressed to her mouth to hide a grin. As soon as she caught me looking, she stashed it. *Nothing,* she'd said when I asked, before telling me that, actually, she couldn't catch a movie later, because she had a "thing" she forgot about. Obviously a lie. It was also obvious who she was really texting. Lily had been trying to edge me out of their friendship for weeks, and even then, some part of me knew it was only a matter of time before she got what she wanted. She always did.

"Well, then, we'll go without you," Piper says, looking to Vivian. "Right?"

Vivian puts her hands on her hips like she's about to ask me to drop and give her twenty. "You seriously have *no* idea what Lily meant?"

I chew the inside of my cheek.

"Look, I know Marty thinks she just ran away, or whatever, but she's my best friend," Vivian continues. "She could be—"

"I know." I take a deep breath in and blow it out.

The thing is, part of me kind of agrees with Marty. Even if no one else can see it, staging her own disappearance seems like exactly the sort of thing Lily LeBlanc would do just to create drama in her picture-perfect life. Because nothing bad ever happens to her. She lives up in her perfect tower, looking down on the rest of us like we're little ants she could fry alive with the glow from her diamond necklace.

But I don't think I can walk away from this. Not because of Lily, but because of that text.

We need to talk about Margot.

Ever since I read those words, I've been flooded with memories of that night. Margot's hand around the lighter, the hiss of the flame. *April, please.*

For a full year, I've tried to forget what we did, how it ended. How I know it's my fault. But now, with Lily's message . . . I can't shake the feeling that maybe I was wrong. Maybe there's more to the story.

The thought is almost too big, too paralyzing to linger on, so I focus on the immediate issue—Piper and Vivian, waiting for my answer. I sigh, reaching for my keys.

"Fine," I say. "Let's go."

If nothing else, I'm not about to let them go traipsing around my darkroom unsupervised.

Beaumont is technically closed for winter break until Tuesday, but for one of the wealthiest schools in the city, they've never been all that concerned about security. They don't have to be—at a school with fifty kids per grade, everyone knows everyone, and it's easy enough to spot someone who doesn't belong.

When we get there, the iron gate by the football field is open, a groundskeeper mowing the grass to Beaumont's standard of perfection. He doesn't bat an eye as we pass, just waves a friendly hand in greeting.

We walk down the brick path beside the football field, and Piper frowns at her phone.

"What?" Vivian asks.

"Wyatt. I guess he just woke up and heard about Lily." There's a slight wrinkle in her nose, like she doesn't approve of slothful habits like sleeping past noon. Then, as she reads further, she looks worried. "He's going to the LeBlancs' to talk to Detective Rutherford."

Vivian gives her a sideways glance. "Was there anything, like . . . weird with them last night?"

Piper's grip tightens on her phone. "What do you mean?"

"I don't know, I just got a weird vibe. Also . . ."

Vivian hesitates, like she's not sure if she can trust us yet—which I guess is fair. We may have gone to school together since kindergarten, but it's not like we're friends.

She sighs. "Right before she left, I saw this text on Lily's phone, from an unsaved number. I didn't see what it said, but she was weird about it."

Piper's jaw tenses. For a moment, she's quiet.

"Okay, so I might have overheard them arguing before they left," she says finally. "It sounded like Wyatt was annoyed that Lily kept texting someone." She glances at Vivian. "Do you have any idea who it might have been?"

Vivian deflates. "No."

"Hmm." Piper narrows her eyes. "Why didn't you tell Detective Rutherford about the text?"

"Why didn't *you* tell him that Wyatt and Lily were arguing?"

Piper holds her in an icy gaze for a moment before turning back to the path. "Because I didn't think it was important. Besides, wouldn't he have just taken that as more proof that Lily ran away because of a 'tiff' with her boyfriend?"

Vivian doesn't answer, but I can tell she agrees. Clearly Piper can, too, because she gives her tennis skirt a self-satisfied brush.

We're nearing the end of the football field, where the massive athletic building marks the beginning of the upper school campus. A breeze reaches under my flannel, and I pull my sleeves over my hands, balling them into fists. Already, I'm dreading having to be back here every day, even though it's technically nice to look at. Beaumont is more like a tiny college than a high school, with red-brick buildings connected by green courtyards and open breezeways, classic French lanterns dangling above them. It's like a brochure come to life, and that's why I don't trust it. It's the kind of beauty that's too symmetrical, too airbrushed. Nothing here feels real.

We walk in what I'm sure Piper and Vivian would consider an awkward silence, but mostly, I'm glad no one's trying to make small talk. Still, when we get to the art wing, I'm relieved.

The classrooms here are clustered around a small courtyard, one room for each discipline Beaumont offers: drawing and painting, ceramics, and—my favorite, obviously—photography. Piper looks around like she's expecting to get jumped, and I wonder if she's ever even set foot here, or if she's one of those straight-A students who thinks any degree that isn't STEM or law is basically worthless.

But what she says is, "I'm pretty sure the classrooms are locked."

I pull a key out of my pocket.

Vivian quirks an eyebrow. "Why am I not surprised?"

"Ms. Ramirez gave it to me," I explain, face going hot. "So I can work on my portfolio after school."

That, and I'm pretty sure she also just took pity on me. *Poor, friendless April. At least let her hide from her peers in this dark hovel where she can, for a brief moment of her day, know peace.*

I'll take what I can get.

But when I slide the key into the lock and twist, it's already unlocked. Weird. I push it open and step inside, greeted by the welcoming scent of photo paper, chemicals, and the lemony cleaner they use on the linoleum. I do a quick scan, but despite the unlocked door, the room is empty. Piper follows me in, and then Vivian, shutting the door behind us.

As we walk deeper inside, Vivian scans the prints clipped to the drying rack, and I realize with an instant burst of regret that they're mine. I shot them at a cemetery in the Garden District, and I've been experimenting with bleaching the film to get a distorted, surreal kind of look, but so far, I haven't gotten it right. The photos always come out messy, and not in an artistic way—just directionless. To someone like Vivian, they probably make me look like a wannabe goth, or worse, a straight-up creep.

The embarrassment must be clear on my face, because Vivian asks, "These yours?"

Reluctantly, I nod.

"They're good."

She sounds surprisingly genuine. Usually, when popular Beaumont girls talk to me, it's with an air of exaggerated niceness, like acknowledging the weird, quiet girl is some kind of tax write-off.

I shrug. "They're fine."

Without giving her any more time to reply, I speed over to the round darkroom door and push my way through to the other side. For a few glorious seconds, I'm alone again.

But the peace doesn't last for long.

"So where do we start?" Piper asks, as she and Vivian shuffle inside, glancing around the room like it's a foreign planet.

My eyes track up to the ceiling.

At first glance, you wouldn't know anything's wrong with it. But when I climb up on a stool, stand on the table, and reach up for the tile, it comes loose, sliding to the side like always.

"Okay, *Mission: Impossible,*" Vivian says, sounding both impressed and a little wary.

I let out a breath. I'd half expected the tile not to open. I haven't let myself check all year, but I'd assumed someone would have noticed the loose tile and fixed it by now. But why would they? No one has hidden anything here since . . .

The memory is so vivid, I'm almost lightheaded. Two years ago, January of sophomore year. The day I walked into the darkroom and found Margot sliding this same tile back into place. The first words she ever said to me:

"What the fuck?"

My hand had frozen around the PB&J I'd swiped from the dining room as Margot stared me down. I was both an underclassman *and* patently uncool, which, in the face of Margot's junior clout, gave me about as much status as a worm. But somehow, before I could stop myself, I'd answered her question with another:

"What are you doing in here?"

Margot raised an eyebrow and sat down on the table. She pulled one leg up to her chest and let the other dangle, heavy Doc Marten bobbing. An amused smile stretched on her lips, revealing her slightly pointed canines. "She speaks."

My first instinct was to back away and flee through the doors, after which I'd pretend that this entire interaction had never happened, but something made me hold my ground. Maybe it was the fact that this was my space, and she'd invaded it.

"What do you mean?" I asked.

She shrugged. "Just observing. I've literally never heard you talk before."

"I'm a sophomore."

"I'm a Gemini. And?"

"I mean we've never had a class together," I said, face hot. "I talk. You just don't know me that well."

My argument was flawed. At Beaumont, it doesn't matter how well you know someone. It's hard *not* to know everyone's full name and life story, no matter how much or how little they talk. Which was pretty little, in my case. Margot was annoyingly right about that.

She pulled at one of the loose curls falling out of her messy bun, twisting it around her finger with an amused look. "What are you doing here?"

If my face was hot before, it could now be a literal fire hazard. I stared helplessly at my sandwich. "Sometimes I eat lunch in here."

"Like, in a Lindsay Lohan in *Mean Girls* way?"

Kind of, I thought.

"No," I said.

She smirked at the NO FOOD OR DRINK sign on the wall. "A rule breaker. I love it."

"I don't make a mess, or anything," I told the floor. Feeling her eyes burning into me, I looked up at the loose tile. "Well, what about you? Do you spend your lunch periods doing sketchy stuff to ceilings, or something?"

She didn't answer. Probably because that was less of a sick burn and more of a lukewarm cough. Finally, I gathered the courage to look at her, and there was a wary look on her face.

"What?" I asked.

"Just deciding if I can trust you. Before, I would've guessed you're like a vault when it comes to secrets, but now that I know you can speak . . ."

For another second, it felt like she was staring through my skin and categorizing my internal organs. Then she hopped up to a crouch on the table and stuck out her little finger.

"Swear you won't tell?"

I frowned, worried she was making fun of me. "A pinky swear?"

She laughed. It sounded genuine. "Would you prefer a blood oath?"

"Kind of." I still wasn't sure if she was just messing with the weird, friendless art girl, but in the end, curiosity won out. I linked my pinky to hers and shook. She grinned.

"I found this spot during class one day," Margot explained as she stood, reaching up to the tile. As her arms stretched out above her, her oversized T-shirt rose to reveal the frayed edges of tiny denim shorts. Way too short, I noted, for winter, and also for the dress code's archaic fingertip rule, but that didn't matter when you were Margot Landry, heir to the biggest energy corporation in the city. Her CEO dad was both literally and figuratively keeping the lights on at this school. At that very moment, the rest of our classmates were eating lunch in the Landry Dining Room. In terms of disciplinary action, Margot was off-limits.

"Thought it was a good hiding place," she continued, sliding the tile aside.

"For what?"

She shot me another wicked smile over her shoulder. "For fun things."

Before I could ask again, she'd reached inside the tile hole and pulled out a pack of cigarettes.

I groaned. "Seriously?"

Her smile fell into a defensive frown. "What?"

"I thought we were past the thing where people think smoking is cool."

She rolled her eyes. "Yeah. I don't smoke them."

"Then why do you have them?"

Margot was picking at the plastic around the cigarette pack, looking almost embarrassed.

"I just think it's fun to get away with shit." She met my eyes and frowned. "It's, like, a statement. This school is so fucking uptight. Sometimes I just like to mess with the natural order of things, okay?"

Before I could think better of it, my jaw dropped into a look of delighted surprise.

Her cheeks tinged pink. "What?"

"Sorry, I just didn't realize you were a John Green character."

She chucked the cigarettes at my head, making me duck. For a stomach-dropping second, I was worried I'd actually hurt her feelings and that she was about to bludgeon me in this darkroom, but when I looked up, her smile was wide.

"Fuck you."

Vivian's voice yanks me back to the present. "You okay?"

I nod. I can't bring myself to lie out loud.

Piper, on the other hand, has no patience for my well-being—which I guess I can understand. She's committed to the mission. "Is there anything in there?"

I reach my hands into the hole in the ceiling, feeling around the edges, but all my fingers brush is dust. With a strange mix of relief and disappointment, I'm about to tell them so when there's a sharp bang from the classroom outside, followed by a loud clatter.

"What the—" Vivian starts, but Piper holds up a finger, silently shushing her with a wide-eyed expression that sends a chill down my spine.

We're not alone.

The classroom door slams, and it's undeniable. Someone else is here, maybe has been this whole time. Panic fizzes under my skin as Vivian runs for the darkroom door.

"Wait," Piper tries. "What are you—"

But Vivian's already pushing through to the classroom, and there's nothing for us to do but follow her.

On the other side, the brightness is jarring. Whoever was here is gone, but they've left a mess behind. The drying rack is toppled over, my pictures scattered on the linoleum floor like dead leaves. I track them all the way to the classroom door, where a crisp white envelope is taped. It's addressed, in fancy looping script, to *The Maids*.

I get there first, tearing it off the door and ripping it open. Vivian and Piper crowd in as I pull out the paper inside. It's thick and heavy like the Les Masques invitations. Actually, it's identical to those invitations, except for the logo. Instead of the Krewe of Deus seal at the top, there's a familiar image: a clown mask with painted lips and jagged eyebrows, one single tear dripping from an eye-shaped void.

A wheel spins in the back of my memory, igniting. I know exactly where I've seen this image before. Margot tracing it with her thumbnail, its chipped blue-black polish. This sad clown is exactly the same as the one on her lighter.

I'm so struck by it that it takes me a second too long to register the message beneath it, neat and handwritten.

My dearest Maids,

Isn't it time we let the dead stay buried?

After all, we all know how hard it is to keep a body underground in this city.

Yours,

The Jester

8

PIPER

DECEMBER 30, 2:00 P.M.

"Shit on a fucking stick," I hiss. "Someone followed us. What the actual . . ."

I reach for my phone, but Vivian's shocked expression stops me. "What are you doing?"

I stare back at her. "Calling the police. Or an adult. I don't know, someone to help?"

"Wait, hold on."

"Why?"

"Just—I don't know. Can we figure out what's, like, actually happening first?" Vivian picks up the invitation, reading the inky script. "*We all know how hard it is to keep a body underground in this city.* What does that even mean?"

"The cemeteries," April says quietly.

"What?" I ask.

April pulls at her camera strap, a haunted look in her eyes as she stares at the mess of photos on the floor. "That's what it's referencing, I think. Since New Orleans is below sea level, and we can't bury anyone underground or else they'd, you know. Float back up."

"That's . . . creepy," I manage. I've also heard that fun little tidbit about the cemeteries—everyone who grows up here has—but I'm a little shocked that April jumped right to the most macabre of conclusions. Although actually, looking at the mausoleums she's apparently chosen to photograph, I shouldn't be surprised.

But that's the least of our concerns. Because this message, combined with the stunt at the ball last night . . .

I reach for the invitation, and Vivian lets me take it.

"*The Jester,*" I read aloud. "Whoever left this is the one who sabotaged the ball. The guy in the costume."

An uneasy feeling washes over me. Yesterday, I thought the stunt with the blood was a bad joke at best. At worst, it was some disgruntled person trying to take a stand against Les Masques and whatever elitism they assume it stands for. But now that Lily's missing, it seems so obvious: what if it wasn't a threat against the organization but against this specific Queen?

"This is about Lily," I say.

"It's about Margot."

We both turn to look at April. Suddenly, it seems, she has a lot to say.

"Lily wanted to talk to us about Margot," she continues. "And last night, at the ball, that was about Margot, too. And this . . ." She brushes the weird clown picture on the invitation. "This exact image was engraved on a lighter that Margot used to have."

I cross my arms. "A lighter?"

April nods.

"That's a weird coincidence, I guess," I concede. "But Lily's the one they threw the blood at." And then I get another idea. "What if the Margot stuff was some kind of threat? You know, like . . . remember what happened to last year's Queen."

It's far-fetched, maybe, but Lily *is* missing, and the possibility is enough to make my skin crawl.

April looks down at her camera. She doesn't argue, but from the way she's winding the strap around her hand like she wants to cut off the circulation, it's pretty obvious there's something she's holding back.

"April," Vivian says carefully, "why did Lily say you'd know where to look in the darkroom?"

I search April's stony expression, wondering the same thing. She practically lives in the photo lab, clearly, but it *is* weird that Lily implied some kind of shared knowledge between them.

Finally, April looks up at us.

"That ceiling tile. Margot used to hide things there, sometimes. And I guess Lily knew about it, too, because—" She pauses. "For a month or so, we were all sort of . . . friends?"

Her face reddens again, like she's embarrassed to have said the word. *Friends.* It makes sense, now, why Lily would have roped April into whatever this is, but still, I'm surprised. I make a habit of knowing what's going on socially at Beaumont—part curiosity, part scoping out the academic competition—and while April ranks low on the list of valedictorian contenders, I've definitely never seen her hanging out with Margot or Lily.

"I didn't realize," Vivian says quietly.

April shrugs. "We didn't really hang out at school, but we'd been friends for a while, Margot and me. Lily didn't come into the picture until the summer before junior year."

"After that Mississippi trip, right?" Vivian asks. "I knew they got close."

Judging by the look on Vivian's face, she wasn't too happy about that.

April nods. "We all hung out that summer, but by the time

the school year started, we'd kind of . . . drifted apart, I guess." She winds her camera strap around her fingers. "And then by December, Margot was . . ."

She trails off, the implication clear.

Finally, it hits me. April was Margot's friend. For me and Vivian, Margot's death was a school tragedy, but nothing more than that. For April, it was personal. I've never been good about grief—for someone whose dad is a psychiatrist, I'm not great at *any* emotions, and that's the most complicated of them all. There's no solution, no easy fix, and so I try to focus on the task at hand.

"There wasn't anything hidden behind the tile, was there?" I ask.

"No," April says. "Maybe I read the message wrong. Or maybe she just didn't leave anything here in the first place."

There's an edge to that second option, like April thinks that's exactly something Lily would do.

My eyes track to the photos on the ground, and an idea starts to form.

"Or maybe 'the Jester' got to it first," I say. "Maybe he beat us here, took whatever Lily left for us, and then . . ."

I notice the closet door, cracked slightly open. It was closed before, wasn't it?

"He must've hidden in there when he heard us coming."

"Shit," Vivian says.

The invitation pulls my gaze. *We all know how hard it is to keep a body underground in this city.* That feeling creeps up on me, just like it did when we found Lily's necklace in the Den. When I knew that something was definitely, distinctly wrong. But just as quickly, I snap myself out of it.

"We need to figure out what Lily left there for us," I say.

Vivian frowns, like she's thinking it over. "Could it have been something about Margot? I mean, that was *her* hiding spot, right?"

She glances at April, who has a distant look in her eyes. Again, I get the feeling there's something she's not saying. But she just shakes her head, like she's not sure.

Well, I'm not waiting around.

"I'm calling Detective Rutherford," I say, grabbing my phone.

"Wait," Vivian starts. "I don't think we should—"

"Someone followed us here and threatened us," I tell her. "I don't know about y'all, but this is the part of the teen TV thriller where I'm always screaming at the main characters to call an adult."

This time, when I call him, no one stops me.

He picks up after two rings. "Hello?"

"Hi, Detective Rutherford? It's Piper. We're at the darkroom, and—" I pause, trying to shape my tone into calm and professional. "We found something."

I put him on speaker and explain it all, from Margot's empty hiding spot to the Jester and his message, as April and Vivian listen anxiously. When I'm done, I can feel a shift, even though the detective is silent.

"You're safe?" he asks finally.

"Yes."

"Good."

He sounds relieved, and so am I. Finally, someone's taking this seriously.

"Well, thank you for calling," he says. "I appreciate it."

"Of course," I say. There's a small silence. "So what do we do?"

"Well, we'll look into this 'Jester' character, of course. It sounds like this could be the same person who pulled that stunt at the ball."

"Right," I say. "But what can *we* do?"

He pauses, like he hadn't expected the question. "Listen," he says, "I'll bet this guy was just trying to scare you. And I'll look into it, I promise, but for now . . . well, I think the best course of action is to be careful, relax, and let me do my job. That sound all right to you girls?"

I don't think he means to sound patronizing, but frustration makes me grip my phone tighter.

"Of course," I say. "Thanks, Detective Rutherford."

"Marty," he says kindly. "And anytime. Y'all be safe, now."

He hangs up, and I let out a sigh. "Well, at least they're looking into it." Then I notice April's scowl. "What?"

"Nothing," she says.

"You look like someone's about to force you to do a deb ball again. It's obviously something."

"I just—I don't know. I don't trust him."

"Why?" I ask.

April swings an arm at my phone, like it's obvious. "Y'all heard him just now. He thinks the Jester is just trying to 'scare us.' He probably still thinks Lily *just* ran away, and Margot was a—" She stops. "I can tell from the way he talked about her. He thinks she was a lost cause."

Vivian shifts. "Marty *is* being weirdly chill about this whole thing. I don't know. He kind of gives me a bad vibe, too."

I tap my nails against the back of my phone case, thinking. Unlike April and Vivian, I don't have an innate distrust of authority figures with *bad vibes,* but they do have a point. Someone followed us here, and Marty acted like it was nothing to worry about, like we're just teenage girls being anxious. It's the same way he's been acting about Lily. Earlier, I might have believed him, but if there's one thing I respect, it's evidence, and right now, it all points to one conclusion: something is really wrong here. And something has to be done.

"Okay." I clap, making them jump. "Sorry. Force of habit when I have a plan."

"Which is?" Vivian asks.

"We do our own investigation. Track down the Jester ourselves."

April frowns. "How?"

"We start with the Dukes. The Beaumont ones, at least. Milford, Jason, and Aiden. They were all up on the stage when it happened, so they must have seen something." Another idea slots into place. "Y'all are coming to the party tomorrow, right?"

April looks like she'd rather dive straight into a tub filled with glass shards. "What party?"

"The one at my house," I say. "My mom sent an invitation to all of the Les Masques Maids. It's a New Year's Eve celebration for the debutantes."

And, as I'm well aware, an excuse for all the kids who show up—and some parents, probably—to get wasted, but that's beside the point.

"Yeah. Me, Sav, and—" Vivian stops herself. Clearly, she was about to say *Lily*. "We were planning to. But . . ."

I roll my eyes. "Obviously, I'm not suggesting we all do shots together. I mean we should use it as a chance to talk to the Dukes. They'll all be there."

Vivian crosses her arms. "You're sure your mom won't cancel, considering?"

I almost laugh. There's no way in hell. For one thing, she

already knows that Lily's missing—I called and filled her in on my way to the LeBlancs' this morning—and she still hasn't made any moves to cancel the festivities. When Genevieve Johnson sets her mind to hosting an event, not even the hand of God can stop her. Literally: once, there was a tropical-storm warning the weekend of a Johnson family reunion, and instead of rescheduling, she rush-ordered monogrammed rain ponchos to hand out at the door.

I shrug. "She's had the caterers booked for months. And anyway, isn't partying, like, the number-one coping mechanism in New Orleans?"

They can't argue, because I'm right. This city literally turned funerals into an excuse to get drunk and parade down the street.

Vivian sighs. "I guess it's better than just waiting around and hoping they find her."

"April?" I ask.

Her mouth opens and closes a couple times, like she's short-circuiting. "Parties aren't really my—"

"Don't think of it like a party, then," I say. "It's an undercover mission. One that we need you for, by the way."

She blinks. "Why?"

I hesitate. Normally, I'm not the best at complimenting people, but in this case, it's merely a statement of facts.

"You notice things," I tell her. "And you have a weirdly good memory. Also, you knew Margot well. That could come in handy if we're trying to figure out how she fits into all this."

April presses her lips together until they turn white.

"Fine," she says.

I can't fight the grin that spreads across my face, the little thrill I get whenever a plan starts to come together.

"Great. Then I'll see y'all tomorrow at eight. Attire is festive casual." And then, with a quick glance at April's baggy bleach-stained clothes, I add, "But let's put an emphasis on the festive."

9

VIVIAN

DECEMBER 31, 8:15 P.M.

By the time Sav and I are standing on the porch of the Johnsons' big white house on State Street, I'm already regretting it. I can tell Sav is, too, from the way she's staring at the golden Deus sign on the front door like it might be a portal to hell.

"This is going to suck, right?" she says.

A weirdly relieved laugh rushes out of me, maybe just because it's nice to hear her say what I've been thinking all day.

"Probably," I say.

Normally, the Johnsons' big holiday parties are the best. Mrs. Johnson is stuffy, for sure, but she's at least a *little* more relaxed once she gets a couple glasses of wine in. Most importantly, there's always an open bar, and even the stuffiest of New Orleans parents tend to be pretty chill with the whole underage-drinking thing.

But tonight, for obvious reasons, I don't think anyone will be having fun.

"I just . . ." Sav hesitates. "I really thought she'd be back by now."

My shoulders tense. It's been almost forty-eight hours. Anyone who's ever watched a crime show knows that's pretty much the end of the window where missing girls get found.

But I force that down. If I think too hard about it, there's no way I'll make it through this door, much less the night.

"Yeah," I say. "Me, too."

"Maybe we give it an hour, and if it's terrible, we leave?" She smiles a little. "We look too good not to at least show it off."

I smile back, smoothing out my black jumpsuit. It's an old staple of my closet, nothing as new or exciting as the gold sparkly dress Sav is rocking, but I like how I feel in it, the way it hugs my curves. I try to let it give me the confidence I don't have that tonight will be okay. That maybe Piper was right, and if we try, we might even learn something that could help us find Lily.

"Deal."

We ring the doorbell. It echoes over the noise of the party, polite conversation and clinking glasses. Piper swings the door open, wearing a navy dress that looks better suited for a Model UN conference than a party, even if she *did* pair it with dangling silver shooting-star earrings.

"Hi," she says, with a look that screams, *You're fifteen minutes late, Vivian, and you will not be hearing the end of this.* "Welcome. So nice of y'all to come. Refreshments are in the dining room." As we step inside, she grabs my elbow tight enough to leave a mark. "Vivian, can I steal you for a sec?" She shoots Sav an apologetic smile. "We're about to take an official Les Masques Maids photo. Mom insisted. Try the bacon-wrapped dates, they're amazing."

Without waiting for an answer, Piper drags me away from Sav and into another room off the foyer. Her dad's office, I'm guessing, from the big wooden desk and shelves of psychology books. April's already here, legs dangling from an armchair like she's waiting to see the principal, her camera still slung over her shoulder.

Piper closes the door behind us and stares me down. "You're late."

"Fifteen minutes."

"Which is late, by most definitions."

I sigh. "Can you explain why we're being held hostage, so I can get back to the friend I just abandoned?"

"We need to make a game plan," Piper says. "I think we should split up to maximize efficiency. We'll each take one of the Dukes. I can talk to Aiden."

Maybe I'm just annoyed by the immediate attack of Piper-ness, or maybe I can't pass up the chance to push her buttons. Either way, I lean against the closed door with a smirk. "Y'all are, like, a thing, right?"

Instantly, she's almost as red as April gets whenever she speaks.

"No."

"Could've fooled me." I shrug, and you know what? Maybe I like watching her squirm. "I saw y'all argue about *Pride and Prejudice* in class one time, and the tension . . ." I mime fanning myself. "Way more entertaining than Jane Austen."

She scowls. "Well, clearly you only read the SparkNotes of *Pride and Prejudice,* because one: it's *very* entertaining, and two: we are not and will never be a 'thing,' so can we please stay on track here?"

I *did* only read the SparkNotes, but I'm not about to admit it. A slow smile spreads on April's face, instantly disappearing when Piper catches it.

I grin. "Fine."

"As I was *going* to say"—Piper gives me a pointed look—"I

think it makes sense for each of us to take our assigned Dukes. So I'll talk to Aiden, you'll talk to Jason, and April can take Milford."

Now April looks like she might be sick.

"I, um—I'm not the best at talking."

Piper sighs. "Fine. I can talk to Milford, too. But you have to be our eyes and ears, then. Keep watch of everyone and listen for anything useful."

April breathes out, relieved. "Okay."

"Good. So our goal is to find out what they saw onstage and if they know who threw the blood. Got it?"

Like it's as simple as that. But I guess it's the only plan we have.

"Got it," I echo.

"All right," Piper says. "Everyone, stay sharp."

With that, she turns and marches out of the office, leaving me and April behind. She's still sitting in the chair, looking so out of place with that giant camera, and something about it makes me sad. Piper has her little squad of AP girls to hang out with, even if none of them seem to like each other that much. But as far as I can tell, April doesn't have any friends at Beaumont. I can't imagine what that's like, going through high school without people like Sav and Lily to make it bearable. Especially if she *did* have a friend, only to lose her.

I think about asking if she wants to hang out with me and Sav, but before I can, April springs out of the chair.

"I guess we should . . ."

"Yeah," I finish, picking up on how much she clearly wants to get out of here. "Let's go."

We split up in the foyer, April heading for the dining room and me off to find Sav. I spot her in the living room with Jason, who's already swigging champagne. Wyatt is there, too, his fist tight around a beer.

My nerves jump, but I try to force them down as I make my way over. *Head up, Atkins,* I tell myself. *Everything's fine.* But just like it has been for the past few months, it feels like a lie.

"Hey," I say. "Sorry, Piper dragged me away." I glance at Wyatt. "Your sister is intense about group photos."

His eyes flick to mine, making me too aware of the exposed skin of my collarbone, the way my hair is falling around my cheeks. I pulled a few strands out of my ponytail to frame my face, and it's not until now that I realize it's almost exactly how Lily wore her hair to the ball.

"She's intense about a lot of things," Wyatt mumbles over his beer, looking away.

"Atkins!" Jason booms, his glass sloshing as he gives me a side-hug. "What is *up,* my dude?"

"Your blood-alcohol content, apparently," I tease, but I'm actually kind of glad to see him. At least he's another friendly face, even if I *am* supposed to be grilling him about the ball. Which, I'm realizing, I have no idea how to start.

"I'm getting another beer," Wyatt mumbles, setting his empty bottle down on the nearest table and sulking away.

"Damn," Jason says. "He's in a mood."

Sav's jaw tightens, and I feel mine doing the same. Wyatt must not have even told Jason about Lily yet. I watch as he broad-shoulders his way toward the bar, and suddenly, it's obvious that Jason isn't the one I should be mining for info.

"Be right back," I tell them, following Wyatt down the hall before I lose the nerve.

I catch up with him in the kitchen, where he's fishing another beer out of the fridge. It's mostly empty in here, besides a few extra trays of hors d'oeuvres. All the other food is arranged in an Instagram-worthy spread in the dining room or being swept around the house by uniformed caterers.

"Hey," I say. "Can we talk?"

Wyatt turns to face me, the beer dripping in his hand. "About what?"

He's going for his usual surly tough-guy crap, but it's hard for him to get away with it when he's facing me head-on. Wyatt towers over Lily, but he's only got a few inches on me.

"Last night," I say. "What happened?"

"Nothing."

"Lily was texting someone, right? Who was it?"

His grip tightens on the beer. "How do you know that?"

"I saw a message pop up on her phone," I tell him, figuring I'll leave out the part where his sister narced on him. "And y'all were both being weird. I know something was up."

"Why do you care?"

"Are you serious?"

He tries to sidestep me, but he's pissing me off, and I know a thing or two about playing defense.

"I care because she's missing," I snap, blocking his way. "And I don't know about you, but I want to find her."

"You think I don't?"

I'm opening my mouth to fire back when Jason appears in the kitchen doorway.

"Whoa," he says in a *break-it-up* tone. "Wyatt, my man, what's—"

Wyatt shoves him hard enough that Jason stumbles back.

"What the hell?" Jason laughs, shocked, like maybe he thinks Wyatt is kidding. He glances over at me. "Is everything—"

But he doesn't get to the *okay,* because Wyatt grips him by the collar so fast it makes my stomach drop.

"Mind your own fucking business," he says through gritted teeth. "Or I'll—"

"Hey, what's going on here?"

The tone is unmistakable: authoritative but somehow still totally chill. Coach.

Instantly, Wyatt releases Jason. "Nothing."

Coach gives Jason a look. "You good, man?"

"Yes, sir." Jason nods quickly, fixing his collar.

That's one of my favorite things about Coach: even though girls' soccer is about as undervalued at Beaumont as any sport besides football, he still knows how to silence a quarterback and a linebacker at the drop of a hat.

"How about y'all cool off, yeah? Take a breath, have a cheese puff," Coach says, his Texas accent slipping in. "From what I can tell, your mom worked real hard on tonight, and I'd hate for it to be ruined by a whole lot of *nothing.*" He gives Wyatt a clap on the shoulder.

Wyatt scowls, but he grumbles a "Yes, sir." He stalks deeper into the house, and Jason scurries off behind him.

Coach sighs when they're gone. "Glad we nipped that in the bud before Mrs. Johnson caught wind. Don't tell anyone I said so, but I think she's just about ready to stab somebody with an oyster fork."

"Piper might beat her to it," I add, even though I'm not totally sure that's an exaggeration.

Coach smiles, but it fades quickly. He runs a hand through his dark curls, which the team always jokes makes him look like a long-lost Jonas Brother. "I, uh . . . I heard about Lily."

I tense.

"Elle heard it from some of the other Deus ladies, I guess." He nods through the kitchen doorway at his pretty girlfriend, who's in the next room, chatting with some other women near a tray of canapés.

My throat squeezes. "Word travels fast."

"You okay?" Coach asks. "I know it must be tough, all this. I can only imagine."

It hits me that he's the first adult who's actually asked me how I'm doing. Even Mom: she's trying her best to stay positive, like anything less hopeful than "Don't worry, Viv, everything's going to be okay" is bad luck. Dad, I haven't even seen since the ball, and he hasn't checked in, either. Since the divorce, anything but Les Masques, school, or soccer seems like dangerous territory for us.

"Yeah," I say. "It sucks."

Coach nods, and I'm glad he doesn't try to offer some "everything happens for a reason" platitude. It's nice to just let *it sucks* be the truth.

"What's your take on all this?" he asks, gesturing at two side-by-side frames on the wall: Piper's Les Masques invitation, and her mom's invitation to be a Maid in the Deus ball thirty years ago. There's an empty space above them, where Piper's Deus invitation will no doubt go in a few years.

"The deb stuff?" I shrug. "It's not really my thing. But my brother was a Duke a couple years back, and my parents are into it, so."

"Elle loves it." Coach laughs. "She's still got her Deus Maid dress in her closet. Her Les Masques one, too, from all the way back in high school. I guess I get the tradition of it all, but I don't know. I've been feeling like a real fish out of water."

"Well, you didn't exactly get the best introduction last night."

Coach winces. "I guess not. But between you and me . . ." He glances at me sideways. "Not really my thing, either."

In the other room, Elle catches Coach's eye.

"Reed," she says, waving him over.

"Duty calls," he tells me, giving her a little salute. "But hey, if you ever need somebody to talk to, you know where to find me."

"Thanks." I smile. "But I think mostly I could use a practice that really kicks my ass next week."

Coach laughs. "You got it, Atkins."

He goes, leaving me alone with the framed invitations. I think again of the one we found in the darkroom, just like these, except with the creepy clown logo and a much scarier message.

We all know how hard it is to keep a body underground in this city.

I turn, suddenly itching to get away from here. Not just the invitations, but this entire night, everyone drinking and stuffing their faces and pretending everything's okay. And the way Wyatt blew up just now . . .

As I step back into the other room, I catch him standing alone, still clutching his beer by the neck. For a second, he meets my eyes. Then he stomps away.

Forty-eight hours, and the only lead I've got is that Wyatt was probably the last person to see Lily before she went missing.

That, and the part where it might be my fault.

10

PIPER

DECEMBER 31, 8:30 P.M.

So far, this party is going exactly as expected. Or should I say, *so far, so drunk*? Which is, for all intents and purposes, a good thing. Drunk people are more likely to tell the truth. Not that my target ever really gets wasted—Aiden Ortiz is far too responsible for that, which would be more relevant if I could actually find him.

I check the living room, dining room, and the sunroom at the back of the house, where Dad is stationed with a thick Alexander Hamilton biography and a glass of whiskey, tuning out the group of Deus dads reminiscing about their time as Dukes way back in the day. Seeing me in the doorway, he lifts his glass in a weary salute. I give one back before swiftly extracting myself.

On my way back down the hall, Vivian comes out of the kitchen, so quickly I stop in my tracks. Seems like I startle her, too, because she visibly flinches.

"How's it going?" I ask, trying not to linger on the fact that she's so clearly unhappy to see me.

"Fine," she says. "Nothing new from Jason. I'm heading to the bathroom."

With that, she speeds away. I'm about to demand more details when I clock my target in the living room—charming a cluster of moms, of course, like he deliberately placed himself there to piss me off. Gritting my teeth, I make my way over, catching the word "Stanford" at least twice as I approach. Maybe if someone says it a third time, a Silicon Valley billionaire in a T-shirt and sandals will appear in the reflection of their champagne glasses.

"Hi, Mrs. Fontaine. Mrs. Kimball. I hope y'all are enjoying the party," I say, flashing a smile as I dig my fingers into Aiden's arm. "Can I steal him for a second?"

"Of course, dear. Don't let us monopolize him." Mrs. Fontaine gives Aiden an adoring wink. "Tell your mom she's done a wonderful job, as always."

"Thank you, I will. And Eugenie looked gorgeous last night. She's a perfect model for Mom's dresses." I grin, just like Mom did at her from across the ballroom, moments after calling her husband an insufferable ass.

I haul Aiden through the living room without releasing his arm.

"Are we on *The Bachelor*?" he asks.

"What?"

"'Can I steal him for a second?' It's a classic line."

"I'm sorry, do you watch *The Bachelor*?"

"I contain multitudes."

"Yeah, multitudes of shit."

We're stopped in the foyer now, which is practically empty.

"Okay, so why'd you drag me over here?" Aiden asks. "Because I was really winning those moms over with my charm and witty repartee."

"I need you to tell me about the ball," I say.

We've wasted enough time. Might as well get to it.

Aiden frowns. "What do you mean?"

"Did you throw the blood at Lily?"

He tenses, all of that irritating ease suddenly gone from his posture. "Whoa, what? I told you before, I didn't—"

"If it wasn't you, then who was it? I know you saw something."

I'm going a little too hard with this interrogation, and it doesn't seem to be working. Lines crinkle around Aiden's eyes, and I'd almost think he was concerned, if I thought him capable of the feeling.

"Piper, is something else going on?"

I cross my arms. "Lily's missing."

He lets out a breath, eyes falling to the floor. "Yeah, I heard."

"Whatever happened to her, I think it has something to do with what happened at the ball. Whoever was in that Jester costume. And I know it's one of the Dukes, so—"

"You think something happened to her?" Aiden's stare snaps back up to meet mine.

"You have a lot of irredeemable qualities, Aiden, but a lack of deductive-reasoning skills isn't one of them. That stunt at the ball was obviously some kind of threat, and now Lily's missing. What else are we supposed to think?"

He sighs, pulling a hand through his hair. "No, you're right. I just . . ."

"What?"

For a moment, he's quiet, like he's weighing his words. "You're good at solving problems," he says. "Personally, I think it's one of your *least* irredeemable qualities. A pretty good one, actually."

There's a little flicker of something low in my stomach, and Vivian's stupid *Pride and Prejudice* thing worms its way into my head. I remind myself this is a perfectly reasonable response to being complimented. Scientific, even.

"But?" I press.

"But I don't think it's smart to get all mixed up in this. I'm sure the police and Lily's family are on it, and the LeBlancs . . ." Aiden looks over his shoulder, like he's making sure no one else is listening in. "They practically run the whole city, and digging around in their business, even with the best of intentions . . ." He shakes his head. "All I'm saying is, families like theirs always have skeletons in the closet. Things that tend to come out when something like this happens. And I think it's dangerous to be the one who finds them."

He seems genuinely worried for me right now, and even worse, I know he has a point. Aiden and I both come from wealthy families, same as pretty much everyone at Beaumont, but there's a stark difference between being a Johnson or an Ortiz and being a LeBlanc. They're the people with politicians and police in their pockets, whose daughters are Queens instead of Maids—they're royalty, and we're just lucky enough to be in their court.

Still, I can't help hearing echoes of Marty in Aiden's words.

"So you think we should do nothing," I say. "Just sit back and hope they find her."

"No, I—" He frowns, but then his gaze softens again. "I just . . . I think you should be careful, Piper."

For half a second, there's that stupid warm feeling again, but it's quickly hammered down by annoyance. He doesn't want me to be careful because he's worried about me—it's because he thinks I can't figure this out on my own. Because he thinks it's not my business.

"Sure," I say. "Thanks for the tip."

"Wait, I didn't mean—"

"Do you have any helpful intel about last night or not?"

Aiden watches me for a second. Then he shakes his head. "I'm sorry, but I really don't know anything else. I wish I did."

"Fine," I tell him. "Thanks anyway, I guess."

I turn around and head back into the living room. So Aiden was a bust. I should have expected that. But at least I can still grill Milford.

Only, finding him might be a challenge, too. Our house is packed with kids from the ball and older Deus members, everyone decked out in their festive-casual finery. I scan the room for everyone my age, all clustered with drinks, bent over their phones—probably planning their next move, because this party is so obviously only a pregame for them, a way to get plastered for free before heading out to one of the grimy college bars near Tulane. One thing I'll never understand: the desire to be anywhere with a sticky floor on purpose.

I spot April in the corner, watching the party with an uncomfortable look on her face. I wonder if I should go check in with her, but then someone tugs on my arm. Jason. I flinch.

"What?" I snap.

"This is Wyatt's," he says, holding out a phone.

I take it, and the screen lights up with his background photo: him and Lily, his arms wrapped around her after one of her soccer games.

"He left it by the beer," Jason adds, lifting his own fresh bottle in explanation. "I'd give it back to him myself, but he's in a hell of a mood. Fair warning."

Before I can ask what *that* means, Jason is lumbering away.

"Shit," I mutter under my breath. The last thing I need tonight is Wyatt on his worst behavior.

I scan the room but don't see him, so I spin around and march down the hall. I'm just passing the staircase when I get an idea. Glancing around to make sure no one's watching, I type our birthday into the passcode keypad.

The phone unlocks.

Classic, I think. He might as well make it "1234." But if we want information about what happened at the ball . . .

Before I can talk myself out of it, I climb the stairs, heart thudding all the way up to my bedroom, where I lock the door behind me.

It's for his own good, I think. Right now, all we know about the hours leading up to Lily's disappearance is that she was texting someone and Wyatt was pissed about it. And if he insists on sulking all day instead of telling me what was actually going on, when Vivian and April probably think he's our prime suspect, then someone's going to have to clear his name for him, and it might as well be me.

I open his messages, scrolling to find his conversation with Lily. When I see it, I wince. It's a parade of texts from Wyatt to her, all unanswered, starting that night at 11 P.M.

Did you get home ok?

Ten minutes later:

I know you're mad but can you at least answer
Did you get a ride home?

Half an hour after that:

Lily come on I'm sorry

Don't do this

Hello??

And then, at 12:30 A.M.:

Fuck this

I'm done

Lily's read receipts show she saw all of them except for the last two. The most ominous two.

And then it hits me. I scroll back up.

Did you get a ride home?

Why would he ask that if he was the one who drove her?

The answer is unbelievably simple: because he didn't.

But Lily's parents said he did, didn't they? Did Wyatt lie to them? To Marty? I shut my eyes and try to think logically. Even if he lied, Wyatt obviously didn't have anything to do with Lily's disappearance. I know this, as well as I know the periodic table or the exact schedule of alarms he sets every morning to get up for school, the third one always ringing at precisely seven forty, when I'm dressed, packed, and passing his room to go down for breakfast.

But I also can't ignore the very real truth in front of me.

Like I said, I'm someone who respects the evidence—and right now, all of it points to my brother.

11

APRIL

DECEMBER 31, 8:45 P.M.

Nearly an hour into this party, all I've accomplished is making a catalog of the best methods of escape. The cleanest would be an Irish goodbye, followed by texting Piper and Vivian that I've been hit with a sudden and severe stomach flu. Both seem like unattainable fantasies, though, because there's too many damn people here, and even an escape through the back door would mean running into people from school, which means risking confused stares or, worse, small talk.

Currently, I'm back in the dining room, wondering if the window in here opens and, if not, what would happen if I simply took a running leap through the glass.

"'Scuse us." Coach Davis gives me a polite smile as he edges toward the appetizer table, a pretty blond woman at his side.

I shove another cracker with crab dip into my face and step aside, watching him load up his plate. I'm not sure if he recognizes me, seeing as I avoid organized sports like the plague, but I remember him sitting with this woman at the ball. For a minute, I listen for anything that might be useful, but all I get is

Coach Davis improvising a song about how much he loves the cheese puffs while the woman looks on, mildly embarrassed.

Drifting toward the dessert table, I glance at my phone again. No updates from Piper or Vivian—which is fine, because I have nothing to report. Probably because I am, you know, hiding.

This detective mission is going about as well as I expected.

"I just can't possibly imagine," I hear a woman croon to another. They're stationed next to the spread of petit fours and mini Doberge cakes that no one seems to actually be touching. I make a mental note to pocket some once these ladies move on.

"It's terrible, isn't it?" the other woman whispers in the kind of scandalized tone that suggests it's not really all that terrible. "And after what happened last year . . ."

"The vandalism?"

I freeze. Already, it's like I can sense what's coming.

"Well, of course, but also what happened to . . . you know."

You know. Like she's just an afterthought. Like Margot's life and death are hardly noteworthy compared to some fucking floats getting destroyed.

The first woman balks. "Oh, but you don't think . . . ?"

"No, no, of course not. Lily's a good girl. It's quite a different situation."

"Well," says the woman. "They'll certainly be in my prayers."

Suddenly, even the idea of Doberge is more than I can stomach. I pull my camera strap up my shoulder and march out of the dining room, taking quick, quiet breaths to stave off the panicked heat burning all over my skin.

New Orleans is the biggest small town in the country, and

news spreads quicker than disease, especially among the present company. But I can't stand the way they were talking about it just now, like some kind of salacious true-crime story, *thoughts and prayers* and a steaming pile of nothing else. And the final, obvious blow: *It's quite a different situation*. As in, something like that could never happen to Lily. As in, Margot had it coming.

The bar table appears in the living room, and before I can think too hard about it, I walk over, pour a glass of champagne, and down it quickly, the bubbles burning.

Screw it. It's time to do some detective work.

It's not long before I catch a flash of bright-red hair moving out of the living room and into the hallway.

Milford.

I move before my anxiety can catch up with my legs, trailing him as he ambles to the back of the Johnsons' house. Drunk, I'm pretty sure. I swallow the lump of panic in my throat. This is good. Maybe I can talk to Milford if he's drunk, if I can tell myself he won't remember.

"Maybe" being a generous term, but now's not the time to overthink it.

Milford passes into the sunroom at the end of the house, and I hang back. A bunch of the dads are congregated there, trading raucous laughter and firm slaps on the back. Milford gets a few as he heads toward the back door.

"Milford Wilcox! What are you getting up to back here?" one man asks, like he hopes it's something illegal.

"Nothing much," Milford says. "Just want to commune with nature."

The man gives a barking laugh. "Hey, your old man coming out tonight?"

"Nah, he has to work."

"Industrious old bastard! Well, don't worry, we won't tell on you. Right, boys?"

The man holds out his hand, which Milford claps before stepping through the back door and into the yard.

God, these men are drunker than the teenagers at this party. I recognize most of them from Les Masques, I think, but none of them are close friends with my parents. They probably won't even acknowledge me if I walk past, because that's the nice thing about being the quiet girl: in the right circumstances, you develop the power of invisibility.

Taking a deep breath, I clutch my camera tightly, hunch forward, and walk toward the door.

"What's up, Annie Leibovitz?" one of the men booms as I pass.

I give my best attempt at a smile, but it's more just pressing my mouth into a flat line, not making eye contact.

"Hey, you chasing after our buddy Milford?" another asks. "Don't take anything he does personally. He takes after his old man."

The men laugh. I rush outside, resisting the urge to flip them the bird as I shut the door behind me.

Outside, the cool air is welcome on my face. Milford has made his way over to the pool, standing next to a magnolia tree. He reaches into his pocket and pulls something out. A joint, I realize, as he sticks it between his teeth. Smoking weed anywhere near Piper's mom feels like a death wish, but Milford doesn't strike me as the type who cares. He pulls out a lighter next, big and silver. Almost like . . .

Recognition seizes me, digging its fingers into my skin.

I reach for my camera. No time to think about it. Milford is cupping the lighter close to the joint between his lips, and I have to know. I press the shutter, instantly regretting using my camera instead of my phone. It was instinct, but now, I can't be sure if I got it clearly. I start to reach for my phone, thinking maybe—

"Uh, did you just take a picture of me?"

Shit. *Shit.*

Milford is squinting directly at me through the dark, and I should have leapt out the Johnsons' window when I had the chance. But no. I have to step up and do this. How hard is it to be a functioning social being for five minutes?

Do it for Margot, I think.

"Your lighter," I force out. "It's cool."

To my surprise, Milford laughs, high and whiny. He lifts it up, examining it in the light, and stumbles slightly, like the change in perspective was too much for his brain to keep up with.

"You smoke, June?"

"April," I correct him, almost inaudibly. He literally escorted me around a ballroom twenty-four hours ago. How does he not remember which month I'm named after? "And I don't really—"

I stop myself. I don't smoke, not since the time I tried it with Margot and spent an hour convinced the statues in her backyard were watching me. But if I get Milford talking . . .

"Yeah," I say. "Sometimes."

I walk over to him, surprised at how calm I suddenly feel. For once, I feel like I have the upper hand.

Milford takes an overly indulgent hit before handing it over. "Another fucking party, am I right?"

I have only the vaguest idea of what Milford means by this, but I nod anyway. It's an opening. "I guess it's weird to be here," I say. "You know. With the Lily stuff."

Milford goes quiet, staring at the pool. Then he nods, like

he's found enlightenment in the rippling surface. "Y'know, she might be smarter than all of us. Just saying screw it. Getting away from all this bullshit."

"You think she ran away?"

Milford shrugs, reaching for the joint again. I hand it back without taking a hit. He brings it to his lips, apparently uninterested in continuing this conversation, but I have to keep trying.

"Can I see the lighter?" I ask.

Milford snickers. "You a pyro, or something?"

I don't laugh. My heart is pounding too wildly. He digs into his pocket and pulls it out anyway, opening his palm for me to see. Some part of me already knew, but still, it's like everything falls away except for that engraving.

The sad clown. It's the same picture that was on the Jester's invitation—on Margot's lighter. I'd seen it a hundred times. In her pocket. On the levee.

In her hand on the last night of her life.

"Where did you get that?" I breathe.

Milford flicks the lighter open and sparks it, the flame dancing in the dark.

"Top secret," he says with a slimy smile.

I reach for it, and he snaps it closed. "That's hers," I say. "That's Margot's."

"What?" Milford looks genuinely confused, even through the daze of weed and alcohol. He takes an unsteady step back, toward the pool. "Margot Landry?"

"Where did you get it?"

"It's mine," he says. "What are you even—"

"Milford," I demand, stepping forward, "*where did you get it?*"

And that's when he loses his balance and goes sailing backward into the water.

12

PIPER

DECEMBER 31, 9:00 P.M.

I hear the splash before I register where it's coming from. I rush to my bedroom window, and looking down, I see it: Milford crashing through the pool's surface, gasping for air, while April stands at the edge.

Goddammit. You take five minutes to yourself to try to process what you found on your brother's phone, and suddenly, the meekest member of your detective trio is drowning guests in your backyard.

I ditch Wyatt's phone in his empty bedroom—he'll find it eventually—and run down the steps, through the house, and to the sunroom, where I push past the cluster of dads and out the door.

"Okay, so this is *not* what we discussed," I hiss at April as I approach.

She stares back at me, wide-eyed. "I didn't . . ."

Milford climbs out of the pool, dress shirt and khakis clinging to his bony frame. He shakes his hair out like a wet dog.

"All good. Just fell." He points at April. "She's scary."

He's slurring, which can hopefully be attributed to drunkenness, because a concussion is quite literally the last thing we need right now. I glance back toward the house, but none of the Deus dads seem to have noticed. Good. I need to fix this before Mom sees and has a conniption.

"Come on." I grab Milford's arm and yank him toward the small guesthouse in the back of the yard. "Let's get you dried off."

April trails behind me like a guilty-looking ghost, wringing her camera strap in her hands. Inside, I instruct Milford to stay put as I march to the bathroom and return with a towel.

"Here." I shove it toward him. "Don't touch anything until you're dry."

He wraps the towel around himself with a fraught expression.

"What?"

"I don't feel so good."

Oh *no*. "Like . . . ?"

Milford nods, a little green, and I fight back the many expletives that I want to throw his way. Instead, I direct him to the bathroom. He scurries inside, shutting the door behind him with a loud slam.

"Just—if you're going to puke, do it in the toilet!"

No answer.

I groan. "Goddammit."

"He didn't hit his head," April says, barely loud enough to hear. "I saw. He's just drunk."

"I'm aware," I snap.

She flinches, looking down.

I let out a breath. It's not April's fault that Milford's an uncoordinated drunk. She was just doing her job.

"It's okay," I tell her, more gently. "He'll be fine." And then I realize. "You talked to him."

She nods, a smile flickering.

"Hell yeah, you did!" I clap, feeling a little like the proud owner of a bird who just learned to recite Nietzsche. With a glance at the bathroom door, I lower my voice. "Did you get anything out of him?"

The smile disappears. "Yeah. I—" She stops midsentence, closing her eyes like she needs to steel herself. "He has Margot's lighter."

"Wait, what?"

April unfolds her fist, and there it is, engraved with a picture I recognize. My breath catches.

"That's the clown from the Jester's message," I say. April already told us it was on Margot's lighter, but still, it sends a chill down my spine. "You're sure it's hers?"

"I'm not positive, but it's identical."

I take it from her, turning it over. A lighter isn't exactly a smoking gun, but right now, it's something. The only clue we have, actually. And handing it back to April, I feel a rush of relief—because whatever this means, it has to be more important than Wyatt's lie about driving Lily home.

I whip out my phone. "I'm calling Vivian. We should fill her in."

As the tone rings in my ear, Milford groans from the bathroom. I wince.

"Hello?" Vivian answers.

"Guesthouse," I say. "Now."

"But—"

"No buts. We found something."

I hang up quickly, so she doesn't have a choice. A few minutes later, she walks in, looking annoyed.

"Okay, this better be good," she says. And then, when

Milford groans again, “Uh, please tell me this hasn’t become a hostage situation?”

“What? No. Who do you think we are?” I ask.

“Just checking.” Vivian holds up her hands in surrender. “But seriously, what’s going on?”

I nod for April to hold out the lighter.

When Vivian sees it, her eyes widen. “Is that . . . ?”

“Margot’s,” April confirms.

“Where’d you find it?”

I swing an arm at the bathroom. “Milford.”

“And he’s . . . ?”

“Drunk,” I say.

“Wet,” April adds.

“But not concussed,” I finish. “Probably. April talked to him.”

“Really?” Vivian looks impressed.

April reddens, but she nods.

“Nice,” Vivian says, like a coach after a good play. “Okay, but wait. Why does Milford have Margot’s lighter? He’s not, like . . . *the Jester*, is he?”

“That’s what we need to find out.” I walk over to the kitchenette, where I grab a glass from the cabinet and fill it with water.

Another moan from the bathroom.

Vivian quirks an eyebrow. “Pretty sure he’s not in any state to be interrogated right now.”

“So we speed up the sobriety.” I hold up the glass.

Vivian stares. “I hope you mean by hydrating him.”

“In a sense.”

“Wait, we have to be careful,” Vivian tries. “We can’t just—”

The door unlocks, and Milford swings it open.

“Feeling better?” I ask.

He nods. "Yeah, I think it passed."

"Did you puke?"

"No."

"Good."

I throw the cup of water in his face.

"Jesus! What the—"

"Why do you have that lighter?" I demand.

"What the actual hell," he grumbles, wiping his eyes and shaking the water off his fingers.

"Keep it in the bathroom. The rug out here is an antique," I order, stepping inside with enough force that he has to move back. I turn to Vivian and April. "Y'all coming, or what?"

"Jesus H. Christ," Vivian mutters, but she follows me inside. After a brief moment of inner conflict between staying out there alone and taking her chances with us, April comes, too.

I lock the door behind us and point Milford to the toilet. "Sit."

"But—"

"Now."

Milford plops down on the closed seat, scowling. "God, you're like a miniature version of your mom."

I catch April and Vivian staring at me in the mirror. They look both shocked and impressed, and I shrug. Sometimes, all it takes is an authoritative, vaguely parental tone for a guy to listen to you. Probably something Freudian in that, but now's not the time for psychoanalysis.

"Why do you have Margot's lighter?" I ask again.

He groans. "I don't know why y'all keep saying it's hers. I got it at a bar."

"What bar?"

He clamps his jaw shut like a little kid.

Calmly, I refill the water glass. "What bar, Milford?"

He doesn't answer. I hold up the glass.

"I can't tell you, okay?" Milford explodes, covering his face so I don't splash it again.

You know, there might be something to this, like spray-bottle training for cats.

Vivian leans against the door like a bouncer. "Why?"

"Because I'm not supposed to talk about it," he says. "It's, like, a 'Carnival secret.'"

Milford puts quotes around it, like he thinks the phrase is silly. I catch April making a face, too. But it's a real thing. The Krewe of Deus has plenty of secrets, like the King's and Queen's identities, which are always closely guarded until they're finally revealed on Mardi Gras Day. Even the Les Masques Queen is supposed to be a secret until the night of the ball, but we all knew it was Lily. Who else would it be?

But clearly, whatever this secret is, Milford takes it seriously enough not to tell.

"So it's, like, a secret bar?" Vivian asks, like that's the most ridiculous thing she's ever heard.

"Is it a Deus thing?" I add. "I've never heard anything about a secret bar. If it's Deus, I would know."

Milford laughs. I grip the water glass tighter, and he stops.

"Care to share why that's so funny?"

"Sorry." He shrugs, sarcasm dripping from his words. "No girls allowed." He stands. "Now can y'all let me out of here before I tell everyone that you kidnapped me?"

I block his path. "Not until you tell us about the bar."

Milford pushes past me, but Vivian is still standing guard at the door. She's pretty good at this, actually.

"Come on," he says. "Move."

But he's clearly a little intimidated. Vivian's got a few inches on him—because while Milford may have been born into unbelievable wealth, height was not part of the deal.

"Sorry," Vivian says. "You've still got some questions to answer."

"Or what?" Milford snaps.

April lifts her camera. "You were smoking weed," she blurts. "I took a picture."

Her face floods crimson as Milford turns to her, narrowing his eyes. "And? It's decriminalized in New Orleans."

He's putting on an unbothered air, but I see where April's going with this. It's kind of brilliant, actually.

"Right," I say sweetly. "But I'm not so sure a picture like this would go over well with your dad's mayoral campaign, will it?"

Milford freezes. We've all seen the ads on TV. Mr. Wilcox is clearly pandering to the family values, tough-on-crime demographic. Milford's even been in a few, looking wooden in a polo shirt, hand in hand with his mom and little sister, walking through Audubon Park like gingerbread cutouts of real people.

He stares at me, and I stare back, a battle of wills.

"Fuck," Milford groans, wiping his hands over his face.

"We won't say a word," I tell him. "As long as you tell us about this bar. Seems like a fair trade, right?"

Milford's eyes dart between the three of us.

"We won't tell anyone we heard it from you," Vivian adds genuinely. "We promise."

I'm not sure how I feel about this gentler approach or a promise being made on my behalf, but apparently, it works.

Milford sighs, flopping back onto the toilet seat. "It's called the Pierrot," he says. "It's just, like, this secret gentlemen's club."

I cringe. "Like a strip club?"

"No, like—I don't know. Just a club for guys in Deus to go to."

"And that's where the lighter came from?" Vivian asks.

Milford nods. "They make branded ones for members."

"Then why did Margot have one?" April speaks up. "If it's men only?"

"I have no idea."

"Bullshit," I say.

"Seriously, I don't. It's like I said: it's just Deus guys. None of the girls are supposed to even know about it."

I feel a twist of uneasiness. Sure, the debutante stuff has a pretty patriarchal history, but it's not meant to exclude women. It's supposed to celebrate us.

"So you've been?" I ask.

A dark look passes over his face.

"Just once," he says. "If your dad's a member, you can join when you turn eighteen."

Has Wyatt been, then? Is this something he and Dad do together, their own secret locked away from me and Mom? The Johnsons are a unit. We don't keep secrets from each other.

Or so I thought. Wyatt's phone flashes through my mind.

"But I didn't join," Milford says quickly. "And I haven't been back. Now can I please leave?"

I don't miss the shift in his tone. Milford hasn't been back because for some reason, he doesn't *want* to.

And I have to know why.

"Sure," I say. "On one condition: you get us in."

"What?" Milford whines. "To the Pierrot? Did you hear anything I just said?"

"Hey, April, how soon can you get that picture to the news?"

"Y'all are insane," Milford mutters.

"Or better yet, you're good at editing. Think we can turn that joint into something more incriminating?"

"Fine!" he shouts. "*Fine*. They're doing a New Year's thing. It's late tonight, like one A.M., in the French Quarter. If y'all can get there, I can try to get you in. But no promises. And you need masks. No one can know who you are. Okay?"

He watches us, desperate, as we exchange glances. April looks anxious, Vivian uncertain, and even I'm not sure this will work. Still, no one argues. I can tell we're all in. This is our best lead—our *only* lead—and if there's a chance the Pierrot is somehow connected to Lily's disappearance, then we can't pass this up.

"Great," I say. "Where do we meet?"

13

VIVIAN

JANUARY 1, 1:00 A.M.

When we get to the address Milford gave us, I'm starting to think we might've been punked.

"Are you sure this is it?" I ask, looking up at the old brick building. It's classic French Quarter–style, with tall shuttered doors and windows, wrought-iron balconies on the top two stories. The door is bright green, and a lantern hangs above it, lighting up the hand-painted sign below: LAGNIAPPE LAND.

Turns out we might have lied to our parents and snuck off to the Quarter after midnight to go to a gift shop. One that doesn't even look open.

"It's the address he gave me." Even beneath her mask, I can tell Piper is pissed.

We're all wearing the same masquerade kind, sparkly and ribboned, like that one episode of *Gossip Girl*. We picked them up at another shop around the corner, which, for some reason, wasn't closed yet. But that's French Quarter logic: it runs on its own time, especially on a night like tonight. The streets are packed with tourists and locals, everyone drunk on giant cocktails and the open-container law.

On a different New Year's, Lily, Sav, and I might be with them, splitting a Hand Grenade and dancing along to the music playing on every corner, live jazz and Top 40 hits all blending together like a chaotic playlist on shuffle. It's the kind of night that reminds me how much I love New Orleans, that makes me sad for everyone who grew up anywhere else.

But tonight, I can't enjoy it. Because Lily still isn't here, and now, we've somehow gone from gently waterboarding Milford to sneaking into a secret society.

Which I'm pretty sure might still be a bad idea. There are some obvious connections between Lily and Margot, but following her lighter to a secret "gentleman's club" full of old Deus guys? There's a very real chance we leave with nothing but a deep desire to bleach our eyes.

Still, it's not like we have any other clues. It's either this or waiting for forty-eight hours to turn into even more, wondering if the worst will happen. If I could have done something to stop it.

"I'm texting him again," Piper says, whipping out her phone.

Next to us, April peeks through the gift-shop windows, fidgeting with her mask, like she's not sure what to do with her hands without the camera. She's looking at a statue behind the glass, a wolflike thing with sharp jagged teeth, glowing red eyes, and pointed claws.

"A Rougarou," I realize. "Like that one they have at the zoo, right?"

April nods. "It was always my favorite part."

"Seriously? That shit gave me nightmares." I shudder, thinking of the swamp exhibit at the Audubon Zoo, where a giant Rougarou figure poses midgrowl, feet crunching over fake mulch, skulls, and baby shoes. As the Cajun legend goes, he hunts children at night, hungry for human blood. So, you know, an *obvious* creature to put on display at a zoo for kids. Somehow, it doesn't surprise me that baby April was into it.

Fireworks pop somewhere over the river, pulling my attention away from the window just in time to see Milford walking up.

"Oh my god, *finally,*" Piper says. "You're ten minutes late."

He shrugs. "Parking here sucks."

His wet clothes from earlier are swapped for the same suit he wore at Les Masques, and I look down at my own outfit, still the festive-casual jumpsuit I wore to Piper's. "Um, a dress-code memo would have been nice?"

"They have stuff you can change into inside."

"Oh, good." I gesture at the closed gift shop. "I've been looking for a WILL FLASH BOOBS FOR BEADS T-shirt."

Milford ignores me, and I can't fight the glare on my face.

"When we get in there, y'all need to be quiet," he says, pulling a mask out of his pocket. It's one of those half-face ones like in *The Phantom of the Opera*. "And don't tell anyone who you are. I gave them fake names for you. Got it?"

"Fine," Piper answers, clearly as annoyed as I am.

Milford puts on the mask. "Come on."

He reaches for the door, and it swings open. Guess it wasn't locked after all.

Inside, Lagniappe Land looks exactly like it did from the window: a boring gift shop. The lights are off, but there's a twenty-something guy at the register, a lamp shining behind him as he scrolls through his phone.

Milford smooths out his suit jacket. "I'm here for the feast."

Sorry, the *what*? I clench my teeth to keep from asking out loud. This is going from weird to full-on cult territory.

The guy behind the desk gives a tired nod and walks over to a nearby shelf of books. He pulls on the edge, and it opens to reveal a velvet-lined staircase, twisting up to somewhere we can't see.

Okay, *definitely* cult territory.

Milford steps through the secret passage, and I glance at April and Piper. They both look a little nervous behind their masks, but I don't think any of us wants to give up now. I'm starting to understand those girls in horror movies who walk down dark halls because they have to know what's in the shadows.

We follow him in. As the desk guy comes to close the door behind us, he gives us each a once-over, lingering on my mask with a small smirk. Then he shuts it, leaving the three of us and Milford alone in the stairwell.

"Okay, what the hell is 'the feast'?" I ask.

"It's just the code to get in," Milford says, tense.

Piper eyes the staircase like she's worried it might fall apart under us. "Is this safe?"

"Y'all are the ones who begged to come here," he snaps. "Look, from here on out, don't ask questions. And don't talk to anyone unless they talk to you first. Okay?"

We all stare at him, silent. Apparently satisfied, Milford turns and starts up the winding staircase. I get a creeping feeling, but I try to shake it off. This is a Krewe of Deus thing. The group is made up of people like our dads and their friends. Plenty of Mardi Gras stuff is culty. How bad can it really be?

The velvet muffles our steps, and as we get closer to the top, I can hear muted jazz. We end up at a small landing with another door, this one manned by a guy who could be a waiter at a fancy restaurant, except for the mask. It's black, with a nose that curves down into a long beak, like one of those old-timey plague masks.

I swallow, trying not to show how skeeved out I am. It's like a game, I tell myself. And if there's one thing I know about winning, it's that you can't let your opponent see your confidence slip.

"I'm here for the feast," Milford says again. "I've brought guests."

The masked man's eyes drift over the three of us. Then he nods, pulling open the door to reveal another small room. This one's lined with the same plush carpet as the staircase, only much darker, almost like blood. Victorian-style wall sconces cast it in fake candlelight. The jazz is louder in here, too. I can almost feel it in my teeth, like drums during a Mardi Gras parade.

We follow the man inside. Without a word, he disappears into an alcove to our left and comes back with three garment bags draped over his arms.

"You can change in there." He nods at the velvet curtain on our right. "One at a time."

Another cult alarm bell goes off in my head, and I shoot Milford a look, but he's fidgeting with the cuff of his jacket. No one else moves, so I step up, taking a garment bag from the man and going through the curtain. Behind it is basically a normal dressing room, only with a weird gothic-vampire feel. Two more wall sconces throw shadows on the long mirror.

I unzip the garment bag and hold my breath. The dress inside is gorgeous, emerald green silk with a slit up one thigh. When I slip it on and catch my reflection, the breath whooshes out of me. It's perfect, bringing out the red in my hair, hugging my curves in all the right places and making me look like some kind of movie star. It's not until I slip on the black heels that come with it, a half size too small, that I stop to wonder why it fits so well, how the man knew it would. Who I'm really getting dressed up for.

This is for Lily, I tell myself. *We're doing this to find her.* But as I step back out of the dressing room, I don't feel any more confident.

Piper goes next, coming out in a sky-blue chiffon dress with a lacy snowflake pattern. It's perfect for her, turning her into some kind of winter princess. April's next in simple black satin, nineties-style with spaghetti straps. She could be the bad-girl star of some grungy teen TV show, if she didn't look like she wanted to dissolve on the spot.

"Shoes," the masked man orders.

April looks down at her feet, the ratty Converse she's still wearing. She swallows.

"We have a dress code," the man adds sharply.

Milford shoots April an anxious look. "Just put them on."

April disappears back through the curtain. When she comes back again, she's wearing black kitten heels, but somehow, she looks even shorter.

"Phones," the man says, holding out his hand.

I grip mine tighter. This is almost definitely the next step in the whole cult thing, but at this point, I know it's not a match we can win. Either we follow the rules or give up on this whole thing. And even though the second option is starting to sound better and better, it's not really a choice, not when that message is still burned into my brain.

We all know how hard it is to keep a body underground in this city.

If there's even the slightest chance that this place has something to do with Lily disappearing, then there's only one thing we can do.

We hand our phones over, and the man slips them into what looks like a row of mailboxes on the wall. He locks them in and then gives us another once-over, seemingly satisfied.

"This way." He leads us to the door and whatever's waiting behind it.

14

APRIL

JANUARY 1, 1:15 A.M.

The Pierrot is an attack of jazz and smoke and noise. It's like stepping onstage at the ball, only so much worse, because all these people are faceless, hidden behind masks, their eyes watching us through the plastic and shimmering fabric like we're the next course in their Michelin-star meal. As we enter, the din of conversation hushes to a low murmur, punctuated by the clink of glasses and the music crackling through invisible speakers.

We're not the only women here. Milford said *no girls allowed,* but there are plenty of us in ball gowns and sparkling masks—now, though, I understand what he really meant. Just like Les Masques, every woman here is on the arm of a man.

Just like Les Masques, it's clear who's really in charge.

One of the men approaches Milford. In one hand, he has a glass of amber liquor, and the other is wrapped around a young woman's waist. A slow grin spreads on his face.

"Well, if it isn't Milly Wilcox!" He releases the girl and pulls Milford into a stiff hug, clapping him once on the back. "I didn't think you'd make it, you son of a gun. Your dad still working?"

The man's face is half-obscured by a deer mask, silver with sharp, menacing antlers, but I recognize him from Piper's sunroom. I scan for other familiar faces, but it's dark, and the men are all stock images of the same type: middle-aged, white, wealthy. It's not until the glint of another man's glasses makes my stomach drop that I realize I'm searching for Dad. But it's not him. There's no way he's here. When I came downstairs to leave tonight, he and Mom were tucked together on the couch watching *Columbo.* I told them I was going to hang out with some friends from the ball, and they were too elated—and mildly wine-drunk from dinner—to care that I was heading out at half past midnight.

"Yeah," Milford says, his shoulders tightening. "I don't think he'll make it."

"Well, good thing you brought friends." Beneath the mask, the man's hazy eyes dance between Vivian, Piper, and me. "Beautiful ones, at that."

Disgust roils through me, and I grab for my camera strap to ground me before realizing I don't have it. My gaze shifts to the woman on his arm. She's watching us with a sort of detached pleasantness, eyes blank behind her masquerade mask. As I look more closely, a chill shudders down my spine. There's no way she's this man's wife. She can't be older than twenty-two.

"Don't go too hard on him tonight, girls." The man chuckles at us. "He's a gentleman." He points at Milford. "Now, I don't see a drink in that hand. Let's fix that."

The man angles toward the bar, and the woman stumbles slightly. I want to do something, say something, but my tongue feels stuck to the roof of my mouth, my limbs frozen.

Because now, looking around, I see the pattern. Every woman

here is young, I'd guess no older than twenty-five. And every single one is with a man who could be her father.

Was Margot one of them? Did she come here?

As soon as the man is out of earshot, Vivian turns to Milford and hisses through gritted teeth, "What *is* this? That girl could barely stand up on her own. And she's, like, *our* age."

"If she's here, it's 'cause she wanted to be," Milford hisses back. "Same as y'all."

"Do my eyes deceive me, or is that Milly Wilcox?"

Milford's head whips toward the voice, which came from a red-cheeked man sprawled across a chaise to the side of the room. His mask is off, dangling around his neck. Probably because, from the looks of it, he's had enough liquor to knock out an elephant. He has a girl next to him, too, just as young as the others.

"Shit," Milford mutters. He waves, putting on a smile, before turning around to whisper to us. "Y'all stay right there."

He hurries away without giving us a chance to protest. Dread burrows deeper into my gut. Even when he was bossing us around just now, Milford didn't sound authoritative. He sounded panicked.

Piper grabs our hands and tugs us forward. "Come on."

"I don't like this," Vivian whispers. "I think we should leave."

"This might be our only chance to look around," Piper says. "We have to."

Before I can protest, she loops her arms through mine and Vivian's, putting on a bright smile.

"Come on," she says. "Let's make the rounds, shall we?"

I want to argue that someone will stop us, demand to know

what we're really doing here, but Piper's already pulling us deeper into the Pierrot. She walks with perfect debutante posture, so assured that I can feel some of it rubbing off on me. And somehow, I don't panic, even as suspicious gazes slide over us. We snake between pairs of laughing men and the masked women on their arms, past waiters with trays of champagne and hors d'oeuvres, like some hellscape version of the Johnsons' party, each of the staff members wearing the same birdlike mask as the man who was guarding the door. But no one stops us.

Once we've crossed to the other side of the large room, Piper lets go. We're in front of a set of tall shuttered doors that open out to a balcony, where two men lean on the railing, one of them lighting a cigarette.

"Let's do a loop around," Piper murmurs.

And then I catch the flame flickering under the man's chin, a silver flash in his palm.

The lighter. I don't need to see it up close to know it's the exact same one as Milford's. As Margot's.

Piper and Vivian drift in the other direction, but it's like a string is tugging me away, pulling me toward the balcony before they notice I'm not following them.

As soon as the two men see me in the doorframe, I freeze, all of the bravery draining from my body. They're both masked, their faces completely hidden. One is a raven, his mask dark and feathered, and the other, the one with the lighter, is a wolf, complete with a fanged snout.

Not a wolf, I think. A Rougarou.

"Looks like we've found ourselves a lost lamb," he says. I can't see it beneath the mask, but it's like I can hear his mouth turning up into a grin. "Now who do you belong to?"

My teeth start to chatter. I clench them.

"Chillier out here, isn't it?" The Rougarou claps the raven on the back. "Be a gentleman. Lend her your coat, huh?"

The raven doesn't move, and the Rougarou chuckles, acrid smoke billowing from beneath his mask.

"Here." He shrugs off his jacket. "You must be freezing."

He holds it out, his eyes slithering down my dress, and all I want is to take the thing and throw it over myself just so he can't see me. But I can't bring myself to touch it. I have a feeling this is the kind of man whose kindness always comes with strings attached.

Suddenly, I wish I hadn't left Piper and Vivian.

"Come on, I don't bite." The Rougarou brings the jacket closer, and I start to take it, just to silence him. As soon as I brush the fabric, he lunges forward, snapping his teeth. I flinch, and he laughs, slinging the jacket back over his shoulder. "No, don't worry. We're all gentlemen here."

There's something familiar in his voice, I think, but a little off, like he's putting on a performance. It's too hard to tell through the muffling of the mask, and too dark to find anything I recognize in the eyes behind it.

A glass shatters somewhere behind us, and I jump.

"Skittish, isn't she?" the Rougarou asks.

"Lay off," the raven mutters gruffly. He glances at me. "She's too young."

"You think?" The Rougarou tilts his head like he's assessing me. "You know, I think you might be right. You look young enough to be in school, don't you?" He laughs. "No, they don't take kindly to that. Against the rules, even here. How old are you. Sixteen? Seventeen?" He looks at his friend. "The other one was seventeen, wasn't she?"

Everything else blurs out of focus except the lighter still clutched in the Rougarou's hand and the beating of my own heart in my ears. *"The other one."* Those three words laced with so much meaning, twisting into memories.

The flick of Margot's lighter. The look on her face that night.

April, please.

"Margot," I force out. "Is that who you're talking about?"

The Rougarou rears back slightly, like her name has a physical force. "Well, shit."

The raven turns to me, and even with the mask, I don't miss the warning in his eyes. "You need to leave. Now."

I don't hesitate. I stumble back through the shuttered doors, my ankle rolling as I slip in my heels. The pain makes me wince, but I keep moving, back into the noise and the music, as far from the masked men as I can get. I run until I almost collide with a wall of blue chiffon.

"Where the hell did you go?" Piper snaps.

"You can't disappear like that," Vivian whispers.

"I . . ." My voice won't come out. Suddenly, this dress feels as tight as my debutante ball gown, threatening to collapse my lungs.

And then I see him.

"April?" Vivian's eyes search mine. "Are you okay?"

I shake my head, and Piper and Vivian turn to follow my stare.

There, on the other side of the room, is a man dressed like one of the Les Masques Jesters. His face is hidden by the hat and plastic mask, its lips painted into a permanent red grin, and he's looking straight at us, like he knows exactly who we are.

Like he's been waiting.

15

PIPER

JANUARY 1, 1:30 A.M.

My first instinct is to laugh. Because of *course*—it's like we're in a bad horror movie, the masked bad guy showing up on cue, and for once, I don't even have my pepper spray.

And then he's moving toward us.

"Shit," I hiss, grabbing Vivian's and April's hands and yanking them in the opposite direction. We sprint as fast as we can in our heels, turning into a narrow hallway off the main room. It's lined with two doors on either side.

I pull on the first one I see, but it's locked. I try the next one. Same thing. I let out a stream of curses under my breath.

"Y'all?" Vivian is looking behind us, where I can just see the Jester pushing into the hallway.

There's nowhere to go but deeper. We haul ass until the path turns to another door, marked LES FILLES in curly golden script.

A dead end. Either we hide out in the bathroom or the Jester catches up with us.

I shove the door open, and once we're all inside, I twist the lock and press my back against it. For a moment, we catch our breath.

"I know they say we always go in groups, but this is a little much, don't you think?"

We all spin toward the girl standing at the sink, toweling off her hands. She's white, petite, and curvy, wearing a lavender evening gown that clashes with her hair, which is the kind of unnatural purplish red that can only be achieved via box dye. Her mask is off, the silver ribbon dangling off the sink counter, so it's even more obvious how young she is. If it weren't for the diamond stud glinting on her nose, which is against the Beaumont dress code, she could walk right into class with us and no one would bat an eye.

"It was unlocked," I blurt. "We didn't—"

"Relax." She leans against the sink, clearly unafraid of water stains on her dress. "Who's the lucky guy?"

"What?" I ask.

"The member you're here with. The one you're running from. Unless y'all have some seriously overactive bladders, I'm assuming that's why you barged in looking like you're regretting every decision that got you here."

Vivian starts to answer, but I cut her off.

"There's someone chasing after us. A man in a jester costume. Do you know who he is?"

"This place has a lot of guys in a lot of stupid costumes. Can you be more specific?"

Someone bangs on the door, three sharp knocks that make us all jump. The girl recovers first, putting on a cheery tone.

"One minute!" she calls before looking back at us, returning to a whisper. "Okay, y'all need to get out of here."

"Wait," April blurts.

I glare at her, but she doesn't seem to notice. April's stare is fixed on the girl, determined, and I know what she's about to ask before it even comes out of her mouth.

"Did you know Margot Landry?"

All at once, the girl's face changes from confusion to outright dread. Then, like she's realized she let the tough mask slip, she frowns, crossing her arms.

"Who's asking?"

"We knew her, too," April says, the words coming out rushed. "We went to school together. And we've been trying to figure out what happened to her. We think it might have something to do with this place." Her eyes turn desperate. "Please. We need to know."

"Okay, yeah," the girl says finally. "I met her here a few times last year. But if y'all go to that rich-kid school, too, then you're *really* not supposed to be here."

A chill crawls down my spine. Margot was here. For a moment, the discovery makes me forget my panic.

"Why aren't we supposed to be here if we go to Beaumont?" I ask.

For a second, she's quiet. "They don't like it when girls from their own circle find out about this place."

My stomach twists, but I press on. "What about you, then? Why are *you* here?"

The girl gives me a look I don't like at all—like I don't understand, and it amuses her. "It pays better than serving coffee to whiny out-of-state Tulane kids, I'll tell you that."

Before I can demand an elaboration, there's another bang on the door.

"Sorry," the girl calls again. "Almost done."

She looks back at us, but before she can tell us again to get lost, Vivian asks, "Was Lily here? Lily LeBlanc."

The girl frowns. "I don't think I know the name, sorry." Then something flickers on her face. "Wait, there was another girl who came around here a couple weeks ago, asking about Margot. She was young, too. Blond, blue-eyed, real tiny?"

"That's her," Vivian says, even though she doesn't need to. I can feel us all holding our breath.

Lily was here, too. She was here because of Margot.

I have so many more questions, but this girl has made an impeccable point: we need to get the hell out of here.

As if to remind us, the knob starts to rattle, someone twisting from the outside.

"Not to cut this lovely chat short," I say. "But can we circle back to the whole getting-out-of-here thing?"

The girl's eyes dart to the lone bathroom window. Quickly, she pushes the thick curtains aside and then curls her fingers under the bottom, pulling. With a scraping sound, the window opens. She sticks her head out and then turns back to us.

"How do y'all feel about balcony-hopping?"

"I'm sorry, *what*?" I crane my head to look outside. There's a small balcony, clearly not well used: the painted wooden floor is chipped, the railing rusty. Directly to the right is another balcony, part of the next building over. They're pressed together in that classic French Quarter style, almost close enough to . . .

"No," I say. "Negative. Absolutely not."

"Do we have any other options right now?" Vivian asks.

"Better than falling to our *death*?"

Another bang on the door.

"Just a second!" the girl calls, giving us a *time is of the essence* look.

"We're only on the second story, right?" Vivian whispers, but she doesn't sound too convinced.

The girl nods. "I've done it before. It's not that bad."

I take another look outside. The balconies *are* basically touching, the railings low enough that we could swing a foot from one to the other, but I don't like it. I'm about to argue again, but Vivian is already pushing past me and crawling out onto the balcony. She bunches up her dress and slides one foot over the railing, testing her weight and then pushing herself up. For a moment, my heart is in my throat, and I'm convinced I'm about to watch her fall to her death. But then she leaps over to the other balcony.

"See?" Vivian says. "Not dead."

"Good." Behind me, the girl exhales, relieved. "Because I've never actually done that before."

I turn to gape at her, but April's already climbing out onto the balcony. She hauls herself over the first railing safely, and I know I have no other choice.

I swallow my fear and put on my best Johnson face, chin up, as I maneuver through the window. Once I'm out, I turn back to the girl.

"Thanks," I say.

"Anytime." She reaches to close the window behind me. "But if I were you, I wouldn't come back."

She slides it shut. I risk a glance down, and my stomach lurches. We're only two stories up, but the asphalt looks impossibly hard and far away.

"Hello?" Vivian waves. "Any day now."

April's already on the other balcony, too, but I'm suddenly frozen.

Vivian crosses her arms. "Piper, you got into a school that

accepts less than ten percent of people who apply. I'm pretty sure the chances of you falling are, like, a fraction of that."

I swallow, trying not to look at the ground below. "It's five point six percent."

"The chance of you falling?"

"No, Vanderbilt's acceptance rate."

"Great. Then buck up and climb over, genius."

She says it like it's that simple, and I guess it is—or it has to be. I slide off my shoes and hand them carefully to April on the other side. Then I hike up my dress and grip the railing, swinging one leg over. Vivian reaches out to steady me as I pull myself to the other side. For a nauseatingly weightless moment, I'm suspended—and then, finally, I touch solid ground.

"Hell yeah!" Vivian claps, and I can't ignore the little fizz of pride in my chest. "Now let's get out of here."

The victorious feeling fades quickly as I realize I'm still barefoot on a random French Quarter balcony. Sliding my shoes back on, I try not to think about the multitudes of diseases no doubt crawling on every surface and focus instead on the building we've escaped to. This balcony is long, wrapping around the side of the building. Another bar, I'm assuming, from the low lighting and live music pulsing through the open door.

We hustle inside and toward the stairs, past a few patrons who throw us vaguely interested glances before returning to their drinks. It *is* the French Quarter on New Year's, I guess—three terrified girls dressed for a masquerade, and we probably don't even crack the top five weirdest things these people have seen today.

As we descend, the music gets louder. There's a band on the first floor, cranking out jazz standards to a crowd who's probably been this drunk—and *vocal*—for hours. We push our way through, and I nearly collide with a woman as her partner spins her around, her hot-pink wig nearly tipping off her head.

"Happy New Year's, dawlin'!" Her New Orleans accent is as thick as the bunch of silver beads around her neck. She takes one off and hands it to me, and I close my hand around the charm emblazoned with the new year. "Y'all look gorgeous!"

I manage a thanks as we hustle past and toward the door, the word catching in my throat. It's such a typical New Orleans interaction, carefree and a little ridiculous, that it makes the rest of tonight feel even more wrong by comparison. Even as we step out into the street, the air feels too hot and close.

The Jester isn't just a name on a message anymore. He's someone who followed us. *Chased* us. And that place . . . I thought I knew how to operate in a place like the Pierrot—somewhere women are meant to be quiet and pretty, to follow orders with a smile. My mom taught me how to turn it into a superpower: how to swallow down the anger and shape it into a sugarcoated *bless your heart*. How to follow the rules so well, the assholes in charge don't even notice when I've made them work in my favor.

But we still weren't safe in there.

Was Margot?

Was Lily?

We all know how hard it is to keep a body underground in this city.

The Jester's threat reverberates through my head as we walk, and with every click of my heels on the grimy street, I'm more afraid I know the answer.

16

VIVIAN

JANUARY 1, 1:50 A.M.

The Pierrot is almost four blocks behind us when Milford finally shows up.

"Hey!" He jogs over, a Lagniappe Land tote bag on his shoulder, and I actually laugh. Does the cult give out party favors? He also looks pissed, and it's really hard to take a man seriously when he's holding a tote bag.

But then I remember the kind of men we just saw in there, and I don't feel like laughing anymore.

"Where have y'all been?" Milford demands, catching up to us. "You can't just disappear like that in there. I was—"

"Is that our stuff?" Piper cuts him off, nodding at the bag.

He frowns. "You didn't answer my—"

"Hand it over," she snaps. "We need to go *now*."

Milford doesn't argue, probably still afraid Piper's going to whip out another glass of water. He hands us our street clothes and, thank god, our phones.

"Those dresses have to go back. Like, ASAP," he says. "I'll get shit from them if they're missing."

I laugh again.

"What?" Milford scowls.

I don't know how to explain it. Lily was *there.* She knew about the Pierrot, and she never told me. She might have been in danger, and she never asked for my help, and now she's missing, and all Milford cares about is getting the ball gowns back. And now I can't keep it in anymore.

"What the hell *was* that?" I explode.

Milford stiffens. "I tried to tell y'all."

"Bullshit."

"I know what it looks like, okay?" he argues. "I didn't want to go back there. *Y'all* are the ones who made me. But those guys aren't bad. They're just—I don't know. Having some fun. My dad says most of them have arrangements with their wives, or whatever. But it's just a stupid Mardi Gras thing. A bunch of old guys playing King for a day, like in Deus. Like Les Masques."

"Les Masques is *not* the same thing," Piper argues. "It's a decades-old tradition about celebrating women. It's not . . . whatever that was."

April scoffs, so quiet I almost didn't hear it. But clearly, Piper did.

She turns on April, arms crossed. "What?"

"Nothing."

"Y'all," I step in. "We need to go."

Because the Jester's still on our tail. I'm not the only one who's thinking it. Piper's already fishing her keys out of the tote bag, and April's scanning the street, anxious.

"Thanks again, Milford," I spit. "Really, you were a *great* escort."

I turn and lead us away.

"Wait," he says, suddenly urgent, and for a second, I think

he's going to apologize. It wouldn't help, not really, but I still want to hear it.

But what he says is "Y'all won't tell anyone, will you? Because I'll deny it. They will, too."

Yeah, I think, shooting him a glare. *I bet they will.*

"Wouldn't dream of it," I tell him through gritted teeth.

We turn and go, leaving him there on the street.

When we make it back to the car, the street is empty. I let out a shaky breath.

And then I realize April is crying. Not hard, just one tear slipping down her pale cheek. She wipes it away, but she doesn't look sad. She looks angry as hell.

Piper's noticed, too, and she's watching April like a cat who wants to befriend a small duck but is sort of worried she might accidentally eat it.

"Hey," I say softly. "You okay?"

April shakes her head. I take a step toward her, but then I remember I don't know her that well, don't know how to comfort her yet.

She wipes another tear. "They knew her. These two guys I saw on the balcony. They knew Margot."

Piper straightens. "How do you know?"

"They said I was too young to be there, like the 'other girl.' And when I asked them if they meant Margot—"

"Wait, you *asked* them? We didn't agree to talk to any of the members. They could have recognized you, or—"

"Let her finish," I tell Piper.

It looks like it takes literally biting her tongue to stop herself, but Piper nods.

"When I said her name, they looked all freaked out," April continues. "Then they told me I had to leave."

There's a new look on April's face now. Not just anger, but like she finally understands.

"This all comes back to Margot," April says. "Lily's disappearance, the Jester—everything. That girl in the bathroom said Lily was at the Pierrot asking about Margot. And Lily wanted to talk to us about her that morning at the Den. She was trying to tell us something before she disappeared. Like maybe . . . maybe there's more to what happened to Margot than everyone thinks."

A chill creeps from my neck to the bottom of my spine. "You mean, like . . . ?"

"Like they did something to her," April says. "Those men at the Pierrot."

There's this look in her eyes now, like she's never been more sure of anything. But Piper shakes her head.

"That's not possible."

"How do you know?" April snaps.

"Because she overdosed. It's not like they could have faked that." Piper pauses, like maybe she's realized how harsh that sounds. "Look, I know that place was bad, but some kind of conspiracy feels like a step too far."

"You didn't know Margot," April says. "I did. And she had stuff she was dealing with, sure, but I never saw her do hard drugs, ever. That was the thing. She liked to be a little dangerous, not reckless. She walked right up to the line but never crossed it. Not until—" She stops. "I just . . . I saw the look in that man's eyes on the balcony. He *knew* her. And y'all saw what it was like in there. It's, like, the most powerful men in the city all in one room. If they did something to her, they'd be able to cover it up, no question."

I don't like it, how true that feels.

"Well, that's still theoretical," Piper says. "We don't have proof."

"It's not a crazy idea, though," I step in. "If Lily was asking about Margot, and she found something out, like . . ." I hesitate before saying it out loud, making it real. "Let's say someone did something to Margot, and Lily knew about it. If it was this Jester guy, that's a pretty good reason for him to be after her."

"Maybe Lily is on the run from him," April says. "Or maybe . . ."

It isn't until now that it really hits me. *Or maybe he caught her.* And if the Jester or any of these Pierrot people are covering up a murder, then there's no telling what they'd do to stop it from getting out. Including making another Queen disappear.

I hug my ribs, feeling suddenly nauseous.

"Okay." Piper steeples her fingers like a therapist, probably something she's copied from her dad. "Okay, so maybe it's not a crazy idea. Clearly, this place is another link between Margot and Lily. But correlation does not imply *murder.* We need to keep looking."

She's right, but it doesn't make April's theory feel any less real. It eats away at me, shutting up any part that's been able to convince myself that this is all some big misunderstanding and Lily will be home in no time.

"We should also probably tell Marty," Piper adds.

"No," April says quickly.

"Need I remind you that we literally just got chased by a masked man?" Piper asks. "We could kind of use a detective here."

"Marty's in Deus," April argues. "Milford said the Pierrot is a Deus thing. And for all we know, everyone in the Krewe is a part of it."

"No." Piper shakes her head. "No way. I don't know about y'all, but there's no chance my dad is a part of that. Do you seriously think yours are?"

"Obviously not," I jump in, creeped out at the idea that my dad would ever set foot in that place. "But April's right. We shouldn't trust anyone, at least until we know what's going on."

Piper juts her chin, like she's thinking of her next snappy comeback, but then she sighs. "Fine. It *does* seem like we'd get in huge trouble if anyone knew we were there tonight."

A firework sizzles a few streets over. Then, deep laughter. We all turn toward the noise, but it's just a group of drunk guys walking by.

"We should go," I say. "It's late."

Piper nods. "But tomorrow, we should make a game plan. Decide what to do next."

I'm not sure how to feel about the fact that we're a "we" now, but to be honest, as horrible as tonight has been, it feels good to be taking action to find Lily. To not be doing it alone.

As Piper climbs into the driver's seat, I turn to April.

"Hey," I start, "if you ever want to talk about Margot . . . I guess I don't know what it's been like for you, not all the way, but I'm here. You know, if you need a friend."

She blinks, and something flickers on her face. Not quite a smile, but a sort of relief.

"Yeah," she says. "Thanks."

Piper's door swings open. "Y'all, get in. Now."

At first I think she's just being typical impatient Piper, but then I catch the fear in her voice.

And then I see the envelope tucked against the windshield.

"Shit," I breathe, scrambling to get in as April climbs into the back seat.

Piper snatches the envelope and slides back into her seat, shutting the door behind her. She hits the lock button, and the click feels louder than it should.

"It must have been here this whole time," she says, tearing it open. "I don't know when he got here. I don't know *how* he—"

"What does it say?" I ask.

Even before Piper slides out the invitation, I know exactly what it will look like: the same fancy paper as the one in the darkroom, the sad clown logo. The same looping script.

"*My Dearest Maids,*" Piper reads. "*I thought we could be civilized, but it looks like you just can't help getting your hands dirty. So let me make myself clear: stop digging, or I'll show everyone just what you've been hiding behind those pretty masks of yours.*"

Dread rushes up in me as Piper reads the sign-off.

"Yours, the Jester."

17

PIPER

JANUARY 1, 2:00 A.M.

The drive home is quiet. I half-heartedly offer the aux, and Vivian puts on a Taylor Swift playlist that doesn't help—just makes it feel like we're in the world's most tonally confusing music video, underscored by the Jester's threat playing in my head on loop.

Stop digging, or I'll show everyone just what you've been hiding behind those pretty masks of yours.

What does he think we've been hiding?

And then the other question, an awful little whisper underneath: Why am I afraid I already know?

"It's right here," Vivian says, nodding at the house on the corner and snapping me out of my spiral. It's small, compared to a lot of houses Uptown, but pretty, with a bright periwinkle front door and an old porch swing. I pull over to the curb.

"Meet up tomorrow morning?" I ask. "We could go to the levee. It shouldn't be too crowded."

Maybe I'm being paranoid, but after tonight, it can't hurt. If April's right about Margot—which I'm still not convinced she is—then the stakes just got a whole lot higher than they already were.

Vivian nods. As she reaches for the door handle, her eyes catch on the Jester's envelope, shoved into the glove compartment, and I wonder if she has a guess about what it means, too. Or April, who's been steadily winding her camera strap around her wrist like a boa constrictor.

Maybe we all have secrets we'd rather not dig up.

"Yeah," Vivian says. "See y'all tomorrow."

I drop April off next, and it's not until I get home that the exhaustion fully catches up with me, settling deep in my bones.

I do my best quick-change in the back seat, heart pounding as every second feels like another chance for the Jester to appear in the shadows. I stash the ball gown in the trunk like a body to deal with later, lock the car, and creep into the house.

There's a brief fifteen seconds where I think everyone's asleep and I've really gotten away with sneaking out. And then I see them.

Mom and Dad on the living-room couch. Waiting.

My blood rushes down to my toes, rooting me to the spot. They don't say anything yet. Mom just puts her phone down and looks at me. Dad closes his book, the same biography he was reading at the party, and it's not enough information for me to tell what kind of moods they're in, how bad this is going to be. They're waiting, I realize, for me to speak first.

"Hi." I try for sheepish, a daughter who snuck out of the house for perfectly benign teenager-on-New-Year's-Eve reasons. "I'm sorry. I was out with friends. I should have—"

"I want you to consider your words carefully," Mom says. "Because we know where you were. And you're too bright to lie to us, Piper. So we're giving you an opportunity to tell the truth."

Everything inside me tenses up into a tight tiny ball. They *know*. How do they know?

The Jester. The answer is obvious, hitting me a second too late. Dad just stares, disappointed behind his glasses, and my mind stutters. Panic mode. I don't know what to say. I always know what to say, but I also never get in trouble. I don't know how to navigate this.

Mom sits back on the sofa, like she's too tired to stay fully vertical. "How about a more direct question: Would you care to explain to us why you were out in the French Quarter tonight with Vivian Atkins and April Whitman, dressed up for some kind of ball?"

"I . . ."

"If you're thinking about denying it, don't," Mom says. "Mrs. Byron saw you from their family's apartment on Royal."

I should have known that I'd never get away with sneaking out, not when Mom is so well connected that she practically has eyes and ears all over the city. But a tiny part of me relaxes. Mrs. Byron is a family friend, not involved in Deus, and she definitely wasn't at the Pierrot. So Mom and Dad don't know—not where we really were tonight, and not about the other thing, what I've been thinking about ever since I read the Jester's latest message. This is bad, but I can fix this.

"We were just going out," I say. "It was stupid. And I'm really sorry. I shouldn't have snuck out, but I just . . ." I pause. "I thought maybe now that I got into college, I could loosen up a bit. Try to have some more fun."

The lie feels more laughable now than ever, because I can *never* take my eyes off the prize. Even if my family hadn't drilled that into me already, it would be clear as day from the Jester's threat. If he knows what I think he does, if he *does* something about it, then everything I've worked for the past eighteen years could crumble.

A line creases between Mom's eyebrows, like it does when she's focusing on a dress, trying to piece the thing together in her mind before it's real.

"I also heard from Betty Wilcox," she says.

Milford, you son of a bitch.

I blink, trying for innocent. "About what?"

"She says Milford came home after the party tonight soaking wet. Apparently, you demanded to know what he saw at the ball and then pushed him into the pool?"

Any chance of hiding my rage dissipates. Of *course* Milford would pull some shit like this. Even though we have that picture of him smoking, he knew how to get a leg up: tattle to my mom like we're in kindergarten.

"I didn't push him in the pool," I argue. "No one pushed him in the pool. He was wasted and he fell, which I'm sure he didn't mention when he ran to Mommy."

"Were you interrogating him?" Mom asks.

I open my mouth and then close it again. "We were asking questions," I say finally, because I don't think I need to include the water-in-the-face detail.

"We?"

"Me, April, and Vivian. We were trying to figure out what happened at the ball. Who ruined it."

It's close enough to the truth that I think they might buy it, but Mom's stare is still icy. "Well, I'm certain there are more *subtle* ways to go about it."

She looks to Dad for backup, and he sighs, a tired but gentle good cop.

"It's great that you want to help, peanut, but Lily's parents and Detective Rutherford are working on it. I know you like to solve problems, but taking this one upon yourself might actually do more harm than good."

"Lily's *missing.*" I know I should calm down, just apologize and deal with the fallout, but I can't. "What happened at the ball wasn't just some prank, and it doesn't seem like anyone's taking it seriously. And all the Margot stuff . . ." I watch her name hit Dad like a cold blast of air, and I instantly regret it. "Someone was clearly threatening Lily that night. I don't know why everyone thinks she just ran away. She's in real danger."

"No, she isn't."

I stare at Mom, stunned. "But—"

"We got an update from the LeBlancs earlier today," she explains. "They tracked down her debit-card activity. Lily withdrew several thousand dollars from an ATM the night of the ball. She ran away, Pipes. And they're trying to find her, of course, but she's not using her cards, and her phone has been turned off, so it's been difficult."

"But they'll find her," Dad says gently.

"Of course," Mom adds.

I'm too stunned to argue. All I can manage is "Lily took out cash?"

"Her parents told us in confidence," Mom says, "so I know you won't go sharing that around, but yes."

"But . . ." I wrack my brain for a way to finish that sentence. But the email Lily sent us. But her necklace, abandoned in the Den. But the Jester. The Pierrot.

Not that I can tell them about those last two.

And then I remember Lily's fight with Wyatt. What if she really did run away? Is that all it takes for a girl like Lily to fall apart?

No, shouts a voice deep inside me—but it's not loud or brave enough for me to say it, too.

"But what about what happened at the ball?" I ask instead. "The videos, and the blood."

"We're still working on finding who did it," Mom says. "But I think your instincts were right. It was probably another vandal like last year, trying to get their misguided point across." She sighs. "We do get people like this every year, you know. People who don't understand our traditions, who think we're 'elitist.' I suppose they've just been getting more . . . reactive, lately."

I want to argue, but again, the words won't come out. Mom thinks it was a vandal. Two days ago, I was thinking the same thing, but now it feels so far from the truth.

"Aren't y'all worried about her?" I ask. "Even if Lily ran away, that doesn't mean she's safe."

"Of course we're worried," Dad says, placing a hand on Mom's knee.

"But we're also worried about you," Mom adds, her steel softening only slightly. "And Wyatt."

The texts I saw on his phone flash through my mind again, spiking my heart rate. Do they know that he lied?

"Wyatt?" I repeat. "Why?"

"His girlfriend is missing," Mom says. "And if something *did* happen to her, god forbid, then you know exactly where everyone's fingers will point."

It's what I thought when I first found the texts on Wyatt's phone, but hearing it out loud, it sounds all wrong. Wyatt lied about what happened that night, and *I'm* the one who's in trouble for trying to find the truth? I know I'm supposed to be careful, to be more delicate, but suddenly, I'm too pissed to keep biting my tongue.

"Did you know he lied about driving her home?" I snap. "I saw his texts. Wyatt left without her, but he told Lily's parents—"

"We know."

I stare at Mom, like maybe I heard wrong. "What?"

"Wyatt told us. It was our idea for him to stick to the story that he drove Lily home."

I'm too stunned—too enraged—to speak.

"We had to think about what's best for our family," Mom continues. "Not just for Wyatt, but all of us."

"So that's what's most important, then?" I explode. "Making sure we look good? Not the fact that another Queen is *missing,* one year after Margot—"

"Of course it's important." Her voice is glass, slicing sharp and clear. "We want what's best for Lily, too. We want her safe as much as everyone else. But we have to think about how this looks."

I cross my arms, feeling like a petulant child now, but I can't stop it. "Why?"

"Why?" Mom looks at me like she can't believe I'd even ask. "Because reputation is everything in this city. *Everything.* How else would your dad and I be doing well enough in our businesses to put a roof over your head and send you to Beaumont? How else would you have gotten into Vanderbilt? Because you work hard, you've built your reputation, and you know the right people. Period."

It stings like spice to the eyes, making them water—even worse because she doesn't know what I've been hiding from her, from everyone.

And she's right. I know she's right. But one Queen is dead, and now another is missing. How can our reputation be more important than that?

"Listen, peanut," Dad steps in. "I know you're only trying to help. You care about things, and that's good. It's none too common, these days."

Despite everything, his words soften my anger the tiniest bit.

"And I know you want there to be some connection here," he continues, "between what's happening with Lily and what happened to Margot. Hell, I did the same thing myself last year, looking for some kind of explanation for why . . ." He stops, shaking his head. "But I'm sorry, peanut. There isn't. Margot was a good kid, but she had a lot of problems. It's tragic, but sometimes, things like this happen. And Lily . . . I know it's hard, but she'll be home soon. I *know* it. We just have to let the right people do their job."

I want to argue, scream that he's wrong, but I can't. Because he's hit me with the one thing I can't ever ignore: logic.

If what Mom said is true, then Lily really *did* run away. Maybe she just changed her mind about meeting us at the Den. And the Margot stuff . . . it's like I told April: we don't have proof. The Jester threatened us, obviously, but that doesn't mean it has to do with Margot or Lily or some kind of murder cover-up at all. What if it's only because we're three girls someplace we're not supposed to be, getting our hands dirty with the secrets of powerful men? And maybe those secrets aren't as dark as they seem. Maybe it's only what we saw with our own eyes: men with younger women, men behaving badly. They do the same thing in the broad light of day, sometimes, unmasked and unafraid. It doesn't mean they killed anyone, or that they made a girl disappear.

Does it?

Dad gets up from the couch, pulling me into a tight hug.

"We love you," he says. "You and Wyatt are what's most important. And your mom and I, we just want you to be okay." He lets go, holding me by the shoulders. "So maybe you just give this thing a rest, okay? Try to focus on school, on getting ready for next year."

I glance at Mom, and I can see it in her eyes, too, even if she doesn't say it. It's never been as easy for her, the mushy stuff—it's where I get it from—but I know she loves me, even if her way of showing it is different: all hard protective edges to Dad's gooey middle.

And that's why I have to make them proud.

"Okay," I say.

Dad smiles. "That's my girl."

In spite of everything, a little ember of pride flickers in my chest.

"Now," he says, with a little clap. "I need my beauty sleep. How about we all get some rest, huh?"

I nod weakly.

He kisses my head. "'Night, peanut."

He starts toward their bedroom, and Mom follows, smoothing my hair as she passes. Her touch is gentle enough that I want to cry, but I tighten my throat, forcing myself not to fall apart.

"Good night, Pipes," she says. "Don't stay up too late."

With that, they disappear down the hall. I trudge up to my room alone, exhaustion mingling with a quickly growing certainty: Margot's death was an accident, and anything else is just wishful thinking, a desperate search for answers that don't exist. And Lily—this whole time, I've been thinking she was trying to tell us something important, that she needs us to find her. But that's ridiculous, isn't it? Because Lily would never want my help. Not after what happened last time. And especially not if she knew what I've really done.

The Jester was right. All we'll get from digging is a mess we can't clean up.

Flopping down on my bed, I check my phone. There are a handful of new messages in our group chat, the first from Vivian.

Everyone home safe?

And then April's response:

Yeah
Piper, you made it?

I press like on the message.

It occurs to me, as I watch the little thumbs-up appear in its bubble, that no one besides my parents ever sent me a "home safe?" text. And then, finally, humiliatingly, I start to cry.

18

APRIL

JANUARY 1, 12:00 P.M.

We meet on the levee. It's empty, just like Piper expected: on a nice day like today, most people will be a few blocks away in Audubon Park, starting off their New Year's resolutions with an optimistic jog or pushing their kids around in expensive European strollers. There, it's gorgeous, all green trees and Spanish moss.

Here, it's as ugly as I remember. I haven't been since Margot was alive, and as we climb, I pick out all the familiar little details. Forgotten beer cans, plastic wrappers, other detritus left behind on the grass. Cars rumbling behind us, the low hum of bugs. I keep my eyes on the trees—a few bursts of scraggly orange leaves, too little and too late for fall—and the Mississippi beyond as Margot's voice echoes in my memory.

Y'all ever think about how the river could just kill you?

Back then it made me smile—such a classic Margot thing to say, bold and blunt but true. Now, though, it feels like some kind of omen. Because not too far off from here is where they found her car.

She died so close to her favorite view. Close, but not enough for it to be the last thing she saw.

I pull my flannel tighter, trying not to think about it. I should have said something when Piper suggested coming here, maybe, but I've gotten good at forgetting.

And maybe today, I don't want to. Because ever since last night, since I said it aloud, I can't let go of the thought: what happened to Margot wasn't an accident, and the Pierrot had something to do with it. The more I think it, the truer it feels. And I need to make up for all the time I've lost believing that what happened to Margot was only my fault.

"So," Piper says, "we should talk about what happens next."

She's using her usual authoritative tone, like this is all under control, but she looks like she's gotten about as little sleep as I have. Vivian, too.

Makes sense, if their nights were anything like mine. The few hours of sleep I managed were full of nightmares—the flicker of a lighter growing into flames that engulfed everything as Margot called out to me, the heat melting her skin like a plastic doll.

I'd shot awake with my heart pounding, the Jester's threat clear and harsh as a bell: *Stop digging, or I'll show everyone just what you've been hiding behind those pretty masks of yours.* I know, all too clearly, what that could mean.

Still, what happens next is obvious to me.

"We have to find those guys," I say. "The ones I saw on the balcony. They knew Margot. And if they weren't the ones who did something to her, then I'd bet they know who did. Maybe even where Lily is, too."

"Right." Piper looks hesitant, her confidence slipping just enough to make me suddenly nervous. "I think we should talk about the Jester first, though."

"Well, yeah," I say. "We need to figure out who he is, too."

"No, I mean—" She takes a small breath through her nose. "We need to think about how safe it is to keep going with this."

The quiet rush of the water behind me seems to get louder. My voice feels too small to compete with it.

"Are you saying we should stop?"

"I'm saying we should consider it. The Jester chased us out of there. He threatened us. That's not something to take lightly."

She's so transparent, I actually laugh. Here I was, thinking Piper was just as committed to this as I am, but as soon as there's the slightest threat of getting in trouble, she balks.

"That message was nothing," I argue. "He said he'd 'unmask' us, or whatever, but what does that even mean? He's probably bluffing."

But even as I say it, I can't deny the way those words haunted me late into the night, tossing and turning around my head until they shaped themselves into memories I've tried to forget.

Vivian shifts her weight. "I don't know. Piper has a point."

I take in Vivian's face, the dark circles under her eyes even more pronounced against her pale skin. I wonder what she was thinking about last night, what she's afraid the Jester might know. I almost want to ask her, but then I remember how kind she was to me after we left the Pierrot. No one has ever asked me if I wanted to talk about Margot, besides my parents.

Besides Lily, in the text that started everything, this whole screwed-up domino collapse.

"But we can't stop," I say, only slightly less forcefully. "The Jester's probably only threatening us because we're close to figuring something out. And y'all *saw* that place. We can't—" My throat tightens, strangling my voice. I shake my head. "We can't just quit."

"I'm not saying we should," Vivian says. "But I do think we should be more careful."

There's a flash of something in her eyes, some hint at whatever it is she's afraid of the Jester knowing, but I let it pass. I'm grateful, at least, that she doesn't want to give up.

"Okay," I say. "Then what's the plan?"

"I think you're right about those guys," Vivian tells me. "We should start with figuring out who they are. What do you remember about them?"

A hollow feeling starts to gnaw at me. "Just their masks. One was a raven. And the other was a wolf. A Rougarou, I think. He had a lighter like Margot's."

Piper scoffs. "Well, that's not much to go on."

I tense, irritated, but mostly because she's right. I could have tried harder, looked closer, but it was dark, and I was scared, and I seriously don't need Piper to make me feel worse about it than I already do.

"Okay, what's your deal?" Vivian asks her, reading my mind.

"What do you mean?"

Vivian crosses her arms. "Are you in this, or not? Because it seems like a no."

Piper picks at a string on the end of her quarter-zip.

"My parents caught me sneaking back in last night," she says finally.

"Oh." Vivian's hands fall to her sides. "Shit."

"A family friend saw us in the Quarter. And apparently, Milford snitched to his mom—not about the Pierrot, but about our . . . you know. Interrogative tactics. So, needless to say, Mom and Dad were pissed."

I wince. As annoyed as I am at Piper, I've seen Mrs. Johnson during our debutante rehearsals, and I wouldn't want to be in the line of fire when she's mad.

"And they also said . . ." Piper tucks a piece of hair behind her ear, a rare anxious tic. "Okay, like, cone of silence on this, obviously, but they heard from Lily's parents, and apparently she took out a bunch of cash after the ball. So, with her car and phone missing, too, they think . . . you know. They think she really did just run."

For a moment, we're both frozen. Then Vivian shakes her head sharply.

"No. No way."

"It makes sense."

"No, it doesn't."

"Look, I didn't want to believe it, either," Piper says, "but maybe we jumped to conclusions too fast."

"What about the Jester?" Vivian argues. "What about—"

"I know," Piper says. "I *know,* okay? But I think, considering how much more dangerous this has all gotten since yesterday, it might be smart of us to take a step back."

Vivian's face hardens, but she doesn't argue.

Well, for once, I'm not staying quiet.

"So let me get this straight," I start. "Lily's missing. Someone's after us, maybe the same person who killed Margot, and you want to just *take a step back*?"

"We don't know for sure that Margot was killed," Piper points out.

"Oh, great, so we're back to this again." I glare at her. "So what? *All* of this is just a coincidence?"

"April . . ."

"What?" This time, I say it like a challenge. Because I need her to say it to my face, what I know she's thinking. What everyone else has already believed for a year: that Margot's death was tragic but not surprising. That you can't mourn a girl who practically signed her own death certificate.

But what she says is "The police said it was an overdose. They never mentioned the possibility of foul play. Her parents moved away and never talked about it. I don't know about you, but if I thought someone had killed my kid, I wouldn't just let it go. I'm sorry, April, but what you're saying is just—"

"Crazy? Impossible? So is this entire fucking thing, and it's really happening."

Angry tears are stinging my eyes now, but I blink them away. Piper's mouth falls open, like she's not sure what to say.

"What?" I demand.

"It's not crazy," she says. "It's normal to want to find explanations when things like this happen, but—"

"Don't therapize me." I wipe a stray tear away with my knuckle. "You're not your dad."

"Hey, maybe we should take a second," Vivian tries, but Piper cuts her off.

"I'm not 'therapizing.' I'm trying to help. I'm trying to say I understand."

"Bullshit," I say. "You're telling *me* I'm coming up with explanations that don't make sense? You're the one who wants so badly to believe there's nothing wrong with Les Masques and Deus and all of the debutante shit that you won't even look at what's right in front of you. You're fucking indoctrinated."

On any other day, the look in Piper's eyes would be enough to make me shrivel, but I won't back down. Not now. She shakes her head slightly, a cross between pity and disbelief on her face.

"Does it make you feel better?" she asks. "Hating everyone

and everything? Acting all aloof and artsy with your camera so you don't have to stoop so low as to actually care about something?"

The question strikes a chord in my chest. One I recognize.

"Okay, seriously, y'all," Vivian says. "Stop it."

Piper holds up her hands. "I'm genuinely asking."

"Fuck off, Piper," I mumble.

"Gladly. But one question first. If the debutante tradition is so evil, then how come your parents are still a part of it? How come *you're* a part of it?"

It hangs in the air, dredging up memories of another conversation, of the night everything fell apart. And I know I can't stay here. That if I do, I'll fall apart, too.

I turn and walk down the levee.

"Wait," Vivian calls after me. "We can talk this out. If we're going to keep doing this, we need to work together."

I stop, lasering on Piper.

"Yeah," I say. "Well, maybe I don't want to be a fucking Maid anymore."

19

VIVIAN

JANUARY 2, 11:45 A.M.

My last first day at Beaumont is even worse than I thought it would be. I was already dreading coming back to a class full of early-decision kids, all rocking their college merch just so everyone knows they got it all figured out by January, while I'm stuck with the slackers who have no idea where we'll be in the fall, or where we even *want* to be. Because maybe some of us aren't so ready to leave our best friends and everything we've ever known to ship off to a campus we've only seen once.

The only good thing was going to be that I wouldn't have to do it alone. Sav still has to audition for all the big theater schools, and now that Lily didn't get into Vanderbilt, we were all in the same boat. We were supposed to get through this as a team.

It wasn't supposed to be anything like this.

"It's official," Sav says, catching up with me on the way to lunch. "I'm pretending to be sick and wallowing at home for the rest of the day. Care to join?"

"But it's meat-pie day," I deadpan. "How could we miss that?"

Sav snorts. Beaumont is always bragging about how fancy our lunches are, and I guess they have a point. Our dining room has oak paneling, white tablecloths, and actual nonplastic silverware. But for all of Chef Bryan's greatest hits, like seafood gumbo or fried chicken, he has a few major duds that he won't retire out of an intense commitment to tradition. Like the meat pies, which Lily refuses to even touch, and which get Sav singing *Sweeney Todd* all lunch period.

"I'm not exactly feeling up to my fabulous rendition of 'The Worst Pies in London' today," she teases, but her face falls. "It's been almost four days, Viv. That's—"

"I know," I say, because I can't let either of us say what it really means. We both know the statistics.

We go silent as we walk, and for a second, I can feel it all about to spill out: the Pierrot, the Jester, his threats. I've been keeping so much from Sav, and it would feel so good to let it out that I almost do.

But then we're almost at the dining room, and it's too crowded. Too late.

Anyway, it's not Sav's mess to clean up. It's mine—and Piper's and April's, even though neither of them has spoken to me since yesterday on the levee.

And deep down, I know there's another reason why I can't tell Sav everything: because then she'd know what I've really been hiding, what I'm afraid the Jester knows.

What I've really done.

When Sav and I make it to the dining-room entrance, Mr. Pierce is walking in, too. He holds the door open for us.

"Ladies first," he says with a polite smile, but it looks strained. Maybe the second missing student in two years is really taking its toll, I think, with a bitter taste in my mouth.

And then I remember Mr. Pierce up on the stage at the ball, trying his best to calm everyone down. Could he be in the

Pierrot, too? I try to picture his eyes behind one of those masks, but Sav is already walking through the door. I snap out of it and follow her through.

"Meat-pie day," Mr. Pierce says cheerfully, as he steps inside behind us, the smell of fried dough and Cajun seasoning already thick in the air. "One of Beaumont's finest traditions, isn't it?"

"Yeah," I say with a weak smile. I don't have the heart to lie to him.

The rest of the day is pretty much torture. I slog through lunch and classes until finally, three thirty rolls around, and there's nothing between me and the only thing I have to look forward to: practice.

I practically sprint to the locker room and change even faster, already making my way back downstairs when the rest of the team is just starting to get ready. I can feel the energy squirming through my whole body, itching to get out. There's nothing I want more than to turn off my brain and lose myself to the field.

"Atkins."

I turn toward Coach, who's walking up with a clipboard tucked under his arm.

"You're early," he says.

I shrug, suddenly embarrassed to admit how badly I need to be here.

"Well, glad to have my best defender back." Coach adjusts his baseball cap, hesitating for a second. "How's everything been?"

It hits me that the last time I saw Coach was only two days ago, at Piper's party. It feels more like years. Lily had only been missing for forty-eight hours, and I'd never even heard of the Pierrot, but now . . . I don't even want to think about it. I could lie, tell Coach I'm fine, but he's one of the only adults at Beaumont who doesn't bullshit. So I don't bullshit him, either.

"Not great," I say. "But it's good to be here. Turn it off for a bit."

He nods, frowning a little. "Still, it's okay if you need to take a step back. I know you always like to give a hundred and ten—it's part of what makes you such a good player—but none of that's worth it if you're running yourself to the ground." He pauses, eyes crinkling. "I guess I'm just saying it's okay to *not* turn it off. You know, let yourself feel it. Talk to somebody if you need."

Suddenly, I feel like I could cry. It's exactly what I needed to hear and also the worst thing he could have told me, because this is what I always do: push things down, keep running, try to forget anything more messy or complicated than the game, than backing my team up. Of *course* Coach has seen it.

And maybe I should take his advice, but I can't. Not here. Because I'm worried if I start to really feel it, I won't ever stop.

And then I get an idea.

"Coach?"

"Yeah?"

I think about chickening out, but I can't. I should have asked him on New Year's, but I was too focused on the Dukes, on Wyatt and his blowup. And now I'm even more desperate.

"Did you see anything that night?" I ask. "At the ball?"

He runs a hand along his stubbled jaw.

"You know, I've been asking myself the same thing," he says. "Thinking it over, wondering if there was anything I might've missed, anything I could've done, but . . . no, I don't think I did."

The regret on his face is so real that it makes me feel awful.

Coach is probably blaming himself, just like I am. She's his player, too. He's supposed to look out for her. But I'm the one who was supposed to know her inside and out, even though apparently I didn't, not the way I thought. And maybe I never will, if the worst happens. If we don't find her.

I force that thought down, too. "Thanks anyway."

But Coach must see the disappointment on my face, because he keeps talking.

"The last time I saw her . . ." He pauses again, and I get the feeling he's holding something back. Then he sighs. "I'd gone out to get Elle's shawl from the car, and LeBlanc was out near the front entrance. I checked in as I passed by, and she seemed fine. Made some joke about the blood on her dress and how that's what she gets for wearing white."

The back of my neck prickles. That's the exact same joke Lily made to Mrs. Johnson, isn't it? Like she had it prepared. Like she was performing even then.

"Then, as I was coming back in, I saw a car pull up, and she got in," Coach continues. "Wyatt, I figured."

He shrugs, like he's sorry he doesn't have anything better to tell me, but something nags at me. When I last saw Lily, she was standing with Wyatt on the path to the front entrance. He said he'd already pulled the car around to the front, didn't he? Why would he have to pull up again? But maybe I'm remembering wrong.

I try to keep my face neutral as I ask, "The silver Honda, right?"

A line deepens between Coach's eyebrows. "It was black. A Mercedes, I think?"

The little nagging feeling grows into something much worse.

"Do you remember anything else about it?" I ask. "The car?"

"No, I don't think so." He looks even more concerned. "Why?"

"No reason." It rushes out of me in a panic before I can think better of it. "I think . . . I think I might actually need to take the day off. I'm feeling kind of lightheaded."

Before Coach can respond, I turn and speed for the athletic building doors, mind racing.

Lily didn't leave the ball with Wyatt. She left with a stranger in a black Mercedes. Coach watched it happen.

And I wasn't there at all.

20

PIPER

JANUARY 2, 3:40 P.M.

The Diet Coke thumps to the bottom of the vending machine, and I slide it out, waiting for the bubbles to settle so I can finally take a pull of aspartame to quell the headache that's been pounding all day. Normally, I love the first day back at school—the routine, the regimented schedule, even the smell of Beaumont's freshly cut grass in the morning. Today, though, I feel like I've just spent the past seven hours dodging land mines.

Probably because I have, in a manner of speaking. I haven't talked to April or Vivian all day, and I intend for it to stay that way, maybe until graduation.

I twist the cap of my Diet Coke, letting a long sip burn down my throat, but the dull throbbing at the back of my skull doesn't stop. Maybe I should consider that the headache isn't caffeine-related at all.

As if on cue, my phone lights up with a new message, and a silly part of my brain hopes that maybe it's the Maids.

Instead, the contact name is "Arch Nemesis."

Meet at the library in 5?

Aiden. I sigh, starting to type out an "okay" before deciding to throw the message a Like instead. Vivian is still in my head somewhere, smirking about her *Pride and Prejudice* crap. Whatever. While, despite what Vivian thinks, I don't relish alone time with Aiden Ortiz, this meeting will be a good distraction. We're both in charge of the Senior Week committee, thanks to a unanimous nomination from the student council, which is not as much of an honor as it sounds. Everyone is always checked out by Senior Week—the famously fun-filled week before graduation—and they'd rather enjoy the festivities than actually *plan* them. I'm pretty sure Aiden and I scored this job simply because no one else is high-strung enough to do it.

At the very least, this meeting means I won't have to run into either of the Maids in the usual after-school exodus.

I hike up my backpack, fighting another stab of guilt as I think of how they both looked at me on the levee. But it's not my fault they're upset, I tell myself as I start toward the library. I made the hard decision, the logical decision. No matter how close we seemed to answers, we were searching for some sort of conspiracy that just doesn't exist. It would only have done more harm than good, even if April and Vivian can't see that. Even if they hate me.

And why do I care? They're not my friends. We were colleagues. Coinvestigators, at best. And it's like it's always been: I don't need friends, at least not more than the surface-level ones I already have. Friends aren't the point of high school. High school is for getting into college, which I've already done. *Check*. I can worry about friends when I get there.

Aiden is already waiting in a study room, irritatingly on time.

"Hey," he says.

"Hey," I say flatly, sliding into the seat next to him at the table.

"No insults today?" He clutches his heart. "But I've grown so used to them."

"Believe me, I've got plenty." It comes out harsher than I mean it to.

I can feel him looking at me but pretend not to notice, focusing on opening my laptop.

"You okay?" he asks.

"Do I not look okay?"

"That's a loaded question."

"Ha-ha."

Aiden is quiet for a second. When I finally glance up at him, he's frowning slightly.

"What?" I ask.

It's hard to tell, but I think his cheeks get a little pink. He reaches for the pencil in front of him, twisting it between his long fingers. "Do you know if they've heard anything? About Lily?"

I shrug. "Nothing new, I think. Why?"

He becomes very interested in the pencil eraser. "I think maybe you were right that there's something more going on. It's been four days now, right? It feels . . . I don't know."

I tense, focusing on my Google Doc, even when I feel his eyes on me again. "They'll find her."

"I thought—"

"You were right," I cut him off. "She probably just ran away."

Aiden nods, shoulders slumping a little. He grabs his water bottle, a new item to fidget with, and after a few seconds, he stands.

"I'm going to go fill this up," he says. "Take five?"

"Fine with me."

Aiden bounds out of the study room, leaving me alone. I stare at the blinking cursor on my screen, a weird hollow feeling in my stomach, then shake myself out of it. I need to focus, do something to keep my mind busy. On cue, my computer flashes with a low-battery notification. Shit. Did I forget to plug it in last night? And how did I not even notice? I reach into my bag for my charger, but it's not there. Shit again. I really need to get it together.

Aiden's bag is open. I'm sure *he* wasn't too distracted to double-check this morning. I don't think he'll mind, either, so I go ahead and grab his charger. That's when I see something else tucked into the laptop pocket.

A folded piece of thick paper.

With a quick glance at the door, I reach inside and pull it out. The paper is heavy, familiar. My pulse thrums under my skin as I unfold it, revealing the sad-clown logo stamped at the top. The message underneath.

> *His Majesty, King Deus, commands your attendance at His Royal Feast, where we shall welcome our newest brothers to the Krewe. January 2nd, ten of the clock. The Pierrot.*

I don't register the door opening again until it's too late. Aiden stands in the doorway, water bottle gripped, eyes locking on the invitation in my hands.

21

APRIL

JANUARY 2, 3:45 P.M.

I shouldn't be here. Taking in the Tulane University campus, I already feel like a shrimp in a sea of collegiate green. Not to mention this plan is totally doomed, because I don't even know her name. If I want to find the girl from the Pierrot bathroom, I don't have anything to go on besides her face and the certainty deep in my gut: now that Piper and Vivian are out, she's my only shot at finding the truth.

Hiking up my camera strap, I scan the courtyard. It's still technically Tulane's winter break, so it's not too crowded. A few students are milling around, jogging by, or snapping pictures of a tree covered with Mardi Gras beads that hang from the branches like rainbow moss.

Margot was supposed to be here with them. Right now, she should be burrowed in the most oversized Tulane sweatshirt imaginable, getting ready for sorority rush or buying her books for the new semester with a massive coffee in hand. Maybe I'd even be with her, learning all the new names and stories from her freshman year.

Now, when I picture her, there's only one image I can conjure up: her face that night. The anger in her eyes, aimed at me like a weapon.

"Excuse me."

A student steps past me, and with a rush of embarrassment, I realize I'm stopped dead in the middle of the path.

"Sorry," I mumble, but they're already long gone.

And suddenly, it's too much, being here in what should have been Margot's future. I'm about to give up and go scurrying back to my car when I see her.

She's ditched the ball gown for platform boots, space buns, and a vintage Bowie shirt that would look try-hard on anyone else, but it's unmistakably her. The girl from the bathroom. She's standing at a bike rack, locking hers up, her hair an even more otherworldly reddish-purple in the sun.

And then she sees me. Her brow furrows before her eyes widen in recognition.

This was a bad idea. One of my worst, actually, and all the nerve is leaving me as quickly as the heat rushing to my face. I scramble in the opposite direction, but I barely make it a few steps before I hear her.

"You're one of the Beaumont girls."

"No," I say, clinging to the possibility that if I walk fast enough, I might develop the power of teleportation.

I don't know how she's so quick in those boots, but in a matter of seconds, she's at my side, her mouth turned down into a scowl.

"What are you doing here?"

"Nothing."

"Are you stalking me?"

"No."

"Do you use words with more than two syllables?"

"Y—" I clamp my mouth shut, face burning. "Occasionally."

She laughs, surprisingly genuine. We're stopped under the bead tree, and I hope that, by some miracle, the shade hides how red and sweaty I must look. I don't think it does, though, because now that she's really looking at me, it's with something like concern, maybe even pity.

"What are you doing here?" she repeats.

It hits me again how close we must be in age. She's too self-assured to be a freshman, I think, but if I had to bet, there's no way she's older than a sophomore.

"I need to talk to you," I tell her.

"Well, you're not doing a very good job."

Her tone is flat, but the corner of her mouth twitches into a slight smile, and somehow, I find the courage to tell her my name.

"I'm April."

She watches me like she's not sure if she should trust me with hers.

"Renee," she says finally. "Look, if you're going to ask me about the other night—"

"You knew Margot." I'm surprised by the ease with which my voice comes now—maybe because I'm desperate. Or maybe because Renee reminds me of her, with her sort-of-raspy voice and tired wisdom, like she's already got the world all figured out and she's sorry to be the one to tell you it sucks.

She chews her lip, not confirming. Waiting.

"You saw Lily, too," I press. "Lily LeBlanc. The blond girl who was asking about Margot. She's missing."

Renee lets out a breath.

"I know," she says. "I looked her up after y'all told me her name. Saw a news report."

"Then you know how important this is. She could be in danger, and Margot—I think something might have happened to her. I know the reports all said she overdosed, but I think someone at the Pierrot—"

At the mention of it, Renee's gaze darts over her shoulder, and I tense. I don't want to put her at risk, but I have to know, and I'm worried I've already scared her off.

Her eyes meet mine. Bright green and probing.

"You were her friend?" she asks finally. "Margot's?"

I nod.

Renee sighs.

"Come on," she says.

"Where?" I ask.

She looks at me like it's obvious. "We can talk. Just not out here." She scans the space around us, the bending oak trees. "I figure we should be careful who's listening."

Renee lives in a dorm that looks sort of like a motel, situated on the second floor with an outdoor walkway overlooking a green courtyard. Inside, it's nicer than it looks—white brick walls tacked with band posters, a bed with deep-purple covers, fairy lights dangling overhead.

"A single?" I ask, because I don't know what else to say.

"Perks of being an RA."

"Do you like it?"

She shrugs. "I like the free housing. Not so much the dealing with drunk and crying freshmen. But you've probably figured out by now that I'm not exactly flush with cash."

Renee hops onto her bed, unlacing her boots. She nods for me to take a seat, so I sink awkwardly into her beanbag chair. My heart is beating fast, but I know I have to bring it up.

"That's why you go to the Pierrot, right?" I ask. "You said he pays. The guy who takes you."

Renee drops a boot onto the ground with a heavy thud. "A damn pretty penny."

"Who is he?"

The other boot thuds to the ground. She eyes me. "I signed a shit ton of NDAs."

A chill slinks down my spine.

Renee must notice, because she adds, "He's harmless, though. Don't worry. He doesn't even try to kiss me or anything. Mostly, I think he just wants a little young thing to parade around for his friends."

Somehow, that doesn't make me feel any better.

"What about the other women?" I ask. "Who are they?"

"Girls like me, I guess. Ones who need the money bad enough to keep our mouths shut."

"But Margot didn't need money," I say. "Why was she there?"

Renee watches me for a moment.

"What happened to your friends?" she asks, sidestepping my question. "The other debutantes?"

I grit my teeth, tensing at the memory of the levee. "I don't know if I'd call them my friends."

Renee is silent.

"Please," I beg, when she still hasn't said anything. "This is the closest I've gotten to answers, and I just—"

It rushes back to me like a gasp of cold water. The way Margot looked at me that night, her hand around the lighter. Desperate. *Please.*

"Something happened," I say. "The last night I ever saw her, I could tell something had happened. She was angry and reckless, but she wouldn't tell me what was going on. And I just—I need to know. Because if I don't . . . then all I'll know is that she needed me, and I left her."

And there it is: the truth. The dark, creeping thought I haven't been able to voice, not even to Piper or Vivian. Some part of me still can't say all of it out loud—what we did that night, the thing I know the Jester might be holding over me, even though it feels like it matters so little now.

Renee brings her legs up on the bed, pulling her knees to her chest.

"I always thought it seemed wrong," she says. "The overdose thing. I only really talked to Margot a few times, but I've known addicts, and I didn't think that was her. She seemed so . . . I don't know. Bright. Fun. And she had this fuck-you attitude, but under all that, there was this . . . joy. Like even though life is full of shit, she was so fucking glad to be alive."

Tears sting my eyes. I've never heard someone describe her so sharply, so truthfully. I would snap a picture of those words if I could, just so I could hold them close.

"I didn't know Margot was a Les Masques girl until after she died," Renee continues. "I still have no idea how she got into the Pierrot in the first place, if anyone there recognized her."

"But one of the men brought her," I say.

"Yeah. I don't really know anything about him, but . . ." She hesitates, and I clock the moment she decides to trust me with whatever she's about to say. "Things seemed different between them. Most of the women, it's clear it's transactional, but this guy and Margot . . . I'm pretty sure they were, like, together."

The memory flashes again: Margot hiding her phone from me. The secretive smile pulling at her lips as she bent over the screen. I was sure that she was texting Lily, that they were laughing at me, conspiring about how to ditch my deadweight.

Now, though, the image shifts, sharpening into higher resolution.

"When did you meet Margot?" I ask.

"Last fall, I think," she says. "Maybe end of summer."

Exactly when Margot was hiding those texts—just before she'd started pulling away, disappearing, busy whenever I tried to hang out. I'd always assumed it was Lily. I *knew* it was Lily. As a photographer, you're supposed to be good at details, weaving images together into a coherent composition, and that was the one that made the most sense. The only one that made sense.

But what if I had been dead wrong?

"Is there anything else you can tell me about him?" I press. "What he looked like, or . . . ?"

"He was the type who always kept his mask on. But . . ." Renee hesitates. "It was this wolf mask."

There's a shift like a storm moving through the room, static all over my skin. The Rougarou's voice curls into my memory like smoke. *The other one was seventeen, wasn't she?*

"I saw him," I say. "On the balcony. I mentioned Margot, and he knew her."

My heart pounds as I wrack my brain for any details I remember about him—his voice, his eyes—but it's like my memory is a deep black pool, so wide and dark that I can't see the bottom.

"Shit," Renee says.

"Have you ever talked to him?" I ask. "Do you have any idea who he could be?"

Renee shakes her head. "I see him every so often, but he's never talked to me or anything, not since Margot died. He barely even looked at me before. I try to stay away, 'cause he gives me a weird vibe, but I never thought . . ." She pauses, dread deepening on her face. "Do you think he really might have done something to her?"

I don't answer. I don't have to. Because it's dawning on both of us now, the horrible truth: I came face-to-face with Margot's killer. I could have torn off his mask, pushed him up against the balcony railing, demanded that he tell me what he did to her.

But I didn't.

I did what Margot always feared I would, what I ended up doing to her in the end.

I ran.

22

PIPER

JANUARY 2, 3:50 P.M.

Aiden starts to speak, but I beat him to it.

"Where the hell did you get this?"

"I—" He stops, and his expression changes from panic to something unexpected. Relief. "You know."

Confusion makes me hesitate, but I won't back down. "I asked you a question."

"It's not mine."

"Bullshit."

Aiden's gaze locks on the invitation in my hand. And then, when he seems to conclude that I'm not letting him get out of this, "If I explain, I need you to swear that you won't tell anyone."

"Why?"

"Piper—"

"Sorry, but this feels like a pretty conditional situation. I can't exactly keep it a secret if you're about to tell me you committed a felony."

"Okay, fair." He puts his water bottle down and slumps into a chair. "If I can swear this isn't related to a federal crime, will you trust me?"

I meet his eyes, searching for a shred of duplicity in their sticky honey brown, but all I see is desperation.

"Fine." Some instinct for professionalism moves me to offer a handshake, and he takes it. When his fingers close around mine, an almost electric current shoots up to my wrist, but I tell myself it's because his hand is cool from the water bottle. Simple physics. "Don't make me regret this, Ortiz. Now where the hell did you get that invitation?"

He lets go of my hand and clasps his own together on the table. "I found it a few days ago, addressed to one of the Deus members."

"Who?" When he hesitates, I press harder. "If your main concern is protecting the anonymity of some old guy, I'm going to have a hard time trusting you."

"I know. I'm just trying to figure out how to—" His eyes drop to the table. "Look, there are things going on inside Deus that you may not . . . know about."

He's speaking like it's physically hard to get the words out, and I realize, suddenly, that he thinks he's protecting me. My fragile image of my family traditions, how glorious and important it all is.

I cross my arms. "Try me."

He finally looks at me. "What do you know?"

"I'm asking the questions."

He gives a small flash of a smile. "You're killing it with the bad-cop thing, but I'm trying to put this together, too. Maybe help me out a little?"

I want to argue, but there's something about the way he's looking at me, all pleading, that makes my brain briefly turn into mush.

"Fine." I smooth my skirt, suddenly unable to look at him,

either. "I may or may not have heard about the Pierrot from Milford on New Year's. Now what do you know about it? Are you a member?"

"No."

"Is your dad?"

Aiden gets this look that I hate—one that says there's something obvious I'm not seeing. "We're not exactly welcome there."

An uneasy feeling squirms in my stomach. I think I know why, but still, I ask, "What do you mean?"

"As far as some people are concerned, my dad shouldn't be in Deus, let alone the Pierrot. I know membership is technically 'nondiscriminatory' now, as long as you've got the money and connections to work your way in, but there was still pushback from the old guard when Dad joined. Some of them weren't too happy about having the son of Mexican immigrants in their little club."

The uneasy feeling deepens. I know about Deus's ugly, racist roots. Almost all of the oldest Krewes were segregated at first. It wasn't until the nineties that the city outlawed discrimination, ordering any groups that didn't comply to forfeit their parade licenses. Most Krewes, like Deus, wised up and changed with the times, but others clung to their exclusionary practices, canceling their public parades and choosing instead to host only private balls. Some of them do to this day, claiming their refusal to be inclusive is some kind of First Amendment right. Still, I thought Deus was different. A week ago, I would have balked at the idea that anyone in our Krewe is so openly bigoted. But now . . .

"I think that's why the Pierrot exists," Aiden continues. "Or at least partly. These old-line guys wanted to go back to a time when they didn't have to hide who they were, so they started a group that would let them do it."

As soon as he says it, I know, without a doubt, that it's true.

"How do you know about the Pierrot?" I ask.

"I first heard about it last semester. The Les Masques invitations had just come out, so Milford's parents invited all the Dukes and their dads over to celebrate."

I remember that night. Wyatt and Dad were there. Mom and I weren't invited, because, like an echo of Milford's annoying lilt when we made him tell us about the Pierrot: *No girls allowed*.

"One of the guys from St. Anthony's said something about an after-party," Aiden says. "At the Pierrot. As soon as he said it, the other Dukes got really weird. Milford changed the subject, but the way they were all looking at me . . . I knew. It was like walking up to a group of people when you know they were just talking about you, only I'd been standing there the whole time. I pressed Milford about the Pierrot later, but he said he couldn't tell me. It was a 'Carnival secret.'"

It's the exact same phrase he used when we cornered him in the bathroom, and it makes my skin crawl.

"I asked my dad about it when we got home, and he had no idea what I was talking about. But I couldn't leave it alone. I had this feeling, like something big was going on right under our noses. So I started doing research. The first thing I found was about Milford's dad. Last year, when he announced that he was running for mayor, a former employee at his law firm came forward to accuse him of sexual harassment."

My blood goes cold. "I didn't know that."

"It didn't get much attention because two days later, that same employee retracted her statements. There weren't any news items about it after that, but I found her on LinkedIn. She was working at a new firm in Florida. I messaged her, pretending to want advice on applying to her alma mater, and we set up a call. When I asked her about the Pierrot, she shut down. Told me never to contact her again. She seemed terrified."

"You think they ran her out of town," I realize.

"I don't know if they paid her off or just threatened her badly enough to make her leave, but . . . yeah, I do. And it's not the first time they've done it. I found two other stories almost exactly like this one within the past ten years. An allegation gets made about a prominent Deus member, it gets dropped, and the person who made it leaves town. And it's not just that. Lawsuits against members' companies disappearing, their DUIs getting reduced to smaller charges or going away completely . . . the past three Louisiana congressmen elected have been pictured at balls or other Krewe events, chumming it up with active Deus members."

I shake my head, like that might make it stop spinning, even though some part of me already knew from the moment I saw that place: they're covering up each other's crimes. Exchanging favors. Maybe even rigging elections.

"And now," Aiden says, gesturing at the invitation, "they're 'welcoming their newest brothers.' It's like a cult. They're building their ranks. Indoctrinating people."

"I know," I say. "I've been."

"What?"

The rest of it rushes out of me before I can stop myself. "They have this club in the Quarter. They all meet there and wear masks and bring these young women and—" I shut my eyes for a second, commanding myself to keep it together. "We think they might have something to do with Lily's disappearance."

"Piper . . ." His face is so full of concern that some instinct in me wants to deny it, if only to make him stop looking at me like that. "How did you end up there? And who's 'we'?"

"Me, April, and Vivian. We've been investigating ever since Lily went missing. We sort of blackmailed Milford into taking us to the Pierrot. And . . ."

I hesitate. It feels like I'm standing on the edge of something, like if I finally accept April's theory, say it out loud, it will make it true. And I still don't know if I can trust him.

But right now, who else do I have?

I take a breath and pray I can rely on the sanctity of the handshake.

"We think someone at the Pierrot might have killed Margot Landry. And Lily might have known about it."

I watch as Aiden takes it in, my hands shaky with adrenaline—not just because I said it out loud. But because now that I have, I realize I might really believe it.

"Shit," he says finally. "So that stunt at the ball, with the projections of Margot . . ."

"We think it's all connected. The Pierrot is the reason Lily's missing."

"Like how they forced those other women to leave town," Aiden says. "Or . . ."

I can feel us both reaching the same conclusion. If Aiden's suspicions are right, then this wouldn't be the first time the Pierrot has run someone out of the city for knowing too much. But there's more than one way to make a girl disappear. And if the Pierrot is truly capable of murder . . .

With a sudden jolt, I realize just how badly I screwed up by telling April and Vivian we should stop investigating. Because Lily knew exactly what the Pierrot was doing. She knew what they did to Margot, and she was planning to tell us that morning at the Den. But if the Pierrot found out, they would have done anything to keep her quiet. Even if, I realize, that meant withdrawing money from her account, making it look like she ran away.

Even if it meant killing another Queen.

April was right. I've been wanting so badly for everything to be fine that I practically covered my eyes as the evidence piled up in front of me. But now?

Now I'm making up for lost time.

"Come on." I push out of my chair and start to shove my things into my bag. "We have to find April and Vivian."

"We?"

I stop. This time, I can't fight the flush as I look back at him, his warm eyes and the little smirk on his face. "Don't feel too proud of yourself."

He smiles wider. "Wouldn't dream of it."

And then his smile fades. The look in his eyes is dead serious.

"What?"

"If there was something else," he says carefully, "something that would hurt you . . . would you want to know?"

My stomach drops as I realize where he's looking. The invitation, still in my hand.

"Tell me," I say.

He takes the sort of breath you take when you know what you say next is going to shatter everything. Still, I'm not prepared for the impact.

"I found that invitation at your house on New Year's," he says. "It was addressed to your dad."

23

VIVIAN

JANUARY 2, 3:50 P.M.

I head straight for the parking lot, not even sure what my plan is besides getting the hell out. All I can think is that Lily left the ball with a stranger, and no one stopped it. *I* didn't stop it. I should have been there, should have done something.

But it's not just my fault. Wyatt was there, too. Wyatt was supposed to drive her home. And instead, he let her disappear.

I dig out my phone, jabbing at my screen until I find his contact, but just before I press CALL, I see him: Wyatt, throwing his backpack into the silver Honda that Lily should have been in that night.

I march over to him. "Hey!"

He freezes with his hand on the car door.

"Why didn't you drive Lily home after the ball?" I demand.

"Whoa, can you keep it down?" Wyatt's eyes dart around the parking lot, where a few other people are turning their heads. But I'm well past caring.

"Answer the question."

"I need to get home." He starts around to the driver's side, but I block his path. He groans. "Vivian, seriously. I'm leaving."

"And I'm seriously going to lie in front of this car if I have to."

For a moment, he holds me in his annoyingly blue stare. But even before he does, I know he'll fold.

"Fine," Wyatt says. "Get in."

I slide into the passenger seat and shut the door. "Start explaining."

He stares at the dash, teeth grinding, but this time, he doesn't try to get out of it.

"We got in a fight. She didn't want to get in the car, and we were arguing, and she—" His voice breaks. "She told me it was over."

I sink back into my seat. Maybe I shouldn't be so stunned, after everything, but I am. "Really?"

He shrugs. "Not like it's a surprise."

But it is. I mean, isn't it? Sure, Lily and Wyatt have been through some rough patches in the past few months, but they're *Lily and Wyatt*. They're the golden couple, the perfect picture of a Queen and her King. He adores her. She talks about their future like it's inevitable.

But then I guess there's a whole lot Lily and I have been keeping from each other.

Wyatt sniffs, turning away from me, and I realize he's holding back tears. And as much as I want to, I can't be mad at him. Because suddenly, I understand where all this has been coming from, the way he's been lashing out: he's as worried about Lily as I am. And he's blaming himself just as much, too.

"I'm sorry," I say. "I didn't know."

The car goes quiet, and even though I'm a little less pissed, I still have to ask.

"Coach says he saw Lily getting into a black Mercedes. Do you know whose it was?"

Wyatt frowns. "Coach Davis?"

"He was outside getting his girlfriend's shawl or something. And you're not answering the question."

The look on Wyatt's face turns into something like dread. "Lily told me she was going to Uber."

I bite the inside of my cheek. Maybe it *was* just an Uber. Maybe I'm jumping to conclusions. But still, I don't relax.

"What if she didn't?" I ask. "What if it was someone else? Someone—"

"She ran away."

He says it so calmly that for a second, I don't think I heard him right.

"What?" I manage finally. "You don't actually think she just—"

"Vivian, I'm telling you." He turns to me with a look I hate, like he's sure. "That night, she told me she was leaving."

It's like the floor falls out from under me.

"What? Where?"

"She didn't say. Just said she was going."

"And you didn't tell anyone?"

"Obviously, I did," he snaps. "I mean, eventually. That night, I was so mad and honestly fucking embarrassed that I couldn't even talk about it. But I told her parents the next morning. They knew. But she was already gone."

Lily ran away. It's what Marty said, what Piper said. But it can't be true. Not with everything else that's happened.

"She wouldn't," I argue. "It doesn't make sense. We found her necklace at the Den. She sent us this email."

"What does it matter? She clearly didn't give a shit about any of us."

"Bullshit."

"Yeah? Then why didn't she give you a heads-up?" His stare burns into me so hard it almost stings.

I turn away.

"You could have told me," I say.

He laughs darkly. "So could Piper."

I force myself to look at him again. "What?"

"I don't know how she found out, but I overheard her ratting to our parents that I 'lied' about driving Lily home, or whatever. I wouldn't be surprised if she knows the rest." He scoffs. "Honestly, I'm shocked she didn't tell you everything. Take every chance she had to act all superior."

Maybe I shouldn't, but I feel betrayed. It's not like I know Piper that well, but I thought we were on the same team. I thought, maybe, we were something like friends. But this whole time, she had a lead we could have used, and she hid it. And maybe it's not the worst lie, but it's one too many.

I shove the car door open. "Thanks for the chat. This was awesome."

"Wait. I'm sorry. I just—" He stops, and as much as I want to leave, I freeze, my heart suddenly pounding. "Look, I know she's your best friend, and you don't want to hear it, but maybe we all need to wake up to the fact that we don't know Lily as well as we think we do. She was never going to let us."

I want to argue that he's wrong. I've known Lily for thirteen years. You can't know a person for that long and not *know* them.

Can you?

I shut the door, and he doesn't try to stop me. Or maybe he knows I won't let him. Either way, I storm back to my car alone, throat burning. All I want is to get the hell out of this parking lot and drive somewhere no one will see me cry.

And then I notice the envelope on my windshield.

"No." I say it out loud, almost involuntarily. But already, like the lead in a horror movie, I'm reaching out to take it, even as the rational person inside me is screaming to throw it away and peel out of here.

But this envelope is heavy. There's something bulky inside it, more than just another threatening message.

I shut myself in my car and rip it open, realizing it's not a message at all. It's a phone. A flip phone, small and outdated. A burner, I think, because it's exactly how I'd picture one, the kind people use in crime shows.

It takes me a second to figure out the buttons, but when I do, I open up the messages. There's only one conversation thread, and it's all from late December. Right before the ball, I realize, my heart skipping a beat. This must be the number Lily was texting that night. But then I notice the full date.

These messages are from over a year ago. December 28, the night of Margot's ball. The night she died.

It starts with a series of texts from an unsaved New Orleans number, sent around two o'clock that afternoon:

Fine keep ignoring me
I literally don't even care anymore
But I'm telling everyone about us
Try and fucking stop me

Whoever was using this phone responded minutes later:

I'm so sorry. Can we talk about this first?

And then, half an hour later:

Margot?? Please talk to me

She didn't text back until a little after midnight.

Meet me at our spot on the levee.

The levee. That's where they found Margot in her car, OD'd. Or so everyone thought. Because now it's clear that that's not what happened at all. Margot met someone that night, hours after she threatened to "tell everyone" about them. That has to mean an affair, right? And whoever had this burner, whoever Margot was meeting, said they just wanted to talk.

But what if their real goal was to shut her up, by any means possible?

My head rushes as it fully dawns on me.

Margot was murdered, and I'm holding the burner phone of the man who did it.

The next question is almost an afterthought: How the hell did it end up sitting on my windshield?

24

PIPER

JANUARY 2, 4:15 P.M.

When I get home, luck is on my side: Mom's and Dad's cars are both missing from the driveway. The one I share with Wyatt is here, but I'll just have to hope he's shut up in his room like he's always been lately.

This is something I need to do on my own.

As I walk into the house, I resist the urge to check my phone to see if Aiden texted. He wanted to come with me, but I shook him off. I was too angry at him for telling me the truth, and even angrier at myself for not being able to handle it.

So handle it, I command myself silently. And I am. I will. All I need is more proof, something to show Aiden he was wrong about my dad being in the Pierrot.

With a deep breath, I push open the door to Dad's office.

I've always loved this room—the smell of the old books lining his shelves, musty and comforting. Most days, Dad works from his office in the Garden District, so he mostly uses this one for the occasional telehealth session or anything else he needs to get done after the workday. Sometimes, though, I think it's his hideaway from the rest of us, which I can understand. Being a Johnson can be overwhelming.

Unless he's not just hiding from you, says a voice in my head that sounds too much like my own. *He's hiding himself. The things he doesn't want you to know.*

I give that voice a swift kick in the throat and tell myself not to panic until I have to.

Settling myself into Dad's desk chair, I tap the mouse of his desktop computer, waking the screen. Instantly, guilt floods my system. His screen saver is a picture of all four of us, one of the family shots Mom wrangled us into taking before the ball. But this one isn't the perfect portrait Mom posted to her Instagram. It's candid: Mom is backing away from the camera, frozen in a hilarious look of surprise because the self-timer went off earlier than she was expecting. Wyatt's losing his battle with an amused smile, and I have a look of pure shock, a white glove pressed to my mouth. And Dad is looking down at me and Wyatt, hands in his suit pockets and undeniable love in his eyes.

A dull ache starts up at the back of my throat. The Dad I see in this picture can't just be a mask, a role he's playing to hide the villain inside. He *loves* us. He's a good person, and I need to prove it.

I type in the password we've always used for everything, and it works. I'm doing this. And now that I've started, I know I have to keep going.

His desktop is pretty standard and organized, folders for work and taxes and not much else. I click on his browser, still open to the portal he uses for patients. There won't be anything about the Pierrot in here, but something scratches at the back of my brain. I navigate to the search bar and type in *Margot*

Landry, stopping before I hit ENTER. Doing this will definitely violate about a hundred different HIPAA laws, but no one has to know. And it's hardly the worst thing I've done lately.

I hit ENTER, and Margot's profile populates the page. After some clicking around, I find the notes from her sessions.

I hesitate. This is wrong in so many ways, but then again, can you really violate a dead girl's privacy?

Yes, my conscience says, but it's not quite as loud as a different, darker thought. If Dad thought Margot was a danger to herself, then maybe that will prove there *isn't* some kind of conspiracy going on. Only what we already knew: Margot had problems, and Margot died. The Pierrot didn't necessarily have anything to do with it.

I open the notes from her most recent session, December 20th of last year, a little over a week before the ball. But reading through it, there's nothing out of the ordinary. From Dad's description, it seems like Margot was a normal girl who struggled with anxiety, which he prescribed medication for. Nothing here suggests a girl on the verge of self-destruction. He wrote that she reported some alcohol consumption since her last session, but no drug use.

I drum my nails on the mouse pad. Margot wouldn't necessarily admit to having a drug problem, but Dad would have noted if something was off, wouldn't he? I click back to previous sessions, but it's more of the same. Dad's notes are brief, but none of it paints the picture of a girl who would be dead before the New Year.

Steeling myself, I open a new tab and navigate to Dad's email. His personal account is already logged in. In the search bar, I type *Pierrot* and hit ENTER. When no results come up in his inbox, I'm relieved. It's not much proof, though. I highly doubt they'd send anything with a subject line as useful as "Murder Cover-Up Action Items."

Going back to the search bar, I type *Margot Landry.*

This time, there's one result. It's an email Dad sent last January, a week after Margot died. The recipient: Detective Marty Rutherford.

> Marty,
>
> Attached is my most recent progress report for Margot Landry. Please let me know if there's anything else I can do to help.
>
> Best,
>
> Stephen

Detective Rutherford worked on Margot's case.

It makes sense—it's literally his job—but a needling feeling won't let me go.

I click on the attachment, and it fills the screen. It's just one page, labeled with Dad's full name at the top. Underneath, the date of the exam—December 20th of the year Margot died—followed by her name and a summary of the session.

> Ms. Landry has exhibited significant regression in the past few sessions. Symptoms of anxiety and depression seem to be worsening, and she described feeling out of control. She also admitted to use of unprescribed drugs, including opiates.

Adrenaline buzzes, making my hands shaky as I click back to the patient portal. Dad didn't write any of this in his notes from that session. He definitely didn't mention unprescribed drugs. I keep reading the rest of the report he sent to Marty, including the medication notes I don't understand, hoping something will make it make sense.

And then, at the bottom, I catch the final line.

> I have shared this information with Ms. Landry's parents, as I am deeply concerned for her well-being. She exhibits signs of psychosis, and I fear that if intervention is not made at home as well as in sessions, she may put her own life in danger.

Everything around me starts to shift. I hold onto the edge of the desk, forcing my lungs to keep up with the frantic pace of my heart.

Think, Piper. Be logical. Because there has to be some logic to this, some explanation besides the dark ones working their way into my head. I check over Dad's notes again, compare them to this report, but it's like they describe two completely different Margots—one who was dealing with the normal struggles of a girl our age, and another who was a danger to herself and others. A girl who couldn't be trusted.

And now I can't deny what's happening here: Dad lied. He falsified this report and sent it to Marty to—what?

I shut my eyes, and memories flood in, lit up by a harsh new light. Dad slumped on the living-room couch as the news played a story about Margot, his eyes glazed and his glass sweating on the table. The quiet sounds of Dad crying behind his locked bathroom door, so muffled and unfamiliar it made me feel like the floor was unsteady under my feet.

I thought Dad felt guilty because he lost a patient, because he couldn't save her from herself. But now, in this new version of reality, there are no shadows to hide in. Only the terrible question, the one that's starting to look like the truth: what if

Dad felt guilty not because he couldn't save her life, but because he *took* it?

Hot tears burn my eyes, and I realize, suddenly, that I'm angry. At Dad, yes, but also at Lily—for disappearing, for making me want to dig around in places I don't belong. But most of all, I'm angry at myself. Because I couldn't let this go. I kept pushing, kept digging, even when I knew I would find things I didn't want to see.

Isn't it time we let the dead stay buried?

Now I've dug so deep that I don't think my hands will ever be clean again.

But I can't just sit here. I wipe my eyes, take a breath, and delete Margot's name from the search history in both Dad's email and his patient portal. I close out of his email, leaving the patient-portal tab open, like it was before. Then I put the desktop to sleep and tuck Dad's chair back in where I found it. All traces of me erased.

I'm walking to the door when it swings open, Wyatt standing on the other side.

I freeze, wracking my brain for some kind of explanation. But then I see the look of absolute fear on his face, and I know instantly it has nothing to do with me snooping around Dad's office. Dread curls out from my center, reaching all the way to my toes.

"What's wrong?"

"Mom just called." He sounds younger than he is. Petrified. "She's at the police station."

"What? Wh—"

But before I can even get out the "why," he tells me, in a voice as distant and frightened as I feel.

"It's Dad. They arrested him."

BREAKING: NOPD MAKES ARREST IN THE DEATH OF MARGOT LANDRY

New Orleans*—The New Orleans Police Department has made an arrest in connection with the death of Margot Landry, 17, which was ruled an overdose last year. Dr. Stephen Johnson, a prominent local psychiatrist, was taken into custody this afternoon after new evidence led police to revisit the case. As of the publishing of this article, no specific charges have been made. This is a developing story.*

25

APRIL

JANUARY 2, 5:30 P.M.

We get to Piper's house at the same time. Vivian and I both climb out of our cars and lock them, staring at each other for a few silent seconds.

"Hey," she says.

"Hey," I echo.

We haven't talked at all today, but now doesn't feel like the time for heartfelt apologies or explanations.

"You saw the—?"

"Yeah," I say. Even if I'd somehow missed the article about Piper's dad, it's all over socials now, too. It would be hard not to know—and clearly, we both rushed here as soon as we heard.

We climb the steps to the porch, and for the first time, my brain slows down enough to think about what this really means. Piper's dad was arrested in connection with Margot's death. I should feel angry and vindicated, ready to beat this door down and demand answers, but instead, I'm hesitant. There's something else, a feeling I can't quite describe. Almost like the pieces don't fit. Like it's all too easy.

But I force it down. There have to be answers inside this house, and I'm not leaving until I get them. I ring the doorbell, and the sound fades into the foyer. Vivian knocks, and I move to the shuttered windows to peer through the slats, and that's when I see it—a little envelope tucked behind them.

"Shit," Vivian says, seeing it, too.

I pull out the envelope. It's addressed to Piper in the Jester's too-familiar script. I rip it open and read the message inside. This time, it's as brief as a puncture wound.

I warned you.

Heart jumping, I go to ring the doorbell again, but Vivian's reaching behind the other shutter.

"They keep a spare somewhere over here," she says. "Wyatt's always forgetting his."

She pulls out a key and slides it into the lock. As soon as we're inside, Vivian's bounding up the stairs.

"Piper," she calls. "Are you up here?" She pauses. "Come on. We saw your car outside."

There's quiet for a few seconds, until a weak voice calls, "Yeah."

We move toward the cracked-open door at the end of the hall. Vivian leads us inside, and at first, we don't see her. Then I spot her feet sticking out from the other side of her perfectly made bed. She's sitting on the floor, knees curled to her chest.

Piper looks up at us with puffy red eyes, somehow still managing her signature glare. "You broke into my house."

"We texted a bunch of times," Vivian says. "You didn't answer. And I know where Wyatt leaves the spare key."

It hits me, suddenly, that Piper must have been alone since

the news broke. No one's come to check on her. We may not be her best friends, but right now, we're all she's got.

"So," she says, "I'm guessing you've heard."

Our silence is an answer.

"Are you okay?" Vivian asks.

"Fantastic," she says flatly. "Never been better."

"What happened?" I ask.

"Apparently, they came to his office. Arrested him in front of everyone." She swallows. "My mom's still at the station. Wyatt went, too, but I can't—I couldn't—" She closes her eyes. "They won't even say what evidence they have. They just took him."

I don't want to ask, but I have to. "Did he kill her?"

"No," she says sharply.

"How do you know?"

"Because I *know*."

The silence buzzes between us. Piper pulls her knees even tighter to her chest, like she's trying to make herself small enough to disappear.

"He falsified a progress report," she says. "About Margot. I found it on his computer. He sent one to Marty that said Margot was abusing pills and showing signs of psychosis, but his session notes didn't say anything like that at all."

My next inhale feels like syrup in my lungs, thick and heavy. I was *right*. I knew Margot wasn't so far gone. She wanted to live, and someone took that from her.

"And . . ." Piper squeezes her eyes shut, like she can't bear to look at us for this next part. "He's in the Pierrot."

For a second, we're all quiet as the truth sinks in: the Pierrot is full of familiar faces, maybe even ones we love.

"Are you sure?" Vivian asks.

"Aiden told me. He found an invitation for an event addressed to my dad. But he didn't do it. I *know* he didn't. There has to be some other reason he faked that report."

I recognize the look in her eyes, that fire of certainty. It's probably how I looked when I told her that Margot's death wasn't an accident.

"I believe you," Vivian says softly, sinking to the floor next to Piper.

I don't know if I do, not fully, but Piper's hurting, and she's maybe my friend, and I think that's all that matters right now.

"You said Aiden told you this?" I ask her, settling down on her other side.

Piper nods. "A few hours ago, after school."

And now she's starting to sound more like herself as she gives us new details at a mile a minute: how Aiden's been investigating the Pierrot, all of the cover-ups he's already discovered. My head is spinning by the time I remember the message in my hand.

"We found this outside," I say, handing it to Piper.

She scans the message. At first, I don't understand the look of revelation on her face, but then it clicks into place.

I warned you.

"They did this," Piper says. "The Jester, or whoever really killed Margot. They got my dad arrested to punish me. They framed him."

I grip my camera strap, trying to ground myself in the swirl of thoughts. But what Piper's saying makes sense. The Pierrot is no stranger to covering up crime, and it would be easy enough to make Piper's dad their fall guy. Still, he wrote that report. He's not innocent. I'm trying to decide if I should say so when Vivian reaches for her backpack.

"There's something else I found," she says, digging into a pocket and pulling out a flip phone. "It was sitting on my car in an envelope after school today."

"From the Jester?" Piper asks.

"I don't know." Vivian hands her the phone. "Read the messages. I don't think he'd want us to have this."

I scoot closer to Piper to read over her shoulder, my chest constricting as I start to understand what it is we're seeing.

"This is him," I say. "The man who killed her. The Rougarou."

"You think it's the guy from the balcony?" Vivian asks.

"I know it is." Breathlessly, I tell them about going to see Renee, what she told me: Margot and the man who brought her to the Pierrot, how they were *together.*

Vivian's eyes widen. "Then this is evidence, right? We could bring it to the police and prove to them it wasn't Piper's dad, or—"

"We can't." Piper stands, like she's too full of energy to sit still. "That's the thing. We *can't* prove who this belongs to. That's probably why the Jester did this. Like he's taunting us, or something."

"And we can't go to the police," I add. "As far as we know, the Pierrot has them in their pocket. Why else would they suddenly arrest Piper's dad when just a week ago they weren't even calling Margot's death a murder?"

Piper nods. "The Pierrot is pulling the strings. Protecting the real killer."

"But why would your dad have been helping them?" Vivian asks. "I mean, if he faked that report, then he was doing it to protect the guy who really killed her, right?"

"Right," Piper says. "So we have to find out who he is."

"I thought you wanted to play it safe." It comes out colder

than I mean it to—maybe because I'm still bruised by everything she said on the levee. "You know, accept that Margot died and Lily ran away and everything is fine."

For the first time, Piper looks almost . . . sorry.

"I shouldn't have said all that," she says. "Or I should have said it in a better way. I was scared, I guess. Of what could happen." She grips the Jester's message, cinching the thick paper. "But whoever killed Margot, he's the reason my dad is in jail right now. He's still walking free, and I sure as hell bet he knows where Lily is, too."

Vivian nods. "We have to find her."

They both have a fire in their eyes now, and I feel an ember of it flickering toward my own, catching.

"And make sure Margot's killer rots in prison for the rest of his sorry little life," I add.

Vivian smiles. "So what's the plan?"

Piper claps with such force that I yelp a little.

"Sorry," she says. "Force of habit again. But the invitation Aiden found . . ." She grabs her own backpack and digs it out, unfolding it for us to read. "This is happening tonight. A 'Royal Feast.' I think they're initiating people."

"You think we should go?" Vivian asks.

"We have to," Piper says. "The Jester, or Margot's killer, whoever he really is—he'll probably be there."

"And what if they catch us?" Vivian asks.

"Maybe we should let them."

They both turn to stare at me as if I just suggested we leap into oncoming traffic.

"I mean, maybe that's how we get him," I explain, the idea taking shape. "We know how to get in and out now. Renee can help us. If we can lure the Jester somehow, then we can trap him. Figure out who he is and what he knows."

Piper grins, and it's in all of us, now. A fire roaring.

"Maids," she says. "Let's fucking assemble."

26

VIVIAN

JANUARY 2, 9:55 P.M.

It's not until we're back on the tiny Pierrot balcony, wearing the ball gowns we never gave back to Milford, that I start to feel like we were a little too hasty with the girlboss detective thing. Here we are, sneaking back into the wolves' den with barely a game plan, and it's looking like our first play might have abandoned us.

"She said she'd let us in, didn't she?" Piper whispers to April, tightening her mask.

"She should be here soon," April says, anxiously watching her phone. Renee was supposed to meet us five minutes ago. "Just give it a second."

Right on cue, the window slides open with a harsh scrape, and Renee pokes her head through.

"Hurry up," she whispers. "If I keep staying in here this long, I'll have to come up with an IBS diagnosis or something."

One by one, we climb through, which is still extra hard in the dresses and heels. Piper's the last one in, and she looks a little green, but I'm not sure if it's from the fear of heights or this entire day. Either way, I don't blame her. If I'd been through what she has today, I don't know if I'd be able to make it out of bed.

April is busy checking her camera, looking relieved when she sees it's all in one piece. Already, she seems much more confident than she did last time we were here, and I wonder how much of that has to do with the camera—or the fact that she stuck to the Converse this time instead of heels.

"Thank you," she tells Renee. "Seriously."

Renee smiles a little, but it fades when she glances toward the door. "Listen, I should warn y'all. Tonight is . . . different."

"Different how?" I ask. A chilly breeze cuts through the open window, ruffling my dress. Renee goes to shut it.

"It's some kind of initiation, right?" Piper asks.

"I don't know exactly." The window screeches as Renee locks it again. "There's a weird energy. They set up a throne out there, and the staff is all gone."

I feel the chill again, even with the window closed. This plan is seeming more unstable by the second. Margot's killer is walking free, maybe even *here,* tonight, and I'm scared we might be too late. That maybe we have been from the moment Lily went missing.

But I can't let myself think that way. I roll my shoulders, remind myself to focus. Lily's still out there, I feel it, and it's time for me to put on my team captain face.

"Thanks for the heads-up," I tell Renee. "Y'all ready?"

I look to Piper and April, who nod.

"You'll take a few minutes' head start, right?"

"Yeah," Renee says, tying her mask back on. "If you don't hear from me after that, then the coast is clear." She checks herself in the mirror and then goes to the door, turning back to give us a final look. Her eyes settle on April. "I really hope y'all know what you're doing."

Without waiting for a response, she slips out of the bathroom. I rush to lock it again as soon as she's gone, pressing my ear against the door to listen. It feels like the longest few minutes of my life, but Renee doesn't come back. The coast is clear.

"Okay," I say, turning to April and Piper. "Let's do this."

We slide into the empty hallway and creep forward, the jazz and low voices getting louder as we go. When I get to the first of the closed hallway doors, I knock. No one answers. I take a deep breath and open the door.

The room is empty. It's small, maybe the size of the bathroom, and decorated like the rest of the Pierrot: red rug over the wooden floor, barely lit except for a little chandelier that hangs in the center, right above a black chaise lounge.

Next to me, Piper scowls. I get it. It's not hard to imagine what goes on in here.

"You know what to do?" I whisper to April.

She nods as she steps inside the room, holding her camera close.

"Be safe, okay?" she whispers before shutting the door behind her.

The lock clicks.

I turn to Piper to check in, but she's already tightening her mask and striding down the hall like a shark tracking its prey. Okay, then. Guess we're doing this.

As soon as we step into the main room, I can see what Renee meant. On New Year's, the energy in here was like a gala for loud fancy drunk people, but now, even though the room is still crowded with couples in masks, the conversations are hushed, everyone watching the throne in the middle of the room like they're waiting for something big.

I catch Piper's eye, knowing we're both thinking the same thing. It's not just any throne. It's the one they used at Les Masques.

And then I realize what else is different. There's still lots of old guys and young women, but tonight, there are younger-looking boys here, too. It's hard to tell with the masks, but based on a quick look around, I think they could be anywhere between our age and early twenties. They're all just milling around, and none of them has a woman with them.

I spot Renee with a man wearing a black mask. He turns, and the light catches its inky feathers and beak. A raven. Didn't April say one of the guys on the balcony had a raven mask?

I grip Piper's arm. "Look, that's—"

"Who are you here with?"

We both spin toward the deep voice. One of the members, hidden behind a silver plastic mask.

I freeze, but Piper gestures broadly at the group of men around the bar.

"Oh, he's getting our drinks," she says in a put-on drawl. It's higher than usual, and she's laying on a thick Southern accent that's sort of, well, country bumpkin, like she's playing the role of someone who could never be an upper-crust Maid. "I just can't get enough of how fancy they are here. Those cute little cherries and everything!"

The man narrows his eyes behind his mask, but if he clocks the lie, he doesn't show it. "Make your way to the throne. The Lieutenant is about to begin."

As soon as he says it, the lights overhead dim and then come back on twice, like they do at Sav's plays when intermission is ending. The men start leading their partners toward the throne.

One man steps forward and faces the crowd. He's wearing a golden cape and matching hat with a ridiculous white feather plume. A gold cloth mask hangs down over his face, covering everything except his eyes, which look through two holes cut into the fabric. He's dressed like one of the Deus Lieutenants, I realize, the guys who ride on horseback in the parade every year, right in front of the King's float, so everyone knows he's coming.

There's something familiar about this guy, the way he's standing, but I can't quite place it. Before I can say anything, Piper loops her arm through mine.

"Come on," she says, still with that smile on her face, but her eyes are alert. "Let's go."

I don't think we have a choice. The man who came up to us watches as we go to stand with the other girls. There's maybe ten of us, and no one seems sure what we're supposed to do. I look at Renee, but she's staring straight ahead. Finally, I catch her eye, but she just gives a small, almost invisible shake of her head.

I look around and realize there's a clear divide between the women and the men now: us in the middle, them surrounding us. It feels like they're watching us through glass, the way rich people do when they're picking out the lobster they want for dinner.

Head up, Atkins, Coach's voice comes into my head. I scan the room for the Jester, but I don't see him. Not yet.

The Lieutenant steps forward, and the other men watch as he reaches into his suit pocket and pulls out something small and shiny. He lifts his hand, and as the light hits the metal, I realize what it is. A cowbell.

The Lieutenant's eyes slide to us, the women crowded around the throne. With the mask on, it seems like that's all he is, just two blue eyes in their circles of pale skin.

He shakes the cowbell once. The metal clangs and then fades away. There's a breath.

And then the noise is everywhere. Cowbells appear in the other men's hands, and they shake them at us like we're cattle, all of them with the same lazy, drunken smiles on their faces. I grip Piper's hand, and she squeezes. For the first time, I can see how scared she is.

The noise builds, high and low pitches mixing together into an attack of sound, metal on metal, until finally, when I think I might scream just to drown it out, it stops, the Lieutenant slicing his hand through the air like a conductor.

"*Omnes nos reges!*" he announces.

"*Omnes nos reges!*" the men echo.

The Lieutenant slides his cowbell back into his pocket, addressing the room like a man who knows he's in charge.

"Welcome, gentlemen, to the Feast. Tonight, as always, we gather for many reasons. First, to honor Deus, our God."

God. I know that's what "Deus" means in Latin, and it's what they've always called the King of the parade, but there's something creepy about the way he says it, like he really believes it.

"We are here," the Lieutenant continues, "to thank Him for the bounty He has rained upon us. To remember the sacrifices we must make to protect it."

That voice. It reaches out and scratches down my spine, the familiar Louisiana twang.

"We are here to thank Him for the beautiful mistresses He has placed at our sides."

I want to yell, run, but I'm stuck, my jaw sealed shut as his stare tracks over each woman, landing directly on me.

Detective Marty Rutherford takes off his mask, a slow grin stretching on his face. "For without them, how could we be Kings?"

27

PIPER

JANUARY 2, 10:10 P.M.

I know Vivian's recognized him at the exact moment I do.

Detective Rutherford, the man who's supposed to be finding Lily, is here, calling himself the Lieutenant and leading this . . . *whatever* this is. I don't have a name for it, the way the men in the crowd are staring at him, enraptured by his speech like he's a preacher at the pulpit and they're his loyal congregation. Is that what this is to them? A church? It has all the makings of the cults I've heard about in documentaries and podcasts, the kind I always think I'd never be dumb or desperate enough to join—only this cult is made up of people I'm supposed to trust.

Glancing around the room, I try to put names to the masked faces, but it's impossible in the dim light. Even the boys, some of whom look young enough to go to Beaumont, are hard to pin down. This room could be full of Dad's friends, or the other Maids' fathers, even our classmates—men who are supposed to be good and smart and capable. Men who are looking at us like we're animals, something to shake bells at.

Men who turned my father in.

I clench my fists, wanting so badly to rush forward and connect them with every face, stomach, or nether region they can find. But we can't give up our cover. We have to play the Maids they want us to be.

I breathe in, out. Lift my chin.

"Today has been a difficult day for our Krewe," Marty says. "We were forced to sacrifice one of our own for the good of the brotherhood."

Dad. He's talking about Dad. I close my fists even tighter, squeezing until my fingers hurt so I don't scream.

"But gentlemen, tonight is not about loss. What Deus takes, He gives. And tonight is a night of celebration. Tonight, we welcome our newest members into the fold."

Marty's focus shifts to the younger faces in the room, and a sick feeling spreads through me. Milford said the sons of Deus members can be initiated once they're eighteen. How many of these boys do I know?

Has Wyatt done this already?

"These young men represent the best and brightest of what our city has to offer. They truly understand what makes a Deus man great: respect, strength, and devotion to their families, to their women, and most importantly, to our Krewe. They herald the coming of our future. A new Deus, stronger and greater than before. Tonight, we welcome them!"

The older men in the room erupt into the kind of cheering they do at football games, breaking from their quiet reverence into raucous masculinity. Marty lets it go on for a while before raising his hands to quiet the congregation.

"And tonight, we have another special cause for celebration. Our very own prodigal son, once fallen from our brotherhood, has returned to our ranks. I invite him to come forward so that we may officially welcome him."

Marty extends an arm to a cluster of men. They part like the Red Sea as one of them takes an uncertain step toward us: a tall man, his face hidden by a wolf mask.

Not a wolf, I think. *A Rougarou.* Just like April said—the man on the balcony, the one who brought Margot here. The one who killed her.

"Come on, now." Marty grins. "Don't be shy."

There are a few whoops and claps as the Rougarou comes closer, until he's face-to-face with Marty.

"We welcome you back tonight as a reminder that for all Deus takes, He has infinitely more to give. May all of our sins be washed away." Marty bows his head. "And as a sign of His mighty forgiveness, we have another gift for you."

Marty gestures to another man, who comes forward with a crown perched on a golden cushion. I recognize it. The Deus crown, the one the King wears every year on Mardi Gras. With a bow, the man hands the crown to Marty, who lifts it like it's made of real gold and diamonds instead of brass and moissanite.

"Tonight," Marty tells the Rougarou, "you wear this crown. But remember, gentlemen, that no matter who serves as Deus, this crown belongs to us all. *Omnes nos reges.* All of us kings."

He sets the crown on the Rougarou's head.

"But lest we forget, no king is complete without a queen to rule. As a final gift, your Majesty, we invite you to select your own from tonight's crop of beautiful mistresses." Marty turns toward us, the women in the center, with a wolflike glint in his eyes. "Though we have welcomed them as guests into our circle, all of our mistresses understand their place: to stand at the side of a king. To share their beauty so that we may protect it. To honor and obey us, and to always be grateful that we have chosen them."

Another grin snakes across Marty's face, and disgust churns low in my stomach. It's exactly what Aiden suspected: these men want to go back to a time when they were in charge, when everything was theirs to own, women included, even as they hide it under the guise of protecting us. *Celebrating* us. Only it's worse—because it's not just the old guard clinging to their ways. They're initiating the next generation. Indoctrinating them.

The anger is so strong that for a moment, I forget my fear. But then the Rougarou comes closer, and I feel us all instinctively press closer together, like a pack protecting its own. I reach for Vivian's hand. She squeezes back, her palm slick.

The Rougarou's gaze skates over the group, lingering, for a moment, on me. My heart nearly stops. His stare isn't predatory—it's vacant. Like he's just moving through choreography, almost outside of his body. His eyes shift from me to Vivian, and then the next girl, before landing on Renee.

He steps toward her, extending his hand like a marionette, and I feel a brief flash of relief that it isn't me before dread fills up my chest.

"An excellent choice. Wouldn't you say?" Marty elbows the man in the raven mask—the one Renee was standing with before—who lifts his hands in playful surrender.

Some of the other men chuckle, but Renee doesn't make a sound as the Rougarou takes her hand, pulling her out of the center.

Vivian's fingers dig into my palm. We have to do something, but it's like my entire body is made of stone. All I can do is watch as the Rougarou leads Renee up to the throne, where they stand side by side. I try to catch her eyes, but she's staring out into the dark room.

"And now," Marty continues, "we invite the rest of our new initiates to come forward and select a mistress of their own."

No. I want to cry out, but any voice I might have had dies in my throat as the other young men approach us. Some are more tentative, like the Rougarou was at first, but others reach for their choice the way they'd pull a T-shirt from a hanger, rough and decisive, expressionless.

There's a tug at my arm, and when I turn to face the boy in front of me, I instantly recognize his muddy eyes. But they don't look dangerous or violent—only regretful.

"I tried to tell you," Milford mutters under his breath.

A small gasp pulls my attention to Vivian, who's just been picked by another familiar boy. It takes me a second to recognize the thick, scruffy neck and football physique, since he looks so uncharacteristically ashamed.

Jason Broussard.

"I'm sorry," I hear him whisper.

Two of the Beaumont Dukes, both getting initiated to this terrible place. Rage burns away at me. It's almost worse, somehow, that they both seem sorry—because they didn't have to come here. Maybe their fathers brought them into it, but they could have resisted. They had a choice.

And so did Dad.

The thought deflates me enough that I don't struggle as Milford loops his arm through mine. We're all paired off now, each girl with an initiate, and I find myself scanning for Wyatt. I don't see him anywhere. That, at least, is a relief.

But it doesn't last long. Marty steps to the bottom of the throne, facing us all with a look of twisted pride.

"Tonight, gentlemen, these mistresses are yours. They are a

reminder of the power you hold as a member of our Krewe: the power to protect and honor, but also"—another slimy smirk—"the freedom to enjoy. For everything we desire is ours by birthright. Don't forget it, no matter how hard some may try to convince us otherwise." He gestures to another man, who hands him a golden goblet. Marty holds it up. "Sons of Deus, do you accept your position in this Krewe and promise to uphold its values, observe its duties, and always, above all, protect its brotherhood?"

"We do," the young men say in unison. Milford's voice is weak in my ear.

Marty drinks whatever's in the goblet and then raises it high.

"Hail, Deus!" he calls.

"Hail, Deus!" the room echoes.

"On your knees," Marty orders, and when none of the men move, I realize he means us. The women. The *mistresses*. "On your knees!"

The command ripples through us like a shock wave, and suddenly, we're all obeying, dropping to the ground. My hands start to shake as I press my palms to the bloodred carpet, like I can't support my own weight. The weight of this.

"Hail, Deus!" Marty shouts again.

This time, the echo is a harsh bark. "Hail, Deus!"

All at once, the cowbells start to clang again, so sharply it makes me cower, getting closer and closer as the men close in on us, shaking the bells right in our ears. My blood pounds, heating my face, and just when I think I can't bear it anymore, I feel another pair of eyes on me, and I look up.

Marty gives me a smile that says, *The jig is up,* that he's seen through my disguise all along. That he *wanted* me to watch this. My mouth opens, the terror and rage rushing up into something—maybe a sob, maybe a scream—but it never gets the chance to decide what it wants to be.

Because that's when the camera flashes.

There's a moment of confusion as everyone turns to find the source, but Marty's stare has snapped directly toward it.

"You." He sneers at April, standing just a few steps into the main room, her camera pointed directly at the throne.

And then a new figure materializes from the darkness.

The Jester, looking like he's been hiding there in the shadows all along, waiting for the perfect moment to strike.

28

APRIL

JANUARY 2, 10:20 P.M.

In the seconds after the flash, I have two thoughts, certain as the close of the shutter. First, our plan worked—the Jester is here, we've got photo evidence, and we've got his attention.

And second: *fuck.*

Because he's coming toward me.

Instinct kicks in, waking up my feet and pushing me back down the hallway, toward the bathroom—to lure the Jester there, like we planned—but I've only taken a few steps before I stop cold.

Renee still stands on the throne, the Rougarou's grip tight on her arm.

I'm not leaving a girl behind. Not again.

I run at full speed toward her, fast and easy in my sneakers. Halfway there, Vivian steps in front of me, blocking my path with her height.

"What are you doing?" Piper snaps beside her. "We have to go!"

The Jester is pushing his way toward us, slowed by the

confused, stagnant pool of the crowd, but not enough that we can waste time. Marty is coming this way, too.

And then someone else appears: Jason Broussard. He's pulled off his mask, wide-eyed with panic. Vivian flinches away from him, but he holds out a hand.

"Wait. I want to help. I—" He looks over my shoulder. "The front entrance. The staff is gone tonight."

I glance at Vivian and Piper, who look like trusting Jason is the last thing they want to do, but I'm not really sure we have another choice.

I look him dead in the eyes.

"Help her get out safe," I say, glancing at Renee. "And don't come after us."

He looks a little confused, almost hurt, but he nods. "Okay. Yeah, I can do that."

I turn to Vivian. "Should we run?"

But she's still focused on the Jester. Waiting, I realize, until he's just close enough that he'll be on our tail. That we can lure him out of here. And then, when he's only a few feet away—

"Go!" Vivian sprints toward the entrance, and we're right behind her, flying down the hallway and through the door with our skirts floating behind us like comet trails. My camera bangs against my hip bone as I run, but I grit my teeth, telling myself it's a reminder that we did it. We have proof: Marty unmasked, the whole terrifying ritual captured in tableau.

At the bottom of the stairs, Vivian shoves the door open, and we tumble into the gift shop. It's empty, lights off. Jason was right: even the cashier is gone. For Marty and the others, tonight must have been too special, too secret, to be shared with anyone outside their immediate circle.

"Everyone okay?" Vivian pauses to check on us, clearly not

even winded. Piper and I, on the other hand, are breathing hard.

"Oh, I'm great," Piper quips. "Cardio? Done. Crushed it. Now what's the plan, since we've clearly deviated from the trap-the-Jester-in-the-bathroom thing?"

In answer, the stairwell door swings open, the Jester barreling through.

"Run!" Vivian shouts.

Like we needed the instructions. In a flash, Vivian pulls off her shoes, and Piper follows suit—and then we're racing again into the night. The Jester's on our tail, but we're even faster now that none of us have heels to contend with. Vivian takes the lead, and we follow her down Royal Street until she takes a sharp turn onto a narrow road. Through the adrenaline, I recognize this as Pirates Alley, a stretch of stone path between the St. Louis Cathedral and the Cabildo. It's one of the many supposedly haunted places in the French Quarter, and tonight, it looks it: deserted, lit only by the glow of the streetlamps, shadows reaching from the iron cathedral fence like claws.

Halfway down the alley, Vivian slows, and I realize that this is where we're doing this. I've barely had time to prepare myself before he's here: the Jester, standing at the opening of the alley, where we entered only moments before. His shoulders heave, probably because it's hard to run in such a ridiculous costume, which might make me laugh if it weren't for the fear burrowing deep in my bones.

For a moment, I wonder if this was a terrible idea—if we're all about to look into the eyes of the man who killed Margot, or at least a man who helped cover it up, only to end up just like her. Gone. Silenced. Three more misbehaved debutantes, girls who just couldn't be saved.

But then I remember that, for once, we have the upper hand here. There are three of us and one of him. And he's pissed, probably afraid of what would happen if my picture gets out, but us?

We're angry. *Enraged*. And we're done with this bullshit.

I step forward, camera raised. "This is what you want, right?"

The Jester comes closer. Piper flinches, but Vivian comes to my side, standing even taller. Then, after a moment, Piper follows suit, lifting her chin.

"Come on," I say. "Come and get it, then."

The Jester is close enough that we can see his real eyes behind the plastic. Blue. He takes two more steps. Another.

And then he lunges.

I rear back, almost tripping over my own feet. Vivian steps in front of me, putting herself between me and the Jester. He reaches again, but Vivian catches his arm. She grasps for his mask, almost getting it, but he shoves her, hard, to the ground. And now that she's down, he's coming at me with the force of a man who's nearly been beaten by a girl.

I want to fight back—need to fight back—but terror has seized my body, my voice, silencing every thought except that he's coming closer. Closer. I brace myself, eyes closed.

And then, a scream. Not mine.

His.

I open my eyes, and the Jester is doubled over, hands pressed to his face. Piper stands in front of him like some kind of war goddess, sparkly pink pepper spray outstretched.

But he recovers too quickly, standing up straight and glaring at us with squinting, teary eyes.

Eyes that are locked again on my camera. On the evidence inside it.

I realize what's happening at the exact moment he pounces, gloved hand outstretched, and suddenly, I'm back in my own body, and I do the only thing I can think of: I swing my camera back and crack it against the side of his face.

He falls back, legs buckling under him as he hits the ground. A shocked gasp hisses out of me, echoed by two more.

"Holy shit," Vivian breathes.

"Holy *shit,*" Piper echoes.

"Holy shit." I stare, gaping, feeling almost powerful. I clutch my camera, giving it a quick check for any injuries, but she's sturdy, the old girl. I allow myself a small burst of pride.

Then the panic kicks in. He's crumpled on his side, not moving.

"Oh my god," I breathe. "Oh my god, I killed him."

But then he moves, pushing himself up onto his side with a groan.

"Jesus *Christ,*" he hisses, locking eyes with me. "What the—"

Piper raises her sparkly pepper spray again, ready to strike, and he holds up a hand in defeat.

"Oh my god, Piper, *stop,*" he barks, and it's so familiar, it stops all three of us in our tracks.

He reaches with a gloved hand to pull off his own mask, and Wyatt stares back at us, a red welt already burning on the side of his face.

29

PIPER

JANUARY 2, 10:30 P.M.

The sequence of emotions goes something like this.

First, stunned. Then, concerned—I *did* just pepper-spray my own brother right before April camera-whipped him in the head—and then, as soon as it's clear that he's not broken or unconscious: *pissed*.

"What the fuck?" I explode. "What the actual living *fuck*, Wyatt!"

He sputters a cough as he sits upright. "Yeah, sure. Help me up. Ask me how I'm doing after you literally maced me in the face."

"I'll do it again if you don't start explaining right now."

Wyatt groans, yanking off his gloves and wiping them across his eyes. "I didn't want to do it."

"What, stalk us? *Attack* us?"

"I didn't attack anyone!" Clearly realizing how useless that sounds, he heaves a sigh. "I didn't want to."

"Then please enlighten us."

Wyatt pushes himself up to standing.

"I was initiated a couple weeks after our birthday. Back in October. I didn't want to—I thought the whole thing was fucked up—but I had to. Dad didn't want to do it, either, but it was part of the deal."

A cold feeling slices through me. "What deal?"

Wyatt rakes a hand through his matted hair. "I . . ."

"What deal, Wyatt?" I demand, my grip tightening on the pepper spray.

He looks between the three of us before landing back on me. "You have to swear you won't tell anyone," he says. "Or . . . or I'll tell everyone what y'all did. The things from the Jester message, the stuff y'all don't want getting out."

I stare him down, a hot ball of anger in my throat. Does he really know, or is he bluffing? I glance at April and Vivian, and they both look to me, like they're waiting for my call. I don't want to risk it.

"Fine," I say. "We won't tell."

He nods grimly. "It was about a year ago, last winter break. For New Year's, we all went out to some of the Tulane bars. Me and the guys, and Lily, Savannah, and Vivian."

Right. Wyatt and his posse spent most of that break getting trashed, while I was holed up in my room, cramming for the February ACT I insisted on taking so I could raise my 34 up to Aiden's 35. Which I did—even if I'm struggling to remember, now, why that mattered.

"After we left," Wyatt continues, "Lily and I were walking home, and she was kind of pissed at me. I was pretty wasted, I guess, and she didn't like when I got like that. So I was already in a mood when this guy comes up to us—this frat-boy asshole—and starts asking Lily if I'm bothering her. If she wants a *real* man. He's just fucking taunting me, and Lily—" He stops. "She's letting him. She's, like, egging it on, just to piss me off. And so I snapped."

Vivian's jaw clenches, her arms folded tight against her chest.

Wyatt clocks it, too, because he adds, "Not at Lily. I would never hurt Lily. But this guy, he got up in my face, and I just lost it. Went at him, started punching. I realized pretty quickly I was a lot stronger than him, but I couldn't stop, even when Lily was screaming at me. I guess I blacked out a little, and the next thing I remember, he's on the ground. Just . . . just fucking pummeled. Bleeding."

Vivian shakes her head slowly, and April's face is blank as she grips her camera. I just stare at Wyatt, some irrational part of my brain thinking he must be joking, but the guilt in his eyes is real.

"And then what happened?" I ask, fighting to keep my voice level.

"Lily was freaking out, and I was panicking, so we just—we left." Wyatt shakes his head. "I tried to forget it, like maybe I was so drunk I imagined it. Lily never mentioned it, either, but I could tell from the way she looked at me." His guilty look shifts to pure devastation. "A week or so later, Detective Marty showed up at our door, and I'm thinking, this is it. They know what I did, and I'm about to get in so much trouble. But then . . ." Wyatt pauses. "Then he sat me and Dad down, and told us that this frat guy was trying to press charges. Apparently he wound up in the hospital. He was fine in the end, but as soon as he could, he went to the police and gave them my description and Lily's. Marty said things were looking bad for me, 'cause they caught me on a traffic cam that night, but . . . there was a way out, if we wanted it."

Dread settles deep in my stomach.

"He wanted y'all to join the Pierrot," I guess.

Wyatt nods. "He made it sound so simple. Dad would have to join and start going to the meetings, and then, when I was eighteen, I'd get initiated, too. We had to hide it from you and Mom, but that was it. That's all we had to do, and the Pierrot would pay off the guy, make him stay quiet. Marty made it sound like this—this brotherhood. This group of guys who had each other's backs. At the time, I remember thinking it was weird that there wasn't a catch, nothing else they wanted from us, but it was too good to pass up. So Dad told him yes."

"But they did want something," I realize. "They wanted Dad to help cover up Margot's murder. That was . . . what? Barely a week after she died?"

He looks down. "I had no idea. I feel like such an idiot now. But yeah, that must have been the deal."

Even though I had already suspected it, it's like the floor drops out from under me. Dad was only trying to protect Wyatt, like he has been this whole time. And maybe he was trying to protect me, too, by keeping it a secret. But I can't fight the creeping worry that maybe he just didn't think I could handle it.

"Do you know, then?" April asks hoarsely. "Who killed her?"

"No," Wyatt says. "Until the last few days, I didn't even put together that it wasn't just an overdose."

"Then why the hell are you in the Jester costume?" Vivian demands.

"Because it was Lily's idea."

That's enough to make us all go quiet.

"What?" I ask after a stunned moment.

"The stunt at the ball," he says. "It was her idea."

My brain is a jumble of thoughts, all of them sharpening into one: Mom was right. She told me she thought Lily knew who threw the blood at her, and when I confronted Wyatt about it, he acted like I was being ridiculous. Still, some part of me doesn't want to believe it.

"That doesn't make any sense," I snap. "Why would she want you to do that?"

"Because, I—" Wyatt hangs his head. "I told her about the Pierrot. Ever since that New Year's, I knew she hadn't really forgiven me, but I still didn't say anything until last month. Things had been getting worse with us, and I just—I thought if I told her about the Pierrot, she'd understand. She was mad, at first, but then she started begging me to take her. She wanted to see it for herself, and . . . I don't know. I can't ever say no to her. I thought it might fix things. So we went. It was a bad idea."

Obviously, I think, but I grit my teeth to keep from saying it out loud. Of course he gave her what she wanted. Even I've been foolish enough to make that mistake.

"After we went . . . I don't know why I thought Lily would just let it go. She couldn't. She wanted to do something about it. She said it wasn't fair, what they were doing to me. So she came up with this plan. She thought if we pulled the stunt at the ball, we could expose the Pierrot without anyone knowing it was us. They'd never suspect it. I thought she wanted to help me. I didn't think . . . I mean, I had no idea the Margot stuff was part of the plan. When those projections started, I was just as confused as y'all. I tried to ask Lily what was going on after the ball, but then she wouldn't talk to me, and then . . ."

"And then you left her there," Vivian finishes, bitter.

"She dumped me," Wyatt argues. "She said she was going to leave town. I thought she just needed to sleep on it, that we could talk it out when she calmed down. But then, the next morning . . ." His face crumples. "I'd barely even had two seconds to process that she was gone before I got this text. It was from a number I didn't recognize, telling me I had to get to the Beaumont darkroom ASAP and take this phone out of one of the ceiling tiles. They told me if I didn't, and y'all got to it first, then our deal was off. They signed it with the Pierrot motto, too, so . . . I knew what that meant. And that's how it started. The texts kept coming, telling me what I had to do."

"That phone." Vivian frowns. "The burner. Why'd you give it to me?"

"What?"

"On my car, in the parking lot. It was sitting there in an envelope."

"I didn't," Wyatt says, confused. "I dropped it off where they told me. I don't know how it got there."

Vivian scoffs. "Right. Just following orders, then."

"I had to," he argues. "They—"

"Did you even stop to think for one second that these people might be the reason Lily is missing?"

It's the first time I've ever heard Vivian really lose her cool, and it clearly shocks Wyatt, too.

"Someone at the Pierrot killed Margot, Wyatt," she continues. "And Lily knew about it. You can't seriously still think she just ran away."

"I know. I know that now. I just didn't think she actually . . ." Wyatt covers his face. "*Fuck.*"

"But you can help us find her," I try, desperate to regain control of the situation. "You have to. You have an in with these guys. If you can convince them you're still on their side, then maybe—"

"Do you honestly think these guys would help me after what they did to Dad?"

His words cut deep, even worse because it's true.

"And maybe Lily really did run," he adds. "Maybe she saw what was going on and just got the fuck out, left us all behind. It's what she always wanted, anyway."

Wyatt's voice is sharp, but in a way I recognize. Because I guess this is one twin thing we share: using anger to cover up the wound, to hide how hurt we feel. I want to do something—slap him, snap him out of it, or maybe just try to comfort him, help ease the hurt—but before I can decide, my phone starts to ring.

"Shit," I hiss. "Mom."

The panic on Wyatt's face must be a mirror image of mine. "I thought she was still at the police station."

"Well, she's calling!"

"Well, don't answer!"

"Obviously I'm not. I'll just let it ring."

For an excruciating minute, we all watch my phone with silent, anxious stares. Then the ringing stops. I breathe out.

Wyatt's phone starts to buzz.

"Goddammit," he mutters, ending the call.

In an instant, my phone is ringing again. A new worry pulses through me.

"Something might have happened," I say.

"Don't—"

I brace myself as I answer, putting on my best attempt at a casual tone. "Hello?"

"I need someone to explain this email to me right now."

I freeze. This was not part of any of the worst-case scenarios that were spinning through my head. Despite her stern words, Mom sounds almost desperate. Scared.

"What email?" I ask.

"To the whole Beaumont list, Piper. Students, teachers, parents."

"Mom, *what email*?"

"It's about you," she says.

I squeeze the phone so tightly my fingers hurt. "What?"

"And Wyatt," Mom continues. "And April Whitman. And Vivian Atkins."

They all stare at me, like they can feel their names through the phone, even if they can't hear them.

"I don't understand," Mom says, her voice tinny in my ear. "It says you sabotaged another student's Vanderbilt application."

My heart starts to pound, my face hot.

They know. Everyone knows. *Vanderbilt* will know, and the Jester did this. Not my brother, standing here like their helpless puppet, but whoever's been pulling the strings.

"It has accusations about each of you," Mom continues. "Piper, is this true? Did you do this to someone?" And then, after a small pause, "Was it Lily?"

Stop digging around other people's secrets, or I'll show the world just what you've been hiding behind those pretty masks of yours.

We forgot about the threat. We got too comfortable, thinking we could outsmart him. Thinking we could win.

We might have unmasked the Jester, but we forgot they could unmask us.

30

VIVIAN

JANUARY 2, 10:40 P.M.

There's a moment where I feel like I'm in the middle of a game: tunnel vision, nothing but my heartbeat and what's in front of me. The phone in my hand. The email on the screen. It's from an address that's just a random series of letters and numbers, but the account name is clear: the Jester. This email was sent to the entire Beaumont list. Students, faculty, parents, everyone.

It's like a ball kicked straight to the stomach: *everyone*. The Jester made good on his threat to ruin our lives, and now everyone will know.

Dear Beaumont Community,

I write to you as a concerned neighbor. It has come to my attention that three of your students—Vivian Atkins, Piper Johnson, and April Whitman—are not at all the well-mannered Maids they appear to be.

Piper Johnson may be one of Beaumont's top students, but she's even more cutthroat than she lets on: under the guise of helping another Beaumont student with their college essays,

Piper submitted a fraudulent application in that student's name, intentionally sabotaging their chances at admission.

Lily. Piper helped her with her essays, didn't she? Judging from the stunned look on her face and the way she's talking quickly into the phone, trying to explain but not denying anything, I'm sure it's true.

April stares quietly at her own phone.

April Whitman is hardly as mousy and quiet as she seems. Last year, she broke into the Krewe of Deus Den and destroyed countless floats and other property, nearly forcing the parade's cancellation with her petty and remorseless vandalism.

The vandalism. I remember everyone freaking out about that last year. But even now that I know her better, know she has good reasons to be angry, it's hard to imagine April doing that kind of damage all by herself.

But I can't think too hard about it, because there, just beneath it, is my own secret, blazing up at me in sans serif.

Vivian Atkins, Beaumont soccer star, is hardly a team player. Her indiscretion is perhaps the most disappointing of all, if only because of how clichéd it is: she slept with her best friend's boyfriend.

Only two sentences, but they almost knock the wind out of me.

I think, *It wasn't like that.*

I think, *Maybe it was.*

I think, finally meeting Wyatt's eyes, *At least he can't pretend anymore. At least he can't deny it.*

And then, another thought.

"Did you do this?" I jab my phone at the air.

"Are you kidding?" he explodes.

And I know from the broken look in his eyes that he's telling the truth. But I should have guessed. He would rather spend the rest of our lives looking right through me, convincing himself it never happened. He's so good at it that sometimes, I could almost believe I made it up, because that would be easier.

I hear the quiet scuff of sneakers on the pavement and turn to see April walking away.

"Wait," I say. "Where are you going?"

"I need to find Renee."

"We'll come with you."

April shakes her head quickly. "I have to go."

"But Marty and the others could still be looking for us. You can't—"

"I just have to go."

She speeds out of the alley, leaving us behind.

I turn to Piper, who's hanging up the call with her mom. "We can't let her go off by herself."

Piper looks like she's pulled a whole all-nighter in the past ten minutes.

"We need to go home," she says to Wyatt.

"Are you serious?" I glare.

"April obviously doesn't want our help."

I shake my head in disbelief, trying to think of some way to talk sense into her. "They only did this because we're close to figuring this out. They want us to stop, but we can't let them win just because they—"

"Because they ruined our lives? I don't know. I'm starting to think maybe we can." Piper's eyes shine with tears. "They got my dad arrested. They just took *college* away from me. I don't know if you understand that, but they did."

"And that's important enough to give up on finding Lily?"

Piper stares at me, chin pushed forward stubbornly even as the tears start to fall. "They're not going to quit," she says. "You heard them in there. 'Everything we desire is ours by birthright.' They're going to keep taking and taking whatever they want from us because they can. So maybe we should just *stop*."

She's right. I know she's right, and still, I'm so angry it feels like something's eating me up from the inside. I look at Wyatt. I don't really want to turn to him for backup, but it's not like I have another choice.

"Lily's still out there," I plead. "We can't just—"

"Do you want a ride or not?" Piper snaps, swiping a tear away with her fist.

I glare at her, but apparently she's suddenly allergic to meeting my eyes. Wyatt's, too. And I get it. She's weirded out. She probably thinks we're both as awful as that email said, and maybe we are. Maybe I've ruined whatever sort-of friendship Piper and I were starting to have. But right now, there are more important things than feeling guilty.

"I'm going to find April," I say.

Piper's face softens. "You shouldn't—"

"Are you coming with me?"

She clamps her mouth shut, glancing at Wyatt. It's enough of an answer for me.

"Fine," I snap. "Safe travels."

I give Wyatt one more look before I go, waiting for him to say something, anything.

But he doesn't.

I shouldn't have expected anything else.

I've barely made it to Jackson Square when my feet start to hurt, the blisters and scrapes from running barefoot through the Quarter finally catching up with me. Still, there's no way in hell I'm putting the heels back on. I tuck them under my arm and force myself to keep moving, scanning the dark street for April as I go.

The thing about being an athlete is you have to learn discipline. And maybe it *is* a cliché, like the email said, but I feel like that's what I've been doing the past two weeks: flexing the same mental muscles I use on game days to push away everything I've been hiding. It's why Wyatt was so good at it, too, I think. He learned it in football.

Or maybe it's just what you do when you grow up in a place like this: forget the uncomfortable stuff, like the rising sea level or a Queen who died too soon.

But now I can't ignore it anymore, and it's right here, as real as the night it happened.

It was winter break, the week before Christmas. That Friday night, we were all at Wyatt's: me, Lily, Sav, Jason, and a couple of Wyatt's other goons. The past month had been brutal. Exams were bad enough, and then early-decision results came out just a few days before the break. I knew Lily was upset when she got rejected from Vanderbilt, but she wouldn't talk about it. She barely responded to our group chat. That night was the first time I'd even seen her since school let out. I was worried, for sure, but I told myself everything was okay now. We were all together again.

Plus, it was warm. It's one of the best things about December in New Orleans: sometimes, winter just isn't a thing. We were out by the pool, and Sav was filling me, Lily, and Wyatt in on the latest theater-kid drama while Jason and two of the football guys, Taylor and Mateo, were dueling with pool noodles.

I barely even remember what we were saying, only that as I looked around, I felt drunk on my friends: Sav with her over-the-top hand gestures and contagious laugh, and Lily with that lit-up look in her eyes, like there's always something going on behind them. Something you want to be in on.

And maybe I was a little drunk on Wyatt, too. The way he looked at Lily like no one else was there, drawing small circles on her wrist with his thumb. Like she was all his.

I knew everything could change when we all went to college. I'd spent all year trying not to think about how I might lose them, worrying that there would never be anything as good as this, my friends, all of us together.

When Lily and Wyatt went inside to get drinks, it was like the air got colder. They were gone for too long. Ten minutes passed, then fifteen, and Jason made some stupid joke about what they were *really* doing in there, but something felt wrong. I know Lily, and I knew she wouldn't disappear like that to hook up with Wyatt in the middle of a party. She'd be too worried about people assuming things, about what they'd think.

I was on my way to check on her when Lily came out alone, walking quickly. She went straight to the lounge chair where she'd left her shoes, slipping them on without looking at us.

"Lil?" Sav asked. "You okay?"

"Yeah," she said, her voice high-pitched, trying too hard to be normal. "I just have to get home. My parents are being annoying about curfew again."

And then I saw her hand drift up to touch her necklace.

Without another glance our way, Lily pulled her keys out of

her pocket and started walking toward the back gate. I got up to follow her.

"Wait," I said, when I was close enough for her to hear me without raising my voice. "Did something just happen?"

Lily looked at me, a tear slipping down her cheek. She brushed it away with the back of her hand. "I'm fine."

"Lily . . ."

"I said I'm *fine,* Viv." It was the harshest she'd ever spoken to me. "Just leave it."

With that, she walked through the gate.

I didn't think it through. All I knew was that Wyatt had just done something to hurt my best friend, and I wasn't going to let that go. Ignoring Sav's worried look, I marched through the Johnsons' back door and up the stairs to the second floor, where I knocked hard on Wyatt's door.

He opened it quickly, looking hopeful for half a second before realizing it was me and not her.

"What the hell just happened?" I asked.

"Nothing."

"Lily just left in tears, so obviously it wasn't nothing."

For a moment, he looked like the five-year-old kid I grew up with. "She did?"

"Yeah. So what did you do?"

"Why are you assuming it's my fault?"

"Because you're an idiot."

He stormed over to his bed and flopped back onto it, pressing his hands to his face.

"A moody idiot," I added. "You should join drama club with Sav. I think you'd crush it."

And then I realized he was crying. "Shit. I—"

"It's over," he said. "She's done with me. I think she has been for a while."

I was too stunned to say anything at first. "Y'all broke up?"

"No." He wiped his tears, staring up at the ceiling. "Not yet. But it's going to happen. I can tell. She's just—" He squeezed his eyes shut. "I've never been good enough for her."

For a second, I thought he meant that Lily's standards were too high, and I felt the instinct to jump to her defense, but then I realized that wasn't what he meant. He meant Lily was too good for him. That he wasn't enough, period. And looking at Wyatt, this golden-boy quarterback breaking down in front of me, I said the only thing I could think of to make it hurt less.

"She loves you."

He laughed hoarsely. "Right."

"She does. The way she talks about you, it's literally disgusting."

Lily *did* love Wyatt. I knew, because the way she talked about him made my teeth ache like I ate too much sugar. It made me want something I didn't even know how to talk about, because I hadn't felt it yet, still haven't: loving a boy and knowing he loves you back.

Wyatt turned to look at me, a soft haze in those stupid ocean-blue eyes. "What does she say?" he asked. "About me?"

I rolled my eyes as I sat on the edge of the bed a few feet away from him. "Oh my god, was this all your master plan to get me to, like, massage your ego?"

"Vivian."

The way he said my name. It was almost the way he said hers, like it meant something.

I looked away. "She says you're, like, the perfect boyfriend.

Like, you're all considerate and nice and basically a goddamn knight in shining armor." My face was getting warm, which made me feel stupid. "She also thinks you're *totally* humble and secure and not at all fishing for compliments, so—"

He sat up, making me stop cold.

The way he was looking at me then . . . it was almost the way he looked at her. Almost, but different. Wyatt looked at Lily like she was some perfect thing he couldn't believe he got to hold in his hands. In that moment, he was looking at me like I was real. Like I was something he wanted.

He leaned in, and I sucked in a breath, my heart thudding against my rib cage. Wyatt's mouth was inches away from mine, hovering there like he was waiting for an okay, like all it would take for him to stop was me telling him to. I *needed* to tell him to stop.

But all I could think of was how Lily had snapped at me outside. *Just leave it*.

All I could think of was Wyatt saying she was done with him. How they weren't broken up, *not yet,* but they would be.

All I could think was how badly I wanted to close the gap.

So I did.

I've never been a girl to romanticize my first time. I always figured at best, it would be fine, and at worst, it would hurt a little. So maybe, I told myself, this wasn't the worst way, doing it with someone who didn't love me. At least he knew me. We knew each other. I'd memorized plenty about him, from the brand of protein bar he always eats before practice to the way he taps his pencil against his knuckles when he doesn't know the answer on a test. And maybe I'd been wondering what it would feel like to be looked at the way he looked at her. Kissed the way he kissed her.

It was quick. He finished. I didn't, and he didn't ask me if I did.

After, I didn't feel any different, at least not in the ways you're supposed to. All I felt was a weight start to settle on my chest as I watched him get dressed again, his back turned to me.

I didn't want to ask, because I already knew the answer, but it came out anyway. "Did you and Lily ever . . . ?"

He shook his head.

The weight got heavier. Wyatt walked to the door, stopping before he opened it. "Don't tell anyone."

"Obviously," I said, not looking at him.

He left. I got dressed. And that was it.

A few days later, Wyatt and Lily were back together, like nothing had ever happened. Besides a few small moments of tension, things I couldn't tell if I was imagining, they seemed exactly the same. As perfect as ever.

And maybe I did imagine it. All of it. It was easier to think of it that way. Easier than *this*. But as terrible as this feels, the worst part is the tiny flash of vindication. Because it *was* real. For a moment, I felt it. The way Lily must have felt when he looked at her.

I stop walking. I'm past Jackson Square now, past Café Du Monde, too, veering into the part of Decatur Street where the crowd thins out and the shadows stretch long from the streetlamps. It hits me how I must look right now, a girl in a dirty ball gown, all alone.

And somewhere, April is just as much an easy target. I pull out my phone to call her, but when I tap the screen, it doesn't light up.

No. I press the power button, and *no, no, no.* The little dead-battery image blinks, mocking me.

Okay. This is fine. I can find a drugstore or something that's open and buy a charger, walk to a bar and beg to borrow an outlet. But then, just as I'm turning around, I see him.

Detective Marty Rutherford stands a block away, his cloth mask floating like a ghost in the breeze. His hands are in his suit pockets, and even through the mask, I can feel the slow smile creeping on his lips.

I run. Heart pounding, wondering how I could be so stupid. Here I am, doing the *one* thing my parents have always told me not to do, walk alone in this city at night, and now this might be how it ends: at the hands of a man who won't get caught, all because I made reckless choices. Is this how Margot felt?

Or Lily?

I just need to get back to the crowd, I think, as I cross the street. Somewhere safe, somewhere—

A car screeches its brakes in front of me, the driver sitting on the horn. I freeze in the blinding headlights, adrenaline pulsing through me as the car skids to a stop, just a few feet from hitting me.

The door opens, and someone climbs out. I still can't see them in the glare of the headlights, but then there's a familiar voice.

"Vivian?"

31

PIPER

JANUARY 2, 11:00 P.M.

When we get home, Mom is waiting for us in the living room with a vodka soda and a stare that could cut diamonds. For a few seconds, she's quiet, taking a long sip as she watches us. I changed out of my ball gown in the car, and Wyatt's back in the street clothes he wore under the Jester costume, but I get the strange feeling that she knows exactly where we've been—not only tonight, but from the beginning of time.

She sets the glass down squarely on the coaster.

"Where should we start?" she asks. "With what you've been doing tonight, or whatever the hell is going on with this email?"

"Does it even matter?" Wyatt snaps. "We're already the family with the dad who got arrested. Might as well commit, right?"

I can't believe he's being so callous after everything that's just happened. I don't even have it in me to defend myself: right now, I feel like someone took one of those oyster spoons and scooped out all of the soft parts inside of me until they could only scrape shell.

To my surprise, Mom laughs, just a small one as she brings her glass to her lips again.

"Well, I suppose you're right about that." Her gaze turns on Wyatt, cold. "But maybe you should think twice about your tone, considering he's only in there to protect you."

The sudden harshness is enough to silence us both. Wyatt curls into himself, his shame obvious. And then it dawns on me.

"You know," I say. "About the deal with the Pierrot."

For a second, she's silent.

"Yes," she tells me. "I do."

I stare, waiting for her to say something, do something, but she just takes another tired sip of her drink. Wyatt looks as stunned as I feel. Clearly, he had no idea Mom knew, either.

"Then you know Dad didn't do it," I argue. "They framed him."

"He made his deal. Without consulting me, I should add. He didn't tell me until after, when it was already too late." She sets her drink down, turning her glass a few degrees on the coaster, like it has to be perfectly aligned before she can continue. "But I can't say I would have told him not to take it."

I don't know what I expected this conversation to look like—rage and disappointment at the both of us, definitely, but I also thought Mom would have a plan, some ingenious way for us to get through this. Because it's always been Mom who's steered the ship. Dad can be softer, more even-tempered, but it's Mom who's kept it all running behind the scenes, stitching our family together as flawlessly as one of her gowns. Of course she knew about the deal.

And something about seeing her now, so detached and defeated, is enough to break the dam.

"You know what goes on at the Pierrot, right?" I explode.

"I know enough. Your father does trust me more than most of those men trust their wives."

"And you let them be a part of it?"

"What else was I supposed to do? Let Wyatt face charges?" Her voice cuts sharply. "And last I checked, your father has free will. He would have done what he wanted regardless. Just like he's doing now."

There's something brimming under those words, more than just resentment.

"What do you mean, like he's doing now?" I ask.

"He told the Pierrot he wanted out," she says. She glances at Wyatt. "For both of you. He knew what would happen if he broke their deal, what they would do, and still, he told them y'all were done."

Wyatt sinks into one of the chairs, his neck straining the way it does when he's trying not to cry, and I feel myself biting back my own tears. That's what being a Johnson is about, isn't it? Fix the problem. Push it down. Be great. Even when it's all built on a rotting foundation.

"So that's it, then," I force out. "We let Dad go down for a murder he didn't commit?"

"Of course not," she says sharply. "We'll fight this. I have an appointment with a lawyer first thing tomorrow, and believe me, I'm not stopping until we've proven this accusation is as flimsy as an underbaked praline." She pauses. "What I'm more immediately concerned with, however, is fixing the problems y'all both created tonight."

Her stare is ice, the implication reflecting back at us in the surface. The email. Wyatt looks down at his hands, the guilt written all over his face. But even his cheating feels small now, in comparison to everything else. And maybe my indiscretion should, too, but a stubborn need to defend myself bubbles up.

"It was her own essay," I say. "All I did was submit what Lily had written before I helped her."

"Jesus," Wyatt mutters. "Like *that's* the most important thing right now."

"She manipulated me. She convinced me to write her essay for her, and then—"

I stop short, suddenly at a loss for how to explain it. Because the thing is, Lily didn't *ask* me to write it for her. She mentioned being stressed about her essays when she was over for family dinner once, and Mom started gushing about how great a writer I am, how maybe I could help, and I knew I had no choice but to offer. Anyway, I figured it wouldn't hurt to have Lily LeBlanc owe me one.

The next thing I knew, we were working on edits in a study room at Beaumont.

"You're so much better at this than I am," Lily had said, flopping dramatically onto the desk, her head in her hands. "Like, seriously. Wyatt's always going on about how you're the smartest person he knows, and he's right."

Something started to tap on my heart at those words, like an egg on the kitchen counter, cracking until the inside oozes out.

Lily turned to look at me. "I don't think enough people get you, you know? They might think you're this, like, high-strung, anal-retentive freak, but it's only because you're not afraid to care."

Now I can't believe I didn't see through that backhanded compliment. I was too caught off guard by her complimenting me at all.

"Anyway," she'd said, turning back to her laptop. "Sorry my essay is such garbage."

"It's not," I told her, even though the essay was, by most objective standards, bad—a puffed-up narrative about her family's debutante tradition that would only make her look spoiled and out of touch to the admissions board. But I couldn't say that. Instead, I said, "It has potential."

The next week, I was surprised when Lily wanted to work at her house instead of at school. Even more surprising: once the hour was up, she asked if I wanted to stay for dinner. Her parents, both busy that night, had left a credit card behind. We ordered pizza and ate it by the pool, talking about school and college and Les Masques. I thought it was a one-off, or maybe just Lily's way of thanking me for the help.

But then, a few days later, she invited me to go shopping with her at the boutiques on Magazine Street, the ones she usually went to with Vivian and Savannah. As we went from shop to shop, Lily offered me fashion advice that I was embarrassed to admit I was grateful for, and the more we talked, the more I realized that Lily was smarter than I thought—she had depth, even though she managed to say things in a way that was more accessible and less condescending than I ever could.

I started to think we could, maybe, truly be friends.

And then, the next week, when we were back in the study room, Lily did something that changed everything: she looked at her new essay draft—still bad, but better—and burst into tears.

"Sorry," she said. "You're helping so much. It's just—my parents are going to kill me if I don't get in. And clearly, I'm a lost cause. I just wish you could, like, crawl inside my head and do it for me, you know?"

She laughed at that last part as she wiped her tears, like it was just a joke, but I felt the idea burrowing under my skin.

"I could," I told her. "Write it for you, I mean."

"Oh my god, seriously?"

Looking back, her performance was flawless: surprise, then uncertainty, followed by gratitude. But in the moment, it felt real.

"That would be amazing. But you really, really, really don't have to."

"It's no problem," I told her. "It'll be easy."

She pulled me into a tight hug. "You're the best, Piper."

So I trashed the debutante crap and wrote her a kick-ass essay, one full of her own words and sentence patterns but better, brighter. I knew it was wrong, obviously—that it could mean disaster for me if Vanderbilt found out—but I was careful. I knew they wouldn't. And some part of me was still aglow in the magic of Lily LeBlanc's admiration. Her friendship.

Friends. I should've known it was bullshit from the moment she came to me for help. But I didn't learn the harsh truth until a few weeks later at school, when I overheard Lily and Savannah talking about their essays in the senior lounge.

"It's truly unfair," Savannah was saying. "Six hundred and fifty words can't possibly express the talents I bring to the stage."

She was mostly joking, putting on an ironic old Hollywood accent, but Lily said breezily, "I know someone who could help."

Savannah paused. "You mean, like, a tutor?"

"Sort of." Lily lowered her voice. "I got Wyatt's sister to do mine. All I had to do was massage her ego and throw her some pity hangouts and she literally offered to write it for me. For *free.*"

Her laugh. That's what I remember, a little twinkling sound

at the end, glitter falling through the air. It wasn't the first time I'd heard laughter at my expense, but it was the first time I hadn't seen it coming.

It was the day before the early-decision deadline, and I knew I had to do something, *ruin* something—because it was suddenly so obvious, how stupid I'd been. Vanderbilt was everything I'd worked my whole life for, and here I was, helping Lily LeBlanc waltz in and snatch it up without breaking a sweat.

In the end, it was even easier than writing the essay. Lily had given me the password to her Common App account. All I had to do was log in, delete my essay, and copy and paste her old one. And just my luck, she hadn't submitted yet—that's what you get for being a procrastinator, I told myself. With one click of a button, it was done.

Now tears sting my eyes as I look at Mom, awash in shame and disappointment.

"She didn't even notice," I say. "She didn't check the application after I submitted it. That's how little she cared."

Wyatt stands abruptly. "This has been a great family chat, but I'm going to bed."

"Wyatt—" Mom starts, but he cuts her off.

"Sorry, but I just—" He chokes up, tightening his jaw. "Lily is still *missing,* and all Piper cares about is the stupid essay, and I can't, okay? I'm done."

He sulks off toward the stairs. Mom just watches, and maybe Wyatt has a point, maybe I'm a robotic, college-obsessed freak, but still, the anger builds and builds until it explodes.

"Why does he always get away with it?" I shout, turning to Mom. "He cheated on her, and I'm the only one who gets a lecture? No, forget the cheating. He beat a guy within an inch of his life, and you're just letting him walk off. Why does he always get someone else to clean up his messes?"

"Because that's what families do." Mom's voice breaks, and something in it breaks me, too, enough to make me go completely silent.

"I don't mean to let him get away with things," she says after a moment. "But what else are we supposed to do? When your kid screws up, you protect them. You fix what you can and pray they learn from their mistakes, because you love them like your own heart outside your body, and what person in their right mind can look at their heart and watch it get crushed?"

My throat tightens, but I feel too guilty to cry. Mom reaches for her drink before changing her mind, setting it back down.

"And maybe—" She pauses again. "Maybe it seems like we're only cleaning up Wyatt's messes because he's the one who makes them. You're always so smart and so together, Pipes. But it isn't fair of me and your dad to assume you've always got it covered. And I know I'm hard on you—maybe because some part of me thinks I'm preparing you. Because the terrible fact of it is that young women, bright women like you . . . when you slip up, you *don't* get away with it." She shakes her head. "But it's wrong. You deserve better."

Quiet tears slide down her cheeks, and all of the anger inside me shrivels up like a dying petal. Because I understand. Mom is teaching me to survive the only way she knows how: by being the best. The brightest. Saying "please" and "thank you" and leaving no room for error, hiding your thirst for blood behind a sweet Southern smile. We both deserve better.

I walk over to the sofa and wrap my arms around her, let her cry. "I'm sorry."

"No." She squeezes my hand. "Never be sorry."

"Is Dad okay?" I ask, and I'm crying now, too.

She sniffs, nodding. "You know him. He was already joking about how thrilled he'll be to have time to read, for once."

I laugh, but it fades into a hollow pit in my stomach. "How long does he have to stay there?" I ask. "Can't we post bail?"

"They haven't set it yet. But we will." Mom squeezes me tighter. "We'll be okay, Pipes. Johnsons are always okay."

And it's only now that a new piece slots into place. A question I'm almost afraid to ask out loud.

"If you know about the deal with the Pierrot," I start, "then do you know what they wanted from Dad in return? Why they needed him to join?"

Something in Mom changes, like a small electric jolt. Then she smooths out her expression.

"I really don't." She shrugs. "Maybe they thought it wouldn't hurt to have a psychiatrist on board—you know, to get access to some easy prescriptions, or get their kids extra time on the ACT even when they obviously don't need it."

She gives a small laugh, like it's just a dark little joke, but I saw it, the slip of her mask. I felt the shift.

"Mom . . ."

Her hand finds my cheek, cold against my skin.

"You're so smart, Pipes," she says gently. "And you're smart enough to know that some questions, you're better off not asking."

32

APRIL

JANUARY 2, 11:00 P.M.

I've walked all the way to the river before I finally hear from Renee. She hasn't answered my calls, but a text pops up on my screen.

I'm safe

Can you meet? There's something I need to tell you

I breathe out, sinking to a seat on the rocks at the edge of the Mississippi. The water churns at my feet as I text back.

Yeah, I'm at the river—where should I meet you?

She responds almost instantly.

Getting my car now, I'll pick you up

I pull my knees to my chest and look out to the horizon, the twinkling spires of the Crescent City Connection.

In the daylight, the Mississippi is ugly and brown, filled

with trash and barges and probably also several creatures that could eat you alive, if the current doesn't get you first. At night, though, it looks different, the surface like a shimmering watercolor in the glow of downtown. It looks, now, like the powerful, monstrous thing it is—a living creature that bent this city to its whim.

This must be how Margot always saw it.

And now that I'm here, now that I feel her with me, I finally let myself think of that night, soaking in the details like salt in a wound.

It was the night of the ball last year, when Margot was Queen. I wasn't there—she hadn't invited me, which was just another nail in the coffin—and so when I saw Margot's name flash across my phone late that night, I jolted upright in bed. It was the first time she'd reached out in months.

I'm at the Deus Den, she'd texted. Can you come?

She didn't have to ask. When I got there, I half expected to find her in her Queen costume, but there she was in a classic Margot outfit: giant hoodie, leggings, and her favorite Doc Martens, the ones she said made her feel like she could stomp on any heart in her path. There was a black plastic bag on her arm, the kind they used at her favorite fake ID–friendly liquor store. From a distance, she looked worried, picking off the pearl-pink manicure that was so unlike her regular blue-black color. But when she saw me, she ran over to pull me into a hug.

"Thank god," she said, squeezing tighter. She smelled like her cotton-candy vape, a gross habit she'd picked up that year, even if the scent was weirdly comforting. "If I had to talk to one more debutante, I swear my head was going to explode."

There was something different about her—a fire crackling in her eyes, this almost frantic energy—but it was so good to hear her voice, to be near her, that I didn't question it. Neither of us brought it up, the rift between us. It was like acknowledging all the time we'd spent apart would break the spell, send us back to real life.

Instead, we went inside. The Den was cavernous in the dark, a forest of papier-mâché creatures looking down on us from their floats. Margot pulled a pint of vodka out of her plastic bag, passed it to me.

"Cheers," she said.

"What are we toasting?"

"The end of my reign."

I smiled, taking the bottle. "Thank god. I've heard you were a bit of a tyrannical ruler."

She smiled back. "Let them eat cake."

For a while, we wandered the Den, laughing and talking and exploring the playground of floats. The whole time, the real questions I wanted to ask her were brimming under the surface, seconds from crashing up for air, but every time I got close, I stopped myself. The night felt almost normal, and I didn't want to ruin it. I didn't want to lose her again.

So when Margot turned to me with a wicked look on her face, I knew I'd say yes to whatever she was about to ask.

"What if we wrecked it?"

I blinked. "Wrecked what?"

We'd only had about a shot each, so the wild spark in her eyes was from more than just the alcohol.

"All of it," she said, gesturing around us. "This whole place."

It was so far from what I expected that I was briefly stunned. "Why?"

"Because it's bullshit." Margot glared at the King's float, its throne empty and waiting. "Calling some old guy a king and giving him a queen young enough to be his daughter. Making him think he's literally royalty just because he's rich and white and powerful."

It was nothing we hadn't said before—Margot knew I thought all of it was bullshit—but there was a twinge of hurt under her words this time, something wounded beneath her confident rage.

"Did something happen?" I asked.

Margot looked away, and I knew then that I'd hesitated too long. For some reason, she needed me to agree to this, and I'd failed her.

"No," she said distantly. "I don't know. I'm just in the mood to break shit. But you're right. It's stupid."

"I didn't say it was stupid," I argued, even though we both knew I'd thought it.

"Whatever," Margot said. "It is."

Her hand tightened around the neck of the bottle, a wall rising up again between us. And I understood, suddenly, what this was. It was like her hidden cigarettes, her sad-clown lighter, all of the rumors about her bad-girl behavior that she ignored or even fueled because it made her feel impenetrable. Tonight, this need for destruction was another mask, a piece of armor to protect whatever was bruised inside. I knew that, and I was desperate to know what was really hurting her—just as much as I knew that wasn't what she wanted. What she wanted, more than anything, was a partner in crime.

And so I said something I shouldn't have.

"Well, maybe I'm in the mood to do something stupid."

She grinned, bright and vicious.

We made a mess together, wreaked way more havoc than two girls would seem capable of. We ripped flowers off of floats, dug under the gold leaf with our nails, hammered papier-mâché faces with abandoned plywood boards, fracturing their skulls. We ripped into bags of parade throws and tossed them around the room, spilling beads, stuffed animals, and light-up toys like brightly colored innards. When we were done, I was almost in awe of it. The damage we could cause together. How good it felt.

And then Margot flicked on her silver lighter, the flame dancing in her dark eyes.

"No," I said, reason taking over. "No way."

"Come on," she said. "They deserve it."

I was silent, still, and that's when I noticed it: the desperation in her eyes. A need that came from someplace deeper. Someplace broken.

"April, please."

"I need you to tell me what's going on," I blurted. "What happened tonight?"

"Nothing. I told you."

"That's bullshit." The words rushed up from deep inside me, some raw, injured place. "You ghost me for months, and then ask me to come do arson with you like everything is totally normal? As if you didn't dump me for Lily fucking LeBlanc."

As soon as I said it, I knew we both heard it. What I really meant. Margot didn't *dump* me. It's not like we were a thing. Margot was my friend—my *only* friend—and I wasn't about to screw that up by catching feelings for a girl who, as far as I knew, was Kinsey scale–certified straight. But there were also times when I knew, deep down, that a part of me was a little bit in love with her. I didn't think she'd seen it, that soft, tender spot, but the way she looked at me then, I knew. She saw me, all the way through.

And I should have said it. I should have admitted it, just to see what would happen, because we were already playing with fire, weren't we? But I waited a moment too long. Because just before I could gather the breath, Margot asked, "Why do you hate her so much?"

And the moment was gone. Just another thing stolen by Lily LeBlanc.

"Because—" I paused, suddenly unsure. "Because she's fake. She's rich and spoiled and everyone loves her for no goddamn reason. And she actually thinks all this debutante shit is important. She's obviously going to be Queen next year, and she's *proud* of it. From the second she popped out of the womb, being a debutante has been the most important thing she'll ever do, and she doesn't even see how fucking sad that is."

Margot stared at me, something simmering beneath her glare. Then she shook her head slightly. "Funny," she said. "You just described me."

"What? No. You know it's all ridiculous. But Lily—"

"You don't even *know* Lily," Margot said. "You haven't given her a chance."

"Because she *sucks,*" I shouted. "Because she's been trying to steal you from me, just because she thinks she can have whatever she wants."

"She's *stealing* me? What, like I can't decide things for myself?"

I sputtered, face hot. "No, that's not—"

"Whatever." Margot snapped the lighter shut, shoving it into her pocket.

"Wait," I said. Panicked, now, feeling her slip through my fingers. "I didn't—"

"Have you ever thought that maybe I *like* having a friend who understands what it's like to be me?"

Shocked, angry tears sprang to my eyes, but I blinked them away, tightening my jaw.

"I understand you," I told her, but my voice came out weak.

She shook her head. "You don't understand what it's like to come from families like ours."

Ours, meaning hers and Lily's. Not mine. My biggest fear, raw and out in the open like a pulsing organ in her palm.

"Oh, so I wasn't born far enough into the one percent to get it?" I spat.

Margot shrugged. "It's like you said. Being a debutante is the most important thing I'll ever do, at least as far as my family's concerned."

"But you don't have to."

"No, you don't get it. I *do* have to." She hesitated. "And maybe I want to."

"You *don't,*" I argued. "You literally just wanted to burn this place to the ground."

"I don't know what I want!" She flung up her hands, her voice so sharp and pained that it startled me. "Maybe I'm angry. Maybe I'm trying to *fix* this. Because maybe I don't think it's *so cool* to fucking despise the place I grew up in."

Her words stopped me dead in my tracks. They were an accusation, plain and simple.

"And don't try to pretend you don't," Margot said. "The second you graduate, you're leaving and never coming back. Right? You say it all the time."

"I—" My voice wilted in my throat. She was right. It was

exactly what Lily had implied that night on the levee, thrown back in my face.

You'll be out of here soon enough, right?

"Me and Lily are lifers. She'll go to Vanderbilt, fine, but she'll come right back here and settle down. She has to. Our families wouldn't let us leave, even if we wanted to. And I don't. This place is messy, and it's full of bullshit, and yeah, sometimes I hate it, but it's *home.* I love it enough to stay and fix the broken stuff. And honestly, April, I really don't understand why you're so ready to just leave it behind."

Because it's doomed, I wanted to say. Because this city is literally sinking. Because it's full of racists and elitists and politicians who think they have a right to tell us who we can love or what we can do with our bodies. People who want to stick us in tight dresses and heels and parade us around a ballroom like it's all we're good for, like it's an honor to be an object.

But it's also full of life and music and joy and people like Margot—people so brimming with it that all I can hope for is to catch a spark, to cup it in my palms like a firefly before letting it go.

But I didn't say any of that. I just stared at her, my mouth dry and my tongue stone.

Margot nodded.

"Lily was right about you," she said.

And that was it. The match that sent the fire roaring until it charred away every last part of this thing we'd built together.

So I did exactly what she told me I would: I left her behind.

The Den never burned, in the end. The Krewe found it wrecked the next day, and there was a brief panic about finding the culprit, about how they'd fix it all in time for Mardi Gras, but all of that was forgotten when Margot's body was found.

The parade still rolled that year, right on schedule. Even a dead Queen, it turned out, wasn't enough to break them.

But our secret has been threatening to break me ever since.

Only, the Jester didn't have it right, not all the way. Because as scared as I was of someone knowing what Margot and I had done to the Den, I was more terrified of facing what I'd done to her. Of knowing that I could have saved her, if only I'd stayed.

Now, at the river's edge, the wind whips by, raising goose bumps on my bare arms. I clutch my camera close, thinking this is the kind of night Margot would have loved. A little chill in the air. The distant sounds of the Quarter, the water rushing past.

And I cry—letting out everything that I've been pushing back, trying to fight, crying until I feel like a hollow husk of myself.

When I'm done, I do the only thing I can think of: I lift my camera, frame the river, and press the shutter.

Already, I know it won't be right. Water is always hard, and it takes more time than I've given it, but it's comforting to know it's there, this little piece of her safe in the square of my camera, where I can hold it to my chest.

Beside me, my phone lights up with a text from Renee.

Here

I wipe my eyes, knowing it's pretty much a lost cause—there's no way they aren't red and puffy—but I don't have time to worry about that. I slide my camera strap over my shoulder and turn back the way I came, finding her clunky gray sedan parked on Decatur.

I climb quickly into the passenger seat, looking over my shoulder before closing the door. Renee is still in her ball gown, and I tamp down the urge to take a picture: my getaway driver, ripping through the French Quarter in tulle and combat boots.

"Hey," she says.

"Hey," I answer, a little breathless, but I'm not totally sure if it's from the walk or the fact that I'm alone with Renee again. Her car smells like fake cherries, an air freshener pumping it through the vents, but it's kind of nice. A miniature sign dangles off a chain of beads from her rearview: BEWARE PICKPOCKETS AND LOOSE WOMEN.

"I'm sorry we ran like that," I blurt. "We should've—"

"April, it's okay. Y'all gave me a chance to get out." She shoots me a soft smile, nodding at my camera. "And that was pretty badass, by the way."

Suddenly, I don't know what to say.

"They're good, too?" Renee asks. "Piper and Vivian?"

"Yeah." I swallow, mouth dry. "I mean, they got out. I think they're both headed home. But someone sort of sent an email to our entire school exposing our deepest, darkest secrets, so are they good in a general sense? Jury's still out."

"Whoa, wait—what? Are you okay?"

"Are you?"

She smiles a little. "You already asked me that."

"You didn't answer."

"Neither did you."

"I . . ." I trace my finger around my camera lens, the circular motion not doing much to calm me down. "I don't know. I'm not sure if I can talk about it. But you're really okay?"

"I think so."

"Good." I pause. "There's something you wanted to tell me?"

For a second, she's silent.

"The guy in the wolf mask," she says. "I saw his face."

I gape. "What? How?"

"After y'all left, I realized it might be my only chance to figure out who he was. The Rougarou. The King. Whatever the hell we're supposed to call him." Her nose wrinkles, like the words have a bad aftertaste. "He's the one who brought her there, who might've killed her, so . . . I had to know."

I can't argue, because I've felt it, too, that need fueling the drive and danger in her eyes.

"So when the Lieutenant ran off after you—"

"Marty," I supply. "Detective Rutherford. That's the guy who's supposed to be working on Lily's case. He worked on Margot's, too."

Renee's eyes widen. "Motherfucker."

"Yeah," I echo, weirdly soothed by her anger.

"After Marty left, your little friend tried to help me get out, but I told him I was fine."

So Jason kept his word, at least. Not that it really redeems him.

"I went off with the Rougarou, let him pull me into one of those rooms in the hallway. He seemed freaked out, like he just wanted to get out of there. Hide. Anyway, we were in there alone, so I got an idea. I acted like I wanted to help, you know . . . calm him down."

Instantly, I pick up on the implication. "You didn't."

"Obviously, I didn't *actually,* but . . . I may or may not have gotten close enough to take his mask off."

My jaw drops, a mix of panic and pure admiration.

"You shouldn't have done that," I tell her. "Gone off alone with him. You could've . . ."

My throat closes up around what I mean to say. *You could've ended up like Margot.*

"Hey." Renee reaches across the driver's seat and cups my chin lightly in her hand. I freeze at her touch, briefly worried I might catch fire from the inside. "I'm fine. I'm here. Soon as I saw his face, I kneed him in the balls and got out of there. And I love that you're worried, but I'm in the middle of a *really* good story, so maybe you let me finish bragging about my badass detecting skills?"

God, this girl is even cooler than I thought.

"Okay," I manage, in a voice that sounds a whole lot squeakier than I'd like it to.

She smiles, dropping her hand. As soon as the warmth of her fingers is gone, I snap back to reality with a cold, creeping dread.

"Did you recognize him?" I ask.

She shakes her head, and I deflate.

"But you're good at faces, right?" She points to my camera. "Seems like part of the whole thing. If I describe him, maybe you'll recognize him, right?"

"I guess so," I say. "Maybe. But—"

"Great." A grin spreads on her lips. "Then it's time to play the most high-stakes game of *Guess Who?* of our lives."

33

VIVIAN

JANUARY 2, 11:00 P.M.

It takes me a second too long to place his voice, maybe because he called me Vivian and not Atkins, but when Coach steps close enough for me to see him, I'm so relieved I could almost collapse.

"You okay?" he asks. "What—"

"I need a ride," I tell him quickly. "My phone's dead, and someone's following me. Could you . . . ?"

"Of course. Yeah, get in."

I glance back one more time, but I don't see Marty. It doesn't make me rush into the car any less quickly.

"Thank you," I breathe, once Coach is back in the driver's seat. "Thank you so much."

He gives me a concerned look and then reaches to grab the water bottle sitting in the cupholder.

"Here," Coach says, handing it over. "You look a little green."

Just the sight of it makes me realize how dry my throat is, and I take a long grateful sip.

"Where should I bring you?" he asks.

I swallow. I'm not sure where's safe anymore, but I know I can't be here. "Home, I guess."

I give him the address, and he nods, pulling back into the street. "You said someone was following you?"

I hesitate. Coach isn't in Deus. I can trust him. He could help. Still, the words won't come out.

"Is this about the email?" he asks gently.

Oh god. In the panic of running from Marty, I almost forgot about it, but of course he's seen it. Everyone will, if they haven't already. My parents, Lily's. Sav.

Coach works his jaw. "Listen, Atkins, I don't know what went on, and I don't need to, but don't you let anybody make you feel like this is your fault, or like you're a bad person. People screw up. And if you're as good a friend as you are a teammate, which I'll bet, then Lily's lucky to have you."

It's like stepping into a hot shower after a game when it's cold out: the sudden stinging shock to your system before the relief so sweet you could cry. I don't even know if I believe him, but I needed to hear it so badly that now I can't stop myself from telling him everything.

"Detective Rutherford is following me," I tell him. "He's the one working on Lily's case, but he's part of this secret Mardi Gras Krewe called the Pierrot, and I think they're the reason Lily went missing. Do you know anything about it? Does your girlfriend, or—?"

"Whoa, slow down." Coach glances between me and the road. "You said a secret Mardi Gras Krewe? Is it a Deus thing?"

"I think so. It's a bunch of Deus members, at least. They did something to Margot Landry, and . . . I think they know where Lily is, too."

Coach nods slowly, taking it all in, and for a second, I'm scared he's about to tell me I sound insane. And maybe I do. Hell, he just picked me up barefoot in the French Quarter wearing a dirty ball gown. I look it, too. But instead, he says, "Listen, Atkins, I don't think this is something you should be taking on by yourself. Have you gone to the police or anything yet?"

"We can't. Marty's running the whole show."

Coach chews his lip, thinking. I remember the dead phone in my hand.

"Do you have a charger in here?" I ask. "I should call April and Piper to check in."

"Yeah, sure. In the glove compartment. I can—"

"Thanks." As I open it, I feel Coach shift. Something tingles at the back of my neck, like I'm being watched by someone I can't see. But I'm just being paranoid, I tell myself.

I plug my phone into the charger, and then take another long pull from the water bottle. As soon as I do, Coach reaches over to close the glove compartment, and it's that exact moment that I catch sight of something poking out, plastic and shiny.

I block the door with my hand before he can shut it.

"Vivian," Coach says. "Don't—"

He tries to stop me again, but I'm quick, grabbing the thing and holding it up to the light. As soon as it's in my hand, time slows down, everything moving with a blurry lag.

A wolf mask.

The Rougarou.

I look at Coach, confusion and rage and fear mixing all together, locking my voice in my throat. His head blurs into two, both with the same sad, pitying look, and distantly, I understand. The water bottle.

"I'm sorry, Atkins," he says. "I didn't want this to happen."

The world starts to fuzz around the edges, and Coach flicks on the turn signal. It ticks away like the countdown of a bomb.

34

PIPER

JANUARY 2, 11:15 P.M.

For a moment, I'm stunned, like maybe I heard wrong, but no. I can read it all over her face, hear it clearly in her tone. *Some questions, you're better off not asking.*

Mom knows what happened to Margot. Or at least she has suspicions she's choosing to ignore.

And I know, suddenly, what I have to do.

Putting on my best good-daughter performance, I tell Mom good night and head upstairs, where I sit on the second-floor landing and listen. It takes forever, but finally, I hear her pad down the hall and into her bedroom. I wait a minute. Another.

And then I walk as fast as I can to the front door, grab the keys, and rush out to the car.

My knuckles are white on the wheel, and I try to breathe, focus on the road as I pull away. Except I don't know where I'm even going. I lift my phone and voice-command it to start a FaceTime with the Maids. It rings and rings, but no one picks up.

"Goddammit," I mutter, trying again.

No answer. What the hell could they even be doing right now? Sleeping, maybe, like normal people.

That's when I get another idea. Probably a bad one. But I'm already starting to drive in that direction, and he's the only other person who sleeps as little as I do.

"*Goddammit.*" I flick the turn signal. "Call Arch Nemesis."

Aiden picks up in two rings. Of course he does.

"Hello?"

"Can I come over?"

I must sound as wild and panicked as I feel, because he doesn't even hesitate.

"Of course. Is everything okay?"

"Can't explain now. And the handshake still stands. Cone of silence, Ortiz."

I hang up before he can answer, willing myself to focus so I don't add a traffic violation on top of this shit sundae of a night.

He opens the door before I even ring the bell.

"Hey," he says. "What's—"

I plow into his house. "Can we go to your room?"

"Yeah, sure. My parents are both sleeping, so we should try to keep it down."

Of course he's worried about not pissing off his parents. His parents are good, law-abiding people who don't join cults or cover up murders to save their son from assault charges.

"Okay, seriously," Aiden says once we get upstairs. "What's—"

A creature leaps from the shadows and directly into my path, so quickly I almost shriek before I realize it's just a black-and-white cat.

"What the hell?" I whisper.

The cat eyes me, unimpressed, and slithers over to Aiden, nuzzling his calf.

"Mr. Mistoffelees," he says. "Don't be offended if he takes a second to warm up."

The absurdly named animal approaches me warily enough that I think it's about to bite me. Then it butts its soft little cat head up against my leg, purring.

"Would ya look at that." Aiden grins wide.

It makes my insides go all warm and buttery for a second. I scowl back at him. "Mr. Mistoffelees?"

Aiden runs a hand over the back of his neck, embarrassed. "From, uh, *Cats* the musical. I had a phase."

"Oh my god." I'm momentarily delighted enough to forget why I came here. "I can't believe you've given me this ammunition. Did you dance around your room in leg warmers? A *tail*?"

"The soundtrack is full of bangers. I don't know what else to say."

"I *knew* I hated theater kids."

"Rude and offensive," Aiden says, pushing open his bedroom door.

And just like that, I'm faced with the reality of his space and the fact that we haven't spoken since I left him in the study room. For a breath, I take it in. It's exactly what I expected: immaculately clean, Star Wars posters, weirdly pleasant-smelling for a guy's bedroom. I also clock the Lego spaceship on his dresser, and I want to make fun of it, but I'm suddenly too anxious.

Aiden closes the door and then crosses his arms, facing me. "So are you going to tell me what's up, or not?"

It hits me that I have no idea how to explain this. I glance down at my phone. Nothing from Vivian or April yet. Mom, either. At least she didn't catch me leaving. But knowing her, she'll probably figure it out soon enough, so I might as well rip off the Band-Aid.

"My dad didn't kill Margot," I say.

Aiden looks relieved—and like he believes me. It makes the rest of it come out easier.

"But you were right," I go on, "that he's part of the Pierrot."

I give him my best abridged version of what I learned tonight: the deal with the Pierrot, how they manipulated Wyatt into being the Jester. Aiden listens with a calm expression, a small worried crease between his eyebrows.

When I get to the end, I hesitate. Once I tell him, there's no going back. There's no guaranteeing that he won't be disgusted by me. That he won't call the police. Worst of all, this is a betrayal. We're supposed to protect each other, Mom said. *That's what families do.* But how far can the lies and secrets go before they rot us from the inside out?

Some questions, you're better off not asking.

I feel the ghost of Mom's hand on my cheek, the warning look in her eyes, and I know I have to give him the truth.

"I think my parents know who killed Margot," I say. "Or, at least, they know it was someone at the Pierrot. I don't know who did it, who killed Margot, but . . . I think they're both part of the cover-up. And I'm worried they might know where Lily is, too."

It's all out in the open now, everything I've feared in the deepest parts of me since the moment I found that report on Dad's computer, and I wait, with a horrible feeling of dread, for Aiden to hate me.

Instead, he wraps his arms around me and hugs me tight to his chest.

"I'm so sorry, Piper," he says.

Tears slip out, hot and quick, and I can't believe I'm crying in front of my arch nemesis. Into his T-shirt, which is as warm and clean-smelling as his room.

"It's just so *fucked*."

"I know," he says, a hand pressed against the back of my head.

I pull away, wiping the mess of tears from my face. "God, what is *wrong* with me?"

"Nothing's wrong with you."

"Then what's wrong with *you*?"

He blinks. "What?"

"Why are you being so nice to me?" I'm maybe 25 percent joking, but there's a dull ache in my throat. "I'm awful to you. You're a cocky jerk to me. It's our whole thing. It works."

Aiden smiles, and I want to slap him, because even his smile is like honey, that asshole. "You're not awful *all* the time."

"Well, you're still a cocky jerk," I quip. "And—" It hits me suddenly. *Shit*. I'd almost forgotten. "And you probably know I sabotaged Lily's Vanderbilt application. Because I'm terrible and vindictive and—"

"Piper, stop." He looks serious now. "I saw the email. And yes, that was definitely a bad call on your part, and maybe there'll be consequences, but you shouldn't beat yourself up. You're a good person."

My mouth hangs open. Does Aiden Ortiz, of all people, have a better opinion of me than I deserve?

"Look, I don't know what's going to happen," he says, before I can argue. "And it sucks that you're going through this with your family. But Lily's in danger, and if there's anyone who can figure out how to save her, it's you. And whatever you're going to do, I want to help."

Never in my life have I been so sure of what I think while feeling so totally at a loss for words.

Yes, I want you to help me.

Yes, I might want something else, too, and Vivian might have been right with her stupid Pride and Prejudice *crap, and—*

"Vivian and April," I blurt as soon as the thought crosses my mind, snapping out of the spell. "I need to find them, and then—"

Before I can even finish my sentence, my phone buzzes. April. I pick it up before it even makes it through one ring.

"Way to disappear when I need you," I snap, and then, overwhelmed suddenly by relief, "You're okay?"

"Yeah," she says. "You?"

"Yes. I'm with Aiden. Where are you?"

Mercifully, she doesn't make any *Pride and Prejudice* jokes.

"Renee just dropped me off at home," she says quickly, and for the first time, I pick up on the change in her voice. She's breathless, wired. "Can we meet up? I think I might have figured out something big."

"What?"

She hesitates. "I think we should talk in person. Just to be safe. But . . . I know who the Rougarou is."

"Shit. Yeah, okay. I'll pick you up."

"Have you heard from Vivian?"

"No, I tried to call y'all, but—"

Right on cue, my phone buzzes again. I look down at the screen.

"Speak of the devil," I say.

I open our group chat, and my heart nearly stops when I see Vivian's text.

Meet me at the Den. I know where Lily is.

"Holy shit," I say.

"Holy shit," April echoes.

"What is it?" Aiden asks.

I'd almost forgotten he was here—which should be a relief to the part of me that was having some pretty ridiculous thoughts about two minutes ago. I want to tell him, but for some reason, I can't make the words come out. Aiden wants to help. I know he does. But this is all coming together so fast, a head rush of information, and something taps at my brain, a little worry trying to get in: something's wrong here. And I know, with sharp certainty, that I can't drag him into this. This isn't his mess, even if he wants it to be. It's not his family that's wrapped up in it.

"I'll pick you up in ten, okay?" I tell April.

"Okay."

She hangs up, and I turn to Aiden.

"I have to go meet April and Vivian."

"What's going on? Do you need me to—"

"We'll be fine, I promise."

Aiden watches me. I can tell he doesn't believe me, just as much as he can tell I've made up my mind.

"Can you trust me?" I ask.

It hangs between us for a moment.

"Of course," he says finally. "Will you text me in, like, an hour to let me know you're okay? And will you share your location? Just so I know, in case anything happens."

I stare at him, a little stunned.

"Sorry," he says quickly. "If that's too much, you don't have to—"

"No, it's okay. I'll share it."

I open my phone's location sharing, hoping he can't read what's really going through my head. He cares. Just like April and Vivian, he wants to know that I got home safe.

And for some reason, in this context, *share your location* is the most attractive thing I've ever heard in my life.

"There," I say, pressing SHARE. "For your stalking pleasure."

Aiden looks embarrassed. "Seriously, I didn't—"

I smile. "I'm kidding." And then, because I can't leave without saying it, without letting him know how much I mean it, "Thank you."

He smiles back at me, those stupid eyes big enough to swim in, and suddenly, I'm pulled by this irrational fear that I'm about to walk into something life-or-death at the Den, that this might be my last chance, so I do the most deranged thing of all: I get up on my toes and kiss him on his stupid mouth.

It only lasts a second, maybe two, but time stretches out and I feel him shift from surprise to kissing me back, bringing his hand under my hair to cup the back of my head, and then I realize how completely and utterly ridiculous this is, so I pull back.

"Bye," I say.

And without giving him a chance to respond, I spin around and march down the stairs on my way to whatever's waiting for me.

35

VIVIAN

JANUARY 3, 12:00 A.M.

When I open my eyes, everything is blurry. I blink a few times, trying to get the world back into focus, but when it does, it still doesn't make sense. I feel like I'm waking up after having too much to drink, but I'm not in my bed, or on an air mattress on Sav's floor, or any of the other places I should be after a night out.

Wait, a mattress. I *am* on a mattress. It squeaks under me, the sheets damp from what must be my sweat. Gross. I groan and sit up to press the heels of my hands to my eyes, holding them there until the throbbing in my head calms down a little.

When I open my eyes again, I notice the other things that don't make sense. I'm on a mattress, but this isn't a bedroom. It looks a little like the scene shop at Beaumont, where Sav and the rest of the theater kids go to paint the sets, only it's smaller and . . . Mardi Gras–themed?

The floor is concrete, and the lighting overhead is bright, almost like a hospital, but the room is crowded with Mardi Gras crap. Racks of sparkly, colorful costumes, towers of cardboard boxes full of who knows what. The walls are lined with framed Deus stuff: old drawings of float lineups, invitations to balls from decades ago, photos of Queens and Kings that change from old-timey to modern, even though the costumes are exactly the same. If you ignore the dirt all over the ball gown I'm still wearing, I fit right in.

The Den, I realize. This must be a storage room in the warehouse. Why did Coach bring me here?

Coach. It starts to trickle back. His car appearing out of nowhere, making me think I was safe. The water bottle. The world blurring. How could I have been so stupid? I feel around the mattress, made up with blankets like a real bed, even though it's just thrown on the floor, but I don't see my phone anywhere.

"No, no, no . . ." I tear off the pillowcases and shake them out. Nothing. I throw them both on the ground. "Fuck!"

"Vivian."

The other voice makes me jump, spiking my adrenaline. But it's not Coach.

I see her first in the mirror that's propped up against the opposite wall, like someone wanted to remind us just how real this is, how screwed we are. She's sitting with her back against a stack of boxes, knees pulled to her chest, chin resting on top of them.

I see her, but I don't believe it until I turn around. Even then, I'm not sure this isn't my brain all mixed up from whatever Coach gave me.

"Lily?"

As soon as I say it, I know this is real. She's here, wearing her favorite leggings and the oversized gray hoodie Wyatt let her steal months ago. She looks terrible. The space under her eyes is the color of a bruise, and her hair is unwashed, stringy around her face, but it's her. She's here, looking at me. Alive.

"Lily," I say again, rushing toward her. "Oh my god, I was so scared you were—"

She flinches as I reach out to touch her, and the look on her face stops me in my tracks. Lily shakes her head slowly, and I realize it isn't just fear in her eyes. It's rage, cold and hard.

"They told you to stop digging," she says. "You should have fucking listened."

36

APRIL

JANUARY 3, 12:00 A.M.

When we get to the Den, we go straight for the gate. It feels like ages since I last punched in the code, even though it's been less than a week. I don't know what makes me say it, but I suddenly feel like I have to.

"I lied before," I tell Piper as the keypad gives a reassuring click, flashing green. "It wasn't my dad who gave me the code. It was Margot. When we . . ."

"Oh," Piper says, eyebrows raising. "Right."

We haven't talked about our respective sins, revealed by whichever Pierrot member sent that email, but it doesn't feel like we need to. If Piper sabotaged Lily's essay, something that could so clearly ruin her own chances at Vanderbilt, then she probably had a good reason to—or at least to believe Lily deserved it. I think Piper knows that Margot and I had a good reason to do what we did, too. And Vivian . . . I don't know, exactly, but things are always more complicated than they seem. And right now, we have much bigger priorities than the ways we've misbehaved.

I open the gate, leading us up to the warehouse door.

"Anything from Vivian yet?" I ask.

Piper shakes her head. "It's weird."

"We should wait, right?"

I scan our surroundings. It's empty out here, dark. The moon casts an inky glow over the street, the overgrown neutral ground behind us littered with abandoned tires and other debris, and I think again how strange it is for a group like Deus to make their home base in the middle of a place like this. A "bad neighborhood," some people would probably call it. But maybe they did that on purpose. Maybe they like to be kings ruling over a kingdom of subjects they believe will never have the power to fight back.

"I have a bad feeling," Piper says.

It validates the queasiness I've felt since all of our calls went straight to Vivian's voicemail on the way here, but it doesn't make me feel any better.

"Maybe we should look around first," I say. "See if her car's here."

Piper nods, and we creep around the side of the warehouse to the parking lot. Worry spreads from the hard ball in my stomach all the way to the tips of my fingers as we approach, and even before I see it, I know.

Two cars are here, but neither of them is Vivian's. And all at once, I understand.

"I don't think she sent that text," I whisper.

But Piper's already bounding back to the warehouse door, and I shuffle to keep up with her, holding my camera strap tight. As she opens the door, carefully and quietly, it hits me with sudden clarity that we don't know what's going to be on the other side. *Who* might be there.

A year ago, fear like this might have sent me running. Last

time, all it took was one dig—*Lily was right about you*—and I left Margot behind. I proved her right.

I wonder what would have happened if I'd turned around and run back inside, if I'd held her close and let her cry, or scream, or just tell me what was really going on. I wonder, if I'd stayed, if we would have burned it all down.

But it's too late to change that now. All we have is the present: our friend inside, in danger.

This time, we're not letting another girl go missing.

We step inside, and the Den yawns before us. The floats are as tall and imposing as ever, giant creatures standing sentinel in rows all the way down the long room. We slip behind the nearest one for cover. It's shaped like some kind of pirate ship, a playhouse for overgrown boys who dream of pillaging on the sea. I breathe in paint and sawdust, the smell so thick and heavy I can feel it on my tongue.

And then, voices.

"This is bad. This is really, really bad."

I bite my tongue to keep from reacting. Coach Davis. I'm certain it's him—as certain as I was when Renee described him to me.

"Calm down." The second voice is familiar, too. Marty, completely devoid of his usual Southern charm.

Piper sneaks past me, moving deeper into the warehouse. I follow as she leads us toward their voices, keeping tight between the floats and the warehouse wall. Every time we step into the open space between floats, I'm seized by a horror-movie kind of fear that Coach and Marty will be there in the gap, waiting. But all we get is open empty space.

"We went too far this time," Coach says.

"Calm *down*."

Piper stops us behind another float. It's classic purple, green, and gold, glittering with shiny paper confetti. At the front of the float, a papier-mâché jester juts out like a figurehead, his lips drawn back in laughter, tongue lolling. The Fool's Float, I realize—one of the legacy floats Deus reuses every year. It's the float Dad always rides on. Piper's dad, too.

Stomach twisting, I put a hand on the side of it to steady myself as we creep toward the open runway at the center of the warehouse, where the voices are coming from.

Slowly, carefully, I reach into my pocket and pull out my phone, opening the camera and switching it to video. They're maybe ten feet away from us, but if they walk into the space between this float and the next one, we'll catch them.

If they don't catch us first.

"I just need to think," Marty says. "I've gotten you out of your messes before. I'll do it again."

Coach sounds desperate. "It can't be like last time, Dad."

We both freeze. *Dad?* But before I've had time to fully process that, Coach says something else that makes my heart nearly stop.

"We can't do to them what we did to her."

What we did to her. Those five words are like the sinking arc of a missile just before it crashes against the earth, shaking the ground in its wake.

Margot. They killed her. I knew it already—maybe should have known from the moment I met these two obvious suspects, both of them wearing their good-Southern-boy acts like cheap masks—but hearing Coach say it, I could almost forget my fear, run straight for them with nothing but a phone, a camera, and my fists. And maybe I would, too, if Piper didn't reach for my hand, giving it a quick warning pulse.

"Tell me, then," Marty says, words laced with condescension. "What would *you* like to do with the debutantes in the storage room?"

Piper's eyes bug out next to me. She dips her head toward the back end of the warehouse, where the storage room is.

And then I realize. *Debutantes,* plural.

With Piper leading, we creep toward the storage room. My heart is pounding so loud in my ears that I don't notice the discarded papier-mâché flower in my path until it's too late.

It crunches under my foot, and I feel it like my own bones snapping.

For a moment, we're suspended, frozen, but it's too late.

We run at full speed toward the storage room, their footsteps pounding behind us on the concrete, and we're almost there, so close I can practically feel the door handle in my palm, when a hand reaches out and closes around my wrist.

"Well, well, well." Marty grins wide, his accent dripping like molasses as his fingers dig into my skin. "Didn't your mother ever teach you that it's impolite to eavesdrop?"

37

LILY

JANUARY 3, 12:05 A.M.

Once upon a time, there was a queen trapped in a castle. It was full of riches and guarded by two dragons with fire on their breath and venom on their tongues, and even though the queen had been in this castle all her life, no one in the kingdom could find her. But that was okay with her. They never could have saved her, anyway, and if they'd tried, she would have warned them: the riches are all made of plastic, but the dragons are real.

And if you're not careful, they can start to feel like home.

Vivian stares at me in horror, like she doesn't recognize her best friend, and maybe she shouldn't. Because I'm not the same.

Or maybe this is who I always was.

"Lily," she says softly, like maybe if she keeps saying my name, I'll be who she thinks I am. "What happened?"

"I got my hands dirty," I tell her. I mean it as a joke, but it doesn't come out like one, and it doesn't change the awful pitying look on her face.

"Coach . . ." She glances at the door. "Did he hurt you?"

I almost laugh at that. Honestly. But she's looking at me so confused and desperate for an answer that I decide to give her what she wants.

"No, don't worry. Besides the kidnapping part, he's been a perfect gentleman." I turn toward the locked door. "Even if the *accommodations suck*!"

I raise my voice on that last part, which makes Vivian tense up, like she might need to fight or run.

"Relax," I tell her. "They won't hear us. These walls are basically soundproof."

Vivian watches me for a second. "They?"

"Everyone's favorite father-son duo." I roll my eyes, but when I look at Vivian again, I realize she doesn't know. "Coach and Marty?"

"Marty's his *dad*?" she asks.

Weirdly, I'm a little disappointed. I know, now, that the plan was doomed before it even started, but still, I thought my Maids would at least put *some* of the pieces together.

"Lily, what happened?"

"You really don't know?"

Vivian blinks at me. "We know that someone at the Pierrot killed Margot and they've been covering it up. Coach and Marty brought you here because you knew, right?"

Now we're getting somewhere. "And?"

She hesitates, like she doesn't want to say it. "And Coach and Margot were having an affair."

And now I actually laugh. I feel bad, but it's just that Vivian has always been like this, straightforward and single-minded—which is great when it comes to things like soccer, but not so much with seeing what's in front of her.

"That *would* make more sense, wouldn't it?" I tell her. "Well, you're almost there, but not quite."

I've pushed her too far.

"Oh my god, can you cut it out with this unbothered bullshit?" Vivian explodes, and finally, there's the fire I recognize, the one she tries to tamp down everywhere but the field. "What is your *problem*? We've spent the past week looking for you and risking our lives and it's like you don't even give a shit." She pauses, like she's just really heard herself. "Sorry. Shit. I'm so fucking glad you're okay, Lil. But I'm trying to figure out what's going on, and you're not helping."

"No, you're right. I guess I wasn't much help, was I?"

I sigh. What does it matter, anyway? She's here, and I'm starting to think that none of it matters, not really, so what's the harm in her knowing the truth?

"Marty and Coach were at the Mississippi house that summer," I tell her. "When I started being friends with Margot. Back then, though, I just knew Coach as Reed, 'cause he hadn't started at Beaumont yet. They'd rented their own house for a week. You know, father-son bonding."

Vivian frowns. "How did we not know that Marty was Coach's dad?"

"*You* didn't," I correct her. I shrug. "But I guess it's not that obvious. Coach's mom remarried when he was little, and he took the stepdad's last name and moved to Houston. Marty wasn't superinvolved in Coach's life, but they'd reconnected ever since Marty helped him get the Beaumont job. Turns out Coach was in a bit of a bind. He'd just gotten fired from his last coaching job when they found out he'd been dealing to students on the side. But Beaumont was willing to overlook that little hiccup, since our lovely Head of School happens to be in the Krewe."

"Mr. Pierce is in the Pierrot, too?"

"Oh, they're everywhere. Like termites. Or ravens circling a carcass, in his case." I roll my eyes, thinking of Mr. Pierce in his ridiculous raven mask, showing off that Tulane student like a new luxury timepiece. "Anyway, one day that summer, Marty offered to take us all out on his boat. Me, Margot, our parents, and Coach. So we went. Watched the grown-ups get wine-drunk and reminisce about the good old days, or whatever. It was all pretty typical stuff, but even then, I could tell. The way he looked at her . . ."

"Coach?" Vivian asks.

"No," I say. "Marty."

I watch it hit her, the same skin-prickling feeling I had when I first saw it happen. We were sitting together, Margot and me, on the white seat cushions of the boat, spray in our faces and sun baking our shoulders, when Marty's eyes caught Margot's over the rim of his glass. Dipped down to her halter-neck bikini top. Flashed, for a moment, with bare and unashamed hunger, before focusing again on his conversation with our dads.

Margot didn't miss it, either.

You see that? she whispered to me.

Gross, I whispered back. *Totally shameless.*

Margot shifted slightly. *I don't know. He's kind of cute, for an older guy.*

She sounded like she was joking. She always had that bold sense of humor, a fuck-you sort of confidence that I'd always been jealous of, even when it bordered on vulgar. Maybe that's why I was jealous—because she *could* be vulgar. Because, despite growing up with the same suffocating pressure and expectations that I did, Margot had a unique power: she didn't give a shit what people thought.

But even then, on the boat that day, I think I had a sense of what was about to happen—something tipping toward a cliff's edge, momentum unstoppable.

"I found them one night," I say. "I'd gone down to the dock to look for Margot, because she'd disappeared, and there they were on his boat together. Alone. Drinking wine, Marty's hand on her thigh. And then . . ."

When he kissed her, I wanted to turn and run, or say something so they knew I was there, but I couldn't do anything except watch, frozen, from the dock. Some part of me needed to see it happen. Needed to know how much of a mess they were about to make.

"I didn't tell anyone," I say. "I just went back to the house and tried to pretend I didn't see anything. For the rest of the trip, it mostly worked. But then, when we got home, they started texting. Margot never said anything, but she was always on her phone, all secretive, smiling. It was so obvious."

Disgusting, too, though I still can't admit it out loud. Not only because of the age gap, the wrongness of it, but because of how *stupid* she was being. That summer, I'd gotten to know her as this strong badass girl, everything I wished I could be, but here she was, doing something completely reckless—and not in a fun way anymore. It was bad enough that I had to fight April Whitman for Margot's attention when we got home, but now . . .

"I kept thinking she'd get over it, get bored, but it went on for months. By Thanksgiving, I couldn't take it anymore. I confronted her about it, told her I'd seen them in Mississippi, and she admitted it. Said he was going to leave his wife for her." I laugh, bitterness burning in my throat. "The thing is, I don't think she even liked him that much. I think she just wanted to see if he'd really do it. Blow up his whole life."

I can still see it so clearly, that gleam in her eyes as she told me. It wasn't love. It was *power,* and she was drunk on it. And I was so angry at her because I understood it, somewhere in the deepest, darkest part of me. Not that I'd ever fantasized about screwing an old guy—ew—but I knew what it was like to daydream about all of the men who thought they owned me bowing down at my feet. Not just some fake debutante-ball version, but *real.*

That's what we were both starving for, I think. Control. Only we dealt with it in different ways: I focused on me, sharpening my self-control like a weapon, and Margot threw hers into the fire, watching it burn.

It's why, I thought, we needed each other. But I guess I was wrong.

"Anyway," I say, forcing down the memories, "Margot basically told me I wasn't her friend if I was going to judge her."

"What did you do?" Vivian asks, her voice hollow.

"What was I supposed to do?" I shoot back. "Tattle to her parents? Mine? They wouldn't have believed me, and Marty would have denied it. He texted her from a burner, like a creep, so there wasn't even real evidence that it was him."

"I know," Vivian says. "We found the burner. It was in an envelope on my car."

Her car? No, that's not right.

"I left the burner for y'all in the darkroom," I say.

"Coach and Marty got to it first." Vivian looks down, guilty. "We told Marty about the email you sent us. That's how he knew where the phone was, I'm guessing."

I grit my teeth. The email—my *one* backup plan in case anything went wrong—and they failed me.

"I have no idea why he would have left the burner on my car, though," Vivian adds. "And I never would have told him about the email if I'd known. I swear, we thought he could help us."

Another bitter laugh works through me.

"Yeah, well. Rookie mistake."

For a moment, Vivian is quiet.

"He killed her, didn't he?" she asks. "Marty?"

A sad smile twitches on my lips. She really doesn't know. I watch her for a moment, waiting to see if she'll put together the last twist in this Southern Gothic fairy tale.

And she should. Because we both know by now that none of my stories have tidy endings.

38

PIPER

JANUARY 3, 12:15 A.M.

I pull harder, but the zip ties won't break. They just bite into my skin, stinging where it's already red and raw from Marty's grip as he forced me up onto the float. The King's Float, specifically, which feels ironic. It's the one that leads the Deus parade every Mardi Gras, and I can picture it perfectly as it rolls down the street: King Deus waving at his loyal subjects from his golden throne, sitting beneath a canopy of yellow and purple papier-mâché designed to look like billowing fabric, the gold leaf glinting in the sun.

It's kind of funny, in a sick and twisted way.

"Something amusing you, Piper?" Marty asks.

April shoots me a warning look. She's on the opposite side of the float, tied to the other harness pole—the wooden posts the riders hook themselves onto during the parade so they don't have one too many beers, go toppling off, and get run over by their own tractor. Coach Davis stands guard, April's camera slung over his shoulder. I hate that he took it from her.

Fear burrows deep into my stomach, but I force my face to stay relaxed.

"Nothing," I say. "Just, when I was little, I always used to ask my dad if I could ride in Deus when I got older, and he said it was only for boys, so this is kind of a vindication for me."

Marty gives me a cruel smile, walking toward the throne and running his fingers over the dusty arms. In the parades, the throne has always looked regal and magnificent, something fit for a real king. Up close, though, it's decaying. The paint is faded, the gold leaf crumpled and falling to the floor like dead leaves. Still, I wonder if this cheap approximation of royalty looks as real to Marty as it once did to me.

"You really did look lovely at the ball," he tells me, almost sadly. "Agreeable. Unassuming. It's a better look for you than this headstrong act you insist on carrying out." He turns to April, his hand slipping into his pocket. "And you. Well, if I didn't know any better, I'd almost think you were the perfect debutante. So . . . demure." When his hand appears again, it's gripping a Pierrot lighter. And maybe it's just the look on his face, but something deep inside me knows it's Margot's—the one he must have taken from her—as he flicks it open, letting the flame dance. "If only it weren't for your little habit of playing with fire."

April locks the lighter in her stare, and I can almost see the flame shifting in her eyes.

"You killed her," she growls, pulling at her ties again. "You—"

"Reed," Marty says, the way you'd instruct a trained dog.

He obeys quickly, drawing back a hand and slapping April across the face. I gasp as if he'd struck my own cheek, but April goes silent, stunned.

And I know, now, the way you know when something's about to crash to the floor, just far gone enough that you can't stop it: this is life-or-death. They killed Margot, covered it up, and they won't hesitate to do it again.

"Please, Detective Rutherford," I say in the soft patient voice Mom taught me, the one I use to hide how badly I want to throttle someone. The desperation is real enough that I'm not pretending when my eyes well with tears. "You don't have to do this. We don't even know what y'all were talking about before. Maybe if you can just explain, we can all—"

"Cut the bullshit." The words have the cool calmness of a blade, and I feel them slice through my whole body. "It's not as clever as you think."

So weakness won't work here. If that's the case, I won't go out with a whimper.

"You can't possibly think this is going to work out. What are you going to do? Kill us? How are you going to explain two more dead debutantes?"

Marty tuts. "You seem to forget, girls, that I'm a very reasonable man. And I'm always willing to reach an agreement." He clasps his hands behind his back, looking out over the floats like he's surveying his kingdom. "The way I see it, there are two choices. Either we come to an understanding . . . or you choose the alternate route. The path we had to take with a certain other Queen."

Marty turns to us, a self-satisfied look on his face, and I know exactly what he means. *Margot.* We aren't too high up, maybe ten feet, but I wonder if it would be enough. If I could get out of these ties, somehow, and if I'd have enough strength to shove him over. If his skull would crack against the concrete floor.

But I force the thoughts down, telling myself to focus. If this is a negotiation, then maybe, *maybe* I can get us out of this.

"What kind of understanding?" I ask.

"Smart girl." Marty smirks. "You were never here tonight. You've never seen or heard of the Pierrot. And, as we are all well aware, Margot Landry was a troubled girl who died a tragic, accidental death. And in return . . . we let you live."

The thought of breaking out of here and never looking at any of it again almost makes me weak with relief. But they still have Vivian, maybe Lily, too, and I know these people. I know how they work, and I'm too smart to believe it's as simple as walking away.

"That easy?" I ask.

He smiles softly. "This Krewe is a family, isn't it? And we protect our family. Of course, family also comes with certain obligations." The smile turns predatory, morphing him into a wolf with bared teeth. "You'll be monitored, just to make sure there aren't any slipups. Any deviations from our story."

"And if there are?"

There's a glint in his eyes, like this question truly delights him.

"It's a shame, really, when such promising young girls lose track of reality. But the signs are always there, once you start looking for them." Marty walks over to the side of the float, where he's stashed what looks like some kind of first-aid kit. He bends down to click it open, examining its contents as he continues in the same soft, almost distant tone. "Reckless behavior. Coaches and Heads of School expressing concern about their grip on reality. Evaluations from their psychiatrist that are, quite frankly, disturbing."

His eyes lock on mine, and my stomach turns. He's taunting me with what Dad did, the lies he wrote about Margot.

"Yes, we all should have seen it coming," Marty sighs, reaching into the kit and removing a small vial. "Poor April was so broken up about the overdose of her only friend that she chose to follow her in the best way she knew how." He sets the vial beside him, reaching into the kit again. "And poor Piper was so ashamed that Vanderbilt rescinded her acceptance after they found out what she'd done. It was the start of a downward spiral that never stopped."

Marty lifts his hand out of the case so I can see what he's holding: a syringe, the needle gleaming in the harsh overhead lighting.

"It was tragic," he says. "Tragic but unavoidable."

Hatred trickles into my blood, mixing with the fear until I'm poisoned with them both.

"That's how you killed her," I force out, eyes locked on the syringe. "Isn't it?"

Marty chuckles. "Quite a stroke of genius, although I can't take the credit. Reed was quick on his feet that night."

I watch it hit April at the same time it hits me. It was Coach. Coach killed Margot. I look to him for some kind of confirmation, but he only stares at the ground, face burning with shame. It's a far cry from his usual self, bounding around Beaumont with the goofy confidence of a family's treasured Labrador.

"Poor boy got a bit of a shock when he found my private messages with Margot," Marty continues. "I'd imagine he was none too pleased to see them, but every father has things he'd rather keep from his son, doesn't he?"

He gives Reed an almost affectionate look, and my stomach churns as the truth sinks in. It was Marty who brought Margot to the Pierrot, who manipulated her into thinking they were in a relationship. Distantly, it hits me that their age gap is similar to that of the twenty-year-old Deus Queens and their sixty-something Kings, and the thought makes me feel even sicker.

"Well, regardless, I'd already handled it. Things were getting too messy. Margot had gotten it in her head somehow that I'd leave my wife, and some of the brothers at the Pierrot were starting to catch on, so I ended it. Politely, of course. Like a gentleman. Her reaction, however, was rather . . . unladylike." Marty frowns. "Threatening to tell everyone about us, to make me look like a fool—to expose Reed's past, too, the unfortunate scandal at his former job. Of course, I knew she'd cool off eventually, but Reed . . . he took her threats to heart. And I can't blame him. I'd just set him up with a fancy little Beaumont job, hadn't I? And if this got out, he thought, if Margot went and tarnished our reputation . . . well, then. He'd certainly be in a bit of trouble."

I stare at Coach, but he's still glaring hard at the ground, neck and jaw tensed.

"So he decided to take matters into his own hands. Even though I had it *handled*." Marty sharpens the last word into a reprimand. "Reed took the phone, pretended to be me, and set up a meeting with Margot. And what happened then?"

He looks at Coach, waiting for him to answer.

"She was angry," Coach forces out. "Crazy. I just wanted to make her calm down and be quiet. I just wanted—"

He chokes out a sob, and Marty lays a hand on his shoulder.

"There, now. No need for that. We cleaned it all up, didn't we? With a little help from our dear friends at the Pierrot."

April shakes her head, her face warped in a mix of rage, disgust, and disbelief.

"And what were those 'friends' doing tonight?" she demands. "Are they seriously stupid enough to join your cult and cover up a murder just because you promised them a fake crown and their pick from a bunch of women who can't say no?"

Marty smiles. "My dear, I think you misunderstand. Tonight was a celebration of our brotherhood. Of Reed's return." He claps his son on the shoulder. "You see, after all of the Margot mess, Reed wanted to take a step back. Our cover story worked, of course, but I think he was afraid it was too . . . open-ended." Marty glances at Coach, who's still silent, face almost blank. "But now the police have their killer, and we can all rest easy. That's certainly a cause for celebration."

He grins, and my blood boils. *Their killer,* meaning Dad.

"Think of it as a passing of the proverbial baton, from father to son," Marty continues. "I even gave him my old mask. He wore it well, if I say so myself."

I want to scream, break out of these ties, and throttle him, but then I catch the look shining in Marty's eyes. Not just evil, but almost . . . proud.

Because that's what's underneath it all, the Pierrot and the lies: fathers protecting their sons. Dad only joined to save Wyatt from the consequences of his own actions. And Wyatt protected him right back—that's what he was doing as the Jester, wasn't it? Trying to keep Dad from going down for a murder he didn't commit. It's what Coach thought he was doing, too, when he killed Margot: saving his dad from his own mistakes. Men protecting each other, over and over and over again.

But we protect each other, too, the mothers and daughters. It may not be as loud or as bloody, but mine taught me how to make even the sweetest of smiles into a deadly weapon.

So I do exactly what she would: I straighten my shoulders and lift my dimpled chin.

"I think we're more than willing to come to an agreement," I say.

"Well." Marty lifts his eyebrows, surprised. "Good." He

looks to April, the syringe still gripped in his hand. "And what about you, dear? Does your clever friend speak for you both?"

Her eyes lift from the ground, searing into Marty with more hatred than you'd think a girl so small would be capable of holding.

"I think you're all sick," she says. "And I'd rather die than do a single thing you say."

Marty holds her stare for a moment, like he's bathing in her disgust. Like he likes the way it feels.

"Well, then. If you're sure." He turns to Coach. "I believe she's chosen option two."

Coach's eyes widen.

"Take it back," I order, but April won't look at me. "Tell them you don't—"

"She's made up her mind." Marty plunges the syringe into the vial, pulls the pump. He looks at Coach. "What do you say, son? Do the honors, for old times' sake?"

With gritted teeth, Coach takes the syringe.

"No," I plead. "April!"

She just stares, her shoulders rising and falling in time with the frantic pace of my heart as Coach moves toward her, the needle poised and glinting in his grip.

39

VIVIAN

JANUARY 3, 12:15 A.M.

I stare at Lily, dumbfounded. She's just explained it all, how Coach found Marty's burner and set up the meeting with Margot, how he killed her. Coach, the only adult at Beaumont I really trusted. Who pushed me, on and off the field. Who never bullshitted me.

Or so I thought. Because not even twenty-four hours ago, when I asked him if he saw anything at the ball, he looked me dead in the eyes and made up a whole story about Lily leaving in a black Mercedes. He acted sorry for not knowing more. Meanwhile, he knew exactly where Lily was. He *did* this. And I trusted him.

I know it's not her fault, but somehow, it still feels like it.

"How do you know all this?" I demand.

Lily tucks a strand of hair behind her ear, still so infuriatingly calm.

"After Margot died, I wasn't sure if I bought the whole overdose story, but I tried not to think about it. I told myself maybe she really *had* just gone off the deep end when Marty broke things off. And then I didn't get into Vanderbilt, and everything fell apart."

I stare at her, but she seems dead serious. "What does Vanderbilt have to do with this?"

"I never wanted to go," she says. "I didn't really know it until Piper submitted that crap essay with my application, but when I realized what she did . . . I was honestly relieved. I'd been basically killing myself to get in, and for what? My parents? So they could keep forcing me to live up to their expectations and then freaking out when I couldn't? But I still didn't know if the essay was enough to get me out of it. Not with my family's connections. So I tanked the interview." A little smile flickers on her lips, almost like she's proud, but it fades quickly. "But Dad found out. Of course he did. He called the admissions office as soon as I got my rejection and demanded an explanation."

In the mess of all the other lies, this one still hurts, somehow. Lily threw her interview. I thought she was devastated about getting rejected, but she didn't even want to go, and I had no idea.

"Once he figured out what I'd done, he was madder than I've ever seen him. Screaming. Threatening to cut me off, make me take a gap year and stay trapped at home while I reapplied. When he sent me to my room, he slammed the door so hard that the wood splintered." Lily's lip twitches, like she can still feel it. "And then, later that night, Marty came over. I could hear his voice downstairs. I waited up in my room until late, after my mom went to bed, and then, when I couldn't take it anymore, I snuck down. My dad and Marty were in his office. The door was shut, but I could hear them talking. They were trying to figure out how to get me back into Vanderbilt. Dad was worried another donation wouldn't be enough, so . . . Marty suggested they use the Pierrot."

Goose bumps break out over my skin.

"They were thinking about recruiting the director of admissions," Lily says. "Marty was digging into the guy's personal life to see if there was anything they could hold over him, but if not . . . the admissions guy had two sons. Marty said maybe they could plant pills on one of them, get them caught cheating at school, something like that. Something big enough that if they went to the admissions guy to offer the Pierrot's protection, he'd have to take it."

"Marty wanted to blackmail him?"

"At the Pierrot, they think of it more like an exchange of favors. Brothers supporting brothers." Her lip curls a little as she says it, like it does whenever she's annoyed but won't admit it. "Anyway, I don't know if they ever got around to it. I'd guess the whole Marty-kidnapping-me thing probably got in the way."

My stomach twists. Somehow, I almost forgot where we are, the dingy mattress and creepy Mardi Gras paraphernalia Lily's been living with for almost a week.

"What happened?" I ask. "How did he . . ."

"After I overheard them talking about the Pierrot, I knew I couldn't leave it alone," she says. "But I needed Dad to trust me again. So I acted all apologetic about the interview, and it worked. He forgave me. Or, at least, he and Mom were too focused on the ball to care about anything else. Then, while they weren't paying attention, I did some digging. I looked through Dad's computer for everything I could find about the Pierrot. And it took some convincing, but I even got Wyatt to sneak me in."

Hearing his name, the email hits me all over again, and so does the guilt. Lily is probably the one person who hasn't seen it. I know I should tell her, but the words won't come out. I can't lose her forever barely an hour after finding her again.

"And once I saw what goes on there . . ."

"I know," I cut in. "We went, too."

Lily nods, looking grateful that she doesn't have to explain it. "I asked some people there if they knew Margot. I had a feeling Marty brought her. But a few of the guys, when I mentioned Margot . . . they got all weird. I knew something was off, but I figured it was just because Les Masques girls weren't supposed to be there. But then, a few days later, I found the burner phone." She buries her hands deeper in her sleeves, wrapping them around herself. "It was in Coach's office. I figured he was probably in the Pierrot, too, so I looked through his stuff, and the phone was in his desk, just sitting there. I guess he was too stupid to ditch it. Or maybe he wanted something to hold over Marty."

A fresh wave of nausea hits. All the times in the past year that I've been in Coach's office, stopping by to ask about the game schedule or even just say hi . . . that burner must have been there. Proof that he killed her, just waiting for someone to find.

"Once I saw those texts, I knew for sure," Lily says. "I had to do something."

"So you came up with the stunt at the ball."

She raises an eyebrow, almost impressed.

"Wyatt told us that was you," I explain.

Now she looks annoyed again. "That was only part of it. I didn't tell him all the details, obviously, but it was supposed to be a distraction. They'd never suspect me of ruining my own big night, so of course they'd think someone else was behind it. I figured Wyatt would be a good fall guy if I needed one."

"A fall guy?" I repeat. "You used him."

She laughs. "Come on. It's not like he's innocent."

For a second, I'm frozen. Lily knows. Did she see the email somehow? Did she know all along? But then she brushes past it, and I realize that must not be what she meant at all.

"Anyway, the ball was only the first step. The real point was to have everyone so distracted that they wouldn't notice what I did next."

"You texted us to meet you at the Den," I guess, pushing down the guilt. "That was the next step?"

Lily nods. "I was going to tell y'all everything. You, April, and Piper. And then . . ." She pauses for long enough that I'm worried she's not going to say it. "I was going to leave."

"Leave?" I gape. "Like . . ."

"Like, run away. Drain my parents' bank account and get the hell out."

And there it is, straight from her mouth. She was going to run. Wyatt told me that Lily didn't care about me enough to tell me, and I wouldn't believe him. I *still* don't believe it.

"That doesn't make sense," I argue. "Why would you leave?"

"Because I didn't have a choice."

"That's not true. You could have told me what was going on. Or your parents. Or—"

"You don't get it, Vivian," she snaps, sharp enough to make me go quiet. "I couldn't do it anymore. This city. My family. They had my whole life planned out: graduate from Beaumont, go to Vanderbilt, be Queen of Deus when I'm twenty-one, which would be the highlight of my sad little life. Then I'd marry Wyatt or some richer, better version of him, have kids, force them to do Les Masques, and be miserable until it's time to bury me in the goddamn LeBlanc mausoleum. There was no other way out. Not unless I blew everything up and ran."

I watch her, the tears in her bright blue eyes. She means every word. I've always thought that from the moment she was born and brought back to that wedding-cake mansion on St. Charles Avenue, Lily had the perfect life. But the way she's describing it, perfect sounds a lot like hell.

But it doesn't make this any less ridiculous.

"So, what—you were going to drop this bomb on me, April, and Piper and then leave us to deal with the fallout?"

Lily wipes a tear away and looks at me hard.

"Y'all would know what to do. I knew you would. Piper's a supergenius, April's this secret badass, and you . . . Viv, you're like the strongest person I know."

Even with everything else she's said, everything she's done, those words melt over me like butter. But it only makes my next question hurt more.

"Then why didn't you give me a heads-up?" I ask. "If I'm supposed to be your best friend, why didn't you just tell me the truth?"

"I was going to," Lily argues. "But just before I left the ball, I got a text from this random number saying they knew what I was planning, and they had information that would change everything."

The text I saw her get outside of the country club. That must be what she's talking about.

"It was Coach and Marty," I realize.

Lily nods. "Obviously, I know that now. But I still didn't have all the proof I needed—not anything undeniable, something the Pierrot couldn't twist against us. So whoever sent that text, I figured maybe they could help. But I was careful about it. I mean, I thought so. I'd already stashed the burner in the darkroom for y'all, and I scheduled that email to send the next morning in case anything went wrong. And I'm glad I did. Because when I got to the Den to meet them . . ." She gestures around us. "Well, here we are."

And then I see it: her hand, creeping up to touch her still-missing necklace. She sees me catch it, and her hand drops quickly, but it's too late.

"There's something you're not telling me."

She laughs. "Well, that would only be fair, right? You've been keeping a pretty big one from me."

Everything stops. She knew. Of course she knew. I should try to explain, beg for forgiveness, but right now, I'm too ashamed even to respond. Even now, when it's already happening, I'm too afraid to watch our friendship burn.

But then it hits me: Lily doesn't even seem mad.

"I mean, it was obvious. Not like I care." She brushes a piece of lint off her sleeve. "I broke up with Wyatt after the ball, anyway. So, really, he's all yours."

Like he's her scraps, the out-of-season clothes she'll lend me, knowing they'll be sizes too small. And it's not even that I care that much about Wyatt, not really. I know, now, that I liked him less than I liked the idea of being with him, of being loved the way he loves Lily. But it's *because* he's so irrelevant that, with all the other bullshit and horror of tonight, I can't let it go.

And then I understand.

"You didn't make this whole plan because you thought me, April, and Piper would know what to do," I say. "You were scared of what would happen if you told everyone the truth, so you left it for us to deal with. You put us in danger so you wouldn't have to be." Finally, it dawns on me. "You were punishing us."

"So what if I was?" she explodes. "You screwed my boyfriend. Piper sabotaged my Vanderbilt essay and thought I wouldn't notice. April hated me for no reason, and Margot *still* liked her more than me. Maybe y'all deserved it." She stands, suddenly serious, and comes close enough to look up at me. "But if you think that's the only reason I did this, Viv, then you don't fucking know me at all."

"Yeah," I say, my voice scratchy. "Maybe I don't."

Before I can fully think through what I've just said, whether or not I mean it, I hear it. A scream.

I move to the door, ready to bang against it, but Lily's hand grips mine, stopping me. When I turn back to her, she's got the look she always gives me on the field when I'm getting too impulsive: *Slow down, Viv.*

"They have April and Piper," I whisper. "We have to do something."

"What are we supposed to do? We're trapped."

I press my ear to the door. I don't hear anything, and somehow, the silence is worse than anything. Before I can chicken out, I reach for the knob. Lily stiffens beside me.

"Wait," she says. "Don't—"

The door gives way, opening with a force so unexpected, I stumble back. For a second, I'm stunned, staring at the open door like it's some kind of fake-out, but no. It's real.

I turn to Lily, expecting her to be just as shocked, but the guilty look on her face tells me she knows what I should have from the moment the door opened.

It was never even locked.

40

APRIL

JANUARY 3, 12:25 A.M.

Coach Davis takes a step, and then another, close enough that I can see the sharp point of the needle, can almost feel it puncturing my skin. Piper screams, I think, but I can't be sure. It's like I'm here, but I'm not—in my body, and also above it all, watching it unfold with Margot by my side. Coach grips my arm, pinching the skin, and through the fear, the racing animal heartbeat of it, I think, *I did it, Margot. I didn't run away this time.*

And then, noise. A door opening. Someone running.

Coach's head whips toward the sound.

"Dad?" he asks, like Marty must be all-knowing.

But he's just as surprised. Marty runs to the side of the float, looking for the source of the sound.

"No," he says, eyes widening. "*No.* Reed—"

Marty doesn't get to finish the command, because a shout cuts him off.

"Don't fucking touch them!"

Vivian.

Icy pinpricks of relief wash over me, and now that I'm not seconds from death, I'm full of a burning need to live. I buck my legs, kicking Coach square in the balls, and he doubles over, the syringe falling from his grip.

Footsteps thunder up the float stairs. Marty grabs for the syringe, raising the needle just as Vivian appears on the deck like an avenging goddess in a ball gown.

Another pulse of relief. She's safe. She's okay.

And then I see the other girl behind her.

"I tried," Lily tells Marty. "She wouldn't listen."

Some part of me knew, and still, my brain won't make sense of it. Lily LeBlanc, here. Breathing. Looking at Marty and Coach like she's defeated, desperate. Like she's on their side.

"I called for help," Vivian says, glancing between Marty and Coach. "They'll be here any minute."

"Admirable effort," Marty says, calm as ever. "But unfortunately, that's quite impossible. I have all your phones."

Vivian clocks the syringe, and the realization drains the color from her face. "No. No, this is . . ."

With a disappointed sigh, Marty flicks a hand at Coach. "Tie them up, Reed."

Coach moves toward them, and for a moment, Vivian stays put, almost like she can't believe he'd really do this. Then he lunges. Vivian jerks away, rushing for the steps, but Coach catches her by the wrist, yanking so hard that she cries out. He pushes her up against the base of the throne, pinning her arms behind her as she fights beneath him.

"Stop," Lily shouts. "You're hurting her!"

"Then she should stop fighting," Marty says plainly. When Vivian doesn't, he adds, "Would you like to choose which of your friends dies first?"

It's then that Vivian goes limp. Not just her body, but her expression, too, like all the fight has gone out of her. She watches with a look of numb betrayal as Coach zip-ties her to another support pole. He doesn't meet her eyes, just pulls the cords tighter than he needs to, like he's trying to prove that he can—whether to himself, Marty, or the rest of us, I can't be sure. He tugs the ties to make sure they're secured, and then he turns to Lily, who holds out her wrists willingly with a vacant, broken stare.

"You're working with them," I say through dry lips.

Lily doesn't look at me. Marty smirks in her direction.

"Lily has been very well behaved," he says. "She knows what's good for her."

Coach pulls the ties taut around Lily's wrists, but she stays silent. Maybe I shouldn't be surprised, but still, my chest burns at her betrayal.

"Now," Marty says, "here's how this is going to work. No one talks unless I've given you permission. You're all going to behave like perfect ladies. Understood?" He waits. "*Understood?*"

The word is like a bullet. We all nod.

"Good." He turns to Lily. "Care to explain why you've failed at your only job?"

Lily's lip quivers, and even now, I can't tell how much of it is an act.

"Y'all are taking this too far," she whimpers. "You said you'd let me go if I—"

"I asked you a question."

She lets out a frustrated huff. "Reed didn't even lock the door. It was open. I couldn't fight her."

Marty pinches the space between his eyebrows, like this is all just a nuisance.

"Reed?" he asks, without even looking at Coach. "Is that true?"

Coach blanches. He looks at the ground. "We said we didn't want her to feel trapped."

Marty scoffs.

"My parents will find out about this," Lily speaks up again. "They'll realize what you're doing, and they'll—"

"Shut your mouth, you stupid girl. You think they're coming to save you?" Marty laughs again. "Then where are they?"

Lily sobs, and some tiny, fractured part of me thinks that maybe this is the reality check she deserves, before I remember where we are. What's at stake.

Coach takes a careful step toward Marty. "We said we'd—"

His voice is sharp and loud, turning like a sudden gust of wind. "Have you stopped for one moment to think and realize, somewhere in that thick head of yours, that maybe things have changed?"

The silence hangs heavy, and I realize how cold it is, the high tin ceilings of the warehouse trapping the cool night air.

Beside me, Piper raises her bound hands like she's waiting to be called on in class. I feel another stab of betrayal low in my gut. How quickly she was willing to give up, to be the good little Maid they want her to be.

"Detective Rutherford?" she tries, when he still hasn't noticed her. "I'm still ready to reach an agreement. I think we can all—"

"Shut up!" he roars, making her cower. "Let me think. I can't *think* with all of your noise."

All of us, even Coach, go quiet, giving him exactly what he wants. And I don't understand. There are *four* of us. We're smaller, maybe, and he has the syringe, but we're double in number. They only tied our hands. We can't just sit here, staying quiet so this man can have the time he needs to *think*. Waiting until he inevitably decides to sacrifice us to save his own skin.

So don't wait, Margot's voice rings in my head.

And this time, I listen.

"Hey, Coach." I look him dead in the eyes. "I said I didn't want your agreement."

"Quiet," Marty orders, but I ignore him, laser-focused on Coach.

"You too much of a coward to kill me?"

"She's baiting you," Marty says, but I watch his grip tighten on the syringe. "Ignore her."

"I want him to say it to my face," I push. "I want him to tell me he's too scared to kill me. Even though Margot was no problem, right? What's different this time? Are you afraid Daddy won't clean up your mess again?"

"Give it to me," Coach says, holding his hand out for the syringe.

"Reed—"

"Give it."

Marty watches his son, tracking Coach's face like he's trying to make sure this isn't a bluff. Then, with a resigned, almost amused look, he hands it over. My heart shudders, every atom of me vibrating with awareness of the needle's sharp point as Coach takes a step toward me.

"April," Vivian croaks.

I can feel Piper's and Lily's stares, too, their silent screams for me to stop, but I ignore them, doing instead what I learned from them both: I lift my chin. Roll my shoulders back, like a queen balancing her crown.

"Just one question first."

Coach pauses, and I feel it surge through me—the power of stopping a man with just my voice.

"Does she haunt you?" I ask. "Because she haunts me. Every night. All the little things I remember. Her laugh. The way her voice got kind of raspy from singing too loud or talking too much." My throat is burning now, but I keep going. "Or the way her boots sounded on the ground, like she was never afraid to make noise. The way she could walk right up to someone and say exactly what she thought like it was the easiest thing in the world."

Another twitch, another crack in his mask.

"I'm asking," I say, "because I want to know how you get through it. How you sleep at night. How you live with yourself, carrying all this guilt around, knowing you killed a girl to protect a father who doesn't even give a shit about you."

"That's not true," Coach says weakly.

I laugh. "Bullshit."

"Stop it."

"Reed," Marty warns.

"You think he cares?" I ask Coach. "You killed for him. If he loves you so much, then why wouldn't he take the fall instead of blaming it on someone else?"

Coach turns to look at Marty, uncertainty flooding his face. "Dad . . ."

"She's getting in your head," Marty hisses. "I saved your life, didn't I? I got you out of this mess. I cleared your name."

"But it was *his* mess," I tell Coach. "Marty started it. You're only mixed up in all this because he couldn't keep his hands off an underage girl. And did he ever once thank you for risking everything to protect him? Or did he just try to make you think it was all your fault?"

The look on Coach's face melts from doubt to woundedness, and I know it's working. I'm getting to him. But Marty just laughs.

"Reed, come on. You don't actually think—" He steps toward him, but Coach flinches. And just like that, Marty's easy, confident mask falls away to reveal a burning rage. "Are you seriously stupid enough to fall for this?"

Coach looks back at me, a wild desperate look in his eyes, and I know this could be the end, but I have to try. If I'm going, it won't be as a good little debutante.

"Are you?" I ask.

And then he lunges. Coach lifts the syringe above his head, aiming the needle directly at his father's neck.

41

VIVIAN

JANUARY 3, 12:30 A.M.

It happens in one swift motion: Marty grabs Coach's arm, forcing it away before the needle can plunge into his skin. Coach rears back like he's going to try again, but then, just as suddenly, he drops his arm to his side and starts to sob.

"I'm sorry," Coach cries. "I'm sorry."

Marty pulls him close. Even though Coach is taller, he shrinks, curling into his dad's chest in a way that's so different from the Coach I know. Still, I see a glint of him in there, too: the Coach who can give an intimidating glare one second and then a soft, goofy smile the next, like we're all in on the joke, because we know he'd never hurt a fly.

"It's okay," Marty says softly. "Give it here, son."

Coach hands over the syringe without a fight.

"It's okay. You're okay." Marty's voice is soothing and a little sad, like he's comforting a kid.

He lifts the syringe.

"Coach!" I scream, but it's too late.

Marty buries the syringe in his son's arm and pushes the plunger.

It's slow, like something moving underwater. Coach starts to stumble, knees buckling, and Marty reaches out to catch him, lowering him to the ground.

"There," he says, still so gentle it makes my skin prickle. "There you go."

Coach's head lolls, his eyes fluttering, and even though I know who he really is now, the things he's done, some part of me wants to save him.

"My son was an addict," Marty says.

At first, I don't get it, but then I recognize his tone. It's the same one he used when he told us that Lily had probably run away. Already, he's spinning his cover story as easily as if it were the kind of fairy tale she always hated.

"He was a good man, but a sick one. I only wish I could have saved him." Marty reaches for the vial and sticks the syringe back into its cap, refilling it. He looks at me. "And I wish, more than anything, that I could have saved those girls."

I fight to break the ties around my wrists, but I'm stuck, trapped here as Marty examines the syringe.

"It's tragic, what happened to them all, but you have to understand." He holds it high, so the needle glints in the light. "It's a sickness."

My mind starts to spin. There are four of us. If we can break out and run, he'll come after us, but he can't get all of us, can he? If I put myself in his path first, let the others get a head start . . .

"Three Maids and their beautiful Queen," he says, almost like it's a nursery rhyme. "Who first?"

Across the float, I catch Piper bringing her hands to her face, clasping them together like she's praying. I didn't think she was religious, but maybe we all start to turn to some version of God when we're facing death. Because that's what's happening, isn't it?

And then I realize: Piper's not praying. She's pulling on her zip ties with her teeth. Tightening them, so tight the skin around them goes white.

I look at Marty.

"I'll go first," I tell him.

Lily gasps. "No."

I reach for her hand and squeeze it, hoping she'll understand. Because even though she betrayed us, and I betrayed her, too, I'm not letting her die. Marty won't bury any more dead girls.

I glance at Piper, who gives a small nod. As Marty turns to face me, she raises her hands slowly above her head.

"How brave of you," he says, stepping toward me with the needle raised. "I'm so very sorry it has to be this way, Vivian."

With a growl, Piper pulls her wrists down, hard, like she's plunging an invisible knife into her stomach. The zip ties snap, and she's free. Marty turns in surprise, just in time for me to slide-tackle his legs out from under him.

He hits the ground, the syringe falling from his grip. As he reaches for it, I slam my foot down on his fingers.

Piper grabs the syringe and tosses it to the side as she darts to Coach and starts to feel around his pockets. He's still breathing, I think, but barely.

Marty crawls to his knees, and I kick him in the stomach, my wrists stinging as the zip ties cut into my skin. He howls in pain but recovers fast, swinging his fist out and cracking it against my jaw. The blow makes me rear back, my teeth clacking together.

"Car keys," I manage through the shock, but Piper's already

got them from Coach's pockets. She rushes back to April, sawing away with the keys at her zip ties until they snap.

My break in concentration costs me. Marty is back on me with even more force, knocking my head against the post I'm tied to before his hands find my neck. He squeezes tighter, his thumbs pressing so hard into my veins and muscle that I'm afraid something will snap.

And then, suddenly, air. I gasp a lungful as April clings to Marty's back, her camera strapped to her shoulder again, back where it belongs. She's scratching and pulling, feral. Exactly the opposite of what he thought she was. In the scuffle, she presses the keys into my palm, and I slice at my ties until they break, the impact pushing me forward.

"Here," Piper calls, crouching beside Lily.

I toss her the keys just as Marty claws out of April's grip. He wheels around, unsteady, and for a second, I think we've won. That maybe he's about to give up and run.

We all spot the syringe at the same time. It's on the ground, rolled almost to the edge of the float. The plunger's only half-pushed. There's still liquid inside, and I'm not sure if it's enough, but there's no time to wonder.

I get there first, but Marty isn't far behind. On the other side of the float, I hear Lily's zip ties snap.

And then Marty is on me, knocking me back into the side of the float. The impact sends a firework of pain across my skull, and I lose my grip on the syringe. He gets it before I can recover, closing it firmly in his grasp and then snatching my arm, pinching the skin.

I'm numb as I realize that this could be the last thing I see. I might be seconds away from death, and I'm not focused on Sav's laugh, or Lily's grin, or Dad's hugs, or Mom's ferocious cheer whenever I get the ball out from under the other team's player and send it flying down the field. I'm not focused on Piper and April and this weird little group we've formed, a friendship that, a few months ago, I would have laughed at because it sounded so absurd.

Instead, I can't focus on anything but Marty's red face, his hot breath, and the cold certainty in his eyes that whatever he wants, he'll get, because this world is his kingdom and it's all for the taking.

Then, just before he plunges the syringe into my skin, there's a click from somewhere behind him.

"Get away from her," Lily orders, and I see something silver shine in her hand. Margot's lighter, slipped from his pocket, the fire dancing.

Marty cranes his head to look at her.

"I'm serious." Lily takes a step toward him. "I'll light it up. Everything."

He laughs. "You wouldn't."

Lily smiles, perfect as ever, as she moves toward the throne, reaching out to touch its glittery draping.

"That's the thing, though," she says, looking at the floats all around us, the monsters and kings, but the sirens and witches, too, the women with the power to make men tremble. "It's all made of paper."

Like a queen waving her scepter, Lily dips the flame and sets the throne on fire.

42

PIPER

JANUARY 3, 12:35 A.M.

It catches fast, snaking from the chair up to the papier-mâché canopy, giving the throne a burning crown. Marty looks on, stunned, and for a moment, I'm just as rooted to the spot, watching it burn.

Then Lily races past Marty and down the steps of the float, and I snap out of it. This isn't just destruction for destruction's sake. It's our chance to escape.

I run after her, April and Vivian right behind me, as Marty scrambles for one of the fire extinguishers stashed on the floats to prevent this exact catastrophe. I jump down to the warehouse floor, a wild laugh rushing out of me. Because Lily was right. They made their little kingdom out of paper. It was always going to burn.

I glance back up at the float, where Marty is spraying the fire, his eyes wide with panic. He turns, seeing us, and I watch the battle playing out behind his stare: stop the blaze, or catch the runaway girls?

"Come on," Lily urges.

She's running toward the next float, lighter in hand. I spot

April making her way toward one of the tractors at the center of the warehouse, the ones that pull the floats on Mardi Gras Day. April reaches down to pick up something beside it, and when I realize what it is, my heart almost stops.

A gas canister.

Not only is the kingdom made of paper, but they literally gave us the accelerant.

April sloshes gas onto the nearest float, the sharp smell reaching deep into my nose. Taking April's lead, Lily searches for another gas canister, and I glance over my shoulder at the float. Vivian hasn't made it down yet. She's still hovering on the steps, watching Coach.

"Vivian," I call. "Let's go."

"We can't leave him here," she says.

But Marty has gotten control of the fire on the throne, leaving it a blackened husk, and now he's running toward her.

"Vivian," I urge.

She leaps off the float as April hands me another canister. I take it, running deeper into the warehouse, pouring gas as I go. Haphazard, careless, no goal except destruction. Behind me, I hear a fire roar to life.

I stop when I get to the Fool's Float.

The flames are raging around us, close enough that I can feel the heat on my skin, but for a moment, I'm frozen, lost in the memories of this float.

When we were small, Wyatt and I used to watch the parade from our Mardi Gras ladder—the ones parents buy and line up on the streets to give their kids a coveted view, higher than everyone else who didn't have the funds or the foresight. Mom stood on the rungs behind us, ready to keep us safe if we stretched our hands out too far to catch the good throws. Not that we needed to worry—because as soon as Dad saw us, he'd toss us a plastic bag full of all the best stuff: stuffed animals and feathered spears, light-up footballs and Moon Pies. I loved how it felt, being up so high, knowing that, even though he was hidden by the mask, all the other kids could tell that that was *our* dad up there, saving all the best stuff for us. That he was special, so we were special.

But he wasn't. He was just trapped in a gilded cage of his own making, pulling us in with him because he thought it made us safe.

I rear back and throw the rest of the gasoline over the float. Lily's right behind me with the lighter, and it ignites. Flames crawl from the jester's face to the baubles at the end of its hat and then stretch even farther, licking at the gold leaf and the decorative flowers dotting the float's rim, making the petals shrivel and curl.

"Stop!"

I spin back around at Marty's agonized shout. He stands in the center of the warehouse, drenched in sweat, his button-down rumpled.

We're all spread out around the rows of floats, taking in the havoc we've wrought. Most of the floats have caught fire, the flames spreading from one to the other with the speed and viciousness of Southern gossip, climbing all the way up to the golden Deus flags dangling from the ceiling, one for each year of the parade. The whole room is thick with the smell of gasoline, smoke, and melting plastic.

There's a wailing sound somewhere in the distance, and it takes me a moment to recognize it. Sirens, growing closer.

Marty coughs, taking another haggard step toward us.

"Do you have any idea what you've done?" he demands.

"Centuries of history. Your family legacy, and you've destroyed it. You'll pay for this. You'll—"

There's a sizzling sound, a mechanical buzz, and then a new angry burst of flame on the warehouse wall, and I remember that this kingdom isn't just made of paper. There are outlets, wiring, all of it as dusty and outdated as the warehouse itself.

"We need to get out," I yell. "Now!"

No one hesitates. The four of us race toward the exit as fire crackles and pops behind us, sparks falling, and still, even as we're running for our lives, I have this fierce, inexplicable thought that I've never felt freer. Three unruly Maids and their vicious Queen, leaving the burning castle behind them, letting it crumble.

The sirens are closer now, red and blue lights flashing through the warehouse door. Just before I get there, I risk a look behind me. Marty stands a few feet away, staring up at the throne, which is burning again, the fire untamable. My stomach lurches as I realize Coach Reed is still up there. Maybe still breathing, still fighting against the drugs Marty forced into his system.

I watch the same realization hit him, twisting his face with horror.

At least, I think it's Coach he's thinking of. Because, as I watch him take it all in—the flames, the floats, the ruined kingdom he never got to rule—there's a part of me that wonders if those are the things he really can't leave behind.

It's a part of me that I choose to silence, snuffing it out like a flame pinched between my fingers. I tell myself it's his son he's thinking about, the chance to save a life, even if it won't make up for the one they took, as he turns and runs back into the burning warehouse.

And then I sprint outside without looking back.

43

APRIL

JANUARY 3, 1:00 A.M.

When it's all over, the outside of the Den looks almost like the aftermath of a parade. Police lights wash the side of the warehouse in red and blue, and the parking lot is littered with some of what the fire department was able to salvage after they put out the blaze: bags of beads and other throws, old costumes and Deus records from their ancient paper filing system. Even now, they're afraid to let it burn completely. I guess it makes sense. Marty wasn't wrong when he said we set centuries of history on fire. It's not so easy to let that go.

A small crowd has formed, too, like the paradegoers who linger on the streets long after the floats have finished rolling. Police, firefighters, and, until a few minutes ago, the EMTs who wheeled Coach and Marty into the ambulance before speeding away, sirens blaring. They're both alive, at least for now—though I heard the word "critical" as they rolled Coach by in his gurney.

The police are talking to Lily first. She's standing across the parking lot with two officers and both her parents, a blanket wrapped around her shoulders like something out of a TV show: missing girl in shock, reunited with her family, who can't keep their eyes or their arms off of her, like they're terrified she'll vanish again.

It's still burned into the film of my memory, the way Mrs. LeBlanc looked when she got here. She pulled Piper, Vivian, and me into a hug much fiercer than I'd expect from someone so dignified, and when she let go, there was a fire in her eyes as real as the one we'd left behind. *Thank you,* she'd said, and then again, like maybe we hadn't understood. *Thank you.*

It should be heartwarming, but I'm still stuck on the way Lily talked to Marty and Coach. Their good little captive. In the end, I know she was the one to light the flame, but I wonder if she still would have done it if they hadn't tied her up with the rest of us. If they'd offered her another way out.

"That was pretty badass with the zip ties," Vivian tells Piper, bringing me back to here, our little cluster in the parking lot.

Piper shrugs, but she can't hide the proud look on her face. "My mom sends me a lot of 'what to do if you get kidnapped' videos. I guess they came in handy."

Vivian laughs. "Point one for Mrs. Johnson."

Piper smiles, but it fades quickly. I get it. Mrs. Johnson knew about the cover-up of Margot's murder, and the thought of seeing her makes me almost sick with dread. I can only imagine what it must be like for Piper, knowing her entire family was a part of this.

"You okay?" Vivian asks me, reading the worry on my face.

"You've been quiet," Piper adds.

"I'm always quiet."

"Yeah, but the part where we almost died tonight is new, smart-ass," Piper says with a tenderness that warms me from the inside.

I shrug. "Nothing decades of therapy can't fix."

"I mean, we were kind of already headed in that direction," Vivian says. "Comes with the whole debutante thing."

For a beat, we're quiet. And then, with a sudden ferocity, Piper pulls us both into a hug. It shocks me, at first, but then I relax into it, squeezing back.

"Hey," she says, sounding uncharacteristically self-conscious. "When we get to school again, are we still friends?"

"Wait, are we *friends*?" Vivian jokes.

"Yeah, I don't do friends," I add.

"Y'all are rude," Piper says, but there's a huge grin on her face.

A car turns into the parking lot, and for half a second, I'm petrified. Even now, knowing Marty and Coach have been caught, I can't shake the fear that more Pierrot men could appear from the shadows, their eyes familiar and threatening behind the masks.

But then Piper straightens, clearly recognizing the car just as Aiden Ortiz climbs out of the driver's seat.

He runs right to her, crushing her into a hug as tight as the one she just gave us.

"You almost gave me a heart attack," he says.

"Hello to you, too." Her voice is muffled by his shirt.

Vivian looks at me with a lifted eyebrow. I return a devious smile.

"Are y'all okay?" Aiden asks, his gaze lifting from Piper to us.

"Yeah," I say. "I think so."

"Did Piper call you?" Vivian asks Aiden, with a look of mischievous delight.

"No, I—" Piper stops, eyes widening. "Oh my god. You location-stalked me."

"You never texted," Aiden says. "And then I called a bunch, and you didn't answer, so . . ." He gestures at the police. "I may have gone overboard. But in my defense, it was clearly worth it."

Piper stares at him, stunned. Then she grabs his face with both hands and kisses him.

Vivian and I gape at each other.

"Holy shit," she says.

"Holy shit," I echo.

Piper pulls back, one arm still around Aiden as she turns to give us both a death stare. "Don't look so proud of yourselves."

Someone clears their throat, and we all turn to find Lily standing beside us, the blanket still around her shoulders. Despite everything, she still manages to look like her usual queenly self. Leave it to Lily LeBlanc to have good posture even after being rescued from a kidnapping.

"Hi." She looks to Aiden. "Mind if we . . . ?"

"Yeah, sure." He gives Piper's hand a squeeze. "I'll wait by my car."

We all turn to Lily, waiting as her hands tighten around the blanket's edge.

"I just wanted to say thanks. And . . . I'm sorry. I—" Her eyes fall. "I know what it looked like back there, but I was there for days, and they got into my head. They said if I cooperated, they'd let me go. I was just trying to survive, and I—" She chokes up, blinking fast like she's trying not to cry. "Y'all saved me. And I'm not sure if I deserve it."

For a breath, no one moves. And then Vivian pulls Lily into the kind of hug that seems like only Vivian can give: fierce, protective, like all is forgiven, and maybe it is, at least for her. There are intricate threads to their friendship that

I don't understand, ones that maybe even this can't break. Maybe that's all it takes.

"Shut up," Vivian says lovingly, squeezing Lily tighter. "Just don't ever disappear again. I need you to kick my ass at practice."

Lily laughs with a particularly unladylike snort. She pulls back, and her eyes meet mine.

"Here." She holds out something for me to take. Margot's lighter, I realize, as the cool metal brushes my palm. "You were always a better friend to her than I was. And I know I said some stuff to her about you, and I'm sorry. I think I was . . . I don't know. Afraid she loved you more. Because I think she did. All the way to the end."

I look down at the lighter, my throat tightening. All this time, Lily and I were afraid of the exact same thing. It doesn't make me forgive her, but at least I think I understand. I close my hand around the lighter, letting the ridges of the Pierrot logo press into my skin, tattooing them there.

Then I hand it back to Lily.

"Keep it," I say, reaching to grip my camera strap.

Maybe because I think she needs it more than me. Because I don't want to remember Margot only by that night, the fire we never lit. Or maybe because I know I carry enough of her with me already—the memory of her laugh, her boldness, the way she struck me like a flint, sparking something that hasn't died.

Lily brings the lighter close to her chest. "Thanks."

Piper shifts, and I notice that, for the first time maybe ever, she looks out of her element.

"I'm sorry," she says in a weirdly professional tone. "About the essay. I shouldn't have—"

"It's okay," Lily says. "Honestly, I never wanted to go there anyway. And I'm sure Dad can get it all sorted out with the admissions people, so you don't lose your spot. We owe you, after you . . . you know. Saved my life."

For a moment, Piper looks unusually lost for words. Then she gives a distinctly Piper-like nod.

"Thank you," she says. "I'd appreciate it."

A white BMW pulls into the lot, and we all turn to squint at the headlights. Mrs. Johnson steps out of the driver's side as Wyatt gets out of the other. For a moment, I watch uncertainty flicker over Piper's face.

But then, in an instant, it melts away. Piper rushes toward her family as they run to her, meeting in the middle in a tangle of arms and tears. Watching Piper's mom, the way she holds her close, speaking gentle words into her hair, I think I can understand it, why her parents did what they did. They thought they were protecting their kids—just like Coach thought he was protecting Marty, like Marty protected him back. When you grow up in a place like this, so suffocated by secrets and ghosts and the threat of rising water, it's hard not to grab what you can and hold on for dear life when the flood starts to come.

I understand it, but that doesn't mean I forgive them.

That doesn't mean that I completely forgive myself.

Vivian shifts beside me, and I realize she's not looking at Piper anymore. She's looking at Coach's car, still parked in the lot.

"Do you think he'll be okay?" she asks.

Another flash of him stalking toward me, the needle raised. I close my eyes, try to reset my brain, remind myself he isn't here.

"I don't know," I tell her.

Vivian takes a breath, her eyes still locked on the car.

Lily shakes her head. "Don't do that."

"What?" Vivian asks.

"Blame yourself. If you didn't go all *Kill Bill* on Marty, we might not have made it out of there. And Coach . . ." She presses her lips together. "We shouldn't feel sorry for him."

Vivian doesn't look convinced.

"It's okay, though," I tell her. "To feel sorry, anyway. For the person you thought he was."

Vivian turns to me. "Can I say something corny, and we'll never speak of it again?"

"What?"

"I like it when you talk. You have some pretty good things to say."

Warmth spills through my chest, as embarrassingly genuine as the smile on my face, but before I can form some sort of insufficient response, another car pulls into the lot. When I recognize it, my breath catches.

"April!" Dad calls, climbing out.

I've only taken a few steps toward them before both my parents are wrapping me in a tight hug that smells like home, Dad's pine-scented car air freshener mixed with Mom's rose perfume. I don't even register what they're saying—only that they're here, and I'm safe.

A throat clears, and I turn to see one of the officers, who looks sorry for breaking up this reunion.

"Would you mind answering a few questions, April?" he asks.

My parents look at me, and I nod. Mom reaches down to squeeze my hand as Dad lays his on my shoulder, giving a protective pulse.

Across the parking lot, Vivian is mushed in a three-way hug with Lily and Sav, her parents nearby. They must have gotten here when I was lost with my own. Piper is with Aiden, Wyatt, and Mrs. Johnson, who eyes Aiden skeptically in the way all moms look at boys who've kissed their daughters in parking lots. Still, her pinched expression softens as she reaches to brush a speck of something from Piper's shoulder, gently smoothing out her sleeve.

There will be conversations, I know. Hard ones, with apologies and questions and answers that may not be enough. But for now, it's just this: all the people we love, here to collect us from the ashes.

And here, in this dingy mess of a parking lot, I think I see a glimmer of it: how Margot saw this city. The part that made it home. The part I need to hold on to, even though I know what this place did to her, and I understand with even sharper resolution, now, all that's broken here. The things I still want to leave behind.

How do you love a home that's sinking?

Somewhere, I think I hear her answer.

Isn't that kind of the point?

For a moment, I lean into my parents' touch, letting it hold me there, floating at the surface. I hold my camera close, too, the evidence still there and waiting for me to develop.

And then I step toward the officer.

"What do you want to know?" I ask.

This time, it will be the truth.

5 Months Later

LILY

The Queen dress still hangs in my closet where I left it, wrapped in plastic to keep out the dust. It feels weird, to be eighteen and already owning one of those dresses—overly expensive, sentimental, the kind I'll never wear again.

I have two of them, actually.

I step in front of the full-length closet mirror and smooth out my graduation dress, enjoying the way it hugs my hips, the white lace fluttering over the corseted top like snow. Beaumont has this weird tradition where we don't graduate in caps and gowns. Instead, we wear white—the girls in long dresses, the boys in suits, like we're at some kind of Southern child wedding. Or a debutante ball.

I twist one of the loose curls hanging around my face, making sure it has that artful accidental look instead of something I intentionally crafted. When I'm satisfied, I move to my necklace, the diamond teardrop Mom and Dad got me for my thirteenth birthday. It feels right, having it back where it's meant to be, framed by my collarbone.

"You're tangled in the back." Mom has materialized in the doorway in her graduation outfit, a designer linen jumpsuit, lightweight to withstand the heat, which is supposed to climb up to the nineties today. Why Beaumont insists on holding graduation outside, I'll never know. Unless it's a calculated move to torture its students one last time.

"Fix it?" I ask her.

"Of course." Mom steps behind me, her cool fingers brushing my neck as she straightens out the necklace chain.

Watching us there in the mirror, I'm hit with a memory: Mom sitting next to me on that gross mattress in the storage room, the necklace in her hand.

The girls found this here, she told me. *They're suspecting things.*

I didn't respond. I was still angry back then. I still didn't understand why they'd done it—even though some part of me knew, even before I walked into the Den on the night of the ball and found them waiting there, that it was my parents on the other side of those anonymous texts. That they'd known about my plan all along.

Vivian was right, in the end, with her weird little lie detector. There was something I was keeping from her. But can she really blame me? I learned it from the best.

The truth is, I never found the burner phone in Coach's office. I was kind of surprised when Vivian bought that it was just conveniently in his desk, sitting there like a smoking gun. But sometimes, I guess we'd all rather accept the easy stories.

The real one is much harder to swallow.

It happened when I looked through Dad's stuff. I wasn't lying about that. I broke into his computer, checked the emails, the texts, looking for anything about the Pierrot.

And then I opened his safe.

I knew where he kept it in the closet, locked with a passcode I'd seen him punch in countless times. He didn't have to be secretive around me. I was his perfect daughter. He trusted me.

I figured I'd just find his guns, maybe Mom's jewelry, nothing out of the ordinary. Still, it couldn't hurt to be thorough.

When I punched in the code and cracked the safe open, it was like the whole room started to sink.

Inside was not only the burner, but evidence. Piles of it. Printed emails and text exchanges between my dad and Marty on the night Margot died, explaining it all. Proving what maybe I should have guessed all along: Dad was in on it. After Coach killed her, Marty went to my dad for help, and he agreed. *Anything for our brothers,* Dad had said. It was his idea to implicate Dr. Johnson, to make him write the fake report. And he'd kept the proof—maybe a sick kind of souvenir, I thought. Or more likely a plan B, just in case he had to throw his *brother* under the bus.

Whatever the reason, that was the moment it all changed. When I knew I had to run.

If only I'd known how impossible that really was.

This isn't you, Dad had told me the night they caught me at the Den. *You just need to stay here for a while. Take some time to become yourself again.*

I wanted to scream. I wanted to throw it in his face, what I knew he'd done. But the words wouldn't come.

Because he was right, I realized. What was I thinking? My plan was ridiculous. Even if I had run away, my parents would have found me, or the money would have run out, or I would have realized what I already knew deep down: LeBlancs always win. We're untouchable, no matter how dark things get. No matter how many sins we commit.

This city is our kingdom, and here they were, offering me a life raft. A chance to come back home.

So I told them everything—where I'd hidden the burner for

the Maids to find, what I'd been planning, all of the evidence I'd gathered and how to destroy it.

Because the truth is, it was easier that way. I'd always been trapped. This was just a new castle. Once I realized that, the shutting of the storage-room door started to sound like the click of my old night-light. Permission to sleep while someone else stands guard against the monsters.

"You look beautiful," Mom says, the necklace hanging perfectly now.

"Thanks." I touch the diamond, smiling a little.

Vivian might have picked up on my tell, but I've gotten better at hiding it. Better at perfecting our story: yes, it was Marty and Coach who kidnapped me. No, I don't feel sorry that they're in prison. Not one bit.

And I don't, to be clear. When my parents brought Coach and Marty in to keep an eye on me at the Den, I thought about fighting it. They were murderers. Dad knew it, *I* knew it, and so did Mom, I'm pretty sure. But then I remembered: technically, Dad is a murderer, too. Or, at least, an accomplice. Still, every time he came to the storage room to bring me a warm blanket or my favorite po-boy for dinner, I knew—Dad thought he was protecting me. That's why he was keeping me there. That's why he called Marty. The Pierrot, their brotherhood, was sacred to him, and I think he trusted that it meant Marty wouldn't hurt me.

So did I, at first.

And maybe that should have made me brave enough to run when I had the chance, before Coach drugged Vivian, and Piper and April came storming in to break us out.

The thing is, sometimes it's just as hard to escape when the door is wide open.

"Y'all ready?" Dad asks, appearing from the hall.

"Just about," Mom answers, smoothing my hair and giving me a quick kiss on the head.

Dad steps into the mirror frame, completing our perfect little family portrait.

"How does it feel to be an almost graduate?"

He squeezes my shoulder. I try not to flinch, smiling instead.

"Weird," I say. "Good."

It's an easier answer than the truth, which is a lot more complicated, even if everything did work out, at least on the surface. The Pierrot is disbanded, but my family is okay. Dad's safe full of evidence came in handy: in exchange for his testimony, he got off scot-free. He didn't get named in the official exposé, either—but I wouldn't be surprised if it took some well-timed donations to make that happen. Piper's dad is okay, too, after they gave him the same deal.

Not so much for Marty. I do wonder, sometimes, if Dad regrets turning his best friend in, but it's like he said: Marty had been a liability for a long time, always pushing for more power, for the chance to be King. It was better this way, with him gone.

So the fairy tale has a happy ending, for once. The bad guys are gone, the dragons are slayed. The Queen and her Maids are free. Piper got to keep her spot at Vanderbilt, thanks to me. Once I swore she didn't sabotage my application, Dad got it sorted out pretty quickly.

April's off to the photography program at NYU. I don't know how long-distance will work out with Renee—they got together a couple months after everything happened at the Den—but they seem happy. April deserves it, I know, even if we'll never be the best of friends. There was never any proof about her vandalism, either—not after Mom and Dad wiped the database of security footage at the Den to cover up their own secrets.

Vivian is heading to Miami, with plans to play soccer. She also won't be too far from Sav, who surprised no one by getting into FSU's supercompetitive musical-theater program. It took some time, but we're all friends again—just maybe not as close as before. Because even though neither of us has a thing for Wyatt anymore, I haven't forgotten the way Vivian betrayed me. Neither has she. But that's the kind of thing, I guess, that you have to learn to live with.

We'll have some space next year, at least: I'll be here at Tulane, which wasn't what I'd hoped for, but I'm glad it worked out this way. It'll be good, I think, to stay close to home.

As far as actual graduation, though, I'm not thrilled. Besides the heat, Piper's giving the valedictorian speech, and even though we're on good terms now, I know it's going to be insufferable, especially since her salutatorian boyfriend, Aiden, will be looking on all googly-eyed.

Not to mention the problem of my ex-boyfriend. Wyatt and I aren't really talking, but at least it feels a little less hostile between us. And he'll be fine: next year at LSU, he'll find some sweet sorority girl who's just as good at playing the part of his girlfriend as I used to be—maybe not better, but at least she'll mean it more.

The main problem, really, is the whispers. Already, I know everyone will be talking today, even so many months later. Lily LeBlanc, the missing Queen, found. The girl who escaped her captors with the help of her three Maids. The girl whose father might have helped cover up a murder, if you believe the rumors from a brave few who don't cower at his feet.

But we LeBlancs are used to being watched. It comes with the territory.

"We should get going," Dad says, checking the time. "Don't want to get stuck with bad seats."

"Can Mom and I meet you at the car?" I ask. "I need her help with one more thing."

"Of course. Just don't be too long." With another smile, Dad leaves.

That's the nice thing about all of this: I've earned their trust again.

Which means I can still occasionally test its boundaries. And Mom seems to know I'm about to do exactly that.

"What is it?" she asks, once Dad's footsteps have disappeared down the stairs.

"It's silly," I say, trying to make it sound casual. "But I've been wondering about one thing. We got Marty's burner phone from Wyatt after he took it from the darkroom, but Vivian said she found it on her car." I meet Mom's eyes in the mirror. "How did it get there, do you think?"

I already know my answer. In the silence that follows, I let it play out—a new story I've been crafting lately, one that feels more like the truth. And it goes like this.

After Mom and Dad got the burner back, they held on to it. This was the first of my days at the Den, when they were hoping I'd change my mind and they'd be able to let me out in a few hours, no damage done.

But then, when it became clear that things were only getting *more* complicated, that maybe they'd taken it a little too far, Mom did something quietly rebellious, almost completely deniable: the burner slipped into an envelope, dropped on Vivian's windshield like a parking ticket. A chance for the Maids to put the pieces together. To carry out my plan as I'd meant for them to.

Because maybe I'm not the only one who felt trapped.

I turn away from the mirror, now, looking at the real flesh-and-bone version of my mother. And the look on her face is all I need to know the truth.

Carefully, she reaches out to adjust one of my curls. She smiles.

"I haven't the slightest idea, darling."

Her phone starts to ring.

"Your father is being impatient, as usual," she says, glancing at it. "Shall we go before he causes a scene in front of the neighbors?"

"Let me just run to the bathroom, and then I'll be out."

"All right."

With one more look—one that feels different, like there's a new understanding between us—Mom turns and goes downstairs.

When she's gone, I go to my bed, feeling under the mattress until my fingers brush silver. I pull out Margot's lighter, trace the engraved logo.

There's an official story about the fire, too: it was electrical. An accident due to faulty wiring that ended up saving our lives, letting us escape. Another half-truth. But that's one we can all agree on—Mom and Dad, too, even though I'm pretty sure they know what really happened. We've never talked about it, but this, I think, is a silent truce we've made: I can forgive what they did to protect me, and they'll forget what I did to escape.

Quickly, I slip the lighter under my skirt, securing it inside the elastic of my biker shorts, where I can feel the metal against my thigh like a blade.

Sometimes it's good to remember the truth. The real story under the fiction. I give myself one more glance in the mirror, letting myself become her: not a victim but a queen. A girl who made things burn.

Maybe it will come out one day. Things in this city never stay buried, after all.

But for now, I paint on the smile I'll wear outside—easy, empty, perfect for a debutante—and I go, feeling the secret pressed to my skin.

ACKNOWLEDGMENTS

Whenever I'm asked to describe myself, one of the first things I always say is that I'm from New Orleans. I think this is because I, like so many New Orleans natives, know (unconsciously or not) how inextricably this city is linked to who I am—even though I haven't lived there full-time since I was the same age as the protagonists of *The Debutantes*. Writing a book about home felt as inevitable as it did daunting, especially one about this particular piece of it.

While I wouldn't describe this book as autobiographical—and there are certainly creative liberties taken—I was once, like a few of these characters, a decidedly unwilling participant in Mardi Gras debutante culture. And, like all of this book's protagonists, I became increasingly horrified as I experienced it firsthand. There was (thankfully) no murder involved, but I *was* absolutely certain that I would one day write about this strange, singular, and deeply unsettling experience. Writing something so close to home was one of the hardest things I've ever done as an author, and I'm endlessly grateful to the people who helped me tell a story about the hometown I love so much, with all of its contradictions and complexities.

To Sarah Grill, my fabulous editor—thank you so much for your care and brilliance in shaping this book and all my messy teens into the best versions of themselves. I'm proud to be a card-carrying member of the Grill Gang for life! Thanks also to Alex Sehulster for stepping in to expertly steer the ship in the home stretch.

A million more thank-yous to my incomparable agent, Claire Friedman. While this book isn't about influencers, I count myself lucky to be a member of the Claire Hype House. And, of course, thanks also to the rest of the wonderful team at Inkwell!

Thank you to Kerri Resnick and Jonathan Barkat for this stunning cover, and to the rest of the team at Wednesday: Alexis Neuville, Alyssa Gammello, Brant Janeway, MaryAnn Johanson, Eric Meyer, Jen Edwards, Melanie Sanders, Diane Dilluvio, Cassidy Graham, and Devan Norman.

One of the biggest thank-yous goes to my family, who I know are terrified this book is about them. (It's not! I promise! Or if it is, then only the good parts.) I love y'all so much. A special shout-out to Dad, who is *much* nicer than most of the dads in this book, and who also sparked the idea for the fire at the Den. And Mom—thank you for holding the giant skirt of my ball gown when I had to go to the bathroom, along with countless other acts of heroism. I wouldn't be here without your support. And, of course, I have to thank Grayson and Eugenie for ~keeping me young~.

To my friends: the Six Stupid People/Book Club/Cheese Club, the SHOFs, the Northwestern crew, the New York crew, and everyone else (you know who you are!): I count myself lucky to be surrounded by such bright, warm, funny, and brilliant people. I hope we all get to know one another forever.

To Mitchell: Thank you for indulging our shared obsession with all things dark, creepy, and little freak–adjacent (and also my monologuing about how hard it was to write this book). I'm really glad we found each other.

To the rest of my New Orleans family: Y'all are the best, and I hope I'm doing you proud.

And finally, to you, the reader: Thank you for giving me a chance. Every day I wake up in absolute awe and wonder that writing stories is my job, and it's all because of you! Here's to more murder, mayhem, and misbehaving girls. And for any of you wrestling with what it means to love a home that's sinking, in any capacity—I feel you. I'm still you. And I hope this helped you feel at least the tiniest bit seen.

ABOUT THE AUTHOR

© Sub/Urban Photography

OLIVIA WORLEY is an author born and raised in New Orleans. A graduate of Northwestern University, she now lives in New York City, where she spends her time writing thrillers, overanalyzing episodes of *The Bachelor*, and hoping someone will romanticize her for reading on the subway. She is also the author of *People to Follow*.